A Win-Win SITUATION

M.PAMELA

*To everyone who's been told that your dreams are too far away -
reach on, defy the odds, and make them yours.*

"Whoever loves something will find a kingdom in it."

— ARABIC PROVERB

PLAYLIST

Undo by Sanna Nielsen
Naked by MaKenzie Thomas
Enchanted (Taylor's Version) by Taylor Swift
This Is It by Oh The Larceny
Lay All Your Love On Me by Dominic Cooper, Amanda Seyfried
Close by Nick Jonas, Tove Lo
Ehsas Jdid by Nancy Ajram
Touch My Body by Mariah Carey
Love Story by Indila
Shameless by Camila Cabello
Ride by SoMo
Safety Net by Ariana Grande, Ty Dolla Sign
Only You by Ric Hassani
In The Stars by Benson Boone
This by Megan McKenna
1+1 by Naika

AUTHOR'S NOTE

To the reader,

Leora & Lucas's story is a steamy slow-burn marriage-of-convenience romance. It's the first interconnected-standalone in the Unexpected Love Series. It follows the journey of two souls who, despite starting on the wrong foot, find themselves in a situation filled with passion and sizzling tension and guarantees a happy ending.

However, it's important to note that this story may contain content that could be triggering for some readers. Please review the following list before proceeding, as it includes:

* Explicit Sexual Activity and use of sexual words
* Some Profane Language
* Mentioning of being abandoned
* Cheating (not by MMC or FMC)
* Sensitive subject matter such as death of a loved one and Cancer.

ONE

LUCAS

THREE MONTHS AGO

I t's funny how, just when you think you have everything figured out, life throws a curveball your way, testing your strength and resolve. They can be anything from small pebbles in your path to large hills that seem impossible to get over and it seems lately, there're some pretty damn big hills in my life. My marketing manager resigned suddenly last week, and now I'm left with all of this paperwork and a hotel opening to plan. A hotel that's opening in six months, which means I need to hire someone as soon as possible.

To make matters worse, James Harlow, the family lawyer, is here.

"As mentioned last week," he starts, "Mr. Ayoub, your uncle, has made some changes to his will, given his rapidly declining health."

My uncle Antoine, who is like a father to me, was diagnosed with lung cancer three months ago. The doctor told him he had a year left at best, but Antoine is a fighter. He hasn't let cancer stop him from living his life - not yet, anyway.

"There's reason to believe that he won't make it the entire

year," Harlow continues, his voice hesitant. My temples start pulsing at his words and I use my fingers to massage the spot. I'm not interested in information I'm already aware of.

I release my fingers from my temples and restlessly tap them on the table before I glance at my watch—a subtle indication for him to hurry up. *I really don't have time for this.*

"Get to the point," I grit out, keeping my eyes on him.

Harlow shifts uneasily on his feet, his previous nervousness heightened by my tone. He takes a deep breath before continuing. "The new clause that Mr. Ayoub has insisted upon is that you . . ." He hesitates for a moment, carefully planning how to continue. "Well, as you know, he's stated that you have to be married before the age of forty." I stare back at him, perplexed. This condition had been made clear to me by my uncle years ago. However, with six years left until I reach that problematic milestone, I can't wrap my head around why Harlow is bringing it up now. His untimely reminder only exacerbates the throbbing in my temples.

Harlow shifts in his seat, keeping his gaze anywhere but on me. "Well, Mr. Ayoub has made some changes. Y-You have to marry before the new hotel opens for you to be eligible to take over the business."

I stare at him incredulously.

"What do you mean?"

He swallows hard. "To take over after your uncle passes, you must marry sooner than expected."

My emotions boil over, and I feel anger building up inside me. It's as if the world is conspiring against me, and I can't catch a break.

To keep my hands occupied, I ball them into fists and look anywhere but at Harlow. Sensing my agitation he scrambles to gather his things and leaves me the new will.

"I will leave a copy for you to look over."

Taking a deep breath, I try to calm myself, although I can't help but think, *What the hell am I going to do?*

I loosen my tie. This whole ordeal has made every attempt to take a real breath impossible. The idea of finding a woman to marry within six months is laughable.

Even if I was willing to, how could any rational woman agree to marry me spontaneously—without love or an emotional connection.

This is a joke.

I let out a bitter laugh. This is going to be a shitstorm.

Remember the hills? They just turned into a mountain.

EVER SINCE FINDING out about my uncle's cancer diagnosis, I've felt this constant knot in my stomach, and it doubles in size every time I visit him at the hotel. Hôtel Ayoub d'Or has been his life's work. Well, that and raising my brother and I.

He took us in after our parents passed, and he slowly began preparing us to take over when he decided to retire. Liam never had much interest in business, so his role is overseeing our international hotels. But from what I've seen, he would rather travel and party, which I find unacceptable, especially given our uncle's illness. We haven't spoken in three months, and that's on him—I'm determined to fulfill my duties to our uncle. Which is why I'm heading to his office. As much as I hate to admit it, I also want to find another way to do it. One that doesn't include getting married.

The door to his office is open, but I still knock. "Hey, Ammo, can we talk?" I ask as I approach my uncle. I've never called him by his name. He's lebanese and in Lebanon, it can be seen as disrespectful to call an elder by their name, and, because I've been raised with Lebanese morals, I call him Ammo—*uncle*. He slowly turns his head toward me and stands up to greet me with his brilliant smile, making the knot in my stomach triple in size.

Ever since he found out about his diagnosis, he's been working harder than ever, trying to lose himself in his work, despite the evident toll it's taking, both mentally and physically.

Even with my ability to see through his facade—the weariness etched into every line of his face— I won't dare tell him to slow down. The last time I broached the subject, he lashed out, the intensity of his anger causing him to be bedridden for two days.

When the discussion about chemotherapy was brought up by the doctors, he adamantly declined it. Despite their offering of a slender thread of hope, a small chance of survival, he dismissed it. His stance on treatment reflected a prideful defiance—an unwavering refusal to submit to a treatment that might extend his time with us. This decision was marked by a stubbornness that both frustrated and pained everyone around him, although his reasoning for rejecting chemotherapy was rooted in his desire to not be weakened during his last few months of life.

He didn't want to sacrifice the semblance of strength and control he clung to, even if it meant potentially extending his time. Even though it breaks my heart into pieces, I tread lightly, always respecting his choices.

"Hi, son." He gestures toward the chair in front of his desk, indicating that I should take a seat. Without a word, I comply, feeling a bit nervous as I settle into the chair. His office looks as it always does—neat and impeccably organized, with stacks of files and papers lining the shelves. On the walls hang photos of Liam and I over the years. I can't help but recall the memories associated with those photos—our laughter, the adventures, and the times when everything felt perfect. But alongside those warm memories, a sense of emptiness and sadness lingers, creating a heavy knot in my chest that makes me rigid. He sits back down in his chair, leans forward, and steeples his fingers in front of his face, regarding me with a patient expression.

"Harlow came by this morning and . . ." I trail off and his smile instantly vanishes.

"You're here to ask me about the will." His voice is low and measured.

I can't get married, but I can't disappoint him either.

"I don't want to get married yet."

"Why is that?" My uncle's expression remains neutral.

"You can't be serious." I scoff. "Firstly, I don't know of anyone that wants to marry me, or I, them, and secondly, I won't marry just for the sake of it."

He chuckles. "*Enta zaki ya* Lucas, and a very handsome fellow, you can easily find a good wife. If not, I will give you a hand."

I stare at him, incredulously. It doesn't matter if I'm *smart*. I thought being "asked" to marry was one thing, but having him arrange it is an entirely different story.

When he sees my expression, he begins to laugh, but it quickly devolves into a wheezy, coughing fit, his face turning slightly red as he struggles. As I stand up to help, he raises his hand, signaling for me to stay. After a few moments, he recovers and speaks again.

"I've taught you well, Lucas. You're a man of pride. A man with goals, and a man who knows how to follow his instincts, but you're incredibly stubborn; a mule has nothing on you," he says with a hoarse voice.

I huff and look away. *I'm not stubborn.* I'm just . . . ambitious.

"I know you'll take good care of my empire when I'm gone. You're doing it already, but I want you to have someone by your side." He raises his shaking hands. "With me gone, who will continue my legacy?"

With me gone, who will continue my legacy?

I know he sees me and Liam as his sons, and as much as the business is his legacy, I know we are too, so the thought of him gone is like a knife to the chest.

I've always believed in upholding our family name, but now, faced with the pressure to marry, it's as if tradition has become a suffocating chain around my neck. It feels like a betrayal of everything I imagined. The dreams of companionship, of building a life together, now feel tainted by the looming shadow of duty. I will continue his legacy, yes, but the idea of being forced into marriage as a means to an end infuriates me. I won't be a chess piece, manipulated for someone else's agenda. I don't want to marry just to secure a legacy.

"I'm not a puppet to be manipulated for your own means, and I won't marry just to secure a legacy," I retort sharply, almost regretting my tone. Almost. "I have my own plans and goals, and I won't let anyone dictate my life. You said it yourself, I'm already taking care of everything. Is that not enough?"

My uncle's smile fades, and his gaze turns icy. "You may be my son, Lucas, but you are also a crucial part of my business."

I shift uncomfortably, knowing exactly where this conversation is heading. "So, would you let what you've built fall into the hands of some stranger if I don't marry?" I ask, trying to appeal to his sense of family loyalty.

"You forget I have two sons," he replies coolly. He's always had a soft spot for Liam. In his eyes, he can't do much wrong. He's just "a lost soul" who needs guidance, but I know Liam would never step up to a responsibility this grand, nor could he. Drinking, partying, and fucking the latest supermodel is what he does best. He knows nothing about business, and as much as I love my brother, I would never allow him to ruin this, and my uncle knows that.

"We both know he isn't fit to lead anything, and he would never agree to marry," I say, feeling a sense of desperation creeping in. This is not the first time my uncle has brought up the subject of marriage. Although, I had hoped that he would change his mind.

"Then it's up to you to make the right decision." His gaze shifts up, away from me, almost as if he's asking God for help. He looks back at me, his face more stern than before. "The news of my illness has gotten out and our stakeholders have started to talk. This is their chance to stake a claim and change the line of succession. When I say they, I mean Michel Beumont. He's like a lion waiting to attack, and my cancer is his greatest opening. Even though the rest of them like you enough, and know I want you to take over, Michel has convinced them that a vote is necessary, that we have to stick to the marriage clause and evaluate you, no matter the situation. That's why we need them to trust you more. This started as a family business and all of the stakeholders are old fashioned. They respect a family man more and they will vote against you if they don't trust you. We can't afford that." His tone is final.

Curious, I press for more details. "Why is that?"

"A family man is going to be more reliable and is often associated with stronger values, like loyalty, dedication, and integrity. Being seen as a loving and committed family man will convey a strong sense of character. They will believe you work not just for the hotels, but also for your family's future. This will strengthen your long-term commitments and stability in your business relationships."

"I'm the same man with or without a wife. Therefore, my choices will be the same."

"You say that now, Lucas, but reality doesn't bend to your wishes. I won't let your stubbornness jeopardize everything I've built. Marrying and securing your position is not negotiable; otherwise, you might as well walk away from everything entirely." There's a flicker of emotion behind his eyes — whether it's guilt or something more elusive, I can't quite discern. However, it doesn't deter him. "Find her, or I will."

I glare at him, seething with frustration. How can he do this to me? My hands flex at my sides as I try to get a grasp on my emotions. He meets my gaze defiantly, refusing to back down. This is completely insane. Yet, deep down, I recognize the weight of his expectations, and I can't afford to disappoint him. Whether I want it to or not, it's happening, and while I won't let him dictate my life, especially when it comes to choosing a wife, I must find a way to navigate this, no matter what it takes.

With gritted teeth, I reluctantly nod in agreement.

"You're making the right choice." A sly smile plays on his lips. "Look on the bright side, son, perhaps you'll find some enjoyment in married life."

Yeah, right.

I don't like people, and I certainly don't like people in my private space. This whole situation means that I'll have to share my apartment. And with the timeline I have, she'll probably be a random woman because asking my ex-girlfriend is out of the question. She's been trying to reconcile since we broke up five years ago but I never loved her, and I don't think she ever loved me.

Inside, a small voice whispers that I don't deserve to be forced into this, but I push it away. This is my responsibility—my duty to the family and our legacy. And I will do it, no matter the cost.

How hard can it be to find a good and respectable woman to marry?

TWO

LEORA

"**Y**ou're fired."

Amazing. Great. Perfect.

"Did you hear me, Miss Davis?"

Agnes, the bitch-boss, was promoted to her manager position a month ago and she's been an ass ever since. She's been at the company for four years; she's talented, but she's always been a little bit of an outsider. I tried to get her to join our Wednesday lunches, but she declined every time, leaving me to assume that she wasn't interested in making friends. I even used to bring her a coffee every morning, but all I got was a stiff smile and a nod. Apparently, coffee is not the way to her heart.

And here I am, sitting in front of her, getting fired.

She shows absolutely no signs of regret or guilt, while my face is probably as white as her sad office walls. Who doesn't decorate their office? There's not even a plant in sight.

"You can't just fire me without reason." I take a deep breath, willing myself to not pass out.

"I actually can, Leora. Your employment is considered 'at-will' which means the company can choose to part ways with you at any time, for any reason. However, in this case, we do have a reason. But on the bright side, now you can take that little vacation with no work hanging over your head." She says the last part with scathing viciousness.

There it is. My vacation.

The trip that was approved *six months ago*.

"Am I getting fired because I'm going on a trip? Senior management already approved my vacation, and so did you," I point out. I always knew she had something against me. This woman has been the bane of my existence since I started this job. And while it might not be my dream job, a job's a job, and a girl's gotta eat.

Right?

As much as I dislike the job and the environment, I'm actually good at what I do. I'm a marketing assistant for a marketing firm, and my workload recently increased when I was given more accounts to work on. I've had the best results, generating the most revenue from each and every account I've been assigned, and I was on my way to a promotion—or at least I thought I was.

"No. I'm firing you because you left internal papers out for the customer to find. Do you know how much I had to scramble to contain the damage you caused? Your actions were a serious breach of company policy, and you jeopardized the confidentiality and security of sensitive information. Unfortunately, your actions have resulted in severe consequences. After speaking with the higher-ups, I have no choice but to terminate your employment at Momentum Marketing."

An icy feeling runs through me as my blood freezes.

What the hell.

I've never left *any* papers out, especially not internal ones. I've always made sure to maintain confidentiality at all times. This must be a mistake. I know I was a bit stressed and tired at the latest event we held with one of my accounts, and I had a few glasses of bubbly to soothe my nerves, but I don't remember leaving any papers out.

At the moment, my muddled mind can't recall anything.

Did I do it? Did I accidentally leave the papers out?

I feel my hands go clammy, and my heart races at the speed of light.

I try to speak up but she isn't having it. "I'm sorry, but this is what needs to be done. Just sign these papers so you can get your severance package—three months in your case—which is more than fair." She taps her fingers on the desk before adding, "Now, if you don't mind, I have a meeting to attend to."

"But I don—"

"If you want to leave the company with dignity and a recommendation letter, I suggest you sign the papers."

I sigh with resignation. I need that recommendation letter if I want to find another job in this industry, so I sign the papers, slowly stand up, and walk through the glass doors only to be greeted by my colleagues—all staring at me wide-eyed. They know exactly what just took place.

"Leora . . ." Mike, my work husband, comes up to me and gives me a sideways hug as he walks me to my desk.

The desk I now have to clean up, once adorned with personal touches including motivational quotes tacked to the bulletin board, and a resilient succulent catching the light. Each item is a small testament to the effort I poured into this space.

"Agnes has lost her mind! You're the best on the team," he says as I lean into him for a second or two before updating him on everything that just happened.

"You would never do that. I was with you almost the whole night," he continues. I come to an abrupt halt as a memory resurfaces. I remember excusing myself to go to the bathroom, but the rest of my recollection is a blur. Did I accidentally leave those papers out?

"I don't know, Mike. I remember asking Agnes for her signature on the agreement, and later, I went straight to the event from the office, feeling completely drained. Everything after that is a blur. What if I accidentally brought the papers with me?"

He frowns. "It doesn't make sense. You're too much of a control freak to do that. She's going to realize her mistake and call you back before you return from Nice, don't worry." He leans in closer and whispers, "I'm going to find out the truth."

I adore this man. Without him, I'm not sure how I would have navigated through everything. We all need a Mike in our lives —preferably a Mike with a husband who bakes the most heavenly chocolate chip cookies, a delightful treat he never forgets to share with me.

"Well, at least I'll get a pre-vacation before my vacation." I attempt to say it positively, but it comes out with a wobbly uncertainty.

"Exactly! You can visit all of those cafés with John now. The ones you've been harassing us about for weeks." He has a point; a few weeks ago, I stumbled upon a list of the top ten breakfast places in town that I've been dying to try out but never found the time for. Not that John's schedule would have allowed it, even if I could manage it.

Now, however, I seem to have all the time in the world.

I TAKE the stairs two at a time, in a hurry to reach my door—to reach *home*. The stairs creak under my feet, reminding me of every horror movie I've ever watched. I live in an old building with an elevator that's a death trap, and I hate elevators.

Three years ago, I got trapped and haven't set foot in it since. Hours went by before I got help; all the while it felt as though the walls were caving in. Every passing minute was filled with an over-whelming sense of dread.

When they finally found me, I was lying in a fetal position, crying.

Looking back, I realize I had my first panic attack that day.

I remember how John, my boyfriend, had carried me home, laid me down on the bed and held me the whole night, comforting me until the panic subsided. He's always been an incredible support system, and I can't wait to get home—because at this moment, I need a lot of support.

That's why I'm climbing six flights of stairs in a pair of high heels, to get home to John.

My heart is racing and I'm having a hard time breathing. My beautiful Aurelie Nude Jimmy Choo's don't deserve this. I got these shoes to celebrate doing a good job at work.

Scratch that. I *thought* I was doing a good job.

My feet ache, but I don't care—I just want to be home.

How am I going to help pay rent? Buy food?

I sigh, hoping that John will be the voice of reason, reassuring me that we will figure it out. That he will help cover bills until I'm back on my feet.

John and I have been through some rough patches this past year. His music career is growing, which is incredible because it means he's reaching his goals, but it also means he doesn't have a lot of time for me anymore.

We met at a bar one night when he was performing, and I was immediately drawn to him. I remember seeing him on stage, so shy and sweet. He walked up to his seat on the stage, barely looking at the audience. I could feel his nervousness, and my heart went out to him.

But then the lights centered on him, and his fingers started plucking on the strings of his guitar. He looked straight at me, with those sparkling blue eyes and a smile so sweet it could rival the warmth of a summer sun. It was as if he drew the courage from me because when he looked back over the audience, he was filled with confidence. I remember being irresistibly attracted to him and wanting him, one way or another.

Since that night, he's grown quite a following, most of whom are beautiful women.

And honestly, some days, I'm not sure I like it.

I'm happy that he gets to do what he loves—he deserves it. But a part of me feels like I always come second and that I'm replaceable. When I dwell on it too much, a sense of uselessness and insignificance consumes me.

My heart beats faster at all these intrusive thoughts, and the failure of today isn't helping. As I approach my floor, a small part of me is nervous to tell him what happened. I know he'll say I deserve better, but it doesn't change the fact that I feel like I failed.

I know I deserve better. I deserve to work at a place where I'm valued—where I can learn and evolve. Momentum Marketing wasn't the right fit. I'm better than them.

When I finally reach my door, my heart is beating way too hard, I'm sweating, and I'm seeing black spots. I really need to start working out.

"John, I'm home!" I call out while setting the box with all my desk belongings on the floor and taking off my heels. The relief is instant, and I release a long, audible sigh.

Mental note, stop being scared of the elevator, or start carrying a pair of sneakers.

No one answers. Weird. John is usually home by now.

"John, are you home?" I call out again.

As I head to the kitchen, searching for the note he always leaves when he goes out, my brows furrow in confusion. There's nothing on the fridge or the kitchen island.

That's strange.

"Oh my god!" a husky female voice screams out, startling me.

Was that . . . ? Is our neighbor getting laid in the middle of the day? She's like sixty years old. I mean, good for her, but I did not sign up for this.

I dash to the failure-box I brought from work to grab my earbuds, but the moaning continues, "Yes. Yes. Yes, right there. Don't stop. DON'T STOP!" The voice grows louder and somehow, it sounds closer.

With a sinking feeling of dread, I question if it's coming from inside the apartment.

Loud groans accompany the moans resonating on the walls—sounding way too clear to be coming from outside the apartment.

There's another moan, this one louder, and it seems to come from my own bedroom.

Did someone break in to get laid? I know we have a great mattress, but robbers wouldn't know about that.

I clutch my phone in my hand, ready to call the police as I walk towards my room.

When I reach the door, I open it slowly.

It isn't the neighbor.

It isn't a burglar.

It's John.

"Oh fuck, baby." His voice is muffled, but not because he's trying to keep himself quiet. No, it's muffled because his head is tucked between a redhead's legs and his dick seems to be lodged in her throat.

I stand there frozen, watching the betrayal unfold in front of me.

It seems I'm not good enough for anything, or anyone, after all.

THREE

LEORA

"That disgusting, *charmout* of a man!" Adeline screams, her Lebanese heritage coming out in the form of Arabic curse words. Most of the time I'm confused, but "charmout" is one word I do know.

Manwhore.

She huffs as she plants herself next to me on the couch. "Haywan!"

Animal.

After I caught him in bed with that woman, I turned around and stormed out of the room without speaking a word to him or the redhead. I always assumed I would be more of a loud and upset girlfriend, seeing as I tend to have a short fuse in certain situations, but in this instance, the only thing I felt as I looked at him, sixty-nineing that redhead, was betrayal. I should be livid for what he did—I have every reason to be angry with him, but I'm not feeling it. Maybe the anger hasn't caught up to me yet.

Not just for cheating.

I'm mad about the cheating, but I'm also absolutely floored that I caught him in bed doing something other than laying on top of—or behind—someone. He never took action with me, and maybe I didn't suggest for us to be more creative, but I wanted it and I wanted him to want it. *To want me.*

I walked away as soon as I saw them, but not before John heard my outraged gasp. He ran after me—naked, might I add—trying to explain that it wasn't what it looked like. Which was funny because his dick was still wet from her saliva.

I calmly told him it was over and to leave. I reached for the door, grabbing my purse before adding that I wanted no trace of him when I came back home.

Which didn't exactly work as well as I wanted it to.

I've been staying with Adeline for the past two weeks and he still hasn't moved out.

He texted me saying he needed a little time to find a new place to live, and I told him that was fine—which Adeline wasn't happy about. The whole "putting my foot down" was harder to do than I thought.

What can I say? I'm weak and a people pleaser. I can't help feeling bad for people when they need help, even if those people are cheating, scumbag, exes.

"What are you thinking about?" Adeline's voice snaps me out of my thoughts.

Adeline is my rock and one of my best friends. She's the most beautiful soul on the inside and out. We've known each other since we were five years old, when we bonded over our love for the Powerpuff Girls—the Buttercup to my Bubbles. A few years later we found Sophie, our Blossom. We've been the perfect trio ever since, and tomorrow we're leaving for *The Ultimate French Riviera Vacation* in Nice. Which I should be incredibly excited about, but the weight of my breakup and job loss has been hanging over me, making me question if going is even a good idea at the moment.

Adeline is convinced this is the perfect way to reset myself and get ready for a new job.

She's also convinced it's the perfect way to get over a cheating boyfriend.

"I don't think I can come with you tomorrow," I say, avoiding making eye contact with her. However, the look of utter outrage is clear on her face, her eyes narrowing and her mouth tightening in disapproval.

"Of course you can. You're not letting that *hmar* stop you from having the best vacation of your life. You'll enjoy it even more now."

"Why do you think that?"

"Do you remember the time we went to Vegas for Sophie's birthday weekend? How he texted you non-stop, asking about what you were doing? He even called you to see your outfits several times. Who acts like that?"

She's right. I remember being so annoyed with him that weekend. We even argued about me going to the club because according to him, *"Girls with boyfriends shouldn't be shaking their asses at clubs in Vegas."* Even though I confronted him and went to the club, his words still bothered me throughout the night. Now that I look back at the situation, I realize that it wasn't okay, but at that moment I didn't see it that way. He wasn't all bad, and after the argument, he told me he only acted that way because he was afraid that something would happen to me, and he apologized profusely. Adeline, however, didn't let that go. She never really got along with John, not fully anyway

Sure, we had our good days, and we all used to hang out. They were cordial to each other, which I presume was for my sake, but some days, I could feel the strain in the air with the way they sent each other scathing looks and the muttered Arabic words from Adeline. Their mutual animosity hung heavy between them, a palpable tension in the air.

That's how my knowledge of Arabic swear words evolved.

I should have trusted her gut instinct. She's always had a sixth sense when it comes to these things. But, as they say, hindsight is always twenty-twenty.

We all make mistakes, some more than others.

"Leora, stop zoning out!" Her fingers snap in front of my eyes, bringing my focus back to her.

"I'm sorry," I mutter as I sink deeper into the sofa, my thoughts spinning around my head like a whirlwind.

When I'm upset, my coping mechanism is to drown myself in work and invest all of my energy into reaching my goals. Now, I don't even have a way to cope.

Fan-fucking-tastic.

The only options at the moment are alcohol or the gym.

Seeing as the latter requires physical effort—alcohol it is.

Adeline moves closer to me, her eyes full of sympathy. I know she wants to help, but I don't know what I need.

"It's okay." Her voice is soft. "You don't have to say anything if you don't want to. Just know that I'm here for you, okay?"

I nod, feeling the tears prick my eyes. Adeline doesn't have to say anything else; her presence alone is enough to soothe my aching heart.

"I'm sorry," I say, gesturing to the mess that is me. My normally sleek, brown hair is now tangled in a greasy knot on the top of my head, my green eyes swollen from crying and my pale skin duller than ever. My clothes, usually neat, are now wrinkled and haphazardly draped on my body. "I know I'm a disaster."

It's a stark contrast to Adeline's beautiful, long, shiny black hair paired with her large, brown, almond eyes. She looks beautiful as always.

Adeline grabs my hand. "No, you're not."

I take a deep breath, trying to steady my racing thoughts.

"It's just that . . . everything feels so overwhelming. I don't know how I'll ever move forward." A tear slowly makes its way down my cheek and I wipe it away with a shaky hand. "I don't want to feel like this."

Adeline nods, her eyes conveying compassion. "It's okay to feel that way," she reassures me. "But you're not alone. We'll figure it out together."

I lean into her, feeling the weight of my troubles start to lift, even if only for a little while. I know that it won't be fixed overnight, but at this moment, with Adeline by my side, I feel a glimmer of hope for the future.

THE SOUND of the door slamming wakes us up, with the credits to *Mamma Mia 2* still playing in the background. I reach for my phone and it lights the dark room. I check the time, shocked to see it's 1 a.m. When did it get so late?

"Honeys, I'm home!" Sophie's voice bellows through the hall-way, accompanied by the rough sound of a suitcase being dragged behind her.

Her blonde hair sways as she runs toward me. "I'm so sorry I couldn't get here earlier. My manager wouldn't let me go," she says as she wraps her arms around me in a tight embrace. She's been out of town for the past three weeks working on an interior design project for a small hotel in New Orleans.

"You are the most amazing person I know," she says, her embrace getting even tighter. "He was never good enough for you, and I hope you know that."

Her words hit me hard and I lean into her warmth.

"What do you say we order some take-out and watch the only movies that make you happy?" Sophie leans back from our embrace and regards me with her beautiful smile.

"We've—" Adeline starts before I interrupt her.

"Thank you, that sounds like a great idea." I don't have it in me to tell her we've already watched the movies, so I sit back and let her press play.

I COULDN'T FOCUS on the movie the second time around. All I could think about was this damn trip. The question of whether or not I should go has been plaguing me for the past two weeks. I already paid for the flight and the hotel so if I don't go, I'll lose the money. On the other hand, there's the cost of food, drinks and activities—which means even if I do go, I'll lose money I don't have. However, if I don't go, I know they won't go either, which will ruin their vacation plans. I guess I might as well go and have fun with them—if nothing else it will keep my mind off of things.

"I need one of you to go grab my luggage from my apartment." If John's there, I'll most likely slap him.

Both Adeline and Sophie's eyes meet mine. "I would go, but I'm not sure he'll be gone. I started packing three weeks ago and I'm almost finished. The only thing missing is some underwear and bikinis, so please throw some in while you're at it."

They both nod in understanding. "Of course," Adeline answers with a certain glow behind her eyes. *She's* probably planning to smack him in the face for me.

I love this girl.

Sophie catches on. "Only to get the suitcase!"

Adeline responds by nodding, robotically, with a maniacal grin that tells me I shouldn't believe that she will leave John's face untouched.

Sophie reassures me they will be as mature as possible, even though he doesn't deserve it.

They quickly head out the door, promising to be back as soon as possible, leaving me alone.

Everything floods back.

I'm a failure.

I'm not good enough.

I always thought I would have everything by now—my dream job, a handsome husband, and a beautiful child. My plan was to grow up, work hard for my diploma, fall in love with a decent guy, get married, and start a family. And considering, so far, I only have accomplished *one* of those things, I feel like I've failed miserably.

I have *nothing*.

My hands tremble as I gulp down a glass of water—anxiety and frustration swirling inside me. Everyone around me seems to know where they're headed, except me. Even Adeline and Sophie seem to have it all figured out.

Honestly, I'm not jealous—I'm incredibly proud of Adeline's success as a *New York Times* bestselling author, and I'm excited for Sophie's potential promotion. Before we know it she will be taking over the interior design company she works for—as she should because she's incredible at what she does. I'm not jealous, but their success perpetuates this feeling that I'm behind everyone in life.

A tear slips down my cheek.

I angrily swipe at it but more follow and I end up cradling my face in my hands, unable to stop the flood of tears.

I hate feeling like this—powerless and defeated.

When the tears subside, I take a deep breath and steady myself against the cold kitchen island, determined not to let these emotions ruin everything. I can't let myself ruin this vacation for the girls, and I won't let myself fall victim to my own negative thoughts. We've all worked so hard to get where we are, and we need to enjoy every moment of our well-deserved break.

"I can do this. I *need* to do this," I whisper to myself, wiping away the last of my tears. Vacation is therapy and I need a lot of it. I'll just put my feelings aside for now and deal with them when we're back in two weeks. That sounds doable.

I mean, at this point, what else could possibly go wrong?

FOUR

LEORA

As soon as we step through the grand, double doors of Hôtel Ayoub d'Or, we're welcomed with warm greetings, a bottle of Laurent-Perrier champagne, and copious amounts of chocolate. The champagne is definitely high quality, and the first sip is pure heaven—the bubbly liquid dancing on my tongue, while the rich chocolate melts in my mouth. The decadence of it is almost overwhelming. I feel like royalty.

My eyes widen as I take in the sheer size and beauty of the lobby. The marble floors shine beneath my feet, and the towering ceilings seem to stretch on forever. The entire space is drenched in natural light, making the already expansive lobby seem even more grandiose.

To my left, there's a seating area with plush armchairs and sofas, arranged in a circle in the center of the floor. Directly above the lavish arrangement is a massive, crystal chandelier that sparkles like diamonds. To my right, there's a sweeping staircase that leads to the upper floors, while in front of me, a long, ornate reception desk beckons.

The walls are lined with priceless works of art, and fresh flower arrangements adorn every corner, filling the air with a lovely, floral fragrance. Soft, melodic music plays in the background, adding to the enchanting ambiance. I take a moment to soak it all in, relishing my luxurious surroundings and the feeling of being somewhere special.

Sophie did an amazing job with the planning. "How the hell did you pull *this* off with the budget we had?" I ask her in awe. If I recall correctly, this was not the hotel we booked—something about needing to change the hotel at the last minute due to renovations—but *this* is completely out of our budget. I wouldn't be able to afford this hotel with a job *and* a sugar daddy.

"I know a guy," Sophie says, leaving us as she heads to the reception desk. Adeline just laughs and follows her. But just before I start moving toward the girls, I glance to my left, my gaze stopping on a man standing by the wall, engrossed in a conversation on his phone.

No, not a man.

Adonis himself.

He's tall, towering over the crowd around him, with olive skin and dark, curly hair tousled in a way that makes it look effortlessly stylish. I can't help but imagine running my fingers through those soft curls. He turns his chin to the side, revealing a profile that is just as striking as the rest of him. His strong jawline is framed by a bit of scruff, and his plump lips are set in a determined line as he speaks into his phone.

He's wearing a crisp, perfectly tailored white shirt that hugs his body in all the right places, accentuating his broad chest and strong arms. The fabric stretches across his shoulders, hinting at the strength and power beneath it.

Wait, what the hell is wrong with me?

I need to focus on something . . . anything else.

"To get over someone, you need to get under someone else," Adeline said as we stepped off the plane. I shut it down quickly, but now I'm not so sure. Maybe it's not such a bad idea after all?

A distraction might be fun.

Still, that detestable voice inside of me is loud. A man *like him* would never even look at a girl *like me*. Especially not when I have my hair in a loose bun, and while I'm wearing simple yoga pants and have a hoodie tied around my waist. Lost in my thoughts, I don't even realize that I have been caught staring until it's too late. I snap my gaze to my feet but still feel a pair of eyes on me, and when I look back up, I see him looking straight at me, sporting an amused expression on his face.

Fuck.

I quickly look away, blushing fiercely, hoping to hide my mortification. A minute goes by—or seconds, I don't even know—but I still feel the pull toward him. I discreetly take a peek back in his direction, hoping he's back to looking at his phone, but I'm met with a blank hotel wall.

Gone.

Where did he go?

Someone behind me clears their throat, sending a shiver down my spine.

Please don't be him. Please don't be him. Please don't be him.

I turn slowly.

"Didn't anyone ever teach you that staring is rude?" He raises an eyebrow, studying me.

Kill me now.

I feel my face flush as his gaze practically drills a hole through me, and I struggle to find the right words to reply.

"I-I'm so sorry," I stammer. "I didn't mean to stare, I just got lost in my thoughts."

He continues to study me, his expression unreadable, but before I can embarrass myself any further, I hear Adeline and Sophie call my name. I turn toward them, relieved by the distraction, and see them waving for me to come over. I look back to him to apologize again, but he's gone. The only thing left of him is the smell of his woodsy cologne—intoxicating and causing my thoughts to run wild.

I take a deep breath, hoping to memorize the smell, before I quickly make my way toward my friends.

"What's up?" I ask, trying to sound casual.

"We're all checked in," Adeline says with a grin. "Let the adventure begin."

APPARENTLY, THE PERSON SOPHIE "KNOWS" helped her book not *just* a hotel room—we have a damn suite the size of my apartment. And that isn't even the best part.

The view . . . *that's* the best part.

We have the most breathtaking view of the beach from our balcony. I can hear the sound of the waves crashing against the shore and smell the salt in the air.

And in this moment, I realize, I'm so incredibly grateful for this—the three of us, on this beautiful trip, in this luxurious suite; it's like a dream come true.

The sitting area connected to the balcony is adorned with tasteful decorations in a neoclassical style that adds to the French Riviera charm. The bathroom is equally impressive, with a massive tub, a separate shower, and premium toiletries we will absolutely be stealing.

My breath gets caught in my throat as I see the large bedroom connected to the sitting area. The room is bathed in a soft, warm glow from the glittering chandelier hanging overhead—thousands of diamonds dancing together. My eyes are immediately drawn to the large, king-size bed that sits in the center of the room, its sheets a crisp, soft white that appears lustrous in the glow streaming in through the windows. My thoughts immediately go to the handsome man I saw in the lobby and how perfect it would be to snuggle up with him as we looked out the French balcony after a night off—

Nope. Nope. Nope.

"That's my bed." Adeline brings me back to reality. She's pointing to the smaller, twin-size bed situated off to the side of the room.

"It's great that you made that choice all by yourself, Addie, because neither myself, nor Leora would actually want to share a bed with you," Sophie says with a hint of sarcasm.

"Heeey! It's because *I* can't sleep next to another person," Adeline fires back. I can't help but laugh, knowing that Adeline's excuse is far from the truth. She's a notorious blanket hog who moves around a lot in her sleep. You'll get kicked at least once or twice during the night. Her choosing the smaller bed is a win for Sophie and I.

"Whatever helps you get through the night, darling." I chuckle, already picturing a peaceful night's sleep in the bed.

After we've settled our luggage in the room, our growling stomachs lead us to search for something to eat. To our pleasant surprise, we stumble upon a gorgeous restaurant located on the Promenade des Anglais. The atmosphere is relaxing and carefree, with the gentle sound of waves lapping against the shore in the background. It's the perfect setting to let go of all our worries and simply enjoy the moment—or at least try to.

"Are you ready to order?" the waitress asks with a lovely French accent.

"I think I want to try the steak tartare," Sophie says, scanning the menu.

"You know that's raw meat?" Adeline asks, scrunching her nose.

"Yes, Addie. Of course, I know. Why do you have that look on your face? You eat raw meat too," she replies with a laugh, looking excited to try something new.

"*Kibbeh Nayyeh* is more than just raw meat, and you love it!" she snaps back. You don't come between Addie and her Meze; I learned that the hard way.

"I'll have the Caesar salad."

"Me too," Adeline says with a grin.

"And we'll have three Pepsi Max, s'il vous plaît," I finish, trying out my rusty French on the waitress, who smiles and jots down our order.

After we finish eating, the three of us settle back into our lounge chairs, enjoying the sound of the ocean, which is like music to my ears. It feels as though I've had a smile plastered on my face since we landed, although it's hard not to when you're surrounded by the beauty of this part of the world. I close my eyes for a second to let the warmth of the sun soak into my skin. The gentle breeze carries the salty scent of the ocean, making me feel alive.

When I open my eyes, I'm met by two pairs of eyes looking at each other with smirks, which can only mean that they're planning something.

"What?" I ask, looking back and forth between them.

"Oh, nothing." Sophie's smile reaches her blue eyes, and it's making me nervous.

Something is going on.

"Well, it's Saturday tomorrow, so we're going to have some fun," Adeline adds.

"And what do *we* have planned?" I ask, curious about their ideas but equally afraid.

Sophie plays with her fingers, a twinkle in her eye. "It's a surprise."

"Oh great." I roll my eyes. "I love your surprises."

Knowing them, this so-called surprise will involve a lot of tequila shots.

Adeline lets out a giggle. "Don't worry, it's nothing crazy. Just something fun and cultural."

I'm not convinced. Although, she's never used the word *"cultural"* when planning a night out before, so I'm actually feeling excited about what they have in store. This might be fun.

"Alright then, let's just enjoy the rest of our day at the beach and take it from there."

FIVE

LEORA

When I think about the words "fun" and "cultural," my mind conjures up images of museums and trying new cuisines. Maybe even exploring this beautiful city.

Standing in line, outside a crowded nightclub on the French Riviera, in a black halterneck dress so tight it emphasizes every curve of my body, particularly around my rounder hips, is certainly *not* what I had in mind.

"Wow, that's a *man*," Adeline murmurs, and I turn around to see the back of a tall, broad shouldered man walk by us. "Stop pulling on your dress, Leora," Adeline snaps, her tone leaving no room for argument and I immediately release the hem.

"When we get in, you're going to talk to one of these hot men. Understood?"

Before I have time to answer her, Sophie chimes in, "You'll go up to him with your hot ass and flirt. Okay?"

I'm not exactly sure *what* she's talking about. *I* don't go up to guys, and I certainly don't have a "hot ass."

My heart starts racing, and I shake my head frantically. "No, no, I can't do that. You know I can't flirt to save my life." The last time I tried doing the cute, doe-eyed, blinking thing, John asked if I had something in my eye. I said yes and ran away. And that was five years ago! If I couldn't flirt then, there's no way in hell I would be able to now. I'm not even sure I remember what to do. Touch their arm? Smile? Blink? Can you even blink in a sexy way?

"Honey, that's your *mission* for tonight," Adeline says with a smirk on her face. I groan inwardly. The *mission* is something we've been doing for a long time. It's a way to push each other to do something outside of our comfort zone, or a way to be assholes. You're allowed to say no to *one* challenge, but I know that if I deny this one, a worse one will follow.

"I hate you guys," I mutter, eyeing them both before winking. "Just wait for *your* missions."

"Nope," Adeline says, making a popping sound. "You know the rules. If I hand out the first challenge, you can't give one back. You'll choose one for Sophie and she'll choose one for me. Simple."

That cocky little—

"List?" The huge bouncer demands, staring us down. Damn, they make the bouncers even bigger in Europe. His eyes narrow, and he wrinkles his nose as he glares at us. Apparently, they're more rude here too.

"Yes, it's under 'Anderson'," Sophie replies, giving me a "what did you expect" look. Of course, Sophie got us on the list. The bouncer nods and checks the list, then unclasps the red rope blocking our way and signals us to walk in. My heart races as I follow my friends into the club, wondering what kind of trouble they'll get me into tonight.

Upon entering the club, my senses are immediately overwhelmed by the beating bass of the music, the colorful lights flashing around the room, and the scent of perfume and alcohol filling the air. The dance floor is packed with people moving, their bodies swaying in unison to the rhythm of the music.

The bar is lined with people shouting their drink orders over the music. There are girls dressed in glittery tight dresses and high heels, dancing on tables with their hands raised over their heads, letting the music take over. I haven't been to a club in a while, but something within me lets go. I'm ready to let loose and have some fun.

I follow my girls through the crowd, feeling the heat of the bodies around me as we squeeze our way toward the bar.

"Nine tequila shots and three drinks of your own choice, handsome, but make them a bit sour," Adeline purrs to the bartender, leaning over the bar. Her curves are perfectly accentuated in her red bodycon dress, and I notice how the bartender's eyes linger a little too long on her chest before he quickly prepares the drinks, his eyes rarely leaving Adeline's cleavage.

"It's on the house."

"Thank you, handsome." She smirks and grabs the shots, handing them to me and Sophie with two lemon slices and of course, salt.

"Here's to unforgettable nights, the bonds of sisterhood, and new beginnings!" Adeline exclaims, looking at me and raising her shot glass. The rest of us follow suit, clinking our glasses together. I slowly lick the salt off the back of my hand before downing the tequila shot. I wince at the sharp burn and quickly suck on the lemon wedge to ease the taste.

Immediately upon finishing our first shot, Sophie hands out the second round of shots before saying, "Here's to chasing our dreams, conquering our fears, and to the endless possibilities that lie ahead." We smile and clink our glasses with hers. This time, the tequila doesn't burn as much.

I take the last round of shots and hand them to the girls, saying, "Here's to the laughter we share, the moments that take our breath away, and the adventures waiting around every corner."

Adeline and Sophie grin and shout, "Cheers to that," before we down the shots together.

The sour drinks the bartender concocted are strong and a tad bitter, but they help soothe my nerves as I take in the scene around me.

"Let's dance!" Adeline yells louder than she needs to.

"You go. I'll be there in a minute," I answer her. So she grabs Sophie's hand and walks to the middle of the dance floor as I take a moment to people watch, savoring my drink before joining them on the dance floor.

And that's when I spot *him*.

The Greek God from the hotel. *Adonis.*

The man I embarrassed myself in front of.

He's standing on the other side of the club with a drink in his hand. His dark hair is ruffled, his eyes intense as he surveys the room. My hands go clammy, and I quickly turn to the bartender, my voice slightly shaky as I speak, "One more tequila shot . . . No, make it two, please." I hope he won't see me tonight, and if he does, I pray he's forgotten about my humiliating staring display from the day before.

The alcohol settles, and I feel the buzz in my veins lead me toward the girls. The pulsating beat of the music vibrates through my body as I sway on the crowded dance floor with Adeline and Sophie. It's easy to let loose, and as the tempo of the music increases, so do our movements. Adeline is swaying her hips in front of me while Sophie stands behind, her hand gently tracing my body. The thumping beat of the music pulses through us, and the warm, sultry air envelops our group. Sophie twirls, her pink skirt flaring up with each spin, the vibrant colors of the fabric catching the dim, hazy lights. We laugh, our bodies moving in sync with the rhythm, lost in the music and the electric atmosphere. The room feels like it's on fire, and I can sense the eyes of others on us, their gazes lingering with admiration and desire. It's intoxicating and hot, leaving me feeling alive and liberated, as if the world revolves around us for these electrifying minutes.

As the music hits its peak, Adeline leans in close, whispering something in my ear, but the noise drowns out her words. I just shake my head and laugh, but she leans in even closer and speaks louder, "I choose *him*." Her finger is pointing in the direction of the bar.

My whole body tingles. I have a feeling I know exactly which "him" she's referring to, and when I turn my gaze and spot him, I curse.

I shake my head. "No," I say firmly. "I can't do it. Not him."

But she's relentless, her finger still pointing to the bar where he's standing. "I choose him," she repeats, her voice teasing and full of mischief. "Don't be a *coward*, Leora."

I can feel my cheeks flushing with embarrassment and frustration. She knows I can't back down from a challenge, and that word is making me want to prove them wrong.

"Do you want to decline this easy, flirting mission and try another one?" Her wicked grin grows wider. "It will probably be worse."

Is it frowned upon to tackle your friend in a busy club? What's the worst that could happen—we'll be thrown out? I have no issue with that.

"Or do you want to take a chance and see what happens?"

I weigh my options, knowing that whatever I choose it won't be easy. But I can't let her win. "Fine," I say, finally. "I'll do it, you asshole."

I take a deep breath and start making my way towards the bar, trying to look confident and in control, even though I may have had one too many tequilas.

This is going to be a long, embarrassing night.

He's leaning against the bar, wearing a pair of chinos and a button-down shirt with a few buttons undone and rolled-up sleeves, which accentuate his broad shoulders and toned arms. The tattoos that had previously been hidden underneath his long sleeves are on display. I can't exactly see what kind of art it is in the dim light, but just the idea of them makes him even hotter. A wave of heat floods through me, and I suddenly feel even more self-conscious in my own skin. He looks like he belongs here, like he knows he's attractive but doesn't feel the need to show it off.

Every inch of my body is hyper-aware of his presence as I draw closer to him, and I have to take another deep breath to steady myself.

When I reach him, I raise my hand and greet him with a loud, "Hi."

His expression quickly shifts to confusion, and I can't help but feel like this encounter is about to become awkward. He leans down and murmurs a hesitant, "Hi," into my ear so I can hear him better over the blaring music. The warmth of his breath against my ear sends an electric thrill through my body.

"Do I know you?" he asks, catching me off guard. When he pulls away, I find myself longing for more.

More words, more physical closeness, more of *him*.

"No, you don't know me." I lean toward him. "Do you come here often?"

Wow, smooth Leora. I should just say goodbye, go back to the girls and strangle them . . . or myself.

He chuckles. "Sometimes. I'm guessing this is your first time?"

I'm slightly shocked at the disappointment of him not recognizing me from yesterday, but on the other hand, I'm relieved. This is my chance to start over with him.

"Leora," I say, stretching my hand out in an attempt to introduce myself.

"Lucas." His hand envelops mine. My God, his hand is big and surprisingly soft. A jolt of electricity shoots through me as our eyes meet.

I can't help but notice one of the tattoos peeking out from under his rolled-up sleeve. It's an intricate design of a pair of wings in black ink. Emboldened by the connection I smile. "Oh, that's a beautiful tattoo."

His features soften, something akin to sorrow, his face taking on a distant expression,as if recalling a memory. "Thank you. It's the first tattoo I ever got."

Neither of us say anything as we continue to eye each other and I find myself lost in the depths of his eyes.

"So, Lucas," I say with a warm smile, trying to shift the conversation, not wanting to pry, "Can I buy you a drink?"

He looks down at the glass in his hand, then back up at me. "Thanks, but I already have one."

Heat creeps up my neck and I can feel it reach my neck.

As if sensing my embarrassment, he leans into me again. "How about *I* get you a drink?"

I smile and nod, still feeling embarrassed but thankful.

He buys me an Amaretto Sour, which is delicious. I sip on it for a few seconds before I look up to find him looking at me closely, curiosity glimmering in his eyes. "What brings you here tonight, Leora?" he asks, with genuine interest.

"Just out for some fun with my friends," I reply, pointing toward Adeline and Sophie. His gaze follows where I'm pointing, and as soon as he spots them, a noticeable change shifts in his appearance.

When he looks back at me, the warmth in his eyes has faded, and his jaw is clenched.

"Do you want anything else?" He leans slightly forward, his brow furrowing as he locks eyes with me, and I blink, completely stupefied by his question. I notice a subtle twitch near his eye, and the tension in his jaw as he speaks, making me wonder if I said something wrong.

"I'm sorry?"

"You got your drink. You can go back to your friends now."

"I don't understand."

"Well, sweetheart, let me put it simply for you: we talked, I bought you a drink, and that's the end of this transaction."

My hand starts to shake, spilling some of my drink as I'm taken aback, wondering again, if I said something wrong. But as I try to collect myself, I realize it doesn't matter—his condescending attitude is not acceptable. Just before he turns around, something in me snaps and I think of something better to do with the drink.

"You can have your drink back, asshole!" I say, tossing the contents of my drink at him.

It splashes his face, causing him to stumble back a step or two, but I don't stay to gauge his reaction. My body is on fire as I storm over to Adeline and Sophie, who have been standing on the sidelines watching the whole thing go down. I grab their arms and drag them toward the bathroom with a scowl on my face.

"Are you happy now? I completed your ridiculous mission," I snap, my voice harsher than I intended. They exchange a guilty look, clearly sensing my frustration.

"Oh my gosh, you didn't just throw a drink in his face!" Sophie says, her hand now covering her mouth in shock.

"That. Was. AMAZING!" Adeline shrieks with a grin, clearly pleased with the outcome. I roll my eyes at her, my irritation simmering beneath the surface.

"I didn't do it for your entertainment," I retort, still fuming.

Adeline's grin fades, and she places a hand on my shoulder. "I'm sorry," she says softly. "What happened?"

I tell them, word for word, how my interaction with the Greek God went and when I finish speaking, the look on both of their faces is enough to know they are out for blood.

"I can't believe he said that!" Sophie seethes, her eyes flashing with anger. Adeline doesn't say a word, which scares me more. She starts to back up toward the door, and I know exactly where she's heading. My hand grabs hers just in time.

"Adeline, you're not going up to him."

"But I just—"

"No. I've already embarrassed myself enough. I don't need my friends fighting any of my battles. Let's look at it from another perspective. I flirted a little bit and completed the mission. That's a win in my book." I give them a fake smile.

"Look at you. This whole mission was for you to break through *your* walls. Fuck him. I'm just proud you did it," Adeline says, surprising me.

Maybe the whole thing wasn't a bust after all. I've always

wanted to throw a drink in someone's face like they do in movies, and now I have.

Adeline squeezes my arm. "You don't need some guy's approval to feel good about yourself," she says. "You're stunning just the way you are. But if you're interested, we can always try again." She winks at me playfully.

I shake my head, feeling grateful for my friends. "Once is definitely enough," I say with a laugh. "But dancing, on the other hand, sounds like a great idea. Let's go!"

We make our way to the dance floor, and I spot him, again, sitting at a table.

Fuck me.

This time, however, his friend is with him. Scratch that; she's practically *on top* of him. She looks like a supermodel in a very short silver dress, her small figure accentuated by its shimmer, and her sun kissed skin contrasting with the metallic sheen of the outfit. Her blonde hair is up in a tight long ponytail and from what I can see, her lips are painted red. She's practically straddling him with her arms wrapped around his neck while her lips hover over his. I hope she squeezes him tight enough that he can't breathe for a few seconds.

SIX

LUCAS

The club is packed, even more so than usual. Julien, my friend, stands by our table, his tumbler of scotch raised over his head as he moves to the music. I've been out almost every weekend since I found out about the whole marriage predicament, and Julien is the friend you call for a good time. However, today I'm not feeling it at all. The clock is ticking and now I have three months to not only *find* a woman but to also make her my wife, all before the vote.

It's an impossible task.

"See anyone you like?" Julien asks as he plops down next to me. I answer by giving him a sideways glance.

No, I don't see anyone I like. There's a bunch of beautiful women here tonight, but no one interests me in the slightest. Even though the whole thing is set up as a business agreement, I still want something to be there. Something that makes me want to choose her—to put my reputation on the line for. Because if this charade doesn't work, I'm screwed.

"Come on man, when was the last time you had some fun with a beautiful woman?" I know what he means by *fun*. I haven't been with anyone other than my fist for the past four months.

Honestly, I've been busy with work, and just like today, I haven't felt a pull towards anyone.

Except for the girl in the lobby.

I shake that thought away. She's only a tourist, and I don't have time for those.

"Why don't you go and dance over there?" I say, trying to get him to leave me alone for a little while.

He laughs at my obvious attempt to ignore his question. "Why don't you join me?"

"Not tonight, man," I reply, feeling drained from my long day at the office. "I just want to sit here and people-watch for a bit."

Julien shrugs, taking another sip of his drink. "Suit yourself. But if you change your mind, I'll be right over there." He points to the dance floor before he moonwalks away.

I nod, grateful for him being so understanding, and settle back into my seat.

As I sip my drink, I watch the crowd, scanning the faces for any familiar ones, but then my eye catches someone.

Her. The girl from the hotel lobby. She's dancing with her friends in the middle of the dance floor, swaying those lovely hips to the beat of the music.

She's gorgeous.

I had been on the phone with Harlow. I was stressed out and trying to keep my cool, but then I caught her staring at me and I couldn't help but notice how beautiful she was. She was wearing a tight t-shirt and yoga pants, which hugged her curves in all the right places. To top it off, she had a hoodie tied around her waist, completing the effortless, yet irresistible travel look.

I had hoped to run into her again at the hotel, but seeing her now feels like fate, like it's God's way of saying, *"Hey, there she is."*

Her eyes sparkle under the lights, and her hair is styled in soft waves that cascade down her back. She's wearing a sleek black dress that accentuates her form, making her look like a goddess among mortals. There's something pure and innocent about her that intrigues me, and I can't stop myself from imagining what it would be like to have her sway those hips against me. But then reality snaps me back to attention.

She looks like a girl who romanticizes life—a life I can't offer right now. I'm not here for love or romance. I'm here on a mission: to find a woman who will sign papers, stay married for a year, and then disappear.

I finish my drink and stand up from the table, ready to continue my search.

It's just business, nothing personal.

But as the night wears on, I can't shake the feeling that tonight won't be the night I find the one. The crowded bar is buzzing with energy, but I feel like an outsider looking in. That's when Julien sidles up to me with a grin on his face.

"What's up, man? Why do you look like someone stole your puppy?" he asks, his laughter echoing around us.

I look at him, my brows furrowing. "I'm not in the mood for this tonight. I need another drink."

I make my way to the bar and after ordering another one, I hear a soft voice. I turn to see the girl standing there, her big green eyes hesitant.

Lobby-Girl.

What are the odds?

"Hi," she says with a small, nervous smile on her lips.

Leaning in closer to her ear, I whisper back, "Hi." Staying close, I continue, "Do I know you?" I haven't been able to shake her from my thoughts since I laid my eyes on her, but she doesn't have to know that.

"No, you don't know me," she says softly, her eyes boring into mine. She tries to flirt with a bad pick-up line, and I can't help but find it endearing.

"Leora," she introduces herself with a soft smile. I take her hand in mine, and I feel a jolt of electricity shoot up my arm as our skin touches. *Leora*, I've never heard that name before.

I like it.

"Lucas," I reply, holding onto her hand for a moment longer

than necessary. Her eyes meet mine, and I can see the spark of attraction that I'm certain is mirrored in mine.

Leora's voice is sweet as she leans in to compliment one of my tattoos. Her eyes fixate on the inked wings adorning my forearm, and a genuine smile graces her lips. I nod, a hint of nostalgia in my eyes as I look at the wings. It's the tattoo I got with Liam, twenty years after our parents' passing.

Leora's gaze softens, and she must have noticed the melancholy on my face. Swiftly, she changes the subject, steering the conversation toward a lighter topic.

"So, Lucas, can I buy you a drink?

I look down at the glass in my hand and politely decline, offering to buy her one instead.

She tells me she's here with her friends and then she points toward two girls at the end of the bar, one with dark hair and the other blonde. I recognize them immediately. They were standing in line to the club when I was walking in. Those two were facing me while the third girl—whom I assume was Leora—had her back turned. I overheard them talking while I exchanged pleasantries with the bouncer. They mentioned some kind of mission and that one of the girls was supposed to go up to a guy in the club. At first, I brushed it off as something silly. Why would any of them need a mission to approach a guy? And for what?

But then it hits me, *she* must have been the girl who got the mission, and I'm *the* guy.

Which means she's only talking to me to complete her mission—to gain some brownie points with her friends. Not because she has any kind of interest in me.

My smile fades as I realize the truth. I shouldn't have let my guard down so easily.

"Do you want anything else?"

"I'm sorry?" Her eyes widen as she blinks, looking completely caught off guard.

I lock my gaze onto hers. "Well, sweetheart," I say, leaning slightly closer, my tone firm, "let me put it simply for you: we talked, I bought you a drink, and that's the end of this transaction."

Before I get the chance to turn around, she throws her drink at me. The liquid splatters all over my shirt, and I feel the sting of the alcohol in my eyes. Leora storms off, leaving me standing there in shock. The people around us are staring, and I can hear someone snickering in the background. My hands curl into fists as I try to control the anger bubbling inside of me. I won't let her get the best of me. As I make my way to the bathroom to clean up, I can feel everyone's eyes on me, but I try my best to ignore them.

I walk back to my table, my shirt still wet, but before my ass even reaches the sofa, a scratchy, drunken female voice reaches me. "Lucas, is that you?"

No way. My already awful night takes a turn for the worse.

As I turn around, I see her—Melina, my ex-girlfriend—stumbling toward me with a drink in her hand, looking as beautiful as always. But the beauty can't mask the toxicity that is Melina.

I brace myself for the worst as she slurs, "I thought it was you. How've you been, baby?"

I force a tight-lipped smile, trying to hide my discomfort. "I'm good, Melina. How about you?" I ask, trying to keep the conversation polite. She plops herself down on my lap, spilling her drink in the process.

"I miss you," she slurs, and I can't help but feel a mix of disgust and pity. As fate would have it, Leora and her friends stroll by at that exact moment, and I catch her friend throwing me a disgusted side eye.

Lord, give me strength.

Leaning in closer to me, Melina continues, "Why did we ever break up?"

I push her away gently, trying not to cause a scene.

"I'm not interested in rehashing the past."

"But I still love you," she protests, taking a sip from her drink while spilling some on me. "Can't we give it another try?"

I sigh, feeling uncomfortable and frustrated. "No, Melina. It's not going to happen. Now if you'll excuse me, I need to go clean this mess up."

With that, I get up from the couch, move her off to the side, and make my way to the bathroom to clean the spilled drink off my shirt, again.

I SIT AT MY DESK, scrolling through the endless list of candidates for the role of marketing manager. I've been at it for hours, but no one feels right. So far, I've met with five candidates, but there's no passion in their eyes. No spark. I need someone who's ready to stand up for what they believe in, someone who doesn't roll over as soon as I say no. I need some push and pull.

I feel my eyes start to glaze over at the dull content, and I quickly close the computer. As I lean back in my chair, I can't help but think about Leora again. No one has ever thrown a drink in my face. While I'm still pissed, I can't help but admit that I like the fire in her. It intrigues me. I've never met a woman like her before.

My phone buzzes. I look to find a message from Julien.

JULIEN

The guys and I are planning on going out for some drinks, you joining?

ME

Send me the details and I'll meet you later.

WHEN I CHECK THE TIME, I realize that I've been at it for far too long. Grabbing my jacket, I head to the office elevator. The office is located on the top floor, which gives us an incredible view of the city and the sea.

As I'm about to exit the hotel, I see three girls walking toward the hotel bar. Among them, one stands out, her sweet voice hanging in the air. I could recognize it anywhere—Leora.

I should probably mind my own business and meet up with the guys at the bar Julien texted me about. What I shouldn't do is follow them, but my legs are already moving on instinct, and I curse myself for it.

I don't know why I just can't leave it alone. A part of me is pissed because she ruined my night, while another part is even more pissed because she's occupied my headspace for the past few days. I don't have time for it and I *especially* don't have time for *her*.

Yet, here I am, wasting my time following them.

As I step inside, the familiar sound of chatter and clinking glasses washes over me. The walls are adorned with vintage photographs and art deco fixtures, giving the space a timeless, sophisticated feel. My eyes wander over to the bar, and I find her in a few seconds. Leora is perched on a stool, surrounded by her two friends, her laughter ringing out above the noise. I don't think she would be laughing if I went up to *her* and threw a drink in her face.

I think about doing it for a second too long before I find a seating area close by that's hidden from their line of sight. I order a whiskey and sit back, trying to listen in on their conversation without being obvious. I find myself trying to catch a glimpse of her and watch as the soft glow of the warm lighting illuminates her face, making her look ethereal.

Why does she have to be so damn beautiful?

It's annoying.

It has to be a test. God must have put her here to test my patience.

"Oh my god. I don't think I've ever seen so many gorgeous men in the same place, and the way they *danced*." Leora takes a sip of her drink while she fans her face with her other hand.

Did she throw anything in *their* faces?

Get a grip.

Another voice chimes in, "Girl, I think I found my first, second, *and* third husband yesterday."

They all laugh and clink their glasses together, the sound echoing in the noisy room. I roll my eyes and take another sip of my whiskey, feeling a sense of disinterest wash over me. A few minutes pass—or maybe more, I'm not sure—and I'm just about to leave when Leora's phone makes a sound, interrupting their conversation. I watch as her face immediately falls as she reads the message.

I lean forward a bit to hear them better.

"It's John," she says, her energy draining. From her reaction, he's probably a dickhead.

"What does he want?" her friend asks with disgust dripping from her tone.

"He's asking when I'm coming back."

The dark-haired friend notices the change in her demeanor and says, "Girl, delete that message and block him. You're not answering or entertaining him. His negativity is not needed in your life."

How poetic.

"You're right," Leora nods and starts typing away on her phone. "Done! The only thing I need now are you two and, hopefully, a new job." Her shoulders drop as she continues, "I actually applied to a few roles before we came here, but most of them rejected me. Apparently, I don't have the 'marketing experience' they're looking for."

I take another sip of my whiskey. So she's unemployed and is looking for a marketing role.

What about the marketing role at the hotel?

I quickly shut down that thought. Why would I do that? Give a stranger a chance to ruin more than just one of my shirts? No thanks.

"It will come, don't worry about it." Her friend soothes her.

"Yeah," she huffs the word out before she jumps down from

her chair. "I need to use the restroom." She stands up and collects her bag.

I turn to look around for the bathroom and lo and behold, the WC sign is right in front of me. *Fuck, my luck is just not it.*

When I turn to make a swift exit, I'm met by Leora's piercing gaze which is locked on me. Her eyes are ice cold.

"Fancy seeing you here." I say with a wry smile.

"Are you stalking me or something?" Her arms cross in front of her chest.

I look at her in disbelief. "Stalking you? Please. I have better things to do."

"Then why are you here, blocking my way?"

"I work here, darling, and if I happen to remember correctly, *you* were the one who was staring at me when we first met. And the second time we crossed paths? *You* came up to me." I lean forward slightly, wanting to make a point. "*You* seem to be stalking *me.*"

Leora opens her mouth to argue back, but then thinks better of it, clearly a bit embarrassed. As she should be.

"Whatever. Just leave me alone, okay?" she says before storming past me to the bathroom, her shoulder colliding with mine on the way.

I really need to start avoiding this girl.

SEVEN

LEORA

It's strange how we can lose ourselves over time, sometimes completely unaware of the negative effects others can have on who we are. It's taken me weeks, but I'm finally coming to terms with the realization that my past relationship had stripped me of some of the things I loved about myself.

I guess that's what happens after being freed from a relationship.

A *toxic* relationship, that is. At least that's what Adeline has been preaching for the past fifteen minutes while we've been perched at this rooftop bar. The atmosphere pulsates with energy as a vibrant crowd dances to the beat of the music, but the energy doesn't match mine today.

"Listen, Leora, John sucks and he was so toxic, you just didn't see it before," Adeline says empathetically, setting her Aperol Spritz aside. Her words pull at something inside me, and I take another sip of my Gin and Tonic, willing myself to listen.

"She's right," I hear Sophie chime in, her voice filled with sincerity. "You always deserved better." I can't help but push back slightly, still feeling a strange sense of loyalty to the man who had been my first love—my first everything. "You make it sound like he's always been a bad person," I murmur. The alcohol courses

47

through my veins, clouding my judgment."No, we're not saying that he was a bad person," Sophie reassures me, her eyes locking on to mine. "Just that you were too good for him."

A lump forms in my throat as I struggle to hold back tears. "He was my first and only love." My voice trembles, and I can sense an emotional storm brewing within me.

"Habibti, I understand that you feel protective over the good memories you shared, but please don't defend him," Adeline says.

Fear gnaws at me as I whisper, "What if I never find another person again? What if he was my only chance at love?" Tears pool in my eyes and I avert my gaze from my friends, taking a long sip of my drink. I signal the bartender for another, even though I know I've probably had enough.

Sophie leans closer, wrapping her arm around me and pulling me into a comforting embrace. It's her warmth and sincerity that finally shatters the dam holding back my emotions.

"Don't breathe air into that narrative. He wasn't your person, honey. Believe me when I tell you that you will find him, and that man is going to treat you like the queen you are."

My voice quivers as I protest, "You can't know that for sure."

Adeline's frustration shows in her next words as she sees my tears. "Yes, we do. Do you know how we know that?"

I shake my head, my curiosity piquing through my emotional haze.

Adeline continues with conviction, "You are, without a doubt, the most amazing person I've ever known. You're not just strong and ambitious; you're the most genuine friend anyone could ever hope for. Anyone who can't see that is the one losing out on something truly special."

I pause for a moment, the words sinking in, "So I did the right thing leaving him?"

"Yes," she responds. She studies me, and she must see a sliver of doubt lingering behind my eyes, because she asks, "What did he say when you got that award for best marketing rookie?"

I think back to that moment, remembering how excited I had

been to share my success with John. A bitter taste fills my mouth as I recall his response. "He said . . . he said I got lucky. That anyone could have done it." I remember how disappointed I was when he didn't applaud me or tell me I did well. But on the other hand, he was right. I did get lucky, and anyone at the company could have done it.

"What did he say to you when you wore that beautiful red dress to Monica's wedding?" Adeline prods, her voice filled with concern.

I take a deep breath, recalling that day when I felt so confident in the stunning red dress I had chosen. My voice trembles as I recount his words, "That the dress made it look like I was trying too hard and that a bold color like red didn't suit me."

Adeline adds to the growing list of grievances, her voice firm yet gentle. "And what about when you wanted to pursue that dream job in London? What did he say then?"

I swallow hard, the bitterness of that memory still fresh. "He said it was foolish to think I could succeed there and that I should just settle for something here, close to him, where there was a bigger chance for *him* to succeed."

Just hearing myself repeat some of his words out loud and recounting the constant gaslighting churns my stomach.

I hate it.

I hate that I let him chip away at my strength.

I hate that I validated his feelings over mine.

I hate that I allowed myself to get lost and lose my spirit.

But, most of all, I hate that I surrendered pieces of my self-respect to such an extent that, some days, I didn't even recognize myself.

I used to be the happy-go-lucky girl, the one known for walking on clouds and always radiating with a bubbly spirit. Yet, over the past year, I feel like I've become bitter—as if the shadows of his toxicity had tainted the sunshine within me. Tears slowly run down my face, unchecked, as Sophie and Adeline wrap their arms around me in a warm, comforting embrace. Their hugs are tight, grounding me in their support, and I feel a sense of safety I haven't experienced in a long time. It's as though their arms are a shield, protecting me from the lingering doubts and insecurities that John has left behind.

I sniffle, feeling the warmth of them enveloping me like a lifeline. "I'm sorry, girls. I'm ruining our night out."

Sophie pulls away slightly to look me in the eyes. "Leora, you're not ruining anything. We're here for you, through the good and the bad. That's what friends are for, remember?"

Adeline nods in agreement. "That's right. We're here to help you heal, and sometimes that means sharing the pain. You're not alone in this."

I sit up, wiping away my tears with a grateful smile. "You two are the best friends a girl could ask for."

Adeline smiles. "We love you and we'll always be here to support you, no matter what."

I take another deep breath, trying to shake off the heavy emotions that had weighed me down. I glance around the lively bar, searching for a way to change the subject and lighten the mood.

"Adeline, that blond guy has been checking you out the whole time we've been sitting here. He even stared at you during the whole cry fest. You should—"

Adeline interrupts me with a playful grin. "Don't finish that sentence, Leora. You know what I think about blond men." We all share a knowing laugh at Adeline's playful aversion to blond men. It's one of her quirks that's been a constant source of amusement among us. I remember her telling me once that even men in her favorite books can't be blond. Not in the ones she writes, or the ones she reads. She's always said that even if they happen to be blond on paper, they'll simply be dark-haired in her mind.

I tease her gently. "You really have a thing against blond hair, don't you?"

Adeline chuckles and raises her cocktail glass. "It's just not my cup of tea, Leora. Now, perk up, my gorgeous friend, and let's cheers to the future rewarding us with what we truly deserve."

I wipe away the last remnants of tears, knowing I probably resemble a raccoon at this point, and raise my glass, joining Adeline in the toast. "To the future," I say, my voice stronger now, filled with hope and determination.

To the future, and to a new, updated version of myself. A girl who doesn't let men step on her, a girl who stands up for herself, and a girl who knows what she's worth.

Also, note to self, invest in some therapy when you're back home.

EIGHT

LEORA

As I stroll back from the beach, the sun kisses my skin with a gentle warmth, and the salty breeze carries a sense of freedom.

I reach the hotel in less than three minutes, and I'm reminded of how close it is to the beach.

What a life.

The hotel looks beautiful as it rises against the blue sky—its pristine, white exterior gleaming in the sunshine. The bellhops welcome me with smiles that match the bright day. When I catch the eyes of the girls behind the check-in desk, they too share in the day's radiance with beautiful smiles. However, as I approach the desk, something unexpected captures my attention—a laminated paper with the words:

Join our team as the Marketing Manager at Hotel Ayoub d'Or - A Golden Opportunity!

Is this a sign?

God, is that you?

If it is, please let this be an opportunity and not a lesson, please and thank you.

"What's that, Clara?" I ask the brunette hotel receptionist.

She lights up. "Oh, Miss Davis. I thought of you when I saw

this." She remembered our conversation from two days ago. I was walking through the lobby, my head buried in my phone, looking through applications when we bumped into each other. She asked me why I looked so stressed and that's when I started word-vomiting to her. She now knows about my failed job *and* my failed relationship. You could say we're best friends.

"You should apply for it," she continues, and as I stare at the paper behind her, I start to realize I *should* apply for it. It's a great opportunity. The only thing is that I might not have the correct experience, or live in the correct country, but hey, I've already received a bunch of rejections; another one won't hurt.

"Yes, I should."

She hands me the paper, and as I touch it I feel a glimmer of hope rekindling within me.

A sudden thud and a surprised cry from Clara makes me turn around to find an older man on his hands and knees.

I don't think for a second before I run up to him. I can see that he's struggling to get up, and his breathing is labored.

"Sir, are you okay?" I ask, extending a hand to help him up. He looks up at me with a grateful expression and nods weakly, his face pale and his eyes slightly unfocused. He must be in a lot of pain.

I try to keep the panic at bay, worrying he may have hurt himself more than we can see. I turn to face Clara and find her face contorted in utter horror, her lips parted as if to speak, but nothing comes out.

"Call an ambulance, Clara," I say.

"No, no, I'm okay," the man insists before a coughing fit interrupts him.

"Are you sure?" I ask while helping him move towards a chair.

"Yes, I'm fine, but may I please have a glass of water?" he requests, and Clara rushes off to retrieve one for him.

As he settles into the seat, he grasps my hand and says, "Thank you, Mademoiselle."

"Is this yours?" A large man joins us by the chair, and when I say large, I mean *huge,* as in the Mountain from *Game of Thrones,* huge. My neck cranes as I look at him and then at the paper in his hand

The job ad.

"Oh. Yes, thank you."

The older gentleman scans it. "Are you applying for the job?"

"Ehm, y-yes. Or at least I'm thinking about it," I say with a smile.

"Then why don't we sit down and have an interview?"

"What do you mean?"

Then the mountain man speaks up, "He's the owner of the hotel, Mademoiselle."

I'm at a loss for words, and I look back at Clara silently mouthing, *"What?"* She replies with a soft nod.

How in the world is this happening today? First the job application, and now I save the owner of the hotel. Okay, *save* is probably too extreme, but he could have broken a hip or something.

God, if this is all you, don't be playing jokes. I can't handle more of them.

"I'm sorry, I don't understand."

"Jacques?" The owner of the hotel calls, and mountain man looks at him. "Can you help me to the sofa and get our applicant whatever she wants to drink?" Jacques's eyes snap to mine. He looks at me as if he's waiting for me to answer.

"Just a black coffee would be great, thank you." *Why did I say that?* I hate black coffee.

The older man across from me exudes kindness. There's weathered lines surrounding his dark eyes and mouth, evidence of a happy life, and his smile carries a reassuring warmth. Yet, I still can't shake the self-consciousness that lingers within me.

I've managed to take five sips of my coffee without spitting it out—that's a win in my book.

"What's your name?" he asks, looking at me curiously.

"Leora," I finally croak out, taking another sip.

"Leora, that's a beautiful and unique name," he says with a smile.

"Thank you," I reply, feeling a little more at ease.

"My name is Antoine Ayoub." The warm smile is still on his lips as he continues, "Tell me about yourself, Leora. Where did you work before? " Antoine asks, leaning forward slightly.

I take a deep breath. "Well, I used to work as a marketing assistant. I was responsible for handling campaigns and overseeing projects. I have experience in event planning, and I've also worked in retail. Retail was fun, but oh my god, people really do *anything* for a sale." I laugh nervously, scolding myself for that last part. I need to stop myself from rambling, which I tend to do when I'm nervous. I take another sip of my nasty coffee and try my best not to scrunch my nose in disgust.

"I don't speak French, and I know I haven't worked as a manager before," I add, feeling a little self-conscious, "but I'm driven, and I'm always eager to learn."

"Everybody speaks English here, so there's not much of a barrier there." Antoine leans back in his chair and smiles at me reassuringly.

"Regarding your previous work experience. While it's certainly valuable, what's more important is who you are as a person and how you approach your work. You strike me as a driven and determined individual, and with that kind of attitude, I have no doubt that you'll be able to learn. Am I right?"

"I think so," I respond with a nod. "I've always considered myself a quick learner, and I'm eager to take on new challenges."

"I'm glad to hear that, Leora. I value individuals who are eager to take on new challenges. Let's move forward with the discussion, I'm excited to learn more about you"

I almost want to cry at his words. No one has ever spoken to me like that. No one has ever reassured me the way he just did.

"Tell me about yourself. What's important to you?" he says, regarding me with genuine interest.

I pause for a moment. How do I answer that? No one's ever

asked me this, especially not during an interview. What if I say something wrong and ruin everything? But on the other hand, *is* there a wrong answer?

Antoine's eyes search mine. He gives me a small smile that lights up his eyes, encouraging me to answer.

"I value people." I say, finally. Antoine's eyes flicker as he nods at my response. "I believe authenticity is important and having a kind heart."

Antoine nods, seemingly pleased with my answer. A sense of warmth spreads through me as I realize that I might have found someone who truly understands me and my values.

"That's a beautiful answer. Your parents must be proud." I stiffen at the mention of my parents.

My parents have never been proud of me. I never *had* any parents to be proud of me. I was unwanted from the start.

"They passed away when I was little." Lies. My mum passed away when I was born, and my biological father couldn't handle the pressure of raising me alone, so he left me at the age of three. I don't know much about them, more than that my father was white, born and raised in New Jersey, and my mother was half Hispanic and half white. I've probably gotten my brown wavy hair from her side. They apparently met in highschool where he knocked her up. So, after he left I was raised in foster care, in a household of ten and had to fend for myself a lot, but I was lucky I happened to have great neighbors. I always say that Adeline and her family saved me. They took me in whenever I needed it. They fed me, played with me, and kept me safe.

A sad expression comes across his face; it looks like recognition.

Maybe he lost someone too?

"I'm sorry to hear that, dear."

"It's okay, I'm now surrounded by people who love me."

He nods at that before asking me a new question, moving the conversation away from the sad stories. "Where do you see yourself in five years?"

Taking another deep breath, I share my hopes and dreams with Antoine, hoping to paint a picture of my ideal future. "To be completely honest, Antoine, I just want to be content in my life. I want to wake up every morning and feel like I have a purpose, like I belong somewhere. I want to be able to go to work and feel like I'm doing something right and that my work is valued and needed."

I look up to find Antoine studying me with a sweet smile on his lips. He nods, and then his eyes gleam in a way I can't make sense of.

"That sounds like a beautiful life," he says, his voice warm and genuine. "I hope you get it all one day." The sincerity in his words makes me feel a bit more at ease.

Just before he rises to leave, Antoine flashes me a playful smile. "And who knows, it might happen sooner than you think."

AFTER OUR CONVERSATION EARLIER, Antoine promised to think about everything we discussed and get back to me later in the day. It's been three hours now and I'm still waiting for his call. Adeline and Sophie are still out shopping, and I know from experience that they can be out all day, which means I know better than to think they will be home anytime soon. So, I'm left alone with my thoughts and keep replaying our conversation in my head.

One part, in particular, keeps nagging me. Antoine mentioned that the role would be here in Nice, and I'll have to stay here for at least a year. He did say that the possibility of remote work could be discussed after that. It's a fair arrangement, but the thought of leaving everything behind and moving here still makes me nervous.

Although, come to think of it, what *would* I be leaving? I have nothing holding me back. No family, no job, no boyfriend. Why wouldn't I agree to this?

You have your friends, a voice in my head whispers. But if I don't seize this once in a lifetime opportunity, I think they will disown me. Just then, my phone vibrates and interrupts my inner battle. I quickly answer, "Hello?"

"Hi, Ms. Davis. It's Antoine." I can sense the smile and excitement in his voice. It's clear that he has some good news to share.

"I wanted to call you personally to offer you the job, if you're still interested," he continues.

"Really? Yes, of course I am," I answer eagerly while doing a happy dance.

"Bravo! I'll get an agreement together for you to sign," he says. I can't help but feel a surge of excitement, but then reality hits me

"Wait, am I even allowed to work here? I don't have a work-permit."

"Don't worry about that. I'll make sure everything is handled." He pauses for a moment before speaking again. "But I have one more offer, a slightly odd one," he says, his tone serious. "Could you please come by my office in an hour? I think this matter is more of a face-to-face discussion."

My heart skips a beat at the mention of another offer, and I put aside the comment about it being *slightly odd.*

What could it be? Is it something even better than the job he just offered me? The suspense is almost too much to bear.

"Sure," I reply, trying to sound as composed as possible.

AFTER REPEATEDLY ASKING every staff member I come across for directions, I finally find someone who agrees to help me—Pierre, the concierge.

Together, we ascend the stairs, as there's no way I'm taking an elevator thirty floors up. However, Pierre seems to be growing increasingly agitated. He's been shooting angry glances my way since the sixteenth floor. Granted, I'm also exhausted and drenched in sweat, but I didn't force him to accompany me on the staircase. He could have easily taken the elevator and left me to my own devices.

Eventually, we arrive at a door with a lock—guests aren't permitted to access the office floors. Pierre leads me through another set of stairs behind the keycard-locked door.

As we walk through the office, I can't help but marvel at its beauty. The space is filled with natural light and the walls are adorned with gorgeous artwork. The floors are covered in rich mahogany, adding warmth to the atmosphere and the furniture is sleek and modern. I feel a little intimidated, like I don't belong here. That feeling is only intensified when we're met by Camille, who looks like she's stepped out of a fashion magazine. She greets me warmly and introduces herself as the assistant to *both* Mr. Ayoubs.

There are, apparently, two of them.

"Thank you, Pierre," she dismisses him and I follow her. We approach a closed door and I hear muffled voices coming from the other side. "They're waiting for you." She knocks on the door and then guides me in.

Upon entering the room, the voices become clearer and I hear someone yelling, "Are you kidding me? I told you I would handle this myself!"

My heart sinks a little at the tension in the room, but then Antoine spots me and his face lights up. I immediately feel relief at seeing a friendly face.

He opens his arms. "Welcome, Leora."

The relief quickly disappears when the angry man in the room turns around, and I feel as though someone has poured ice-cold water down my back.

"You!" We exclaim at the same time

In front of me stands none other than the handsome asshole, Lucas.

NINE

LUCAS

My uncle rescheduled our mid-day meeting, and my body fills with rage as I enter his office.

"You're not *choosing* a wife for me."

"I've already chosen one, and she'll be great for you."

"I won't marry a random girl you've picked," I say through gritted teeth. "You don't even know her yourself. You just met her *today.*"

"You forget that I've lived much longer than you, and that my eyes have seen more people than you could ever dream of. You don't succeed in life without learning how to read people and understand their hearts."

I shake my head at his words. My uncle has been spewing Arabic proverbs about understanding people since I was young, with his favorite being, *"The heart knows what the tongue can't say, and what the ears can't hear."* He's always encouraging me to learn how to understand a person through their eyes and determine if they're trustworthy. But he seems to forget that times change and people are much more calculated nowadays. Eyes don't speak the same language anymore.

"I'm not interested in this girl," I say, crossing my arms in defiance like my younger self.

"You should give her a chance. At least meet her and see for yourself."

I sigh at his words before answering with, "I'll choose my own wife."

"It's been over three months, Lucas, and you only have three months left. From my perspective, it doesn't seem like you can. Besides, she's on her way here now."

Fire courses through my veins. "Are you kidding me? I told you I would handle this myself!"

My uncle just laughs, seeming very pleased with himself.

Suddenly, the door opens and my uncle speaks, "Welcome, Leora."

Leora.

I know that name.

That name belonged to the infuriating woman that threw a drink in my face.

That name . . . is here to be presented as my potential wife.

There's no way in hell.

I turn, my attention immediately drawn to the woman entering the room. It annoys me that she looks even more beautiful now than she did in the club, but her aura still screams *warning*. Her eyebrows furrow, and her gaze turns harsh as she spots me.

"You!" she exclaims.

"You!" I respond as we recognize each other.

A sudden realization strikes me. Is this why she approached me in the club, pretending to be innocent and afraid? Was this her plan all along? She must have known who I was and found a way to slither into our lives. Maybe she already knew who my uncle was, and helping him today—an action that warmed my heart up until a few seconds ago—was only a scheme to get her foot in the door.

My anger flares up again, and I can't take it anymore.

"Absolutely not," I say, moving toward the door to leave.

But my uncle's voice stops me in my tracks. "Lucas Christian

Ayoub, you do not walk away from me. Sit down and listen!" His words are loaded with disapproval and authority, and for the first time in a long while, he calls me by my full name, making me realize the severity of the situation. I reluctantly comply, sitting back down in my chair.

"You too, Leora," he adds, motioning for her to sit as well.

She complies with his request, looking a bit startled, and says, "I don't understand."

My uncle looks between us. "Have you met before?" I size her up and find her doing the same to me, but neither one of us answers his question. He huffs before he turns his attention to Leora and begins speaking. "Leora, I did my due diligence on you. I know that you were let go from your previous job." She stiffens beside me at his words.

I knew she was looking for a job but not that she was fired.

"I also found out that your previous boss has been spreading negative feedback about you, bad-mouthing you to anyone who listens. However, we do need your skills, and I'm still offering you the job if you agree to one more condition."

Leora looks surprised, before sadness overtakes her. "Why would you still want me?" she asks.

"Because I believe in giving people a chance," he replies. "And because I see potential in you. You have a lot to offer, and we could use someone with your talents and values."

Leora looks thoughtful for a moment—there's a sheen to her eyes.

Oh god, don't tell me she's going to cry. I feel a surge of discomfort as I shift in my seat, unsure of what to do. I hate when people cry. I don't even remember the last time I shed a tear.

"Okay," she whispers, discreetly wiping away a tear that almost fell before she smiles. I can't help but stare at her in awe. *She's good. She's really good, my uncle is eating this up.*

Uncle Antoine smiles, relieved. "Great, we'll work out the details later. But for now, let's get back to business."

Leora looks at him, puzzled. "But why is *he* here?" she asks, pointing at me. There's not a single tear left in her now sharp eyes.

He takes a deep breath, contemplating his words carefully. "As much as you seem to need us, we also need you," he says. "You see, I'm dying"—straight to the point, making the knot in my stomach twist again at the reminder—"and Lucas is my heir. But he can only take over the hotel if he gets married. That's where you come in."

Leora's expression morphs into a look of sheer confusion. "Oh, I know I said I've done some event planning, but I've never done a wedding. I meant more business events."

"No, Leora, you misunderstand," my uncle clarifies. "Lucas, here, needs a bride."

"What does that have to do with me?" she asks, still not connecting the dots. Her eyes dart between my uncle and I, and I can feel my frustration bubbling up. How can she not see what we're getting at?

My uncle takes a deep breath, choosing his next words carefully, "We want you to be the bride."

Leora's eyes widen, and she looks back at me with a mix of shock and uncertainty. As if looking at me will make any sense of this situation. She's beginning to understand what my uncle is offering, but for some reason, it looks like she's not fully there, which means I have to jump in and explain it to her. My eyes roll on their own accord before I speak up. "In short, we need you to marry me so that I can take over the hotel without having our stakeholders riot because I ignored a clause in the company's contract. I know it's a lot to ask and believe me, I'm not thrilled about this either. But my uncle is adamant that this is the best way to secure the future of the business."

Leora's mouth drops open, and I can tell that she's finally grasping the seriousness of the proposal. "Marry you? But we barely know each other," she protests, her voice wavering with uncertainty and something else.

"I want you to know that I didn't plan for this, and certainly not with you," I continue, her brows furrowing at the truth in my words.

Before she can snap back at me, my uncle speaks, giving me a sharp look. "We don't expect you to give an immediate answer. Take the time you need to think it over. I promise we'll do our best to make this as painless as possible for you."

Leora seems to be echoing my feelings of unhappiness with this situation. I can see her emotions playing out on her face, and it's clear that she's struggling to process everything. I shift uncomfortably in my seat.

How did all of this get so complicated? Why couldn't we just skip the formalities and bend the rules this time?

But my uncle doesn't back down. He speaks earnestly to Leora, explaining the gravity of the situation and the trust he's placed in her. "Leora, I have given you all of this information because I believe in you. I saw something in you when we spoke, and I truly meant every word I said to you. I trust you to keep this between us, whatever decision you make."

Leora's gaze snaps back to me, and she lifts her small hand, pointing her finger at me again, a gesture I'm starting to dislike. "What about him?" she asks, her voice tinged with frustration. "He doesn't want to marry me."

My uncle's response is direct and unsympathetic. "He has no choice in the matter. He needs a wife, making this your choice and your choice only," he states firmly, leaving no room for negotiation.

The tension in the room intensifies, and I grit my teeth, knowing deep down that my uncle is right. I have responsibilities and obligations to my family, and it seems like fate has tied me to this unexpected and unwanted situation.

To this woman.

Leora doesn't answer; she just looks around, stunned, before taking a breath, leaning back and staring at the ceiling as if in a trance.

I catch my uncle's eyes, and he looks as confused as I am.

What's wrong with her?

She mumbles something, and all I can hear is the word "*God.*" I assume she's praying for God to make something fall on my head.

"Dear, if you decide to take on this role, not only will you be rewarded with a well-paying job that will significantly advance your career, but you'll also receive compensation that extends beyond six figures. Additionally, you'll of course recieve coverage for your room and board, as well as a provided car if you want. It's a win-win situation." He says the last part with a smirk. I don't know if I want to slam my head into the wall or sink through the chair.

Leora stiffens at the mention of money.

"For how long?" she asks. My uncle looks to me for answers, which is his way of reaching out a hand in this insufferable situation.

"A year should be enough," I offer. "That should give us ample time to persuade the stakeholders before and after the vote."

"Leora, does one year sound feasible to you?"

Leora takes a deep breath, processing everything that has just been revealed to her. She looks at me and then back at my uncle, a mixture of emotions playing across her face. After a few moments of silence, she speaks up.

"I appreciate the offer, but I won't marry someone I barely know for a job," she says, her voice firm.

My uncle's expression darkens, disappointment etched on his face. "Leora, I understand this may seem sudden and overwhelming, but please take some time to think about it."

"I'm sorry, but I have to decline," Leora replies, standing up from her chair. "Thank you for the job offer, but I don't think this is the right fit for me."

My uncle looks like he's about to protest, but I cut him off. "Uncle, I agree with Leora. This is too much pressure to put on her. We can't force someone to marry me for the sake of a hotel." I mean, of course, it's unfair to *me*. But by shifting the focus to her, might make my uncle feel a hint of guilt.

He regards me with a mixture of surprise and desperation. "Lucas, this is not just about the hotel. It's about our family legacy; we can't just let it fall apart."

All this talk about family legacy doesn't sit right with me. It's too much, too desperate. Something else is off.

Both Leora and I tense up, and she instinctively grasps the back of the chair.

"What do you mean, Ammo?"

He doesn't try to hide his emotions. I've never seen him look this beaten down.

"We will lose the hotels. They will vote us out."

My whole body feels as though it's been hit by an arctic blast and I don't know how to catch my breath.

"They can't do that. It's your hotel!" I force out.

"They can do whatever they want if a majority agrees and from the whispers I've heard, there will be a vote soon."

"When is the vote?"

"Around the opening."

"Is this some kind of joke?"

"No, it's not," my uncle responds firmly.

"Are they doing it because of *me?*"

"They are going to be *your* hotels, Lucas. However, they're investors, which means it's also their hotels by extension"

Leora stares down at her hands, seemingly lost in thought. I can tell she's trying to process everything that's happened. But when she starts looking around the office, her eyes freeze on the pictures of me, Liam, and Ammo Antoine standing in front of different hotel doors. I notice something behind her eyes: guilt, and maybe longing.

Her leg moves up and down rapidly as she fidgets with her fingers. It's as if she's holding something back, but I can't quite tell what it is. I feel a sense of unease wash over me when I try to read her expression, but she finally speaks up, her voice soft but firm. "I need some time to think about it."

I study her intently. *Is she feeling bad? Or does she realize how much power she has in her hands—meaning she can get more money?*

My uncle nods understandingly. "Of course, take all the time you need. But please keep in mind that we need to put this in motion soon."

Leora nods, her gaze shifting between my uncle and I. I can sense her discomfort, and I know that I'm not the only one unhappy with this situation.

"I understand," she says, standing up from her chair. With that, she turns and walks towards the door. I watch her go, feeling a mix of relief and disappointment. Relief that she hasn't said yes, but also disappointment at her aversion to the proposal. Is the idea of marrying me that terrible?

My uncle turns to me, his eyes filled with concern. "Lucas, I know this is not what you want. But we have no other options."

"I know," I say, my shoulders slumping defeatedly.

My uncle sighs. "You have to trust me on this."

I nod, knowing he's always had my best interest at heart.

"We'll give her some time to think about it," I say. "But if she says no, what do we do then?"

My uncle fixes his gaze on me, his brows furrowing in a show of deep concern. "We'll cross that bridge when we get to it. But for now, let's concentrate on persuading her to say yes."

THE REST of my day drags on—my body moving through the motions while my mind remains fixated on her. We simply can't afford to lose the hotels; failure is not an option which means it falls on me to make her agree, no matter what it takes. I don't have a clear plan yet, but I know I must convince her to marry me.

"Monsieur Ayoub, line three for you." Camille's voice reverberates and I pick up the phone, pressing the button for line three.

"Yes?"

"Hi." A sweet voice on the other end speaks softly, but I can hear the hesitation in her tone.

It's her.

I take a deep breath, trying to calm my rapid thoughts before speaking.

"Are you calling to give me an answer?" I ask, my tone flat and emotionless.

There's a brief moment of silence before she replies, "You're not Antoine."

"I'm not."

"Well, I want to speak to him."

"You've got me. Now, answer my question."

She lets out a shaky breath. "I . . . I have some conditions."

I resist the urge to roll my eyes. Of course she has conditions, and they probably have everything to do with money.

My fingers drum on the table, voice curt and clipped. "And what are they, Leora?"

There's another pause on the other end of the line before she speaks again. "Could we meet up and discuss this like civilized people?"

"Very well," I reply, my voice still controlled. "How about you come up to the office?"

"No, not the office. There's a café close to the hotel. Let's go there."

I agree, and we set a time for later in the day.

Maybe I can reason with her and negotiate some terms that work for both of us. Whatever happens, I know I can't afford to mess this up. The fate of my family's hotels rests on my shoulders, and I'll do whatever it takes to save them, even if it means marrying Leora.

TEN

LEORA

Adeline's face contorts with disbelief. "I'm sorry, back up, they did *what*?" she asks, her voice high-pitched and incredulous. I chuckle nervously, feeling the weight of the situation.

"They offered me a job *and* a marriage proposal," I repeat, my voice trailing off at the end. "And I think I might say yes."

Adeline's eyes widen in shock, and Sophie's jaw drops in shock.

"What?!" they both exclaim in unison.

"Are you insane?" Adeline adds, her tone bordering on hysterical. I can't blame her for her reaction, I'm still processing the proposal myself. But the job offer is too good to pass up, and the idea of a fake marriage doesn't seem so insane anymore. Besides, after hearing that they might lose the hotel I can't possibly say no now—I'll look like an asshole. The look on sweet Antoine's face broke my heart, and I'll get a chance to try out marriage before I do it for real. A test run of sorts. Guys always talk about testing a car before they buy it, why can't I do it for marriage?

Who knows, maybe I'll hate it and never want to get married again. I'll become one of those aunts who travel the world, drink a lot, and have the best stories for her nieces and nephews.

I let out a sigh. "I know it sounds crazy, but think about it. I lost my job, and the ones I've applied for haven't responded. However, now I know Agnes might be the reason for that. I can't believe she would sabotage everything for me. This is my opportunity to get my life back while saving their business. I can't say no to that."

"Leora, if you say no, they'll find another bride. Don't put that much pressure on yourself," Adeline says reassuringly, and she has a point. They'll probably find another woman, but then I'll still be unemployed.

"This is also my chance to start fresh in a new country, with no cheating ex-boyfriend around, and a job that will give me *something*." I try to reason with them, hoping they'll see my point of view. I don't know why, but I need them to support my decision. I need them to be on my side because if they don't agree, I can't do it.

I might be weak for it, but I *need* them to say *yes*.

"But Leora, marrying someone for a job is insane!" Adeline exclaims, shaking her head.

"Addie, you're usually the superstitious type. Don't you think this is a sign after all that has happened?"

"I'm not superstitious."

"When we were younger, you didn't allow me to step over you because that meant you would stop growing, and every time a shoe is upside down you have to flip it around."

Adeline crosses her arms over her chest, looking offended, with her brows furrowed and lips pressed into a tight line. "I'm not superstitious enough to let you marry a stranger. And a shoe upside down brings evil and bad luck, that's different."

Sophie, who has been quiet up until now, speaks up. "Girls, back to the subject. I see where you're coming from, Leora. It's not ideal, but it could be a good opportunity for you. You just have to think it through and make sure it's what you really want."

Adeline turns to her in surprise. "I'm sorry, have you two been taking the same crazy pills? She wants to marry a *stranger*. Not only that, but a guy that has been nothing but an ass to her!"

I roll my eyes at Adeline's comment and turn to Sophie. "Thank you for being the voice of reason here," I say with a grateful smile.

Sophie ignores Adeline and returns my smile before she continues with, "I mean, it's not like you're being forced into anything. You have a choice in the matter. You'll both have to sign a contract and have your own conditions, but what's the worst that could happen?"

Sophie's comment prompts Adeline to chime in, her tone sharp with disbelief.

"Are you serious, Sophie? How can you even entertain the idea of Leora marrying someone for a job?"

Sophie raises her eyebrows. "I'm not saying it's a perfect solution, but let's be practical here. Leora *needs* a job, and this is a good opportunity. And who knows, maybe they'll even fall in love."

Fall in love. With *Lucas*? Unlikely.

That man seems to walk around with a stick up his ass and I'm not going to be the one who pulls it out.

Adeline scoffs. "Oh please, stop romanticizing everything. This is a business arrangement, nothing more and Leora shouldn't have to compromise her values just to get ahead."

Oh.

Sophie rolls her eyes. "Adeline, stop being so bitter. You're supposed to be the romantic one, and not everyone has the luxury of turning down job offers left and right. This is a great job. She would have to work for at least three years back home before she would be offered a job at this level."

"I write *fiction*, which isn't this. Accepting a job offer is one thing, but marrying someone for a job is another," Adeline retorts.

"Guys, please . . ." I try to interject, but they don't seem to hear me anymore. It's starting to piss me off that they're talking about me like I'm not sitting right next to them.

"And what happens when the job ends, after the one year mark? She'll be stuck in a fake marriage with a stranger!"

Sophie rolls her eyes again. "It's not like she's signing her life away. If it doesn't work out, they can just get divorced."

Adeline shakes her head in disbelief. "I can't believe you're being so cavalier about marriage. It's a serious commitment."

"I know it's a serious commitment," Sophie retorts, "but she has an out if she wants one."

"Guys, please stop. I appreciate your concern, but ultimately it's my decision to make."

Adeline stands up and walks a few steps before she faces me again. "The only thing we know about this guy is that he has an office at this hotel, that he parties and likes to turn down beautiful girls at clubs before putting blondes on his lap. Is that what you want, Leora?" she snaps. I feel a sting of hurt at Adeline's words, but I try not to let it show.

"Would it make you feel better if I told you that I've looked him up?" I respond defensively. "He actually seems like a good guy. I'll show you." I quickly pull out my phone and show them what I spent the day doing. After our meeting, I went back to our room and started researching like my life depended on it—I guess it sort of does.

"His full name is Lucas Christian Ayoub. He's thirty-four years old and has a younger brother named Liam, who's also very handsome," I add before continuing. "Their parents passed away in a horrible car accident when they were kids. According to the article I read, Lucas had been in the car with them but he didn't suffer any major injuries. Then they were adopted by their uncle." I have to admit that it broke me when I read about his parents, and in a way—not that I'm excusing his rude behavior—it made me understand him a little bit more.

"That's awful. Poor kids," Sophie murmurs in a compassionate tone, her hand gently pressed against her heart. As I glance at Adeline, I notice her eyes widening with empathy, a soft frown forming on her face in response to the heartbreaking news.

I pause, allowing the information to settle, then share, "He later got his MBA from Cambridge University, and his uncle has been training him to take over ever since. "

But that wasn't all I found out.

"Okay, so he has a degree. Good," Adeline comments.

"Lucas is also heavily involved in multiple children's charities, something that really caught my attention. He started his own charitable organization to help orphaned children—allowing him to provide assistance to kids who are facing the same challenges he once did." It's a full-circle moment and it's incredible. So incredible, it's hard to believe that Lucas, 'Mr. Ice Block,' has a heart.

I look up from my phone to see Adeline and Sophie studying the screen intently.

Adeline's face relaxes a bit.

"I know it sounds insane, but I have a good feeling about this. And there's one more thing," I add. "He's half Lebanese. I thought you'd appreciate that."

Adeline softens more at this revelation. "Well, I guessed that when I heard his last name."

I smile at her, relieved that I finally found a positive angle to the situation. "So, what do you think? Do you think I should go for it?"

Adeline opens her mouth to speak, but before she can say anything, Sophie stops her. "No more arguing, Addie."

They share a look and Adeline takes a step down, telling me that she's only worried about me but that she will support any decision I make. She also adds that she will cut off Lucas's balls if he tries anything, which I agree to let her do. With that, we all settle into our seats on the balcony, the tension in the air slowly dissipating. Sophie pops open a bottle of the champagne we love from the hotel, and we cheer for new opportunities.

As soon as the clock strikes five p.m., I get dressed in a pair of jeans-shorts, a white t-shirt, and my sneakers before I head down to meet Lucas.

As I descend the last flight of stairs, I see him standing by the elevator, waiting for me, *I think*. He's wearing a pair of slacks with his white shirt tucked into them. His blazer is folded neatly over the crook of his elbow, making him appear like the businessman he is.

The elevator door opens and a family of five steps out. From a distance, it looks like Lucas' shoulders relax.

Is he nervous?

As I approach him, he looks up, his eyes widening just a fraction. I can't help but notice how handsome he looks with his dark hair neatly styled and his sharp jawline perfectly outlined. His eyes are a deep brown, almost the color of melted dark chocolate, and they seem to be studying me intently. He doesn't smile, instead he looks me up and down. A smile now and then would brighten up his features. But no, he has to look all serious and judgy. I look down at my outfit and feel the heat of a blush creeping up my neck, suddenly self-conscious under his gaze.

"Good evening, Leora," he says in a deep voice that makes goosebumps appear across my whole body.

"Good evening, Lucas," I answer in the same formal tone.

"Shall we?" He raises his arm towards the exit. I fall into step beside him, feeling my nerves start to fray.

Are we doing this?

Is this happening?

Should it be happening?

We walk in silence; the only sound is our feet hitting the ground. I try to gather my thoughts, but my mind is a jumbled mess. We reach the café and he leads me to a cozy table at the end of the outdoor seating area. He pulls my chair out for me, ensuring I'm comfortable before he takes his seat across from me.

John would never.

"Mr. Ayoub, welcome!" The young waitress looks surprised to

see him but she hides it well under a sweet smile. "Can I get you started with anything to drink?"

We both place our orders—Lucas opting for a black coffee, even though it's in the evening, and I opt for a cappuccino. As our drinks arrive, we settle in for a conversation that will change my life forever

"What are your conditions?" he says after he takes a sip from his cup. *Straight to the point, I see.*

I square my shoulders, taking a deep breath before launching into the weighty conversation ahead.

ELEVEN

LUCAS

She's striking.

I don't know what it is about her, but there's something hidden beneath her infuriating layers—like a buried treasure waiting to be discovered, and as much as I despise it, I'm already prepared with a shovel.

I still can't wrap my head around why she agreed to this. I get that the job is enticing, and great for experience, but to marry a stranger for it? I don't quite believe it. There's something she wants—money I suppose, but then again, why would that bother me? I'm the one who *needs* her, and we would be paying whomever agreed to this proposal anyway.

It leaves me feeling confused and unsure of what to do next. There's a part of me that wants to get closer to her, to unravel the mystery of who she is, but there's another part that warns me to be careful. I can't let my guard down; we are here to agree on conditions to make this marriage as clear as possible—that's it.

She sips her coffee carefully, as if every sip needs to be savored and foam clings to her full lips. My eyes are glued to her, watching as she gently licks it away. An unexplained sensation sparks within me as her eyelids flutter closed, lost in the taste of it. I watch her closely, captivated by the moment.

Her brown hair is up in a tight ponytail, showcasing her beautiful face. As I observe closely, I notice a tiny, perfectly round birthmark over her right eyebrow.

Her hairstyle accentuates how long her hair is, probably long enough to wrap around my fist twice and those eyes . . . I have to stop myself before the heat in my body rushes south. Those thoughts will have to take a backseat—*for now.*

I take a deep breath, preparing myself for what's to come. After all, this is just a means to an end. If she agrees, we'll keep it civil, and I'll have to keep her at arm's length.

"What are your conditions?"

She swallows before she speaks. "Right to the chase—I like it." A nervous smile spreads across her face. When I don't answer, she clears her throat. "I want it written in the contract that another job, at this level, will be waiting for me back home when this whole thing is over. It doesn't have to be in the hospitality business, but a job nonetheless. I know you have contacts."

I respect that. "I'll do my best."

"No. I don't want you to do your best. I want you to do it without fail. If you can't find me one, I want to keep this one, working remotely until you find me another one."

"Okay."

"I also want a recommendation letter, preferably from your uncle, but you will do, too." I scoff inwardly at that remark. A letter from me would give her a great job with benefits she could only dream of.

Her fingers tap against her mug, a sign of her nervousness and her eyes dart around the café, avoiding my gaze. I can feel her anxiety building as she waits for my response.

"Sure."

My own heart is pounding in my chest, a feeling I'm not used to, and I'm unsure of what to expect next. I'm used to discussing *business* conditions with stiff men in suits, not marriage conditions with beautiful women in shorts that expose their stunning, tan legs that would look perfect wrapped around my waist.

I clear my throat, straightening in my seat, trying to compose myself. Lord, I really need to focus on anything other than her legs; otherwise, this meeting will end up going in a completely different direction.

"No touching," she says in a low voice that snaps me out of my thoughts. I let her words sink in. How are we supposed to pull off looking like a married couple without touching each other? She reads my face and quickly adds, "I mean, no touching *in private*."

"I hadn't planned on touching you, Leora. Not more than I have to when we're out and about."

Lies. Every time I see her, my brain seems to conjure up all sorts of situations where we are certainly touching.

"Is that all, Miss Davis?"

"No." She takes another sip of her coffee before continuing, her voice a little more confident now.

"No cheating."

Her request catches me off guard again.

"Cheating? How would I cheat on my fake wife?"

"I know this whole thing won't be *real* in our eyes, but other people will believe it," she says firmly, taking yet another sip. "I won't be embarrassed like that again, even though this is a fake relationship. If you need to scratch an itch, you do it yourself, or find a way to be very, very discreet," she adds, her hands slightly shaking as she speaks.

Again? Did someone cheat on her? If so, it makes sense why it would be one of her conditions. Regardless, I despise cheating in all forms. There's something incredibly weak about a person who chooses to stab another in the back. It's simple, if you want to fuck someone else, you leave the person you're with first. Easy.

I can see her eyes studying me, trying to gauge my reaction.

"There will be no cheating, real or fake. I'm not that kind of man."

Her eyes widen slightly for a second before she nods, relief evident in her expression. *Did she think I would argue in favor of cheating? Why does she look surprised?* This woman clearly has the wrong impression of me, and for some damn reason, I want to rectify every wrong thing she thinks of me.

"But it goes both ways, Leora." My tone bears no argument. "You'll be married to me and *only* me."

I pause, studying her face for any sign of reaction. After a moment, she lets out a breath and replies softly, "Okay."

"Is that all?" I ask.

"Yes." Her response is hesitant but affirmative.

A small smile forms on my lips. "So you agree?"

Again, she nods. "Yes."

I take a deep breath, my heart racing with anticipation and uncertainty. "You'll marry me?"

"Y-Yes," her response is low, but it's a yes nonetheless.

"Perfect, we'll get married this Saturday. I need some time to get all the papers together, and you'll also have to sign a prenup."

The sooner, the better. We need to get this over and done with so we can focus on work.

She stares at me in disbelief. "Saturday? As in, two days from now?" She exclaims.

I nod. "Yes, that's what I said."

She looks at me with a mix of surprise and apprehension, clearly not expecting things to move so fast. I notice her body tensing up.

"But don't worry," I continue, trying to put her at ease. "It's just a formality. A quick ceremony at the town hall, and we'll be done in no time," I say, my attempt to appease her falling short. Trying to calm her down is like trying to slow a wave during a storm—it's not possible. Leora swallows, her eyes still wide with surprise. I can tell she's nervous, but I need to keep her focused and moving forward with the plan.

"Oh, that reminds me," I say, trying to sound casual. "We need rings; an engagement ring for you and wedding bands for us both. " I take out my black AmEx and slide it toward her, assuming she'll want to choose her own ring. "Please get yourself whichever diamond ring you'd like. Make sure it looks like it came from a man like me."

Her nose scrunches for a second before she relaxes, and I'm immediately struck by how *cute* she is.

Why do I think she looks cute while looking disgusted with me?

"You also need something more elegant to wear. As *cute* as your dresses are, you'll need more elegant attire for people to believe you're my wife."

Leora's expression shifts to one of bewilderment and a hint of offense as she gazes at the card in front of her. After a few seconds, her green eyes rise to meet mine. There's an unmistakable intensity in her gaze—she's angry.

"First of all, what the hell is wrong with my clothes? Second, I don't need your money," she says firmly.

Arching an eyebrow, I offer a measured response. "This is only about appearances. We have to consider the bigger picture if we want this arrangement to succeed, and right now, you don't look the part. That responsibility falls on me, so take the card and get yourself some new outfits and rings. If you need anything else, get that too."

A retort, seemingly poised on Leora's lips, falters and evaporates. The momentary hesitation in her expression briefly raises my concern. She inhales deeply, rising from her seat, and reaches for the card.

"Will do, *fiancé.*" Her words drip with a frosty detachment as she begins to pivot away. Then, she abruptly halts, turning to me, saying, "I almost forgot. I want it written in the contract that when this is all over, I don't want any money from *you*. The job is enough."

No money? I'm left puzzled, my mind struggling to catch up with the abrupt change. *Isn't that the whole reason she's agreeing to this?* I had thought she found out about me being a billionaire. Maybe this is her way of testing my sincerity or, perhaps, a subtle way to show who she is.

But I don't ask her. I don't press. I only nod.

"I'll call you with the details tomorrow," I say as she turns to leave.

"Great," she snaps back as she stomps away.

Her fire is back, and I can't help but feel curious about what that fire is capable of. There aren't many who dare snap at me. My employees seek validation, while everyone else wants attention. But Leora doesn't care, not in the slightest. This marriage might turn out to be more interesting than I initially thought. However, it hits me after she's left that we haven't discussed her moving into my apartment. She must know that's going to happen, as we're getting married, and married people live together. But I push it aside; we'll discuss it later.

I finish my coffee and before I leave, I call my uncle, letting him know the hotels' future is safe.

TWELVE

LEORA

As cute as your dresses are, you'll need more elegant attire for people to believe you're my wife.

I'm classy. I'm classy as fuck, *normally.*

But I'm on vacation now, so all he's seen of me is what I look like in yoga pants, a short black dress for a night out, or in someting as simple as jeans shorts.

Moreover, why did I have to add that I don't want any money after this is over? I *need* the money. Even though I'll have a job after this, the extra money could help me buy a new apartment. I'm an idiot.

After his remarks, however, I decide to actually do what I'm told and max out his credit card.

I stomp my way up the stairs, sweating my ass off, until I reach our floor and open the door.

Adeline greets me as I stop into the room. "Well, hello to you too. Where have you been?"

"Did you do it?" Sophie asks.

I walk by them and go straight to the bedroom. "It looks like I'm getting married on Saturday."

Both of them scramble off the sofa and rush after me.

"This Saturday? As in, *the* Saturday we fly back home?"

Fuck, I had forgotten about that. How the hell am I going to do this without them?

"I can't do this without you. This is a mistake. I should call him back and tell him I changed my mind."

"No. No. No, don't freak out. You decided that you'd do this and you will." Sophie reassures me, but the unease lingers.

"Habibti, listen, I know I was against this idea in the beginning, but I'm coming around. It's going to help you out a lot in your career, and whenever you doubt this, remember you're doing it for the experience."

I'm doing it for the experience; I repeat the mantra in my head. Whenever we're unsure of something, Adeline always says, "*Do it for the experience. You're the main character and whatever moment —good or bad—is merely a plot point leading you to your end chapter.*"

Adeline caresses my hair and I relax into the feeling. "On the bright side, if this doesn't work out, you've given me the perfect premise for my next book."

I gently push her away. "I hope I'll get twenty percent of the royalties if you ever write it." She laughs and Sophie and I join her.

"What's that in your hand?" Sophie asks me, curiously. I completely forgot about his credit card. I raise it, showing it to the girls, giving them a rundown of what happened.

"Who wants to come engagement ring shopping with me tomorrow?" I smirk, waving the black card in the air.

THE RINGS sparkle in all sorts of ways. Adeline looked up a few jewelry shops in the area, and this is the second one we're visiting. My heart is pounding as the reality of it all settles in.

What am I doing?

"Leora, come on!" Adeline calls, waving me over. I take a deep breath and follow them into the store, my eyes drawn to the sparkling diamonds and colorful gems.

The saleswoman greets us warmly and asks us what we're looking for. I swallow hard, feeling overwhelmed. Noticing my unease, Adeline takes charge, explaining that we need an engagement ring for me and wedding bands for Lucas and I. The saleswoman looks at us incredulously, probably surprised that *I'm* the one buying the rings, but I laugh it away by explaining that my fiancé is very, very busy with work and that I'm very particular when it comes to jewelry. She nods, not saying anything, as she shows us a variety of rings, each with its own unique cut and carat.

I try on rings in yellow gold and white gold, princess cut and square cut, but none feel right. If I'm being honest, I should just pick one and get it over with, but there's something in me that wants to relish this moment. What if I'll never have the chance to wear an engagement ring again?

"This is one of our most spectacular rings. I've seen several celebrities wear it." She brings it out and takes my hand in hers before pushing it onto my ring finger. It's a square-cut diamond, at least 5-carats with a halo of smaller diamonds surrounding it. It sparkles when it catches the light, but it's way too big and extravagant for my taste. I don't want something that screams, *"Look at me, I'm engaged!"* because in reality, I won't be engaged or married for long. Nonetheless, Lucas said I needed to get something "believable"—whatever that might mean—and he's paying for it

Sophie notices my hesitation. "Maybe something less in-your-face. Do you have anything smaller?" The saleswoman lets out a small huff, probably tired of my ambivalence.

We move on to a display of oval-cut diamonds in different settings, but they don't quite catch my eye either.

Then we come across a round-cut solitaire with a few smaller diamonds on the band, and it immediately feels more to my taste. The center diamond is smaller, just over a carat, and yet it's beautiful in its simplicity. But then my eyes find another ring—a ring that makes me think of Lucas's words again, and I smile.

"This is a beautiful piece," the saleswoman states, noticing how my eyes light up and I nod.

"It is, but I want that one." I point at a smaller, solitaire ring. It's modest and delicate, something I doubt Lucas will like. Which is exactly why I want it.

Sophie leans in. "But you seemed drawn to that other one with the slightly bigger diamond."

I shrug. "I want this one."

The saleswoman nods hesitantly and takes it out. "This is a 0.2-carat diamond with an excellent cut and an IF clarity."

"Great, I want it."

It's perfect, because Lucas is going to hate it. Excitement bubbles in my stomach. I can't wait to see Mr. You-Have-To-Look-the-Part's face when he sees this ring.

I leave the jewelry shop with the little engagement ring on my finger and with two wedding bands stuffed in a white bag. A simple platinum ring for Lucas and a matching, single-row, diamond-covered ring for me. It was too beautiful not to buy.

As we walk toward another boutique, this time to find some clothes, Adeline stops us in the middle of the street. "I seriously don't understand why you didn't get the bigger ring. He's the one paying. Let's go back."

"Because I have a feeling he'll hate this ring and seeing his reaction will be better than owning the largest rock we could find."

We step into the boutique, my eyes scanning the racks of clothes for something eye-catching. Lucas had demanded that I go on a shopping spree to buy new, *elegant* attire. So here I am, using his card, already taking on the role of his "wife".

I move from one rack to another, examining the various styles and fabrics before picking up a few dresses, and holding them up to imagine how they would look on me. A sweet sundress catches my eye, and I add it to my pile before remembering what Lucas said. Returning it to the rack, I go for a few staple pieces instead: little black dresses, evening dresses, and some work attire. I also purchase three new blazers and blouses, along with two pairs of jeans. It's a good start but I will have to do a lot more shopping after the wedding.

Every time I think about that word, *wedding*, my stomach rolls and I feel as if I'm about to vomit.

"What are you wearing on Saturday?" Adeline asks as she looks through the racks of clothes.

"I don't know. We're only going to the town hall."

"Okay? But you're getting married, so you still need to wear something suitable. What about this one?" She pulls out a white midi-dress with bare shoulders. It's simple, which makes it the perfect piece. I take it from her and hold it up to my body.

"Go try it on," Sophie says, and I listen.

I stand in front of the mirror in the boutique's dressing room, examining my reflection. The dress is fitted and it accentuates my curves. I feel beautiful and sexy, but then that familiar voice creeps into my head, *"Babe, you know I think you are beautiful, but maybe a super tight dress isn't the best choice."*

That voice makes me look in the mirror through another set of eyes. The dress is beautiful, but it could look better if I had time to lose a little weight.

I shake my head, stopping myself from giving any attention to the unhealthy and unnecessary thoughts. Who cares if I don't have the flattest stomach or that I'm rounder around my hips?

I take a deep breath and remind myself that I'm beautiful just the way I am. I deserve to feel confident and sensual, and I can't let anyone else's opinions bring me down. The most important thing is that I value myself.

I think that's what the article, *How to Love Yourself in 12 steps*, said.

With that thought in mind, I decide to step out of the changing room and show the girls.

Both Sophie and Adeline look up, their faces breaking into wide smiles at the sight of me in the white dress.

"That. Is. Perfect," Adeline exclaims as she rushes toward me, her hands landing on my waist.

"You look beautiful." Sophie joins Adeline, her hand raised over her mouth. "Why does it feel like I'm going to cry?" she wonders aloud.

"Thank you. I think this is the one for the occasion." I give a little twirl, and both Sophie and Adeline clap their hands in excitement.

"Lucas is going to go crazy when he sees you," Adeline exclaims, her initial reluctance now replaced by enthusiasm.

"Do you think so?" I give them an uncertain smile.

"I know so." Sophie adds.

As much as I don't want to care about his opinion, something in me seeks his validation.

I guess we'll see on Saturday.

THIRTEEN

LUCAS

I spent my entire Friday morning making calls and preparing the necessary documents for our marriage. Thankfully, everything seems doable. Although Leora's long-stay visa is not yet secured, I'm confident that it will be obtained before her ninety-day visitation period ends. The visa requires various documents as evidence, such as proof of accommodation *(my apartment)*, proof of financial means *(which I've taken care of by arranging her new job and salary)*, and proof of marriage *(will be obtained tomorrow)*. The remaining details will be handled by my lawyer.

As I'm reviewing some finances, I come across a purchase from a jewelry store—the rings, I suspect—but I do a double take at the amount as it doesn't make sense.

A knock on the door interrupts me.

"Come in!" I call out.

"My apologies, Mr. Ayoub," Camille says as she enters my office. "Miss Davis is here and she claims to have—"

"Let her in." I interrupt. Leora strides in with confident steps, wearing a pair of tight jeans that look painted on, and for a split second, all I want is for her to spin around. She holds a small bag in her hand, but something else catches my attention. Something small around her finger.

"Are you kidding me?" I mutter under my breath.

"Hi, fiancé," Leora greets me with a sarcastic tone.

I immediately point to the shiny object on her ring finger. "What is that, Leora?"

"Oh, this thing? It's the engagement ring you bought me. Isn't it cute?" She smiles as she brings her hand up, showing off the ring.

"It would be cute if I could see it," I retort, feeling the familiar knot start to build in my stomach. No one can see her wearing a ring like that. She's going to ruin everything before it even starts.

My irritation grows when she doesn't answer. "I'm waiting for you to pull out the real one."

She seems unfazed by my frustration. "It seems this ring is doing wonders to your ego."

I try to maintain my composure. "*Leora*, you need to buy another ring. I told you to get a good one."

"Well, *Lucas*, you weren't the one buying the ring and I like this one—it's simple," she insists.

"Keep the same design but make it bigger. That ring on your finger looks to be less than half a carat," I counter.

"That's because it's point-two carats," she corrects me. I want to drag that ring off her finger and throw it out the window.

"Even worse," I snap.

"Lucas, the ring is not going to be the dealbreaker. If anything will, it's your behavior."

This back-and-forth is unfamiliar to me, and I'm not sure how to respond. Typically, people don't challenge my decisions or engage in such ridiculousness. It's as if the usual script I'm accustomed to is being rewritten, and I find myself navigating uncharted territory.

"Leora, just go exchange the ring for another one you like, but bigger," I say through gritted teeth. "Or I'll send Camille to pick one out for you."

"You're such a control freak, and it's not a good look on you." She sneers as she places the bag on my desk. "I'm not getting a new ring, and I think what you meant to say was . . ." She stands taller, her hands on her hips, before she starts talking, in a mocking tone. "Thank you so much for getting the wedding bands, Leora. Thank you for also buying yourself the engagement ring *I* should have bought. I mean, it's the least I could do after being an asshole." With that, she turns around and heads towards the door. My eyes immediately go to her round ass. At least I have something nice to stare at.

Deep breaths Lucas, you aren't married yet and you can't scare her away.

"My uncle wants to take us for dinner. Be ready at six," I say as I try to calm myself down.

"Yes sir," she salutes me over her shoulder.

I stare at the door as it shuts behind Leora. I haven't been this frustrated with a person in a long time and that's saying something. She bought that ring with the sole purpose of going against my request. It's like she's daring me to call her out on it—almost as if she enjoys pushing my buttons. And yet, even with how much she drives me crazy, there's something about her that draws me in.

Maybe it's the way she carries herself, or the fire in her eyes. Or maybe it's the way she challenges me, refusing to be controlled. Whatever it is, I can't deny that I find myself thinking about her more often than I'd like to admit.

AFTER A GRUELING SESSION at the gym—my attempt at cooling down after my discussion with Leora—I make my way back home. My penthouse apartment overlooks the beach and the city, offering a breathtaking view. I grab a cold bottle of water from the kitchen and take a long sip, relishing the refreshing taste. As I look out the floor-to-ceiling windows that stretch from here to the living room, I feel a sense of peace wash over me. I take another long drink, feeling the cool liquid soothe my parched throat, before I make my way to my bedroom. The muted gray and blue tones create a soothing atmosphere, and the king sized bed dominates the room, inviting me to rest.

But the true gem of my bedroom is the balcony overlooking the ocean. As I step outside, I feel a gentle breeze caress my skin, carrying the salty scent of the ocean. The sound of the waves crashing against the shore is a symphony for my ears, and all my worries and stress fade away. It's my favorite part of the apartment —a sanctuary within a sanctuary.

Will Leora like it?

My own thoughts surprise me. I've never been one to fret over someone's opinion so much. Leora's a tempest herself—a whirlwind of opinions, and a force that seems unstoppable. She challenges me, questions me, and for some reason, that's unsettlingly attractive. Every jab, every witty retort serves a purpose. But I've seen enough in life to know that letting someone in, and allowing them to get to know you, often leads to pain. And I've had my fair share of that, which is why I won't be letting her in.

Still, the thoughts gnaw at me. *Will she be comfortable? Will she feel at home? Will she warm up to me?*

It's not like I care about her approval—not really. The arrangement is what it is, and we both know it. We're bound by a contract that has nothing to do with emotions. But her comfort, strangely, matters to me in a way I'm not ready to admit.

I've spent a lifetime perfecting the art of detachment, keeping everyone at arm's length; everyone except for my uncle and Liam. It's how I've survived and maintained control. Leora, though, she's like a chink in my armor, a crack that lets the light in. And it both infuriates and intrigues me.

I shake my head, dismissing the thoughts as I stand up. This apartment is just another piece in the elaborate puzzle that is our arrangement.

I head to the ensuite bathroom and step into the glass-enclosed shower. When I finally step under the hot water, I let out a groan of relief as I wash away the tension. I lather up my body wash, enjoying the way the scent fills the room. Before I get the chance to relax, Leora pops up in my mind and all I see is her ass in those jeans. My body reacts immediately, and I push away the urge to touch myself to thoughts of her. Instead, I turn the lever to cold and stand under the freezing water, cursing her. The shock jolts me out of my thoughts.

Why can't I get her out of my damn mind?

This is ridiculous. I've always prided myself on being in control, on being able to compartmentalize emotions and physical desires. But ever since Leora entered the picture, it's like a switch has been flipped. I can't seem to escape the way my body reacts to her presence—the subtle quickening of my heart rate, and the distracting twitch of my cock. My thoughts wander when I should be focused on more important matters, lured away by the magnetic pull of her presence.

She's been annoying me at every stop—I shouldn't be thinking about her this way, dammit.

I take a deep breath, forcing myself to focus on the cold water beating down on me. It's a sharp contrast to the heat that had been building within me, a reminder that I need to regain control. This situation, this arrangement—it's difficult enough without adding unnecessary complications. Leora might challenge me in more ways than one, but I can't afford to let her affect me like this.

I turn the water off and step out of the shower, grabbing a towel to dry myself. As I stand there, I make a silent promise to myself: I won't let thoughts of Leora distract me. I'll keep up the act, maintain the distance, and ensure that this arrangement remains strictly business. Because getting tangled up in emotions and desire would only complicate things further, and that's the last thing I need.

After my shower, I get dressed in a dark blue Armani suit and a simple white button down. I check my reflection in the mirror; my curly hair looks unruly per usual, but I don't bother trying to tame it. According to some, it's part of my charm. My mum was one of them; she always used to let my hair run wild, insisting it showcased my wild spirit.

I slip on a pair of brown leather shoes and make my way to the living room, grabbing my keys and phone on the way. I step out of the elevator and into the parking lot, heading towards my car—a sleek black Mercedes-Benz, and unlock it with the press of a button.

Around the rearview mirror hangs my mother's rosary; it's white and gold, and I touch it just like I always do before starting the car. The engine roars to life, and I navigate my way through the busy streets to pick up my new fiancée. Pulling up to the hotel, I see Leora waiting outside.

Let's get this evening over with.

I get out of the car and walk towards her, feeling a surge of pride and possessiveness as I take in her appearance: her black dress hugs her curves in all the right places, and the sight of her toned legs draws my attention more than I care to admit. Her brown hair cascades in waves down her shoulders, and there's a glint of determination in her green eyes, a reminder that she's not one to be underestimated.

"Leora," I say with a nod. "You . . . look good." I shift uncomfortably, my attempt at a compliment falling somewhat flat. "I mean, it's a great dress."

She raises an eyebrow, the tension between us palpable, but she replies with a tight smile, "Thank you, Lucas. You're almost charming tonight."

I ignore her jab at me, my eyes drifting to her lips as she speaks; they look sinfully full. They're painted a shade of pink that complements her complexion perfectly. She must have been a siren in a previous life, luring men into the deepest of waters before drowning them.

I don't think she's aware of how much of an effect she has on the male population, considering she's completely oblivious to the hungry look coming from one of the hotel's doormen. He's practically undressing her with his eyes, and I don't like it. I don't like it at all.

Instinctively, I wrap my arm around Leora's waist and glance towards the doorman once more, my expression hard, a silent warning: *She's with me.* He quickly averts his gaze, suddenly finding something fascinating on the marble floor.

Exactly.

"What are you—" she begins, clearly taken aback. But I don't let her finish.

"Let's go," I say firmly, my voice leaving no room for arguments.

I guide her towards the car, my arm still wrapped protectively around her. There's a surge of possessiveness within me that surprises even myself. I can't stand the thought of someone else eyeing her that way when she's supposed to be my fiancée.

I open the door to the passenger seat and when she steps closer to me, before lowering herself into the seat, I can't help but lean in slightly to smell the sweet scent of her perfume—*vanilla*. I close my eyes before closing the door and making my way to the driver's seat.

Her soft voice surprises me, and I turn my head to look at her.

"Are you sure about this?" she asks, motioning between us with her hands. "About this whole thing?"

My mind races. Would anyone be sure in this situation?

"No," I say truthfully, before turning the key in the ignition.

"Me too." I can feel her eyes on me as I drive, but I don't look at her. The weight of unspoken questions hanging in the air, questions I don't yet have the answers to. Yet, I can't help but wonder what she's thinking.

Will she be able to pull this off?

Will she convince the others in the restaurant that what we share is real?

Will I?

My uncle chose this restaurant because he knew a few of the stakeholders would be here tonight.

Tonight is about us making our public debut.

The questions swirl in my mind as we pull up to the restaurant. I step out of the car and make my way around to open her door, but apparently Leora is in a hurry. She's halfway out of the car by the time I reach her, my hand extended. Her shoulders tense, and a furrow forms in her brow before her eyes meet mine, and she takes my hand.

"You don't have to do that," she says sweetly, like she's not used to being treated this way, and that bothers me. I was raised to take care of the women around me, and more than that, I *want* to treat her that way.

"Yes I do." I offer her a stiff smile. Her gaze lingers on mine, searching for something, and, for a brief moment, the air is charged with something I can't explain. The moment seemingly passes as she nods and steps fully out of the car, her hand still in mine.

As we step into the restaurant, Leora subtly links her arm through mine, one hand gripping my bicep, and the other lightly resting on it. I feel her weight shifting towards me, as if trying to make our body language look natural and intimate. It's a small gesture, but it's enough to make me feel a bit nervous and unsure of what's to come.

When we spot my uncle, he's wearing his usual black suit, a stark contrast to his white hair. I feel her grip on my arm tightening. *She's nervous.*

He greets me with a warm smile and then his eyes land on Leora. I don't think I've ever seen him this enchanted by someone.

"Hello, dear."

I watch as she raises her hand slowly, unsure of what to do. He takes it and leans in, giving her three kisses on the cheeks—a Lebanese custom that I will have to teach Leora. It's one of many customs I will have to teach her if she's to play the part of my wife.

As we take our seats at our usual table, Leora sits down next to me with my uncle on the opposite side.

Before we even have time to order our food, I notice Michel Beaumont—one of our investors—making his way over to us. He's a middle-aged man who exudes sleaziness and I barely tolerate him. When he reaches us, his beady blue eyes immediately scan over Leora's form, and it pisses me off. I feel a protective instinct flare within me as I mentally prepare to fend off any of his unwanted advances.

I reach below the table to find her hand, quickly intertwining mine with hers. With Michel's gaze still locked on Leora, I place our intertwined hands atop the table in a display for him to see. Leora's eyes widen in surprise as she looks at our interlocked hands.

"Lucas." He nods towards me and then towards my uncle. "Antoine." He returns to staring at Leora, and I feel her tensing up next to me.

"Who is this beautiful lady?"

"My fiancée, Leora," I answer.

"She's also our new Marketing Manager," my uncle adds, and I immediately know it's the wrong thing to say to Michel.

Michel's gaze lingers on Leora, a sly smile tugging at the corners of his lips, as if he's relishing a secret amusement. "Fiancée, you say?" he drawls. "Well, Lucas, you've certainly got yourself a catch. But didn't Antoine warn you not to mix business and pleasure?" His eyes travel down to her breasts, and Leora shifts in her seat, a subtle unease causing her to play with the hem of her dress as Michel's gaze becomes intrusive.

"Tell me, *dear*," Michel continues, "do you have any experience in the business world? Or are you just a pretty face for Lucas to show off?" His words are loaded with implication, and I can feel my blood beginning to boil. Leora's hand tightens around mine. She opens her mouth to respond but I beat her to it

"Actually, Michel, Leora has extensive experience in this field. That's why I decided to hire her." I turn my face toward Leora, a warm smile playing on my lips as I gently lift her hand. The soft texture of her skin and the delicate intertwining of our fingers send a reassuring warmth through me. "She's not only qualified but *also* the most beautiful woman I've ever seen." My lips graze her hand, a subtle touch that raises goosebumps on her skin. When I raise my gaze, our eyes meet in a silent exchange. Her green eyes are soft and there's a small smile on her lips. A smile that tugs at something within me.

"I see that the lady can't speak for herself." It's spoken like a dare, his words laced with condescension. The low hum of conversation in the upscale restaurant becomes a distant buzz as Michel's words hang in the air, creating an uncomfortable hush around our table.

Leora's expression tightens, a mixture of indignation and resolve flashing across her features.

"I'm quite capable of speaking for myself, and while I appreciate your interest, my value as a professional has nothing to do with my physical appearance." Michel's smirk fades as Leora's words sink in. She pauses and looks at me, the softness in her eyes morphing into determination.

"I'm here because I love Lucas and believe in the work we're doing together," she adds. Leora's hand tightens around mine, a subtle yet powerful show of solidarity. I can't help but feel a surge of pride as I watch Leora confidently finish scolding Michel.

Atta girl. I'm relieved to see that her fire isn't solely reserved for me.

"Well then, I suppose I'll have to take your word for it. But I must say, I'm intrigued." He lingers for a moment longer before finally turning to leave, his gaze still fixed on Leora.

"Good job." I lean in to whisper in her ear, unable to resist inhaling her delicate vanilla scent. She smells divine.

As the adrenaline settles, her body relaxes and her eyes widen as she comprehends the significance of the encounter.

"Was that rude? I shouldn't have spoken like that. Is he going to see through this entire charade? Did I just jeopardize your business?" She fires off questions without taking a breath in between, her words a rapid cascade reflecting the whirlwind of thoughts in her mind.

"No, no. You handled him perfectly, dear," my uncle interjects, a proud smile stretching across his face.

Leora hastily releases my hand. A chill replaces the warmth of her skin, so I quickly return my hand to my side

"Did I overdo it with the whole 'love' thing?" she asks, her uncertainty written across her face.

"No, that was great. Bravo." My uncle chuckles. "I guess you'll have to keep up the act of being madly in love with Lucas from now on," he teases, leaving us to grapple with the unforeseen consequences of our performance.

FOURTEEN

LUCAS

The waiters arrive with our food and begin arranging an assortment of plates on the table. I take a moment to appreciate the vivid array of dishes laid out before us.

"I ordered the full *Meza* before you arrived. I hope you don't mind." My uncle's voice breaks the silence.

"Not at all," I reply, and Leora's eyes light up with enthusiasm.

"Oh, I love tarator djej," she exclaims, pointing excitedly at the dish placed in front of her. My uncle and I exchange surprised glances, taken aback by her familiarity with the cuisine.

How did she know how to pronounce it?

She glances between us, sensing our astonishment. "My best friend is Lebanese, and her mother basically adopted me and made me an honorary Lebanese." She explains with a cheerful grin before she grabs the pita and scoops up some of the dish.

My uncle catches my eye, a knowing look shared between us, and his eyes twinkle with approval. "*Smalla, aeleya,*" he says, and a smile naturally curves my lips as I begin to eat.

Indeed, *good on her*.

As the meal progresses, I find myself becoming more and more lost in Leora's company. She laughs at my uncle's jokes and engages in lively conversation, and I can't help but feel a sense of pride seeing this play out and seeing him smile. I haven't seen him this excited in a long time.

While we eat, Leora seems to be thoroughly enjoying all the different flavors of the Meza. She comments on the tanginess of the Tabbouleh, the spiciness of the batata harra, and the creaminess of the hummus. I'm glad she's enjoying the food and the company, and I find myself starting to relax. She isn't as infuriating as I expected.

"We've decided to get married tomorrow," I announce confidently, watching as my uncle's eyes widen in surprise and Leora coughs, a piece of bread catching in her throat. My hand swiftly finds its way to her back, giving her a gentle pat to help her clear it.

"Tomorrow?" he repeats, his eyebrows lifting in genuine surprise and a pleased smile spreading across his face. The news seems to draw him in, and he leans forward slightly.

"Yes, we understand it's sudden," I reply, trying to maintain my composure, "but we both agreed to the arrangement. Why delay the inevitable?"

My uncle's gaze shifts between us, considering our request. Finally, he says, "I think this is a great idea. Like you said, why delay it?"

I don't know why I thought this hastiness would make him change his mind. As if the reality of the situation would make him see how insane it is. But, of course, if anyone would be excited, it would be him.

"But isn't one day too short to plan a wedding?" he sits back, studying both me and Leora.

Leora and I exchange a nervous glance, but I quickly recover. "Oh, don't worry," I say confidently. "We will just head to the town hall to get it done."

His gaze turns to Leora, his attention completely ignoring me as though my opinion holds no significance. "Is that what you want, dear?"

"Yes." Her voice is confident, yet something tells me not to believe her. But despite my lingering doubts, I ignore it. A town hall wedding is the right way to go. Swift and uncomplicated. A means to an end.

"Well then, I suppose that settles it," he remarks, raising his glass of wine in a toast. Leora and I mirror the gesture, the clinking of glass filling the air.

Later, after we finish our meal and say our goodbyes, my uncle leans in closely, his words a hushed whisper, "Son, consider getting her a new ring. A woman like her deserves more."

My teeth clench, a resurgence of the previous annoyance bubbling to the surface. This is exactly why I asked her to exchange the damn ring.

Tomorrow, Camille *will* be getting her a replacement.

"Yes, Ammo."

WALKING TOWARDS THE CAR, my hand finds its place on Leora's back. She turns to me, her green eyes shimmering in the moonlight.

"Thank you for tonight." Her voice is soft, genuine even. "I actually had a wonderful time. Your uncle is quite the gem."

I can't help but smile, relieved that the evening went well. "I'm glad you enjoyed yourself. And yes, he certainly is."

I open the door for her, watching as she gracefully climbs inside. I make my way to the driver's side, my thoughts churning as I start the engine.

Leora stares out the window, lost in thought, and I struggle to find the right words to say. The need for a conversation hangs heavy in the air, but the question remains: how do I initiate it?

I've never been good at small talk, not in my youth and certainly not now. The mere thought makes my skin crawl, yet for this charade to work, we must get to know each other. Or at least agree to some fabricated story. As much as I detest the situation, we're in it now and we'll have to do our best for it to be believable.

At last, I break the silence. "We don't really know each other that well."

Leora nods in agreement, and I sense her relief. "True. What would you like to know about me?"

A smile creeps onto my lips, the tension easing slightly. "Let's start with something simple. What's your favorite color?"

Leora lets out a musical laugh—a sound I already yearn to hear again. "I know, I know, it's a bit cliché," I admit. "But hey, we've got to start somewhere."

Her smile widens. "Blue. My favorite color is blue. What about you?"

"Black."

"That's not exactly a color, come on." She challenges.

"What's the color of your dress, Leora?" I raise a brow.

"Black."

"There you go."

"Alright then. Other than black?"

I pause for a moment, thinking. "Red." Feeling the urge to push the boundaries, I add, "Red would look good on you."

Her surprised expression doesn't go unnoticed as a slight pink hue sets on her face.

"Red is a bit too bold for me," she confesses timidly.

"Bold is good," I say and I truly mean it. I envision how enchanting she'd look in a vibrant red dress, but as I glance at her, there's uncertainty etched on her face. In that instant, I decide that I'm getting her a red dress for the hotel opening.

I wait for her to ask something in return but she doesn't, so I continue. "What do you like to do for fun?"

Leora's face lights up. "I love to read. What about you?"

"Work."

"That doesn't count as something you do for fun," she retorts and the playful laugh is back.

"Okay, fair enough." A hint of a smile tugs at the corners of my lips. "I enjoy cooking."

"Really? Am I fake marrying a chef?"

"That's a stretch," I say, and she smiles. "But I must confess, I can whip up a mean crêpe."

"I can't wait to taste it."

My smile widens at her words.

I can't wait to make it for you. The thought catches me off guard. *What the hell is happening to me?*

"My turn," she interjects, and I internally thank her for it. "Any siblings?"

"A younger brother, Liam. What about you?"

She hesitates for a moment. "Nope, only child." That brief pause indicates something, and I put it away in my mind to hopefully ask about it later.

Without realizing it, I pull up at the hotel. This might have been the fastest car ride in a while. I step out of the car and open the door for Leora. My eyes linger on her for a moment, taking her in, catching the way she bites her plump lower lip between her teeth.

"I'll see you tomorrow. Be ready at twelve," I say, my voice steady before I let go of her hand. Tomorrow isn't just any day— it's the day we're getting married. I'm becoming a husband. Regardless of whether it's fake, we'll still be tied to each other in others' eyes, and in my eyes.

"Goodnight, Leora."

"Goodnight, Lucas," she whispers, and I watch as she disappears inside the hotel.

FIFTEEN

LEORA

I'm getting married today.

I still can't believe I agreed to this. The reality of the situation hits me in waves, each one more nerve-wracking than the last, and I'm unsure if I should try to escape the waves or let them engulf me.

With a deep breath, I finally force myself to rise and head to the bathroom to begin my preparations.

To my surprise, both Sophie and Adeline are standing there, one holding a bag filled with makeup and the other with a curling iron.

I come to a halt. "What are you doing? I thought you'd be packing."

"Do you think we would miss our best friend getting ready for her big day?" Sophie puts the curling iron on the bathroom floor before coming up to hug me.

"It's not my big day."

"You're getting married, real or fake. It's an important day," Adeline points out.

Tears prick in my eyes, and my whole body, which was tense a few seconds ago, relaxes at seeing my best friends.

"Now, now, Habibti, don't cry. Jump in the shower, and then

we'll help you get ready." Adeline wipes away a tear that escaped the corner of my eye.

"Okay." My voice comes out in a whisper, but I do as she says.

I step into the shower, letting the warm water wash away any traces of apprehension and doubt. I take one of those do-it-all-showers where you wash, scrub, and shave *everywhere*. Why exactly do I do it all? I don't know. It's honestly comical considering it's not like I'm having a normal wedding night. No one is making sweet love tonight—especially not me.

While Sophie dries my hair, my mind drifts back to yesterday —a surprising and enjoyable day. The dinner with Antoine was delightful. He's undoubtedly the sweetest man I've ever met, emanating a sense of familiarity. There's a softness in his eyes that makes me feel secure, as if he sees something worthwhile in me.

The drive back home with Lucas wasn't entirely unpleasant either; in fact, it turned out to be quite good. Although it started with a bit of awkwardness and silence, he eventually initiated a conversation, trying to get to know me. During our talk, he displayed a sweetness that surprised me. He even smiled and, *oh my god,* his smile. It could only be described in one way: *beautiful*. No wonder he keeps it under lock and key. With a smile like that, he could take over the world but if I'm being honest, it's better that way. Grumpy Lucas should be easier to resist; his scowl acts like a buffer. But smiling Lucas . . . that's an entirely different story. Smiling Lucas makes me want things. Things I shouldn't want from a man who's essentially a stranger.

So, maybe it's best if he stays rude and distant. It's a defense mechanism. I get that. Deep down, I want to know his story, but I can't. Being left in the unknown serves as a safeguard, preventing me from making foolish and reckless decisions, like starting to enjoy spending time with my husband.

I STUDY my reflection in the mirror, thoroughly impressed with the girls' work. Adeline, the makeup guru, skillfully aimed for a soft, glowing, bronzed look, while Sophie, my hairstylist for the day, expertly crafted a curly half-up, half-down hairstyle.

Lastly, I slip on the pristine white dress I bought just two days ago. The midi length gracefully drapes over my frame, and the snug fit accentuates my curves, enhancing my figure. The bare shoulders add a touch of allure, completing the elegant look, and I find myself wondering if Lucas will see me as beautiful today, or at the very least, if he might find this whole arrangement a bit more bearable.

"Wow," Sophie says with a hand over her mouth, eyes glistening as she steps closer. "You look so beautiful."

"Do you think he'll think so?" I cringe at the desperation in my voice.

I catch Adeline's eye in the mirror as she furrows her brows slightly. "You don't need his validation. You are absolutely gorgeous." She smiles. "However, I know he'll think so too."

I gently take her hands in mine, squeezing a little bit—a silent thank you for her support.

"I wish this was real," Sophie adds, a hint of longing in her voice.

I do too.

"Don't worry. It's only going to be for about a year, then I'll get back to my life and hopefully find a nice guy to marry for real. Then you two will be bridesmaids like you're supposed to." I offer them a reassuring smile, which both return.

"So, what's the plan for today?" Sophie asks.

"I'm not entirely sure. He told me he would pick me up, and then we'd head to the town hall to get it over and done with. Afterward, I think we're coming back here," I explain.

"Okay, so we'll see you after?"

Oh, I thought they would be leaving for the airport soon.

I furrow my brow, asking, "Don't you have a flight?"

The smile on Adeline's face broadens. "We managed to switch to the evening flight."

I exhale, relief washing over me as a grateful smile plays on my lips. "I can't believe you did this for me."

"Don't be ridiculous." She laughs. "We tried to extend it further, but there are no flights tomorrow, and our jobs declined our requests for an extended vacation," Adeline huffs out the last part.

"It doesn't matter. Just having you for a few more hours means everything to me."

As happy as I am at this moment, realization seeps in.

I'll be completely alone after this evening.

WHILE I WAIT for Lucas to arrive, I try to distract myself by taking in my surroundings.

The lobby is bustling with activity as guests check in and out of the hotel. As I watch them, I try to imagine their stories—the tired family with kids in tow, the couple who look like they're celebrating something special, the businessman tapping away on his phone like the world depends on it.

But my mind keeps going back to Lucas. Every so often, my gaze drifts towards the entrance. It's like a reflex, really. I tell myself it's because I'm eager to get this over with, but deep down, there's a little flutter of nerves that I can't ignore. Is he going to act like he did yesterday? Will he smile some more? Maybe I'll just crack a joke to see if he's capable of it.

Finally, I catch a glimpse of a familiar figure making his way toward me.

It's him, looking every bit as dashing as I'd expected—he exudes an air of authority. He's dressed in a sharp, black suit paired with a crisp white dress shirt, and to complete the look, a stylish, black bow tie. He looks so handsome.

As he gets closer, I remind myself that this is just a business deal—a transaction. But no matter how hard I try, my heart seems to skip a beat or two.

It's because of the situation we're in, I tell myself over and over again.

His face is expressionless, devoid of any emotion or warmth. They say *"don't judge a book by its cover,"* but he's like a book without any damn pages: expressionless and unreadable. I was secretly hoping for a smile, a small sign of approval, but I guess that's too much to ask for.

However, he proves me wrong when he reaches me. He greets me with a small, yet soft, smile. "You look beautiful." This time, his compliment sounds genuine.

"Thank you." I smile at him. "You look quite handsome yourself."

"Are you ready?" he asks. I quickly nod and together, we walk towards his car.

We make our way to the town hall, the silence in the car almost suffocating. I try to break it up with some small talk but it's like trying to empty the ocean with a teaspoon. Lucas seems lost in his thoughts. His jaw is clenched so tightly, I half expect to hear the sound of grinding teeth.

I glance at him, concerned and uncertain about everything. Finally, after what feels like an eternity, he sighs deeply and speaks, "I never thought it would come to this." The strain in his voice is evident. I've been so immersed in my own feelings that I forgot about him. He must be grappling with a whirlwind of emotions as well.

"Neither did I."

He nods, but the tension remains and the silence continues. I take a moment to study him out of the corner of my eye, noticing the lines of worry etched on his face and the way his hands hold the steering wheel with a white-knuckled grip.

When we arrive, the gravity of the situation hits me. This is it —the moment when everything changes, whether it's for show or not.

We sit for a moment, staring at the imposing building, and just as I'm about to open the door, Lucas stops me, his hand gently touching my arm.

"Wait." He reaches into his suit pocket and pulls out a box. "I asked Camille to return to the jewelry store and find a more suitable ring for you."

Ah, yes, the grump is back. But seriously, why didn't he just go get the ring himself? Before I have time to ask him, he distracts me by opening the box. I blink in surprise at the sight of the solitaire ring nestled inside, the same one that caught my eye in the store.

How in the world did she know?

I shake my head, pulling myself together. "It's beautiful, but I like the one I have on."

He doesn't seem satisfied with my answer. His lips purse, a furrow knitting his brows as he grabs my hand and demands attention.

"Leora, be serious for a second. You can't genuinely prefer that small one over this."

I clench my jaw to keep from blurting out something I might regret. The idea that he assumes I'd favor the bigger, more expensive one grates on my nerves—even though I adore the ring he's holding.

I pull my hand away from his, irritation making my voice sharp. "I like mine."

"Leora." He grits his teeth in frustration.

"Lucas," I fire back, locking eyes with him. It's like a battle of wills, and right now, I'm standing my ground.

And in the end, I win.

"Suit yourself," he grumbles as he steps out of the car and walks around to open my door. The gesture has become quite endearing, but at this moment, my irritation overrules any swooning sentiment. I intentionally ignore his outstretched hand and step out of the car. I don't need his help, thank you very much.

We walk through the big double doors of the town hall, this time I allow his hand to take mine. It's almost comical, like we're trying to convince the world that *"the lovebirds are here,"* even though that's nowhere near the truth.

The hallway that greets us is beautiful, with high ceilings and hardwood floors that echo our footsteps. Lucas stays by my side, guiding me through the doors where the dimly lit room is tucked away. At the front of the room, a man—probably the mayor—is seated, his presence commanding. Beside him stands an older woman, whom the mayor explains will be our witness since we didn't bring our own. Had I known the girls would stay beforehand, I might have insisted on bringing them. But on the other hand, I'm a little bit relieved they're not here. This isn't real. In the future, they'll witness the real deal, not some warped wedding ceremony in the name of business.

Lucas wraps an arm around me and grins as he confesses that we were so eager to get hitched that we forgot about the whole "witness thing."

The woman eyes us with curiosity and maybe a hint of admiration, as if she's in awe of our love. As if the sweet, innocent couple in front of her is so in love, nothing could come between them. *Oh, if she only knew.*

When the time for the ceremony finally comes, we stand before the mayor, facing each other. Lucas takes my hands in his, and I meet his gaze. It's strange how his eyes seem softer now, when just moments ago they could have drilled holes into me.

The mayor clears his throat. "Nous sommes réunis ici aujourd'hu—"

"En anglais, s'il vous plaît," Lucas interrupts, gesturing towards me, indicating that I'm the one in need of translations.

"Bien sûr, je suis désolé." He nods, before continuing in English. "We're gathered here today to celebrate the union of two people who have chosen to join their lives together in marriage. It is a joyous occasion, filled with happiness and hope for the future," the mayor starts, sounding like he's reciting lines from a well-worn script.

"Today marks the beginning of a new journey—a journey that will be filled with love, commitment, and companionship. As we witness the union of Lucas Ayoub and Leora Davis, we are reminded of the beauty of love and the power it holds. May they find joy, fulfillment, and strength in each other's company, and may their love continue to grow and thrive for years to come."

A giggle escapes me before I can stop it and I instantly catch the daggers Lucas shoots my way forcing me to bite my lower lip, squelching the laughter. As I glance up again, his dark eyes remain unyielding, but something has shifted. There's now a strange tension between us. A quiver of anticipation courses through me at the intensity of his gaze, making my heart race with a mixture of fear and an odd desire to challenge him further. I've never felt boldness like this before, and in a way, I like what it's doing to me.

"Lucas, do you take Leora to be your lawfully wedded wife?" the mayor prompts, peering over his glasses.

"I do," Lucas responds, his tone devoid of any romantic sentiment.

"Leora, do you take Lucas to be your lawfully wedded husband?"

It's my turn. I take a deep breath, focusing on the big picture. This is for my future.

"I do."

"I now pronounce you husband and wife." I breathe a sigh of relief. *It's finally over.* "You may kiss the bride."

Kiss? The word echoes in my head like a dreadful chant. Oh no, *the* kiss. How did I forget that part? We're supposed to touch . . . with our lips!

I sneak a glance at Lucas, and his uncertainty mirrors mine. He looks even less interested in kissing me than I do him. I didn't think that was possible.

How are we even going to do this? The only lips I've been kissing for the past five years have been John's. What if those are the only lips I know how to kiss? What if I'm a terrible kisser? I can't have him hold that against me later on.

My gaze lingers on his lips. They're full and perfect, almost too perfect, with a cupid's bow that I find myself envying. I can't help but wonder how they would feel against mine, how he would kiss me. Would it be controlled, like him? Powerful and assertive? He steps closer, his chest brushing against mine. Heat blooms where our bodies touch and his hand cups my cheek. I lean into his touch, my body craving any sort of contact, in stark contrast to my conflicted thoughts. It feels like time slows as he leans down, his lips brushing mine in a quick, chaste kiss. Then, just as suddenly, he pulls away, avoiding my gaze.

Well, that was . . . underwhelming.

For a fleeting moment, I wish that touch, that connection, could have lasted just a tiny bit longer.

"Are we done here?" Lucas's voice cuts through the air, abrupt and impatient. His gaze flickers, almost as if he slipped up, revealing a vulnerability beneath the façade he's been maintaining. In an attempt to regain control, he manages a strained smile, "I promised we'd meet up with my uncle."

WHEN WE RETURN to the hotel, a cluster of four people wielding cameras sprints towards us. My initial response is to shield my face, caught off-guard by the onslaught. Despite the chaos, Lucas stands tall, his grip on my hand tightening, providing a grounding touch.

"How did they find out?" Lucas mutters, more to himself than to me, his brows knitting in genuine confusion.

I had assumed he and his uncle were well-known, but not to this point. Is it because of their wealth? Their business? Or is it simply because Lucas is one of the most sought-after bachelors?

Correction: *was*. He *was* a bachelor, before me.

The paparazzi are loud, their voices blending into an incomprehensible cacophony. I'm not sure if it's the language or the situation that renders me unable to fully grasp what's happening.

"Monsieur Ayoub."

"Regarde ici!"

"Souriez pour la caméra." The pleas from the paparazzi are almost drowned out by the chaotic noise of shutters and shouts and they move even closer, crowding us against the car. My whole body freezes. It doesn't feel safe. I find myself instinctively leaning into Lucas, seeking refuge in his protective presence. To my surprise, Lucas's arms wrap protectively around me, guiding me to stand behind him. The gesture catches me off guard. His large presence is shielding me from them.

"Pardon." One of the paparazzi pushes the others to take a few steps back. "Une photo s'il vous plaît."

Lucas stiffens a bit. He hates this too.

He turns around to face me. "Are you okay?" As I look into his dark eyes, I feel safe, so I nod.

His arms circle behind my back, pulling me back to stand next to him. He smiles, but his eyes betray a hint of discomfort.

"One photo, then my wife and I will need some alone time." Hearing the phrase *"my wife"* on his lips leaves me feeling a certain way, making me comply immediately, as I attempt to muster a smile for the camera amidst the blinding flashes. He's holding me close to his body, my hand on his chest. We maintain our connection, gazing into each other's eyes. The intensity of the flashes briefly blur my vision, yet, I focus on him, and as quickly as it began, it's over.

Lucas thanks them, his tone polite but with an undertone of reservation, and then we start walking towards the entrance, his grip on my hand remaining reassuring.

"What was that?" I murmur to him, still shocked by the whole scene.

"It doesn't happen very often, someone must have tipped them off," Lucas replies cryptically, leaving me with more questions than answers.

Who would have tipped them off?

What the hell have I married into? I wonder as we make our way into the hotel.

I'm someone's *wife.* How the hell did that happen? How did I go from being cheated on to standing here as someone's wife?

Here we are, married and steeped in mutual discomfort. It's like we both got handed a script for a rom-com, but we can't decide if we're the protagonists or the comic relief.

At least I have Antoine on my side. I like him. I think he'll help us navigate this and help us get along for the year.

We reach the hotel lobby, and Antoine is there to welcome us with his infectious cheer. He bursts into a song that sounds vaguely familiar but I can't quite place it. His arms are wide open, and I can't help but smile at his genuine excitement.

"Mabrouk Mabrouk ya hayat albi Mabrouk," he sings, and I catch snippets of the words, realizing they're Arabic for *congratulations.* His arms engulf me in a warm, fatherly hug. It's an embrace that feels foreign, yet comforting, and I allow myself to savor the feeling of it.

"I finally have a daughter-in-law," he says as he pulls away. I blink rapidly, straightening my posture and swallowing down the unexpected surge of emotions. I can't afford to get emotional now. If I do, I don't know if I'll be able to stop.

"Thank you, Antoine," I manage to say, my voice slightly hoarse.

He hugs Lucas as well before turning to both of us, mischief twinkling in his eyes. "I might have done something."

I can practically see Lucas's patience running thin which I find confusing. How could anyone be upset with this man?

"What did you do?" his tone is wary, like he's bracing himself.

"I *might* have invited some people," he admits, wearing a sheepish look as he continues, "stakeholders, investors, and friends for a surprise wedding lunch." As he shares the news, his eyes flicker with a mix of excitement and hesitation.

"Ammo," Lucas warns, his voice dropping an octave. Antoine

shrugs nonchalantly. "Well, I thought it would be nice to celebrate you getting married. Plus, it's good for business, no?"

Lucas massages his temples and takes a deep breath, as if trying to contain his frustration. I can tell he's not happy about the surprise, but he also doesn't want to cause a scene in the middle of the hotel lobby.

"Fine, but I hope you kept it low-key. We don't need a big fuss." Lucas finally concedes.

Antoine beams triumphantly. "Of course, *mon fils*. You'll love it, you'll see." He turns around and walks away, expecting us to follow.

"I doubt that," Lucas mutters under his breath as he places his warm hand on my upper back, urging me to move forward. The contact leaves a swirl of conflicting emotions. Confusion mingles with intrigue, leaving me momentarily caught off guard before continuing to walk.

SIXTEEN

LEORA

The wedding lunch turned out to be much larger than expected, with Antoine inviting practically half of the French population. Despite feeling overwhelmed by the sheer number of guests, I'm thankful that Sophie and Adeline are here, sitting at a nearby table with Antoine. They both look as beautiful as ever, with Sophie in a pink, midi-chiffon dress and Adeline in a green silk dress.

Lucas and I, however, are seated at the sweetheart table, where all attention seems to converge. I can feel curious eyes on us, scrutinizing, wondering who I am, and how I've managed to land Lucas. When I walked past one of the women earlier, I caught her whispering, "She must be after his fortune."

If that's what people think, we're screwed.

"Can you at least try to look like you want to be here?" Lucas whispers to me through a tight smile, his arm draped casually around my chair. He's playing his part, thanking everybody for their well-wishes, and his act is almost convincing. *Almost.* I see right through it though, his smile doesn't reach his eyes, and there's a tense edge to him.

He's really good. The man could be an actor, I'll give him that.

I catch myself staring at the dimple on his left cheek, a new discovery for me. It makes an appearance every time he graces us with a rare real smile. It's disarmingly adorable, a tiny feature that adds a dash of boyish charm to his otherwise stoic façade. It's a small detail, yet it gives him an unguarded look that's inexplicably appealing. It makes my heart beat a tiny bit faster. But I can't get lost in moments like this, where he seems almost human rather than a walking iceberg. It's not the time to be distracted by his charming dimple or his attempts at polite conversation. I need to keep up with his act, plaster on a fake smile, and try not to over-think when he's acting so husbandly.

Suddenly, the sound of a clinking champagne glass fills the room. I lift my gaze to find Adeline tapping her flute, excitement dancing in her eyes. A ripple effect ensues as Sophie mirrors her action before they both stand up.

"Hi everyone, my name is Adeline, and this is Sophie. We have the incredible honor of being the best friends of the stunning bride. When we first met Leora, we never could have imagined that we would be standing here today. But here we are, and we're happier than ever. Leora, you deserve everything the world can offer, and your happiness is all we wish for."

I shoot them both a grateful smile as Adeline continues, her tone warm and sincere. "Together, I hope you can give each other that." She glides her gaze toward Lucas, a silent warning conveyed through a subtle arch of her eyebrow. I chuckle, earning a side-eyed glance from Lucas.

Sophie is the next to speak, and there's a nostalgic smile painted on her lips. "Back in the day, when the world was a bit simpler, the three of us used to play Powerpuff Girls in Adeline's backyard. Leora, who is the kindest and sweetest soul I've ever met, played the role of Bubbles. Every day we were saving the world from imaginary villains with our superpowers. As we grew older, we met real-life villains. But Leora learned how to fight them off too. Whenever any of us needed her, we found her by our side. To help us, and to protect us. Wherever we turned, we knew Leora would be by our side. And now, Leora has found a new partner in crime. Lucas, I hope that you will take on the role of the person who protects Leora. To help her fight off supervillains. Just as we once did in our childhood games, may you stand by her side in the face of any challenges, real or imaginary."

The memories she mentions bring tears to my eyes. I'm transported back to those carefree days when everything was simpler. Even though my life wasn't ideal, I had the two of them and they made me feel loved. They're the gift that keeps on giving.

"Let's raise our glasses to the lovely couple," Adeline chimes in, her eyes twinkling mischievously. "May your days be filled with laughter, your nights with shared dreams, and your life with . . . well, let's just say, may it be an adventure worth remembering."

The entire room raises their glasses, and so do Lucas and I. But before the glasses hit the table, someone in the back yells, "Kiss her!"

My eyes widen, and they instinctively dart to Adeline, a momentary lapse that proves to be a mistake. Her mischievous smile widens before she too joins the playful chorus, exclaiming, "Kiss her! Kiss her! Kiss her!" Soon, the entire assembly of guests joins in, creating a lively choir of encouragement.

I feel my cheeks heating up with embarrassment as hundreds of eyes bore into us.

"I'm going to kill you," I silently mouth at Adeline, but she just blows me a kiss in response.

Just then, Lucas leans in, his warm breath brushing against my ear. "Let's get this over with," he murmurs.

Move aside Shakespeare, there's a new romantic in town.

"Yes, just give me another little peck and we'll be done," I murmur in response, not exactly sure why I had to mention the previous kiss.

I turn my head and find him extremely close to me, and I'm momentarily trapped in the intensity of his dark gaze. His eyes challenge me, as if daring me to break character and it takes all of my willpower not to roll my eyes. But his hand on my back grounds me, while his other hand gently grabs the back of my neck. My breath catches at his closeness, the charged air between us igniting a strange feeling I can't explain. Held captive by his magnetic gaze, the world begins to fade away until it's just us in this moment

Then, his lips are on mine.

At first, it's a soft, hesitant touch, and I assume it will end like the chaste peck we shared at the town hall, but Lucas surprises me. His lips don't leave mine after the first taste. Instead, the soft hand on my neck tightens slightly as he pulls me in closer. His kiss turns firm, confident, and shockingly real. I'm taken aback for a moment, my body going on autopilot. But my initial surprise melts away as the kiss deepens, and I find myself leaning in, my eyes fluttering shut. Every movement of his lips is met with a corresponding one of mine, igniting a series of reactions within me. The warmth of his mouth against my own makes a tingling sensation spread through my body—it emboldens me as I attempt to match his fervor. Our breaths become one, mingling in the small space between us, creating an intimate rhythm.

When the kiss deepens further, my fingers instinctively find their way to his chest, feeling his heartbeat beneath my touch. My senses heighten, and I'm aware of the warmth radiating from his body, and the taste of champagne on his lips. His hand cradles the back of my head, his fingers tangling in my hair. Any animosity we had toward one another evaporates in this moment.

The sound of applause breaks our trance. We slowly pull away, both breathless, our eyes locking for a heartbeat. Lucas's hand lingers on my neck for a moment longer, and I can see the hint of a small smile on his face before he licks his lips and turns to face the crowd.

I feel my cheeks flush as reality crashes back in, and I hear the hushed whispers and giggles from the crowd. I look for Adeline and Sophie. When I find them, they appear just as shocked as I feel, their eyes wide and their mouths hanging open.

What. The. Hell. Was. That?

It was a kiss.

A *real* kiss.

A real, good fake *kiss*, I remind myself.

The only reason he did it was because we had to show off in front of the audience. If it's less than believable, they would all see right through us. Both Lucas and I agreed to commit to this, and we're going to be the sweetest damn couple these people have ever seen. Which means that the kiss didn't mean anything.

Just because I felt the kiss down to my toes doesn't mean I want more of it, even though a twinge of electricity still lingers on my lips.

I mean, I wouldn't be upset if it happened again. After all, we're doing this for show and I need them all to believe it if I want to secure this new job. A little kissing here and there is necessary to maintain the illusion, but I must admit that I'm relieved he's good at it. But a nagging thought worms its way into my mind: did he think it was a good kiss? Did he think I was a good kisser?

Insecurity creeps up on me at that thought. What if the intensity I felt was one-sided?

Ugh, snap out of it, Leora. It wasn't real, it was just an act. Stop overthinking it.

Besides, who cares what he thinks?

His touch on my back nudges me gently, his lips brushing tantalizingly close to my ear as he murmurs, "Leora, if you keep acting so surprised every time I kiss you, we might have a problem."

What an *asshole.*

"I'm not surprised, and you didn't have to kiss me for so long." I whisper back with a feigned smile, even though a shiver runs through me at the promise in his words.

Every time I kiss you.

A smirk tugs at the corner of his lips as he leans in closer, his face dangerously close. His voice is a low and intimate whisper, intertwined with the soft music playing in the background as he retorts, "Well, *wife*, I do have a reputation to uphold. I can't afford to disappoint you now, can I?"

His tone is a playful blend of arrogance and amusement. This time, I actually do roll my eyes, unable to suppress the hint of a smile.

THE NEXT FEW hours are a blur of smiles, and small talk with strangers. We continue to play the part of the happy couple, dancing and mingling with the other guests. Lucas's eyes meet mine every now and then, and in those brief moments of connection, I sense that he's as eager as I am for this charade to be over. But every time his fingers brush mine, or he leans in to whisper something in my ear, I feel a flutter of a butterfly deep within.

I know it's silly, and it makes me feel like that naïve little girl who always wished for fairy tales to come true. The girl who yearned for love and comfort in a world that felt so cold. Sophie's words echo in my mind, *"Can this turn into something more?"*

I try to shake off my irrational thoughts. But the reality is that I had the perfect fairy tale—until I didn't. And that's when I realized fairy tales aren't real.

As the evening starts to wind down, Adeline and Sophie approach me, preparing to say their goodbyes. They have to catch their flight back home, and my heart sinks at the thought of being left alone.

I don't think I can do this without them.

No, scratch that, I *know* I can't do this without them.

"Breathe sweetie. You can do this," Sophie soothes as she brings me in for a hug, and I instantly feel better in her arms.

"I don't think so," I whisper back, doubt and apprehension evident in my tone.

Untangling from our hug, she grabs my face, her eyes reflecting a mixture of empathy and encouragement. "Yes, you can. Remember, we're here for you. I have no problem jumping on a plane to come see you if you ever need anything."

Adeline wraps me in a tight hug, her words filled with genuine affection. "I love you."

I smile. "I love you, too."

Adeline then turns her attention to Lucas, her face void of all previous emotions. "Oh, and Lucas," she says, her voice stern, "if you hurt her in any way, I'll be back to cut off your—"

"Adeline!" Sophie cuts her off mid-sentence, a look of horror on her face.

Adeline, however, doesn't back down, raising two fingers to her eyes before pointing them at Lucas in a clear threat. Lucas's chuckle only seems to offend her further, so she continues, in Arabic this time, "Yel'an—"

"I guess congratulations are in order," a deep voice interrupts, and we all turn toward the source of the voice.

"I'm disappointed, Lucas. Not even a call to share the happy news?" That same voice is laced with a touch of amusement, yet, there's an underlying tension.

Lucas's whole demeanor changes as he visibly tenses beside me and I'm afraid the glass of whiskey in his hand will break. The man standing before us is tall, almost matching Lucas's height, and his eyes resemble the same dark color as Lucas's. He's wearing a leather jacket over a white t-shirt that's paired with dark jeans, and his hair is short, almost like a buzzcut. I look between them, but no one notices as they seem to be in a staring contest.

They kind of look alike.

No, I take it back, they *do* look alike.

They continue to stare at each other, oblivious to my presence until finally, Lucas speaks up, breaking the tension.

"Liam," Lucas says, his voice rigid.

"Lucas," Liam responds.

The intensity of their stare is tangible, and I feel like an outsider witnessing an intimate moment.

Wait. Liam.

Of course, Liam is his brother.

The air is thick with unresolved issues, and I can't help but wonder why. My hand instinctively slides into Lucas's and I have to gently coax his hand open from its clenched position. He eventually yields to my touch and intertwines his fingers with mine.

"Hi Liam, it's nice to finally meet you. I'm Leora," I say with a warm smile, hoping to ease the tension in the room. "I've heard so much about you."

Liam's gaze shifts from Lucas to me, and the intensity in his eyes softens.

"Leora, I guess you're my sister-in-law now," he says, taking my free hand and brushing his lips across my knuckles. It's obvious he's a charmer, and he knows it.

I look back at Lucas to find his gaze has narrowed slightly. His fingers tighten around mine as he slightly pulls me back to him.

"I'm happy to meet you too, but I doubt you've heard much about me." The corner of his lips quirks. "At least, not anything good," he adds with a playful wink.

His gaze drifts to Sophie then, lingering a second too long to be just a passing glance. She forces a smile, but I can see the uncertainty in her eyes.

"Well, I'm sure you aren't that bad," I say with a small smile, trying to diffuse the situation. There's a lot more to the story, but I decide not to press any further. At least not for now. I can feel Lucas's hand tightening almost painfully, and I instinctively respond by giving his hand a reassuring squeeze, which seems to relax him a bit.

Adeline looks between Sophie and Liam, sizing him up as if he's some new enigma, before tugging me away from the awkward staring match. "We have to go, but keep us updated." Sophie smiles reassuringly and adds, "Don't hesitate to call us if you need anything. Okay?"

I nod, trying to keep it together. They give me one last hug before making their way to the airport. Then they're gone.

"How long are you staying this time?" Lucas asks a bit

abruptly, breaking his silence. Liam's gaze flickers back from watching Sophie walk away to his brother and I can see the tightness in Lucas's jaw as he awaits an answer.

"I'm not sure yet," Liam finally answers. "I just got in today and haven't made any plans."

Lucas nods, and I can feel his hand relaxing in mine. I give it another squeeze, trying to provide some comfort.

"Well, you're welcome to stay with us as long as you need," I offer with a smile, not exactly knowing why. I'm hoping Lucas won't take offense, though I'm not entirely sure there is an "us" to stay with. We haven't talked about accommodations. If it's up to me, I'll just stay here at the hotel—on his dime.

My hopes are smashed when his head jerks in my direction, his eyes flashing with anger. I choose to ignore his reaction, focusing on Liam, who returns my smile with a hint of gratitude in his eyes.

"Thanks, Leora. I appreciate the offer, but I'll stay here at the hotel. Speaking of which, I'm going to go and say hi to Ammo Antoine. It was nice meeting you, Leora."

As Liam walks off, an awkward silence envelops Lucas and me. I turn to face him, our fingers still intertwined. His jaw is clenched tight, and he takes a swig of his whiskey. His demeanor has changed; the hint of warmth in his smile from a few moments ago has morphed into the pensive curve of his lips.

"Are you alright?"

Lucas grunts in response, his gaze locked on the amber liquid in his glass.

"Are you sure?" I press gently, hoping to break through the wall he's built up. With that question, he lets go of my hand, and I feel a pang of coldness where his warm fingers were.

"I'm fine," he mutters before downing the last of his drink in one swift motion. I try to ignore the sinking feeling in my chest and concentrate on the task at hand: making him relax.

We can do this. *I need this to work.*

This is my chance to start over, to prove that I can make something of myself. Lucas is the ticket to that future.

I take a deep breath and reach for his hand, hoping to offer him some comfort. But he pulls away, leaving me feeling foolish and rejected. I watch as he retreats further into his own thoughts, pondering whether we'll ever manage to bridge the gap between us. Or if this is what the next year will look like, two strangers, bound together by a piece of paper and selfish desires, counting down the days until it all comes to an end.

SEVENTEEN

LUCAS

He's actually here.

How did he even manage to show up? When did he arrive? And most importantly, *why*?

It's been six months since we last spoke, and I can't help but feel a twinge of resentment towards him, even though I know I should be the responsible older brother and support him. But then again, he's a grown man who claims he doesn't need anyone to tell him what to do.

After our conversation—if one can even call it that—I couldn't focus on anything else.

Not even Leora's attempts to comfort me could break through the haze of my thoughts, so I chug what's left in my whiskey glass. There's a fleeting pang of guilt from when I caught the hurt in her eyes, but right now, there's not much I can do.

Whatever it is that she wants to know, I'm not ready to talk about just yet.

For the next hour, we put on a show for our guests, as if nothing ever happened—holding hands, exchanging smiles, and engaging in light conversation. Whenever a question about how we met comes up—a conversation we've yet to have, mainly because I hadn't anticipated a wedding—Leora smiles and says something about social media and how I "slid into her DM's." Whatever that means. I'm not a big social media guy, and I'd rather live without it, but I have to say, I prefer that narrative over the truth. I'd rather be the stalker she paints me to be than the weird man who propositioned a woman to be his fake wife in exchange for money and a job.

The press would have a field day with that one.

As the event draws to a close, my attention lands on Leora, who's standing next to my uncle, laughing at whatever he's saying. I maneuver through the crowd, making my way towards them. Strangely, seeing her beside him almost makes me happy about the situation we're in.

"Let's go," I say abruptly, catching both of them off guard.

"Go where?" she says with a puzzled look on her face.

"Home."

"What do you mean? I'm staying here."

"I mean," I say, my voice determined, "that you're coming home with me." Her expression shifts from surprise to disbelief. She turns to my uncle, seemingly for confirmation, but he simply looks back at me, a glimmer of approval in his eyes.

Her arms cross in front of her chest as she retorts, "No, I'm not."

I can practically feel the stubbornness radiating off her, and a headache is starting to form, but I try to keep my tone composed, despite the need to drag her out of the hotel. "Yes, you are."

Leora shakes her head, her voice laced with a challenge. "Why can't I stay at the hotel?"

"I'm not going to argue about this. You're staying with me." I lower my voice. "How do you expect people to believe we're newlyweds if you stay at my hotel?"

I watch as her shoulders tense up, and her demeanor shifts as if she's about to start an argument. But then, after a second, she relaxes slightly, probably coming to her senses and realizing I'm right, or she's simply too tired to argue. She concedes with a resigned tone. "Fine. But I need my stuff."

AFTER WE'VE GATHERED "HER STUFF," which consists of *one* suitcase, we make our way to the car.

This is it. Leora is my wife, and now my roommate.

I can't help but feel a sense of unease wash over me. This is the first time I've ever lived with a woman, let alone a significant other. And the idea of not knowing how it will play out is making me nervous. I sneak a sidelong glance at Leora, her gaze fixed on the passing cars outside the window. She seems distant, her posture tense and her fingers restlessly fidgeting in her lap. She's clearly uncomfortable with the whole "living together" arrangement. What had I expected? Of course she's uncomfortable, but I'll try my best to make her feel more at home.

I wish I didn't have that whiskey during the wedding because if I were sober, I could've been driving. Which would have allowed me to focus on the road rather than the woman sitting next to me, or on the kiss we'd shared.

As soon as the crowd started chanting, I knew I had to put on a show, but when my lips brushed hers, I couldn't stop. It was as though my lips already knew hers. All I craved was more of that sweet taste. Unfortunately, the memory also leaves me with a semi every time I think of it.

Eventually, we arrive at my apartment building, and as I pick up Leora's suitcase from the trunk, I can't help but notice that it's light. A feeling of annoyance washes over me as I recall asking her to buy some clothes just two days prior. However, I had a feeling she wouldn't listen. So, I took it upon myself to ask Camille to do some shopping and hang the new clothes in her room.

We step into the elevator that takes us to my penthouse, and I sneak another quick look at Leora. Her eyes dart around nervously, taking in her surroundings. There's a slight tremble in her hands as she adjusts her grip on the strap of her purse. Her breathing seems to have quickened, and her eyes won't meet mine, as if she's afraid to look at me.

I let out a frustrated huff. I understand she's nervous about moving in with me, but this level of fear seems unwarranted. It's as if I've forced her into marrying me at gunpoint. If anything, considering her fiery nature and history of throwing things at my face, *I* should be the worried one.

As soon as the elevator doors open, she practically rushes out. I follow closely behind, noticing the relief in her eyes as she steps into the apartment. Taking the lead, I guide her into my space, trying to project a sense of calm, despite the tension that seems to be lingering between us.

Again, I can't help but notice her gaze darting around, taking in the details with a mix of wonder and trepidation. Gradually, her shoulders seem to lose some of their tension as she moves through the hallway and into the expansive living room that connects to the kitchen.

"It's so big." There's an awe in her voice as she looks around at the floor-to-ceiling windows surrounding the sitting area.

"It is quite spacious," I respond, a faint smile tugging on the corners of my lips at her chosen words. A moment of stillness settles and I find myself captivated by how the natural light streaming in casts a soft glow on her face. She almost looks angelic.

"We'll have plenty of room for ourselves," I offer, aiming for lightness, but her answering smile seems strained, not quite reaching her eyes.

I clear my throat. "Let me show you to your room so you can change out of your dress."

I lead her to one of the guest bedrooms, choosing the door closest to the living room. My own room is strategically located on the far side of the penthouse, a considerable distance from hers. It's the best case in this situation. That way I can keep her at arm's length and have my own space. The truth is, we don't need to hang out that much when we're in private. Our roles are set. Out there, we act; in here, we exist.

Her room is cozy and well-appointed, with a comfortable,

queen sized bed, soft linens—egyptian cotton, of course—and tasteful decor. A small sitting area by the window, that offers a nice view of the beach. I remember she told me she enjoys reading and that spot is perfect for it.

I turn to Leora and gesture toward the room.

"This will be your room," I try to sound as welcoming as possible, but when we step in, we both freeze.

"You really went all out, didn't you?" she says, this time with a genuine smile on her lips, but as beautiful as it is, my mind is preoccupied with what's in front of me.

On the bed lay a bunch of rose petals forming the shape of a heart, and there's candles scattered all around the room.

"Camille," I hiss through my teeth. Leora's giggle turns into full-blown laughter, and she almost topples over with amusement. Camille is my most trusted employee, the only one who knows the truth about this arrangement.

"I'm going to fire her," I grumble, though a small smirk tugs at the corner of my lips. Despite the awkwardness of this situation, her laughter is infectious, and for a moment, I forget about the complications and just enjoy the sound of it.

All I had asked Camille to do was to buy Leora some outfits and shoes. Simple.

Apparently not for Camille. Instead, what she managed to do was raise my blood pressure through the roof. Attempting to mask my annoyance, I nonchalantly shrug, trying to dismiss the situation.

"Camille wanted to surprise you," I say, trying to justify her actions.

Leora chuckles, her eyes dancing with amusement as she teases me. "Well, it looks like she surprised you even more."

I take a deep breath, reminding myself to keep my composure.

This day has been overwhelming.

I've married a stranger, been surprised with a wedding reception, then had to kiss said stranger. Even if my body seems to long for another taste of her lips, it still doesn't change the fact that this whole situation is nowhere near ideal.

"There are some new clothes for you in the wardrobe," I say, changing the subject, fully expecting a retort about how she doesn't need my help or my money. But to my surprise, Leora remains silent instead.

She nods, her expression a mix of gratitude and nervousness.

"Thank you," her voice is soft as she steps deeper into the room.

"Is there anything else I can do for you?" I ask, genuinely wanting to make her feel at ease in my—*our*—home.

Leora shakes her head, her eyes avoiding mine. "No, I'm fine," her voice is barely above a whisper. "Thank you for showing me around."

I give her a small, reassuring smile. "All right then. How about you settle in," I say, gesturing toward the room with a nod. "If you need anything, just let me know."

Leora nods in agreement and begins unpacking her suitcase. With that, I leave the guest bedroom and head toward my room to shower and change out of this suit.

I spend more time than I intended in the shower, lost in thought as I try to devise plans for Leora and I. Other than the various business events and dinners, we'll need to be seen together in public, so we could go on a few "dates" to places where we might be spotted.

The idea of taking Leora to Paris for a weekend crosses my mind. That's something people in love would do, right? I always hear about how going to Paris is so romantic. Which means it will be great for us, and I bet she would even be happy to visit. Isn't Paris on every woman's bucket list?

The wedding day stretched on longer than intended. As it's almost six o'clock, I quickly change into a pair of sweatpants and a t-shirt. Grabbing my laptop, I settle down on the sofa to go through some emails. However, my eyes keep returning to Leora's closed door.

She's probably getting settled in. As new as having a room-mate is for me, it will be even more of an adjustment for her. Not only does she now have a husband, but she also moved to another country and into someone else's home. I sigh and try to return to my emails, noticing one from Michel Beaumont.

A cold rush goes through my body at the sight of his name. I hate that man.

Dear Mr. Ayoub,

I hope this email finds you well. I want to extend my congratula-tions to you and your new wife, on your recent nuptials. Although, its last-minute nature did come as a surprise to many of us.

Unfortunately, I was unable to attend the hastily-arranged wedding reception hosted by your uncle.

Nevertheless, I would like to extend an invitation to you and your wife to join us for brunch on Monday at 11:30 a.m.

We would be honored to have you both as our guests.

Best Regards,
Michel Beaumont

Fuck me.

As if it couldn't get any worse, now I'm going to have to spend a day with a bunch of stuck-up men, including Michel. I'm going to have to answer his email, pretend to be delighted and accept the invitation on our behalf.

This might turn out to be a shit show because we still have so much to discuss and decide. However, there's also a chance it could work in our favor. If I know Michel well enough, he will have invited a few more stakeholders, and if I read the email correctly, he's doing this to prove a point. Meaning we'll have to put on such a convincing show of being in love so that he will have to eat his words.

I try to compose my response, carefully choosing my words to convey gratitude and enthusiasm. *All lies.* I express our delight at the invitation and accept it graciously on behalf of Leora and myself. I make sure to mention our upcoming honeymoon we will be taking after the hotel opening, hoping it will add an air of authenticity to our situation.

It's time to show Michel, and everyone else, that Leora and I are a united front, regardless of the initial doubts we garnered. Hopefully, it will make them back off.

I knock gently on Leora's door, not wanting to disturb her too much. "Leora?"

"What?" Her muffled voice reaches me through the closed door.

I enter the room and find her sitting on the bed with her phone in her hand. She's changed into a cute pair of white pajamas with red cherries, showcasing her toned legs. I can't deny that I find it attractive—any man would.

Any man. The mere thought of another man looking at her now that she has my ring on her finger unsettles me. It's irrational, considering our unconventional situation, but the idea of anyone else showing interest in her bothers me. She may not truly be mine, but to the outside world, she is. Still, the question lingers, why does the notion of another man looking at her bother me? I shouldn't care, yet something inside me does.

I quickly shake off the thought and refocus on her, reminding myself that we have important matters to discuss.

"I didn't say come in," she says sharply.

"You didn't say *not* to come in either."

"What do you want, Lucas?"

"We need to talk"—I gesture between us—"about this whole thing. How we met, why we got married, your likes and dislikes. I need to know more than just your favorite color, which, by the way, I remember is blue." I add the last part before she has the chance to ask.

Her response is blunt. "You slid into my DMs, I found you hot and we fell in love. End of story. A modern day fairytale." She's testing my patience, which is already wearing thin.

I take a deep breath and try to keep my composure as I motion for her to follow me to the living room. To my surprise, she does so without arguing. That's twice today, and if it happens a third time, I think I'll have to reward her in some way to encourage this behavior.

As she walks past me, I can't help but steal another glance at her legs, tracing the smooth lines, the gentle curve of her calf, and the delicate arch of her ankle—it's impossible not to stare. However, when I notice she's glanced back at me, raising her brow at my unintentional staring, I quickly avert my eyes.

She sits down on the far end of the sofa, as far away from me as possible, leaving a subtle scent of vanilla lingering in the air. It remains, heightening my senses and sending a tingling sensation coursing through my body.

"Before we start, let's order some food. Do you want sushi?" I propose. But as soon as the question leaves my lips, I see her wrinkling her nose and her face contorting in disgust. Sushi is clearly not on her list of favorite foods, and she doesn't hesitate to let me know.

"I hate sushi."

"Noted," I reply. "Alright, what about pizza then?" I suggest, hoping for a more favorable reaction. This time, she nods in agreement.

Perfect, pizza it is. I proceed to order one Diavola for myself and one Margherita for her.

Shifting gears, I mention, "We've also got an invitation for a brunch on Monday, courtesy of Michel Beaumont—the guy from the restaurant last night."

"I don't like that guy. Do we have to go?" She crosses her arms over her chest like a stubborn child, and I'm getting a sense that this is her signature move.

"Yes."

Leora looks at me defiantly—her eyebrows furrow and her lips press into a thin line. "Then, what's the story?" she asks me as I sit back on the sofa.

"Well, you already decided *how* we met, but we haven't decided when."

"Six months ago, you were feeling incredibly lonely around Christmas," she says with a playful smirk. "You were scrolling through Instagram, and *BAM*, you stumbled upon me, and you just *had* to get to know me."

The vivid imagination of this girl. I don't even have an Instagram account, but I guess I'll have to create one for the sake of this story.

I look at her, and there's a smug smile on her face that wasn't there just a few hours ago. I have to admit, I like seeing her smile. It's unexpected, but it brightens her face in a way I hadn't noticed before, and I can't help but smile in return.

"Two months after that fateful DM," she continues, "you were so obsessed with me that you hopped on a plane to meet me."

I raise an eyebrow, intrigued. "Oh, is that so?" I ask, playing along.

She nods enthusiastically. "You had it all figured out and surprised me with the largest bouquet of roses, hundreds of them." She pauses and points a finger toward me. "Although, I must admit, I'm more of a tulip girl, but for the sake of the story, I'll accept the roses."

I let out a genuine laugh at her witty comment, then decide to take our fictional narrative up a notch.

"Little did I know," I begin, with a playful glint in my eye, "that you had an even bigger surprise for me."

Leora raises an eyebrow, intrigued. "Oh really? Do tell."

"You went down on one knee and proposed to me right in the middle of the airport."

Her eyes widen in mock surprise, and she bursts into laughter. "You're kidding, right?"

I play along, enjoying the absurdity of our invented story, "You even serenaded me —it was incredible."

She throws her head back in laughter. "You're insane! Firstly, I would never be the one proposing, and no one would even believe that. Secondly, serenading you? Come on. Thirdly, who proposes to someone they just met, for the first time, in the middle of an airport?"

I join in with her laughter, enjoying the absurdity of our made-up story. She's right, of course—no one would ever believe that story. I wouldn't like that either. Yet, as much as I had been against this marriage, the idea of someday proposing to someone has always been in the back of my mind. I remember the story of how my father proposed to my mother, a story I've cherished for years.

Mom had flown back to her hometown in Lebanon, to visit my grandmother. With my uncle's help, my father had flown all the way from the United States to surprise her.

Instead of just driving up to her favorite place, Harissa, my father had planned something more adventurous: he took her on the cable car. When they reached about 500 meters above sea level, he went down on one knee, making the whole cable car shake, and my mum cry out in fear. They always joked about how my mum probably agreed to marry my father because she was afraid. When she died I kept her ring; it's a precious memento of their love that I will cherish forever, and I've saved it for when my time comes.

Someday, I'm meant to find my match, but in recent years, I've simply been too preoccupied to actively seek her out.

"Okay, but let's be serious for a second." Leora's voice snaps me back to reality. The reality where I'm married to a girl I barely know. I can't help but think that my mom would be disappointed in me, even though I'm doing it for the sake of our name and our hotels. She had so much love in her heart and she disliked anything business related—she thought it ruined people; that when money was involved, it took away from their values and morals.

Have I turned into the type of person she despised?

The thought leaves me with a pang of guilt. But I gather myself and give Leora a more realistic story we can use. "We started talking six months ago. I happened to find you on social media and thought you were beautiful, so I 'slid into your DM's.' We started talking every day—joking and sharing parts of ourselves we've never shared with anyone else, and in the process, we slowly fell for each other. During my business trip to New York three months ago, we finally got to meet each other. We knew then and there that we wanted to be together. When you know, you know. So I took you to a beautiful rooftop and proposed to you under the stars. You accepted, and now you're here. We both decided not to have a big wedding, but Antoine surprised us with the small gathering."

There's a disappointed look on her face. The playful glow that was there earlier seems to have vanished.

"Okay." Her eyes are on me, quizzical. It's as though she felt the shift in me and wants to know why. "Lucas, are you—"

My phone chimes, interrupting her. I glance at my phone and see the front door calling.

"Looks like our pizza's here." I quickly excuse myself and tell them to send the pizza up. As I hand over the money, I can't help but feel relieved for the interruption.

"Got the pizza," I say, setting it down on the coffee table. "Hungry?"

Leora smiles, and her large, green eyes light up as she nods. "Starving."

I go to grab a bottle of wine. "White or red?"

"White, please." I choose a *Chapoutier Roussanne* and bring it to the table with two glasses.

We dig into the pizza, and as we eat, the previous tension dissipates and the conversation flows easily between us. I learn that

Leora dislikes seafood and black coffee—she prefers a Cappuccino —and has a peculiar obsession with a movie called *Mamma Mia*. When she found out I had no idea what she was talking about, her face lit up with enthusiasm as she launched into an animated description of the movie and how we have to watch it together. Listening to her talk about it with such passion was oddly endearing, and I found myself getting drawn into her excitement. To be honest, the movie sounds good.

When the conversation winds down, she turns to me, her eyes trying to hide their apprehension.

"Lucas, can I ask you something?"

"Sure"

"Did you recognise me when I approached you in the club?" Her question catches me off guard.

"No, I didn't," I reply, trying to sound casual, not wanting her to feel uncomfortable that I did, in fact, initially recognize her. I remembered her the moment I saw her. How could I forget a face like hers?

I see her shoulders slump and her gaze shift to the plate in her lap, a shadow of disappointment crossing her features. Fuck, wrong answer.

"Oh."

She doesn't say anything for a few seconds, seemingly lost in deep thought. When she looks up at me, her brows are furrowed and her spine is stiff, as if she's gathering her courage.

"Then why did you act like a complete douchebag?" Her voice is tinged with some anger, and there's fire in her green eyes.

Me?

Douchebag?

Okay, let's back up.

"You threw the drink at *me*," I retort.

"Because you were rude!" Her voice rises slightly, and the girl who looked sad just moments ago is now replaced with a hostile one.

"Do you throw drinks at everyone who's rude to you? Or just

the guys chosen for your 'missions', Leora? Is that how you handle things when you don't get your way?"

"Excuse me?"

"I overheard you and your little friends. You only came up to me to complete a dare—to use me." I state matter-of-factly, my words hanging in the charged air. People have used me before, when I was younger, either for money or for a jump in their career. Then they dropped me as if I were a burning match. It's a pattern I've grown accustomed to, and I won't let it happen again.

Her surprise is evident, and I smile inwardly.

Lucas, one.

Leora, zero.

At my comment, her eyes darken, and they almost match the intensity of mine. She stands up, her teeth gritted, and her hands balled into fists.

"I wasn't using *you*?" she snaps, pointing a finger at me. "That 'dare' was for me to gain some confidence by talking to a man after my ex cheated on me."

Her ex cheated on her?

Suddenly, I remember the conversation I overheard about a certain John—whom I had assumed was a dickhead—and it seems like I was right. I feel my jaw tightening.

Her eyes are flaring. If looks could kill, I would have been incinerated on the spot.

I try to ease the tension so we can talk it out. "Leora, how was I supposed to know about—"

"Save it," she interrupts, her voice cutting through the tension. "That doesn't excuse your behavior."

The room falls silent, heavy with unspoken words and at this point I don't know exactly how to react.

EIGHTEEN

LEORA

"I understand you're upset. Maybe I didn't handle things well, but can you see it from my point of view too?" he says with a slight calmness to his tone.

I didn't want to use him. I just wanted to talk to him.

"Lucas," I say firmly, "you had no right to assume the worst of me and treat me as you did. I didn't deserve that." He looks taken aback, but I continue, my voice unwavering. "I approached you at the club because I wanted to talk to you, not because I wanted anything from you. I have my own money. I can take care of myself, and I don't need you. But you didn't even give me a chance to explain before jumping to conclusions."

His eyebrows raise, and he takes a step toward me, towering over me. Suddenly, my whole bravado disappears, and my nerves take over. My fingers tingle, and my stomach flips as I try to stand my ground, but his imposing presence makes me feel so small.

His eyes lock onto mine. "And you don't think your behavior was wrong?" My body involuntarily tenses at his confrontation. A surge of adrenaline courses through my veins, setting my heart racing and creating a subtle discomfort. I know I was in the wrong, but a stubborn part of me yearns for him to acknowledge his wrongdoing first and offer an apology that would soothe the ache of our recent clash.

With an airy touch, he raises his hand and uses his index finger to brush away a stray strand of hair that has fallen across my face.

"Aren't you going to apologize?" I try to sound composed, but it comes out as a whisper.

Lucas lowers himself, so we are eye to eye, and a charged silence hangs in the air. His gaze locks onto mine, and for a moment, the world seems to pause.

His eyes are so dark, they're almost black yet in his right eye there's a speck of gold, a captivating anomaly that draws me in.

His lips curve into a subtle, mysterious smile, and he leans in just a fraction closer, leaving me breathless. My heart races as I struggle to maintain composure. "We're not going to solve this today. Be ready tomorrow at ten. We're visiting Ammo." The warmth of his breath sends a tantalizing shiver down my spine. Without another word, he straightens, turns his back to me, and walks away from the living room. I'm left standing there, caught in a whirlwind of conflicting emotions.

What the actual—

I had hoped we would resolve this, but it looks like we won't. It takes me back to when John and I would argue. He would simply dismiss me left and right, not allowing my feelings to be validated. Whatever he had done, I was always in the wrong, whether it was because I actually did something or because he had hurt my feelings. It was always, *"You provoke me into saying stuff I don't mean,"* or, *"Why are you upset? What about my feelings? Do you ever stop to think about them?"* Then, I was the one feeling guilty, which led me to apologize unnecessarily. I'm not going through that again, real or fake. That's why I want him to apologize first. It might be childish and wrong, but I need it.

At the thought of my past, a surge of emotions lights me up, and with renewed determination, I follow Lucas into a hallway.

"Lucas." My voice is filled with conviction. He turns to face me, his expression guarded.

"I won't apologize," I say firmly, looking him directly in the eyes.

"I didn't ask you to."

"But you—"

Lucas's jaw tightens, and he gives me a piercing glare as he takes a few steps toward me. Fuck, I think I just poked the bear a little too much. Despite his aggravation, he still looks incredible, and it's frustrating because I'm supposed to be upset with him, not turned on. His presence makes me want to forget everything and succumb to the attraction that lingers between us, even amidst an argument.

"But what, Leora? I should apologize just because you want me to? That's not how it works, darling," he says the word *"darling"* like it's poisonous. "My patience is wearing thin. I thought we were having a good night." He brushes a hand through his hair, sighing, "I'm not a mind reader—I wasn't then, and I'm not now. For you to assume I should be aware of your past is unfair." Lucas crosses his arms, his expression still guarded.

I take a deep breath, trying to calm myself down and keep my voice level. "I was angry and hurt, and I wanted to make a point." I try to gauge his expression but get nothing, so I continue. "My friends wanted me to feel confident again, and walking up to a guy that looks like you and getting a response will give a girl some confidence. I never wanted to use you in any other way than to talk."

Lucas's jaw clenches, and for a moment, I think he's going to say something else to fuel the fire. But then he sighs heavily, his hand once again going through his already messy hair. "Leora," he says my name with so much concern, his voice a gentle touch in the midst of the tension. "It's been a long and intense day for both of us. Can we put this conversation on hold and discuss it when we've had a good night's sleep?" He's right. It's been an intense day. Maybe that's what's fueling my emotions. Though I had wanted to solve this now, I nod in agreement.

He turns and walks toward his bedroom, his shoulders

slightly slouched. I watch him go, his every step echoing the weariness he carries. As he disappears from view, I turn and head toward my own bedroom, my mind turbulent with thoughts and emotions. The heaviness in the air lingers, a silent testament to the weight of the day on both our shoulders.

As I enter my room and shut the door behind me, I take a deep breath, attempting to calm myself down. The argument has left me drained and exhausted, yet I know it's not over. There's still a lot to talk about, and I just hope we can work things out.

If nothing else, I learned something about my husband tonight: Lucas might be even more stubborn than I am.

I SLOWLY OPEN MY EYES, blinking against the brightness. The soft light from the window filters through the curtains, casting a warm glow across the room. It paints the walls in hues of gold and shadows dance across the floor. I stretch my arms above my head, feeling a pleasant tingling sensation as my muscles awaken from slumber. As I sit up, I notice the faint scent of the salty ocean in the air, carried in by a gentle breeze that rustles the curtains. The chirping of birds outside adds to the serene ambiance. It feels as though I'm living a dream.

My heart sinks as the memory of yesterday's argument floods back into my mind, shattering the peacefulness of the moment. I got one minute of peace before my memories of him ruined my morning. I don't know how to move forward from this, and I don't even know if I want to. Part of me wants to hold onto the anger and resentment, to not give in and admit any wrongdoing. But another part of me, a softer part, wants to find a way to bridge the divide and start to build on a relationship.

I huff. What relationship? This whole ordeal is for others to see and believe. In reality, it doesn't matter if we argue or dislike each other behind closed doors. We just have to make it look as if we love each other.

I inhale deeply and reach for my phone on the nightstand. The first thing I do is open up the group chat between the girls and I, and find a few messages.

> **ADELINE**
>
> We're home now, habibti.
>
> How are you?
>
> **SOPHIE**
>
> How's the new husband treating you?
>
> **ADELINE**
>
> They've probably killed each other, that's why she's not answering

> **ME**
>
> Good morning my loves.
>
> I'm fine and nobody has killed anyone...yet. but if I don't answer any more messages today, I'm probably in jail for causing harm to my "husband." In that case, I love you.

My eyes go to the clock on my phone, 9:40 a.m. *Dammit*, I only have twenty minutes to get ready.

I swing my legs over the side of the bed and rush to the en suite bathroom. I splash my face with cool water, feeling the refreshing sensation wake me up completely. I quickly go through my skincare routine, applying serums, moisturizer, and sunscreen —I never forget sunscreen—with practiced efficiency. I glance at the clock on the bathroom counter, realizing that time is ticking away faster than I thought. I rush to my walk-in closet, which had been filled with clothes when I arrived. He had prepared every-thing, from formal dresses to jeans and t-shirts.

At first, I was slightly annoyed. It felt like a way for him to control me, for me to wear "fitting" clothes as he had put it. But after our argument yesterday, I took a look at the clothes and everything lookes amazing; it looks like *me*. Which both pisses me off and makes me extremely happy at the same time. There are even a bunch of sundresses in various lengths and colors. And don't get me started on the shoes or I will cry. There are rows of beautiful heels, flats, and sneakers.

It's a dream come true, and I'm utterly confused.

Yesterday, he told me we were going to meet with Antoine, and I'm quite excited to see a friendly face, especially after yesterday's ending.

My hair still has some curls from the wedding, so I only focus on getting the perfect curtain bang before I do my make up. I keep the look soft with a touch of pink lip gloss and a hint of blush.

After I finish, I opt for a black silk, midi skirt paired with a black tank top, completing the look with a pair of stylish Chanel flats. As soon as I saw the beige, tweed flats, I knew I had to wear them. They're simply gorgeous.

I look at myself in the mirror one more time and spritz myself with my favorite vanilla perfume before I leave my room.

Of course, Lucas is already waiting in the kitchen, leaning against the kitchen island with a coffee in his hand. I curse under my breath when I see him looking as handsome as ever. His outfit is casual; he's wearing a pair of dark jeans and a t-shirt.

Our eyes lock as I walk toward him, and Lucas's gaze slowly travels over my body. I become acutely aware of his attention, and my body reacts to his lingering stare. My heart skips a beat as a flush spreads across my skin.

Why does he have this effect on me? I don't understand; we don't even know each other enough for me to react like this.

All I ask is that he doesn't notice how my traitorous body reacts. I lick my lower lip nervously, and I catch Lucas mirroring my action, his eyes zeroing in on my lips.

Yep, he totally noticed.

To my relief, his eyes move back up to meet mine. The intensity in his gaze is unmistakable, and I can see a flicker of something there.

He takes a sip from his coffee cup. "Did you sleep well?"

I stop in front of him, leaning in ever so slightly to smell his cologne. It smells woodsy and manly, and my breath catches in my throat. For a reason, my voice can't seem to come out, so I nod. *What's wrong with me?* Why can't I seem to act like a normal person in front of him?

Lucas blinks, and I take a step back, feeling embarrassed.

I try to shake off the tension that still lingers in the air as I busy myself with getting a glass of water.

Remember you're still mad at him.

I try to dig up the feelings from yesterday, but now there's something else that has been added to the feelings.

Guilt.

I might have overreacted, *I think.*

Lucas clears his throat and looks away, and I can tell that he's trying to regain his composure.

"We should get going, We don't want to be late."

I nod again, take a last sip from my water, and follow him out of the apartment and into the death trap.

NINETEEN

LEORA

My heart is racing as I step into the elevator with Lucas. I don't know if the stress is adding to my usual fear, but I can't breathe. Lucas's eyes are on me, yet I can't bring myself to look at him.

I can tolerate him disliking me. But pitying me? I can't handle that.

My palms start to sweat, and I feel like I'm going to faint. It feels like someone's hand is wrapped around my throat, squeezing it tighter for every second that passes. I'm suffocating, like the walls of the elevator are closing in on me. My chest tightens, and I struggle to take a deep breath.

Lucas turns to me with a concerned look on his face. "Are you okay?"

I don't answer. I can't, because if I open my mouth, I'll break down. Instead, I try to calm myself down, repeating to myself that I'm okay, that this is just a small space, that I'll be out soon. But the panic is overwhelming, and I can't seem to shake it off.

Finally, the elevator doors open, and I rush out, gasping for air. I try to compose myself as best as I can, but my hands are still shaking.

A large hand softly lands on my back. "Leora?" he says my name with a tone of concern, as if he's worried.

I manage to take one large, calming breath before I nod at Lucas. With a weak smile, I say, "I'm fine, don't worry." But the truth is, it hasn't been this bad in a long time. I usually don't freak out this much when other people are with me.

I take a few more deep breaths, trying to regain control of my racing thoughts and calm my body. I don't know why, but I don't want him to know this about me. It's so silly. Even though I have a feeling he wouldn't judge me for it, I just don't want him to know.

Who's afraid of elevators at the age of twenty-eight? It's embarrassing.

"Leora?" he presses with more concern in his voice and it fills me with a warm feeling.

"I'm good. I just got a little dizzy."

Lucas wears a confused frown, his hand, a source of comforting warmth, remains on my back, tracing soothing circles.

"You sure you're okay?" he asks gently, "Maybe we should take a moment."

I appreciate his support, I hadn't expected it to feel so tender.

"I'm alright," I assure him, though his lingering concern doesn't escape me.

Lucas seems to be lost in thought, his grip on the steering wheel tight. We seem to be back to silence.

I hate it.

John used it against me as a form of punishment. It didn't matter if I was the reason for the argument. In the end it was always my fault.

Silence makes me feel small. It makes me feel alone and I don't like it.

I glance at him through the corner of my eye, hoping to see a change in his expression. He's still grasping the wheel, his jaw set and tensed. I notice a little curl that has fallen over his forehead, softening his features. It's cute, and more than anything, I want to brush it away.

However, now does not seem like the right time for that. I shift my gaze to the dangling object hanging around the rearview mirror that Lucas had touched when we sat down in the car. It's a delicate rosary, with pristine white beads that reflect the soft interior lights of the car. On the bottom, a small golden cross dangles gracefully, glinting in the sunlight. It sways gently with each movement of the vehicle. It makes me want to touch it—maybe it will give me some strength to endure this marriage.

My hand reaches out, fingers almost brushing against the beads, but just before I make contact, his head turns to me, his eyes meeting mine with a mix of curiosity and a hint of something unreadable. I snatch my hand back, my heart pounding as I wait for him to say something—anything at all—but he doesn't.

I try to distract myself by looking out the window, but my mind keeps going back to our argument. A part of me wishes I could take back my words and start fresh, but I know that's not possible. Maybe I should apologize—try to make things right—because I won't be able to stand this for long. However, once again there's another voice telling me that he's the one who should apologize first, not me.

Before I know it, we're pulling up to a building and Lucas puts the car in park and turns to me. "We're here."

He grabs my hand as we walk toward a large house, and I can't help but feel a sense of wonder at its beauty. The house is elegant, overlooking the shimmering Mediterranean Sea. The exterior is painted a pristine white, with terracotta tiles covering the roof and cascading bougainvillea climbing up the external walls.

As we approach the grand, double doors, adorned with intricate wrought-iron accents, I can feel the warm breeze carrying the scent of sea salt and lavender. We knock on the door, and it's not long before a stylishly dressed man greets us with a welcoming smile. He ushers us inside the villa, revealing a spacious foyer with high ceilings and elegant furnishings.

The interior of the villa is just as breathtaking as the exterior, with marble floors, grand chandeliers, and ornate furniture. The walls are adorned with priceless works of art, and the floor-to-ceiling windows provide breathtaking views of the sea and the rolling hills.

He leads us through the hallway and out to the backside of the villa, where Antoine seems to be resting. The outdoor area is a tranquil oasis with lush greenery and a serene fountain at its center. Antoine is sitting on a chaise lounge, looking tired and frail in a way I've never seen before. I can see the exhaustion etched on his face.

He looks so small, not like the Antoine from a few days ago or even yesterday, when he was happily introducing me to everyone he knew. He coughs and a wave of sadness washes over me as I realize how sick he actually is.

As soon as Lucas spots Antoine, he goes rigid, clearly shocked by the severity of his condition. When I look up at him, the beautiful olive tone of his skin has morphed into a pale white, a stark contrast to its usual warmth. I squeeze his hand gently to offer him comfort; the tension from the argument set aside for this. But he withdraws as if he's suddenly realized we were holding hands.

Why is he pushing me away? I know he's upset, and I try to focus on the fact that this is about his uncle and not me, but I can't help but feel a little hurt at the rejection.

It's clear that Lucas is struggling with the reality of the situation, and I feel powerless to help him. Despite his tough exterior, I can see the pain and sadness in his eyes. The state of Antoine has shocked him, he didn't expect him to be this bad. As we approach Antoine, I try to stay strong, but my heart breaks seeing him so frail and weak. When he notices us, he stands up, or at least he tries to.

"No, Ammo, sit down," Lucas says as he runs to help him but he's already up, raising a trembling hand to Lucas's shoulder.

"*Ya ibni*, I'm happy you came to visit."

When he spots me, a smile spreads over his face. "Leora, come come sit."

After giving him a hug, I take a seat. "How are you, Antoine?"

"I'm doing well. I'm just a little tired today after being on my feet for the past few days. Don't worry, a quick nap and I'll be back to normal." I can sense the strength and determination in his voice, and I hope that he's right.

He looks between Lucas and I. "So, how has married life been so far?" A chuckle escapes his lips as he winks at me.

Lucas's expression remains blank, as if he doesn't know what to say or how to react. I take the initiative and joke back. "Well, it's been twenty-four hours and we haven't killed each other yet, so that's a positive." Antoine laughs in response to my comment. Lucas finally cracks a small smile, but it quickly disappears.

"That bad?" Antoine turns his head toward Lucas with a fake, scolding look on his face. "Lucas, you must take care of your wife. You know what they say: happy wife, happy life."

Antoine's voice trails off into a coughing fit, and I can see the concern and worry in Lucas's eyes as he reaches out to steady him. There's a glass pitcher of water on the table, so I pour Antoine a glass and hand it to Lucas. He helps him take a few sips, gently patting his back to ease the coughing. Antoine eventually recovers and offers us a strained smile. "Did you also get invited to Michel's brunch?"

Lucas returns to my side. "Unfortunately."

"Remember that Michel is the main reason there's going to be a vote, meaning that this invitation is to prove something."

We both nod, understanding the gravity of the situation.

"I know," Lucas replies.

"You two will have to play the part there. You can't act like you are right now. I can see right through you."

I feel a pang of discomfort at his words, wondering if it's

really that obvious. Lucas shifts beside me, avoiding any eye contact with Antoine.

Lucas and I exchange a look, silently acknowledging the truth in Antoine's words. We both know what's at stake, and we can't afford to let personal issues get in the way.

Antoine continues, "I know it's not easy, but for the sake of the business, we need to present a united front. Michel is a shrewd businessman, and he'll take advantage of any weakness he sees."

Lucas nods in agreement, and I chime in, "We'll do our best."

Antoine smiles, the warmth returning to his eyes. "I know you will. I have faith in you."

His gaze shifts to Lucas. "And you, my boy, have to prove to everyone that you are worthy of leading this company—that you have what it takes to continue my legacy. Remember, *He who is patient, achieves.*"

Lucas nods determinedly. "I know, Ammo. I won't let you down."

Antoine smiles at us. "Good. Now, let's not dwell on this any longer. We have much to celebrate today. Let's enjoy ourselves."

And with that, the conversation shifts to lighter topics.

WE WATCH as the sun begins to set over the sea, signaling the end of our visit. Antoine hugs me tightly, whispering, "Be patient with Lucas"—he pauses and looks at Lucas, his eyes filled with concern—"he may come across as stubborn, but deep down, he's a good man."

I nod. We say our goodbyes to Antoine and make our way back to the car.

"Are you okay?" I ask, concerned for him.

Lucas looks at me with a blank expression, "I'm good."

It's obvious that he's still upset with me, but I think seeing Antoine this tired made him realize the severity of the situation he's in.

We're in.

It makes you realize that small arguments really don't matter—who says "sorry" first doesn't matter. I summon the courage to initiate a conversation, attempting to offer an apology.

"So, about yesterday . . ." I start.

"Leora, I'm not in the mood to argue right now." His words cut through me, and a knot forms in my stomach. He looks at me, his eyes stern and black. On any other day, I would shy away from a gaze that harsh. I would feel small and scolded, but not today.

"That's not what I was trying to do," I reassure him, still trying to reach a hand out.

The darkness in his eyes morphs into weariness, and there's a small comforting smile on his lips. "Can we talk about it tomorrow?"

"Sure," the whispered word leaves my lips and I turn to look out the window, watching the passing scenery, feeling a pang of regret in my chest. *I should have just kept my mouth shut.*

The silence is broken only by the soft humming of the car engine and the sound of my heartbeat pounding in my ears.

He stays like that until we reach his apartment building. The silence is like a blank canvas and I'm waiting for him to fill it with color and purpose.

When we reach the penthouse, not even the fear of the elevator could fill the space. Every unspoken word feels like a weight pressing down on my chest, suffocating me slowly.

"Goodnight, Leora." Lucas breaks the silence, but nothing follows as he walks toward his room and I stand still in the hallway, like the previous evening.

The sound of his door closing makes me jump. It's as if the closing of the door was the punctuation mark on the end of an awkward, and uncomfortable conversation that never happened.

As I lay in bed, staring up at the ceiling, my mind races with thoughts of what I could have done differently. Maybe if I had just kept quiet, or maybe if I had apologized yesterday . . . But it's all too late now, and I can't shake the fear that this tension will linger for the rest of the year.

The night passes slowly, with the weight on my chest refusing to lift. I toss and turn, unable to find a comfortable position, until finally, the first rays of dawn start to filter through the window.

TWENTY

LEORA

For today's brunch, with the very not-charming and untrustworthy Michel, I dress in an adorable white Zimmerman embroidered sundress with puff sleeves and I pair it with light beige Saint Laurent sandals.

I look at myself in the mirror, taking a moment to admire my outfit. It looks sophisticated and elegant; my hair is up in a ponytail and my makeup is light. Thanks to my tan, a little blush and mascara goes a long way.

Will he like it? The thought crosses my mind but I try to push it aside. I take a deep breath, trying to remind myself that what matters is what I think and today, I think I look great.

Before leaving, I grab my favorite accessory—my bag. The closet is not short on bags either, and I choose a Saint Laurent Mini Cassandra bag that matches my shoes perfectly. I slip on a pair of sunglasses but before I make it out, I hear a soft knock on my door. Opening the door, I'm met by an effortlessly handsome man in his white linen shirt and beige chinos. Lucas completes the look with matching boat shoes and Ray-Bans tucked into the collar of his shirt, exuding a sense of refined style.

His gaze scans me slowly, and there's an approving look in his eyes.

However, the tone in his voice is curt. "Let's get this brunch over with."

"Somebody woke up on the wrong side of the bed," I mumble under my breath.

"Excuse me?" Lucas arches an eyebrow, catching my muttered remark.

I respond with a fake smile, feigning innocence. "Oh, nothing, husband."

Lucas quirks a corner of his mouth at my sarcastic tone but chooses not to engage. With a casual gesture, he leads the way toward the elevator.

While we wait for the elevator to arrive, the mounting silence becomes too much this time and I can't help but blurt something out, "So, is the rest of the year going to be this awkward?" Lucas looks at me, his expression shifting to one of confusion.

"I'm sorry?"

Realizing he didn't catch on, I press further, "I said, are you going to keep giving me the silent treatment and only talk to me when you have to?"

His response is swift, his tone sharp, "I'm not giving you the silent treatment."

"Yes, you are."

Lucas watches me, a hint of irritation crossing his features. "If you'd pay more attention, you'd realize that not everything is about you." The words hang in the air, a weight settling on my chest. I don't respond, but I look at him, silently questioning if he's right. Am I selfish?

The elevator doors open with a *ding*, saving us. We step inside, as always I take a deep breath to try to calm myself down, but it's pointless because of the fact that I might die from this elevator. I can't seem to continue the conversation which builds up my frustration even further. *Stupid elevator fear.*

I'm just grateful I'm not alone in the elevator. If it gets stuck, at least there's two of us—we could put our heads together to come up with a plan. Oh, who am I kidding, I'd be on the floor crying.

As we exit the elevator to the garage, a sleek black car pulls up in front of us, and the driver steps out to open the door for us.

"You're not driving?"

"No, I need a drink or two to get through this brunch."

We climb inside and settle into the leather seats. I try to sit as far away from him as possible, needing space, but he follows, choosing the seat in the middle and caging me between the door and himself.

"I really don't like you today," I whisper so the driver won't hear.

"Yeah?" he says, his arm wrapping around my waist as he tugs me closer to him, his lips brushing the shell of my ear. "I don't like you much today either." I feel a shiver run down my spine as his breath tickles my ear. I push him away, but he only chuckles in response.

The car ride is quiet, and I feel the tension between us growing with every passing minute. This time however, there's another type of tension mingling in the air as well.

I stare out the window, trying to distract myself from the uncomfortable situation. I've caught him glancing at me a few times, although I'm sure he has noticed my own glances as well. Until I impulsively blurt out, "We need a safeword."

What the hell am I saying?

Lucas turns to me with a raised eyebrow, looking intrigued by my sudden suggestion and amusement glimmers in his eyes before he adopts his usual stern gaze again.

"Continue."

"Let's say we're talking to someone and suddenly we don't know what to say, we use the safeword for the other to jump in and save the situation."

"Wouldn't it be obvious to know where to jump in?"

He has a point. If we're next to each other, then we'll probably know if the other is struggling.

I pause for a moment, thinking. "Okay, what about when you are talking to someone else and I need you? What then?"

"Okay, we can have a safeword if you need it. What do you want it to be?" he asks curiously.

Well, I hadn't thought that far ahead yet. I ponder for a moment, trying to come up with a suitable word. I want it to be something natural and discreet, like a fruit or something common.

After a brief pause, I smile as an idea comes to mind.

"How about 'pineapple?'" I casually suggest.

Lucas looks at me with furrowed eyebrows, an expression that I interpret as a silent "no."

"Okay, then what about 'ocean?'" I press on.

"Leora, we live on the French Riviera; the word *ocean* will pop up quite often." He states in a tone that makes me feel utterly ridiculous, but to my dismay, he has a point.

"Then you come up with one if you're so smart," I say a little defensively, crossing my arms over my chest.

"How about 'coconut'?"

I scrunch my nose, considering his suggestion.

"You like 'coconut' but dislike 'pineapple'?"

He stays silent for a few beats, lost in thought, and I watch him. When he's focused, he scrunches his forehead and a little wrinkle appears between his eyebrows. Before I can stop myself, my lips turn up. He's adorable.

A knowing smirk spreads across his lips. He watches me, clearly happy with what he came up with.

"How about 'amaretto' then?" he suggests.

"Amaretto it is," I agree, rolling my eyes.

TWENTY-ONE

LUCAS

"Amaretto."

We arrived at Michel's lavish estate merely twenty minutes ago, and Leora has already downed two Mimosas and used our safeword about five times. I try to hide my chuckle every time because seeing her in a panic is one of the cutest things I've seen. Even cuter than her scrunching up her nose when she disagrees with something I've said. It's a big problem because I'm still pissed off about our argument and I can't go around thinking she's cute. It doesn't make sense. I need to remember her being annoying, loud, and stubborn.

Emphasis on the loud and stubborn.

I didn't mean to be short with her yesterday, especially not after her attempt to extend an olive branch, but witnessing my uncle's declining state shifted something within me. All I wanted was to be alone, but then she spoke and her soft cautious voice made me feel guilty. It was too much.

Despite my annoyance, I can't help but notice how beautiful Leora looks today. Her hair is up, showcasing her delicate neck— its subtle curve is begging to be touched, and the dress she's wearing fits her perfectly. For a moment, I forget all about our exchanged words and find myself admiring her from afar.

When she catches me staring, I quickly avert my gaze. I can't let myself get distracted by her beauty. I tell myself that I need to keep my distance and avoid getting emotionally invested. The way her laughter weaves a melody, filling the air with warmth, is a detail I shouldn't be captivated by, yet inexplicably, I am.

This is only a business partnership. I need to stay focused on the task at hand and get through this day without any further arguments or distractions.

But deep down, I know it's easier said than done. Something about Leora's fiery spirit and unwavering determination intrigues me, and despite our differences, I can't deny the chemistry between us. God, all I wanted to do when I saw her this morning was shut her up using my mouth.

It's infuriating.

I've never seen eyes be so mesmerizing when they're irritated. It makes me want to push her buttons even more. But I can't do that. Being attracted to my wife is not what I need at this moment. When she opened the door in her gorgeous white dress, memories of the kiss we shared during our wedding flooded my mind. All I wanted to do was stay home, and I'm ashamed to admit it because it feels pathetic.

I'm pathetic.

We're only on day three of this marriage and I'm lusting after her like a high school boy with a crush.

How am I going to survive this?

I'm either going to have to hide every time we're alone together or get it out of my system. But that's the tricky part. She told me not to cheat, or to be discreet.

I think about it for a second, but it's not what I want or stand for.

One year. I can control myself and my urges for one year; it's a challenge, and I thrive on that.

One year without fucking anyone should be doable. That's what my hands are for.

Not when you're living with someone who looks like her.

As soon as we stepped into his garden, Leora's eyes grew incredibly large, looking as though she were in a trance. Her gaze swept over the meticulously-tended grounds, taking in the blooming flowers of all shapes and sizes. They painted the landscape with a kaleidoscope of colors. Michel's house is nestled in the enchanting Villefranche-sur-Mer, with the Mediterranean Sea stretched out before us in all its glory.

I watched her in awe, captivated by the way her eyes sparkled with childlike wonder, and how her lips parted slightly in amazement.

The thought of that makes me realize I want nothing more than to see her like that every day.

I catch her eye while we wait for the host. She mouths our safeword to me subtly, all while staying engaged in conversation with another one of our stakeholders, Gérard Moreau. He and my uncle have been working together for as long as I can remember, and they both have a warm and welcoming quality in their gazes that draws people in and makes them feel safe.

I'm a few meters away from her at the bar Michel has set up, grabbing an orange juice for myself and a third Mimosa for her. I changed my mind about the alcohol when we got here—I need to be as alert as possible. I still haven't spotted Michel and that makes me nervous.

I respond with a subtle nod and a smirk. With that, her smile fades slightly as she looks at me with a furrowed brow, silently pleading for my assistance. It's time to continue acting like I genuinely like my wife. A voice inside whispers *"It's not an act."*

"Ah, Lucas! I've been getting to know your lovely wife and she's just magnificent."

Ah, my lovely, *stubborn* wife. I wrap an arm around her and press her against my body and Leora smiles gratefully, playing her part by leaning into my embrace as I answer, "Am I not the luckiest man in the world?"

I see her eyes begin to roll at my comment before she snaps back to her part as the sweet wife.

"Tell me, son, why isn't your brother here?"

Leora's gaze shifts to me, her eyes searching mine, silently conveying why she asked for help.

"Unfortunately, my brother couldn't make it," I say smoothly. "He's caught up with work commitments. You know how it is."

Gérard seems satisfied with my explanation and moves on to another topic with the other guests around us. Leora visibly relaxes. She leans her head on my shoulder, and in the spur of the momentum I press a soft kiss to the top of her head.

The gesture shocks me as much as it does her, and I quickly pull away, my heart hammering in my chest. What am I doing?

"If it isn't the newlyweds, welcome, welcome!" Michel's voice bellows through the garden and we both turn around. I feel a sudden tug on my hand as Leora grabs it, a subtle attempt to keep up the charade. He slowly makes his way through the party and stops when he reaches us.

Leora and I share a quick glance, and I can see the slight unease in her eyes, pleading for me not to leave her side. I give her hand two quick squeezes, reassuring her that I will stick by her.

As Michel reaches us, he opens his arms and wraps them around Leora in a hug, momentarily breaking our connection.

I watch with a clenched jaw as he hugs her. An unsettling sensation claws at my chest, a desire to pull them apart bubbling within me. It's an unfamiliar feeling, threatening to engulf me entirely.

Leora seems uneasy in the embrace, and a surge of possessiveness urges me to draw her close. However, I resist, refusing to let the impulse create a scene.

Finally, Michel releases Leora from his grip, and she steps back, regaining her composure. I instinctively reach for her hand, seeking a physical connection to ground me. Our fingers intertwine, and in the warmth of her touch, I find my calm.

Michel pats me on my shoulder. "Congratulations."

"Thank you. We're very happy." My gaze is still fixed on Leora, who nods in agreement with a big smile plastered on her face.

"Of course you are, with a beauty like that on your arm how could you not?" Michel says with a hint of jealousy, his eyes narrowing on Leora. "Although, Lucas isn't the only one who should be happy, right, Leora?" he continues, his tone dripping with poison.

"I'm truly blessed. Lucas is an amazing husband," Leora says, patting my chest with each word.

"He is. He's also very rich and can offer women jobs they don't really have the experience for," he says with a sneer on his face. "Oh yes, Leora. I've heard about your previous job and the gossip circling around about you."

Leora's expression hardens, and I can feel my blood starting to boil. I quickly step in, placing a protective hand on her back.

"That's enough." I glare at Michael but he just smirks, clearly enjoying getting a rise out of me. It was probably his plan from the beginning to provoke me into starting a scene in front of everyone, as if to prove something.

"Oh, I'm just playing around. Right, Leora?"

Before I can say anything else, Leora speaks up, her voice steady and composed. "I married Lucas because I love him, not because of his wealth or the job opportunity." Her eyes flash with determination. "Unlike some people, I value genuine connection and mutual respect in a relationship."

Michel's smug expression falters, seemingly taken aback by Leora's response. He opens his mouth to retort, but Leora cuts him off with a polite yet firm nod. "If you'll excuse me, I need to find the ladies room." She smiles at me before she walks away toward the house.

I watch her leave and I'm left seething with anger. I clench my fists, resisting the overwhelming urge to punch Michael in the face.

But then he speaks, a self-satisfied expression on his face. "Women are so emotional, am I right?"

That's it. I can't hold it back any longer.

In a split second, I grab a fistful of Michel's shirt, yanking him towards me, my voice low and dangerous as I speak through gritted teeth, "Speak to my wife that way again, and you'll regret the day you ever crossed paths with me."

I can feel the tension in my muscles; everything in me is screaming to make him understand.

Nobody talks to her that way. She's wearing *my* ring. To him, she's my wife in all the ways that count, so for him to jab at her is the same as jabbing at me.

Michel's earlier arrogance fades, replaced by surprise and a hint of fear. "Is that a threat, boy?" he counters, trying to regain his composure. I keep a tight hold on him, sensing his subtle shifts beneath my hand.

I hold his gaze, unflinching. "No, it's a promise," I say firmly, my voice resonating with quiet intensity. "I won't tolerate disrespect toward my wife or anyone in my company. Consider this your only warning."

After a tense pause, I release my grip on Michel's shirt and take a step back, my chest heaving with anger. I look around, gauging how many eyes witnessed my confrontation. When I don't spot anyone, I shoot him a final warning glare before I walk toward the table that's been set up at the other end of the garden. My gaze shifts towards the mansion, and I catch a figure in one of the windows.

It's a woman wearing white, and my mind goes to Leora straightaway.

Did she witness what just happened?

Is she upset? I don't like the idea of someone upsetting her. I'm the only one who's allowed to challenge her—no one else.

I need to find her, talk to her, and make sure she's all right.

I reach the table and sit down, my mind racing with worry about Leora, but a screeching voice interrupts my thoughts.

Melina.

"Oh Lucas, there you are. I'm happy to see you."

Unlikely—she's almost as conniving as her father. If not for the vote, I would believe this whole charade was her idea.

"Are you here alone? I don't see your wife," she hisses like the snake she is.

"Don't worry, she's here," I reply calmly, trying to hide my irritation with her.

"Who would have thought that Lucas Ayoub would get married out of nowhere? I certainly didn't peg you as the type of man who settles." Melina sneers at me, her voice dripping with venom.

I raise an eyebrow at her. "Settled? I don't settle, Melina."

She scoffs, "Please, Lucas. You're not fooling anyone."

I lean toward her, my voice low as I say, "I'm sorry to disappoint you, Melina, but my marriage is none of your business."

She attempts to sit down in the empty seat next to me, but I stop her, giving her a tight-lipped smile. "You can't sit here."

"Oh, I didn't know we had designated seats."

"Every seat next to me is reserved for my wife, and my wife only."

Her face flushes with anger, but before she can respond a voice interrupts.

"Hello."

Leora's voice comes out soft and polite as she introduces herself. Melina's eyes scan her up and down, probably trying to find something to criticize, but she can't come up with a single thing.

"Oh, the wife," she says in a condescending tone. A knowing look graces Leora's face. She remembers her from the club.

Melina's gaze lingers on Leora's hand, and a mean smirk grows on her face. "Cute ring."

"Thank you" Leora says quirking a brow. "Now, would you please move? That's my seat."

Melina rolls her eyes. "Whatever." She huffs and moves to another seat, shooting daggers at us both with her eyes.

I can't help but feel a sense of satisfaction as Leora calmly takes the seat next to me, not even acknowledging Melina's comment

"Who was that?" she asks, pretending not to remember her.

"That was Melina, Michel's daughter," I reply, trying to keep my tone neutral.

Leora's eyebrows furrow in confusion. "Why was she so rude?"

I grimace. "Melina is also my ex-girlfriend."

"Your ex?" Leora's eyes widen in surprise, but she quickly composes herself. "I see."

I can tell she's trying to process the information, but before she can say anything else, the person on Leora's left introduces himself and they start to discuss our wedding. I can see Leora nodding and smiling politely, but her mind seems to be elsewhere. Her hands are clutching her bag in a death grip. Weird—*very weird.*

What's wrong? It's possible she's just nervous or anxious?

When their conversation dies down, she turns her gaze toward me, and a warm smile graces her lips. In that shared glance, her eyes soften, and I feel a sense of relief washing over me.

"Are you okay?" I ask to double check.

"Yes, I'm fine."

Fine. The word rings in my ears, and I know it's not always as straightforward as it seems when it comes to women. Fine could mean a multitude of things—hurt, upset, or disappointed.

Fine means "I'm *upset* with you."

She probably notices the look on my face because she tries to assure me, "I promise, I'm fine."

"Are you sure?"

She nods, her smile widening. "Do you think they'll serve pain au chocolat?"

When she mentions the sweet pastry, I can't help but smile. Pain au chocolat is my favorite—it's the only dessert I truly enjoy.

In front of us, the table is adorned with china plates and crystal glass, showcasing an ostentatious display of wealth. I'm not surprised; it's in typical Michel fashion to show off. There are croissants with various fillings, Quiche Lorraine that seems overly rich, and smoked salmon with cream cheese that looks too pretentious for my liking. Fresh fruits, assorted cheeses and charcuterie are carefully arranged on platters, adding to the opulence of the brunch spread. There's also a silver tray filled with macarons in all colors, dark coffee brewing on a silver coffee press, and a few bottles of expensive Champagne chilling in the ice buckets.

As the servers come by with the last of the spread, I catch the smell of freshly baked pain au chocolat, and my senses immediately perk up. I can't help myself. Even though I'd rather be indulging back at home, I reach for one and hand it to Leora before I grab one for myself.

As I chew, I notice how the others at the table are engrossed in the food and conversation. Michel, in particular, seems to revel in the attention he's getting and Melina sits next to her father, occasionally glaring at us.

I look at Leora, anxious to see if she's enjoying the food. To my relief, her smiles are even bigger now. With each bite she takes, she wiggles in her chair as if she's dancing with delight—I don't think she's noticing it herself.

She's adorable.

I quickly wipe away my smile, trying to suppress any feelings that may be growing.

Stop looking at her that way. You're doing this for Ammo Antoine.

"It's so delicious," Leora says between bites. When I look at her, I find her eyes on mine, glimmering in the light.

I swallow hard, the taste of the food suddenly less significant. *I'm screwed.*

After a few minutes of eating, I find Leora's eyes darting

around, and she's still got that big smile on her face. I can't help but chuckle. There's a mischievous glint in her eyes, and a feeling of suspicion creeps in. She's up to something, and I'm certain she's done more than just enjoy her meal.

"So, what did you do, Leora? It looks like you've got a secret up your sleeve," I whisper, playfully nudging her.

"What? Nothing?" She blinks innocently.

"Leora," I warn.

"Lucas," she echoes.

Our gazes lock, and we find ourselves in a tense staring contest. I'm instantly captivated by the intensity of her eyes. The way her green eyes seem to shimmer in the soft light, resembling precious stones of jade, leaving me mesmerized.

I lean in, my teasing grin widening. "Come on, Leora, you can't fool me. I know you've done something." I pause before I mock-gasp, pretending to be scandalized. "Don't tell me you threw a drink at somebody!"

Leora slaps my shoulder lightly, before she looks around, making sure no one else is within earshot. Then she leans in closer to me, her breath warm against my ear. "Okay, fine. But you have to promise not to be mad," she says, her eyes sparkling with mischief.

I raise an eyebrow, intrigued. "I promise, now spill."

Leora takes a deep breath, her excitement barely contained as she opens her bag, revealing its contents to me. My curiosity peaks as I lean in to get a closer look.

Inside the bag, I see an array of colorful forms.

They look like turtles.

They *are* turtles.

What the hell is that and where did she find them?

She picks one up and hands it to me under the table. My fingers brush against its smooth surface. It's like touching silk, but with a slight grip to it.

I take a better look at it and turn it in my hand.

It's fucking soap. More specifically, *turtle soap.*

"Leora, why am I holding a turtle made of soap?" I whisper.

Leora leans into me, laughing. "I took all the soap they had in the guest bathrooms. That'll teach Michel not to be rude to me."

"You did what?" I say, unable to contain my smile, my eyes crinkling at the corners. This is the silliest thing I've ever heard, but it's hilarious. My head falls back and I let out a laugh attracting everyone's attention. Leora giggles along with me. She looks triumphant, as if she's just pulled off the most brilliant prank. The thought of her sneaking around, collecting soap from the guest bathrooms, just to get back at Michel, makes me laugh even harder. The ridiculous thing is that he'll never notice it—not even his wife will.

As our laughter dies down, I wipe a tear from my eye and look at Leora, still grinning. "You're absolutely mad. That's some next-level revenge right there. Is that why you left?"

Leora smirks, clearly proud of her impromptu plan. "No, I walked away because I was about to say stuff that would cause a scene. But then I found these cute soaps and thought stealing them would teach him a lesson. And besides, who needs that much soap anyway?"

I laugh and shake my head. "Am I next on your revenge list?"

Leora draws closer, her voice softening with a twinge of threat. "At this particular moment you're on the 'okay' list, but watch your back, big guy."

The "threat" catches me off guard. Is she *flirting* with me? I quickly dismiss the idea—surely she's just excited by the moment. When it wears off, she's probably going back to her normal state. But despite my efforts to brush it off, a sense of disappointment lingers. To anyone observing us, we must look like a blissful newlywed couple, inseparable and madly in love. We're close together, our bodies angled toward each other. We exchange whispers and glances, and share secret smiles. But little do they know the real topic of our conversation.

She brushes her hand against mine as she takes the soap back, and with a playful smirk of my own, I murmur, "Well, in that case, I can't wait to see what other tricks you have up your sleeve."

Leora's smirk turns into a seductive smile, and I can't resist the urge to reach out and brush my thumb against her hand, feeling the softness of her skin.

Her breath hitches at my touch. Our faces are merely centimeters apart. "Oh, you have no idea," she whispers, her voice husky with promise. My gaze roams her beautiful face and lingers on her lips. They're calling to me. I want to feel them on mine, and right now is my shot. As long as we have an audience, I can do whatever I want—and I need to get this burning desire out of my system.

As I reach out to cup her cheek, I note the confusion and anticipation in her eyes. I lean in slowly, our lips almost touching, but I stop just shy of her lips. "Play along, Michel and Melina are watching," I lie, hoping she doesn't see through my ruse. In response, she whispers something I can't hear. Instead of answering, I savor the moment, the undeniable electricity sparking between us. Our lips graze for a brief moment before I give in and kiss her softly. It's frustrating to hold back, but I can't kiss her the way I want to right now.

Despite her anger toward me, her desire for me now is unmistakable. I notice the disappointment in her eyes as I pull back from our brief kiss and I know it's mirrored in mine.

"Are they still looking?" her voice is mellow. I don't bother looking to confirm, instead, I give her a subtle nod before our lips reconnect. I find myself gently licking the seam of her lips, exploring the taste of her, probing her to open up. When she does, our kiss deepens. I kiss her for another second or two, or three; I'm not sure because I lose track of time before I reluctantly move away. This is anything but professional. I'm at a brunch surrounded by stakeholders, and yet I don't care. I catch a glimpse of her, a little shocked, her eyes wide. She licks her bottom lip before straightening. In that moment, the desire to feel her bottom lip between mine again becomes an irresistible urge, something I ache to fulfill as soon as possible.

Our moment is interrupted by Michel's cheerful voice as it booms across the table and I internally curse. We sit back in our chairs, my arm finding its place along the back of hers, keeping her close to me.

He raises his glass and offers a toast. "To Lucas and Leora, the newlyweds, and the bright future that lies ahead of them!"

His eyes briefly meet mine, and I catch a hint of something menacing behind them, but he quickly masks it with a smile as he joins the rest of the table in raising their glasses in celebration.

SHE HASN'T LOOKED at me once since we sat down in the car and it's driving me insane. I want to grab her chin and make her look at me. I don't understand how she can just turn it off like that. I know I messed up yesterday and the day before—I should have been calmer. I know I have to apologize, but the words refuse to come out of my mouth.

However, I thought we shared something during brunch.

It went well. It went *more* than well, actually. The kiss and the laughter felt more than an act. I actually had fun for the first time ever at an event like that, and she is the reason for that.

But apparently, she's a great actress and, as provoked as I am, I can't fault her for that. That's why I married her. The whole reason she's in my car this second is because I need someone to play my wife.

As we pull into the driveway of our home, the tension in the car is suffocating. I let out a sigh of relief, grateful to finally be off the road. Leora unbuckles her seatbelt and opens the car door, ready to escape the confined space. She stops halfway out when she notices that I haven't moved a millimeter.

I can't stay here, not with this tension between us. I need some time alone to sort out my thoughts. If I stay, we're either going to argue or I'll break one of her rules by touching her in all the ways I'm craving. It's frustrating to be in this limbo, not knowing where we stand or how to move forward. But for now, I need space to breathe and clear my head.

Without a word, I take out the key and the magnetic fob for the elevator from my pocket and hand them over to her. Her eyes are fixed on me, watching my every movement and searching for a hint of emotion. I keep my face neutral, not wanting to give her any inkling that this marriage is already affecting me.

"Take these," I say, my voice low and steady. I check the time on my watch. It's only three o'clock, so I have plenty of time to clear my head before I come back.

Leora looks at me, her eyes wide with surprise and a hint of vulnerability. "You're not coming?"

I shake my head, trying to keep my emotions in check. "I'll be back this evening."

"Where are you going?"

"I have some work I need to get done."

She pauses for a moment, her eyes flickering between me and my hand. "Okay," she says softly, taking the keys.

I watch as she gets out of the car and walks toward the elevator.

I don't drive away yet. I'm watching her closely—how her body moves with every step she takes. When she reaches the elevator, she hesitates.

Come on, Leora, use the pad to make the elevator door open. She complies, but as the doors slide open, she hesitates, not stepping inside. Instead, she turns to the left and heads to the door that leads to the staircase and I watch her disappear.

What is she doing?

Why would she take the stairs when there's a perfectly fine elevator right in front of her? There's more than twenty flights to reach our apartment. Is she seriously climbing them all?

I sit there in the car for a few minutes, debating whether to follow her or leave. Then realization dawns on me. Every time she steps into an elevator, she hesitates. She almost shuts down during the ride and her breaths grow heavy. When we reach our floor, she rushes out of the enclosed space.

When I asked if she was alright yesterday, she told me she was fine. She almost had the same reaction when we rode in the elevator together the first time. Is it a coincidence? If she had any issues, she would have told me, right?

You fool. Why would she tell you when you're in the middle of an argument?

I shake my head. Maybe she just felt like taking the stairs.

With that, I drive away to the office.

TWENTY-TWO

LEORA

I'm a fool.

A complete moron.

I hate stairs, almost as much as I hate elevators at this point.

I mean, honestly, what is two to three minutes of anxiety, when I can keep dry and have a heartbeat under one hundred and sixty beats per minute? But now, as I trudge up the seemingly never-ending steps, I'm drenched. My dress is sticking to my skin, I have boob sweat, and I'm even sweating in places I shouldn't be. This is not the wet feeling I normally strive for.

My poor Saint Laurents are hanging from my hands as I walk up this hell of an incline, barefoot, contemplating why I hate myself so much. I thought it would give me some time to think about Lucas and why he's being so weird, considering he didn't speak to me the whole ride back home and then he just left me. I thought the brunch went well, except for his ex showing up.

When I came out, I immediately recognized her as the blonde who straddled him that night at the club. What I hadn't known, however, is that she's Lucas's ex. Much like last time, she seemed desperate to get his attention, and I didn't like it. I didn't like it at all.

It's not like I'm jealous, if they want to they can get back together when our agreement is over. But right this second, he's connected to me through this marriage. Which means he isn't hers to take just yet. It's a bit of a slap in the face, though, the amount of disrespect you have to harbor to flirt with a married man.

I try to shake off the feeling of irritation as I walk up the stairs. I don't need more problematic people to think about, so my mind floats back to Lucas and the brunch.

I thought we were on the same page and that we'd both moved on from the argument, but that's clearly not the case. The brunch was our first real test, other than the wedding, and I thought we worked great together.

Two puzzle pieces finally falling into place.

I'm still shocked over how he treated Michel after I walked away. I didn't hear what he said, but I watched from afar as the scene unfolded. Even though I don't know him that well, it felt like I was witnessing a completely different side of Lucas. It felt good to see him stand up for me that way; it made me feel safe and protected, and the moment we shared at the table felt genuine.

I clutch the bag of soaps closer to me, chuckling a little bit at the memory, before another hits me.

The kiss.

My fingers instinctively go to my lips, reminiscing about the electric, sweet sensation of his mouth on mine. To say I crave more is an understatement, but no matter what, Lucas must remain unaware of that desire. To be fair, he had mentioned that Michel and Melina were watching, suggesting that the kiss was prompted by their presence rather than his own wish.

When I finally reach the door to the twenty-third floor, I'm panting and gasping for air. I really need to start working out because this isn't even slightly healthy. I'm practically dying.

I use the fob to unlock the door but instead of opening, the keypad lights up with the word CODE.

What damn code is it talking about? I don't have a code, and

Lucas didn't mention anything about one. I take my phone out of my bag and send him a text.

ME

I need the code for the door

LUCAS

What door?

ME

The door to your apartment from the staircase

A minute or two passes and I still haven't received a code. A little flutter of panic runs through me and it escalates when I start to overthink. *I'm going to die here. I'll stay here forever.* Lucas will come home and he'll probably worry—*I hope*—then call the police and after further investigation, they're going to call me a missing person.

My phone buzzes in my hand. Okay, maybe I'll make it out of here after all.

LUCAS

*950915#

As I press the last button, the sound of the lock clicking echoes through the hallway. Relief floods through me as I push open the door and step inside, finally escaping the endless staircase. My whole body is aching after that grueling workout so I head straight to my bathroom, eager to wash away the sweat and exhaustion with a soothing shower.

After I finish washing up, my mind once again drifts to Lucas.

Is he alright? And why did he leave me here, alone, when we really need to talk?

I sit on the edge of the bed and pick up my phone, scrolling through social media. I come across a French gossip site and the first image I see is a picture of me and Lucas. It's one of the photos the paparazzi captured of us outside the hotel.

He's holding me close to his body, and I'm leaning against him, my hand on his chest. We're gazing into each other's eyes, smiling.

Wow.

We look like a real couple—anyone would believe it. I close down the website and just before I put my phone away, I notice an unread message from twenty minutes ago, just before my shower. It's a message from Lucas.

LUCAS

And it's our apartment.

The word *"our"* lingers in my mind as I stare at his message.

Our apartment. Not just his, but ours. It's a small thing, but it means a lot. The word *"our"* hasn't crossed my mind once, especially considering it won't be "ours" forever.

IT'S ALMOST ten o'clock in the evening and Lucas is still not home. I've had time to make food, eat it, organize my stuff, watch a movie, take a nap, and now I'm reading the book I brought with me on vacation. Or, at least I'm trying to read, but my mind keeps wandering to Lucas, wondering where he is. I keep telling myself to stop being so worried. He's a grown man who can take care of himself.

I try to focus on the words on the page, and I somewhat succeed when I finally reach the part where the couple give their relationship another go. I love a second-chance romance, and this one is keeping me on my toes. The spice in it is immaculate—their desire and hidden love for each other almost palpable.

The male main character's dirty talk is incredibly arousing to me. Whenever I read it, I can't help but wonder if there are actually men out there who desire their partner so passionately and who genuinely crave their satisfaction.

The sound of the elevator opening interrupts my reading. I

look up from my book and see Lucas walking in, appearing a bit disheveled and tired. His steps are a tad heavier than usual, and his eyes carry the weight of the day, a weariness that reflects in their subdued gaze. His tie hangs loosely around his neck, and his curly locks appear thoroughly tousled from his hand running through them several times.

My heart skips a beat at the sight of him, but I quickly compose myself and ask, "Where have you been?"

"Had some work to finish up. Lost track of time."

I want to believe him, but something feels off.

I close my book, set it aside, and sit up to make room for Lucas on the couch. It's a silent plea for him to sit next to me. I'm left feeling simultaneously grateful and disappointed as he takes a seat but says nothing. I look over at him and meet his gaze, his eyes are filled with an emotion I can't identify precisely. I open my mouth to speak, but before I can say anything, he beats me to it.

"I'm sorry for what I said yesterday, and the day before, and for not giving you a chance to explain. I overreacted, and I am sorry for any hurt or misunderstanding I may have caused. You didn't deserve that." His tone is gentle and apologetic, and there's now a softness to his eyes that conveys his regret. The weight of his words settles in the air and I can't help but feel a sense of relief washing over me. Are we finally going to move past this mess?

I nod, accepting his apology, and a small smile tugs at the corner of his lips.

"Thank you for apologizing; I was afraid we would tiptoe around each other for the rest of the year."

"I don't think I could handle that."

"Me neither," I admit, "and I'm sorry for raising my voice and for throwing that drink at your face. It wasn't okay, I shouldn't have acted that way."

"I understand why though, I was an ass."

"Well, yes, you were. And to be honest, I was quite upset that I didn't finish the drink. It was delicious."

"I'll get you another one if you promise to drink it this time." Lucas lets out a little chuckle, his dimple on full display.

He's so beautiful, it hurts not to raise my hand and caress his face the way I inexplicably crave to.

"Friends?" I say, extending my hand as a peacemaking gesture, hoping we can move past the tension and start over.

Lucas momentarily stares at my outstretched hand, then, his lips stretch into the most breathtaking smile, and a flurry of butterflies take flight in my stomach.

"Friends." He reaches out to shake my hand. An electric zap courses between us as soon as our hands touch, causing us to startle and pull our hands away.

He tilts his head, looking at me with curiosity and amusement. My eyes go to his smile, focusing on his soft lips. My mind drifts back to the kiss we shared and it's begging me to do it again.

As Lucas's gaze lingers on me, I can't resist the pull I sense toward him. With a surge of courage, I raise my hand and gently move the loose curls away from his face with my hand—something I've been wanting to do since the first time I laid eyes on him. His hair is so soft to the touch.

Lucas closes his eyes, savoring the sensation of my fingers in his hair. A low groan escapes his lips, and my body reacts at the sound. I feel a rush of desire between my legs, and I shift in my seat, trying to alleviate the sudden ache. It's been building up from reading my book, and having him sit next to me is only adding to my arousal.

When he opens his eyes, the look he gives me sends a shudder through me. It's a look filled with hunger and longing, and I know, without a doubt, that he feels the same attraction that I do.

For a few moments, we sit there in silence, lost in our own thoughts and desires. I want him, I *need him*. This lust between us has to go somewhere, it can't just keep building.

I'm torn between the desire to lean in and kiss him, and the fear of ruining everything this marriage pact is for.

So I make a choice, and snap out of the magical moment, pulling back as I let go of his hair, breaking the physical contact between us.

Lucas seems to sense my hesitation, and he gives me a reassuring smile.

"We should sleep. It's your first day at your new job tomorrow." His eyes glimmer, and I nod at him as we both stand up.

"Goodnight, Lucas," I say softly, my voice barely above a whisper, trying to ignore the butterflies still dancing wildly in my stomach.

"Goodnight, Leora," he replies, his voice husky.

Time seems to stand still for a moment as we gaze into each other's eyes, the air charged with unspoken emotions. He gives me a half-smile, his dimple, once again, visible. I turn around, my steps a bit unsteady, and begin walking toward my room.

As I'm about to take another step, his voice stops me in my tracks.

"Leora." I look over my shoulder.

"Remember when you told me that you came up to me to feel a bit more confident?"

I simply nod at him, holding my breath as I wait for what he has to say.

"A girl like you doesn't need a guy like me to be confident," he says softly, before he turns around and walks to his room.

That might be one of the sweetest things anyone has ever said to me.

Do I believe him?

No.

But I still appreciate it. Lucas seems to be much sweeter and more considerate than I originally thought. He's more than just a pretty face, and tonight I actually feel that we can make this work while still enjoying each other's company.

We might become friends after all.

TWENTY-THREE

LEORA

There's a knock on my bedroom door, and when I glance at the clock, it's two am. Despite the late hour, I open it, and there stands Lucas.

"It's the middle of the night, Lucas." He doesn't answer, only stares at me with an intense, dominant look on his face.

What does he want?

"Lucas, what do you—" My question morphs into a yelp as his arms sweep under my ass. He walks toward my bed, throws me down, and I land with a thud.

"Just say it, Leora. Say it and I'll give you everything." Lucas whispers as he slowly climbs over me, his eyes glowing with an animalistic intensity.

"S-Say what?" I breathe out, feeling his touch all over my body.

"Tell me I'm allowed to touch you in private," he says, his intensity almost too much to bear. My body responds to him, but I'm scared of what it might mean.

"What?" I whisper.

Lucas leans down and kisses me softly, his lips brushing against mine in a gentle caress. "I'll make you feel good, I promise."

His words soothe my soul, and I nod in agreement. "Touch me." I say, my voice shaky. "Please, touch me."

A mischievous smile spreads across his face, and he begins to explore my body with his hands, sending waves of pleasure coursing through me. He moves from my chest to my waist and down to the hem of my panties, tugging them down.

"Look at you, all needy. Do you want me that bad?" he teases.

"Lucas, please." I'm panting at this point, needing his hands on me.

"Please, what?"

"Just touch me, dammit." I've wanted him for so long. I need him to take this ache away.

He chuckles at my lack of patience as he bends down, hovering over my core.

"Do you want me to touch you here?" He uses his finger to touch my most sensitive spot, and I huff impatiently as his laugh grows huskier.

"My impatient girl."

He licks his lips and bends down, but stops a breath away from the place I need him most. "What's that?"

I hear my phone ringing, but I'm so into what's to come that I don't want to stop.

"What?" I breathe, my voice shaking with need.

"Your alarm—turn it off and I'll make you feel good." Lucas pulls away and looks at me with a quizzical expression.

My alarm?

What alarm?

I wake up with a start, my heart racing and my body covered in sweat. I take a deep breath, trying to calm down and clear my head.

It was a dream . . . and it felt so real.

I can still feel his touch on my skin, his breath on my neck, and his finger on my—

I shake my head, trying to rid myself of the memory, but it lingers.

Did I really just have a sex dream about Lucas?

I bury my face in my hands, trying to shake off the feeling. It was just a dream, nothing more. It's okay to have dreams like that; especially when you live with a man that looks like Lucas. I'm just feeling a little bit frustrated and lonely. But it doesn't mean anything.

I really need to get myself a toy or something, because if I have more of these dreams, I'll probably be the one pounding on his door in the middle of the night, begging him to take the edge off.

We can't have that.

I get up and stretch, feeling the stiffness in my muscles from the tension of the dream. I make my way to the bathroom and splash some water on my face, trying to shake off the last remnants of the dream before I take a cold shower.

When I emerge from my room dressed in black slacks, a blouse, and my new favorite black Manolo's, a pleasant scent of cinnamon and vanilla fills the air, making me feel at ease. As I walk toward the kitchen, I'm momentarily stunned by the sight of Lucas—shirtless, wearing only a pair of gray sweatpants, and with damp hair from his morning shower.

Did he take one because he usually showers in the morning? Or because he *needed* one in the same way I did?

My gaze shifts to his back again. I notice the way his muscles ripple as he moves around the kitchen, expertly flipping a slice of French toast in the pan. When he reaches up to grab a plate from the cabinet, his back muscles contract and flex, drawing my attention to the defined lines running down his spine. His shoulder blades protrude slightly, adding to the aesthetic appeal of his toned physique. He must work out a lot because there's muscle *on* the muscles. He leans over slightly for something on the counter and I can't help but sneak a peek at his ass, which looks firm and perfectly shaped in those gray sweatpants. The way he moves is almost hypnotic—I'm both drawn to him and a little lightheaded.

This show is exactly the opposite of what I needed this morning. I need him to dress in very oversized clothes, preferably all day, every day.

I clear my throat to announce my presence, and he turns around, a smirk forming on his lips as he takes in my outfit.

"Good morning," he says, his voice sweet. "Are you ready for your first day at work?" He's genuinely trying to act friendly, but I can't focus. It's taking a lot of energy not to blatantly stare at his tattooed chest. He has a full sleeve that continues on to his chest. Every single one of his tattoos is a work of art. There's a beautiful rosary that wraps around his arm, mirroring the one in his car. However, the one that grabs my attention the most is on his pectoral. Two doves are nestled closely together, with the number nineteen ninety-five elegantly written underneath.

A blush creeps up my neck, and I avert my gaze, trying to focus on something else. "Is that French toast I smell?" I ask, attempting to change the subject.

He nods, grabbing the plate he just brought down and expertly placing a stack of golden-brown slices on it. "Yes, I thought I'd surprise you with breakfast."

I can't help but smile at his thoughtfulness. "Thank you, Lucas. That's very sweet of you."

He hands me the plate and I take a seat at the kitchen island. I take a bite and, my God, it's heavenly. I close my eyes, savoring the aroma and the delicious taste of the French toast. Lucas places a cup of coffee in front of me on the island before he sits down across from me, his own cup of coffee in hand as he scrolls through his phone.

As I continue to eat, I find myself stealing glances at Lucas, and every time he catches me, my heart beats a little faster. He gives me a playful smirk, and I can feel the heat rising to my cheeks. We continue to exchange furtive glances until Lucas looks up from his phone and our eyes meet again. This time, we hold each other's gaze a little longer, and the tension between us grows. It's as if we are both searching for something in each other's eyes, something we both seem to be yearning for.

"Did you like it?" he asks me, and I look down at my plate. It's empty; there's not a single crumb left.

"Yes, it was delicious. Where did you learn to cook like this?"

"My aunt," he says and then adds, "Antoine's wife."

I perk up at that. I would love to meet Antoine's wife.

"She passed away a few years ago." A shadow darkens his expression as he shares the news of her passing. Immediately, I feel terrible. Why did I have to ask? He already told me he liked to cook before—I could have kept it at that instead of prying further.

"I'm sorry to hear that. May she rest in peace," I offer.

"Thank you," he replies.

I pick up the cup of coffee he made me, and as I smell it, I realize it's a cappuccino, my favorite. Bringing it to my lips, I take a sip, savoring the perfect balance of espresso and frothed milk before letting out a satisfied sigh.

"This tastes amazing, Lucas. Thank you."

He smiles, his eyes crinkling at the corners. "You're welcome."

As I take another sip, enjoying the warmth spreading through my body, I notice Lucas's gaze on me. "What?" I ask him.

He shakes his head. "Nothing. I'm going to get dressed, and then we'll leave for the new office."

"New?" I ask, curiously.

"They're doing some renovations to the old one, so we have to work at a temporary location for a while," he explains while getting up from his seat. "I'll be ready in five minutes." With that, he heads toward his room, leaving me to finish my coffee and gather my wits.

STEPPING OUT OF THE CAR, I look up at the towering building before us. Sleek and modern, it presents a stark contrast to the historic architecture of the city.

He grabs my hand and leads the way, his long strides easily

eating up the pavement. I try to keep up while taking in the sights and sounds of the bustling street.

We step into the lobby—it's grand and opulent, with chandeliers and marble floors. It's busy with people, but Lucas expertly navigates us through it. We walk past the elevator and I stop, pulling on his arm.

A puzzled expression crosses his face. "What's wrong?"

"Aren't we going up?"

"No, this way." Lucas leads me to a grand staircase at the end of the lobby. We begin our ascent, only climbing up two flights of stairs before arriving at our destination.

As Lucas pushes open the door, I step into a spacious, airy office with high ceilings and large windows that let in plenty of natural light. The walls are painted in a soft shade of beige, with a few colorful accents in the form of artwork and plants scattered throughout the space. The floor is made of polished concrete, adding to the modern feel of the office. All the employees are already at their desks, working away. They glance up as we enter, and I sense their curiosity and interest in me as they try to sneak glances.

Lucas turns to me with a dazzling smile. "Welcome to our new office space, wife." The last word reminds me of who I am to him in public, and I wrap the hand that isn't interlocked with his around his bicep.

"Listen up everyone. I'm very excited to introduce you to your new Marketing Manager, Leora Davis." He pauses to gauge everyone's reaction, before continuing. "I truly believe that she will do wonders with all of your expertise. Additionally, some of you might already be aware of this, but Leora isn't only your Marketing Manager, she's also my wife. So, take care of her." He ends with a wink.

I'm really enjoying seeing his different sides and learning about him. This side is confident and in control—it's clear that he's respected by his employees, but he's also more relaxed around them, which makes me feel more at ease.

I feel a wave of excitement and a hint of nervousness as all eyes turn to me. "I'm thrilled to be joining this talented team as your new Marketing Manager," I say, trying to project confidence. "I may be Lucas's wife but I can assure you that will not interfere with my ability to lead this team."

I see some surprised and curious expressions in the crowd, but also a few friendly smiles and nods of welcome.

"Also, know that everything you say to me will stay between us. I won't tell the big guy over here," I say in, what I think, is a playful tone while elbowing Lucas next to me. However, no one laughs or even dares to breathe.

Why am I like this?

I catch Lucas watching me with a confused look, the corner of his lips almost tugging up, before he continues, changing the focus. "Our first priority is to finish planning the hotel opening, and I'm confident that Leora's expertise will be invaluable in making it a success. So, let's get to work."

"Leora."

I recognize the voice and follow the sound to find one of the few people I've met before. A blonde bombshell runs toward me, her arms spread wide before they wrap around me.

Camille.

The hug is warm and familiar. "I'm so happy you're here!" she exclaims in her French accent before she pulls away and looks at my face with a big smile.

"What do you think of the new office? It's better without elevators, no? Lucas told me that you don't—"

The man in question clears his throat, interrupting her just as she's about to tell me something interesting, "How about we introduce her to Simon?"

My eyes narrow at Lucas, knowing he's trying to divert attention away from what Camille was about to say, but I want to know what he told her.

I look back at her, trying to give her the *"tell-me-later"* look, but she only purses her lips while directing a lingering gaze at Lucas.

"Okay, follow me," she huffs and turns her back leading us toward a sweet looking man wearing round glasses.

"Leora, this is Simon, our marketing coordinator. You two will probably be working close together."

I regard Simon with a warm smile and extend my hand to shake his. "Nice to meet you, Simon. I'm Leora."

Simon takes my hand in his. "Nice to meet you too, Leora."

"You two will be working closely together to make sure the opening event runs smoothly," Lucas explains, clapping Simon on the back before leading me to my own office. We reach a door to a cozy-looking office, complete with a large window that overlooks the ocean, and there's also two beautiful plants set in the corners.

"Here it is, your own little space."

My jaw drops as I take in the room in more detail. There's a brand new laptop on the desk and next to it, I notice a vase of tulips. My eyes widen in surprise and delight, and I can't help but let out a small gasp. *He remembered.*

Tulips have always been my favorite flowers, and it's such a thoughtful gesture for someone to have put them there for me. If I ask Lucas, he'll say it was Camille, but I know deep down that he did it. He's the only one I've told about the flowers. Warmth spreads through me as I approach the vase and bend down to inhale its sweet fragrance.

I turn toward Lucas, his eyes almost black as he studies me with an intense expression. I can't quite read his thoughts, but there's a slight flutter in my chest at the way he's looking at me. I straighten up and move my gaze to the walls. They're the same beige as the rest of the office, however, one of the walls is adorned with three, blue picture frames.

Once again, Lucas is the only one here who knows my favorite color is blue.

He must have done this, but when? We've been together the whole weekend.

Except for yesterday, when he came home looking completely drained.

I walk toward the wall and study the pictures—two of the images are of Sophie, Adeline and I. One features us wearing our PowerPuff girl pajamas, each of us dressed in our respective characters. I smile; we're supposed to be grown-ups, but for some unknown reason, that show holds a special place in our hearts.

I move my gaze to the other picture of us three. My eyes narrow slightly as I tilt my head, how did he get this picture? It's a picture we took at the club, right here in Nice.

The last picture is slightly bigger; it's of Lucas and I.

It's the picture I saw on the French gossip site, the one where we actually look like a happy couple.

"Sophie sent those to me. I felt your office needed some personalized touches," Lucas says, breaking me out of my thoughts.

I nod slowly, still trying to process everything.

"When did you do this?" I ask.

"They got it done yesterday."

Not they, you, I think to myself, but I say nothing. I allow him to deny credit for this wonderful gesture.

"Thank you," I say, grateful for the effort he put into making my office feel more personal.

"You're welcome," he responds with a gentle smile.

My phone buzzes. I take it out of my bag to find a few messages from an unknown number.

UNKNOWN NUMBER

Did you seriously get married?!!

Did you?

Please say it's just gossip.

It was a mistake. I told you I was sorry.

I had a feeling about who it was, but the last text confirms it. It's clearly John.

ME

Delete my number.

And yes, I'm married. Stop texting me before my husband gets upset.

I block his number again, praying to God that this time, he'll leave me alone.

TWENTY-FOUR

LUCAS

I leave Leora to get accustomed to her new office, and I can't help but think that I'll never tire of her smile. Her smile could light up the darkest of nights, and warm up the coldest of rooms. She probably doesn't even know the effect *she* has on people. Her ex must have screwed her up royally if she thought she needed *me* to feel better.

So, I decided to set a personal mission for myself: by the time our agreement ends, she will have learned to love herself as she truly deserves.

As for yesterday, once I left her at the apartment, my plan was to head to the office, get some work done, and indulge in a glass or two of my twenty-five-year-old whiskey. I needed to think and I needed to plan, but the only thing that ran through my mind while I was driving was how Leora had chosen to take the stairs. I started thinking about why. Every time we had been in an elevator together, she seemed out of it, never making eye contact with me and always fidgeting until we reached our floor. That's when it dawned on me that she must hate elevators and therefore, that's why I decided to move our offices. Our old one needed a renovation, so I used it as an excuse to call up an old colleague of mine who is now the owner of this building, and he made everything happen. The new office space is perfect. It doesn't have the same view as the one at the hotel, but it will help Leora feel more at ease for now.

Today is slightly better than yesterday, but it's still clear that she's afraid, even if she's too stubborn to admit it. While on the elevator, I tried to keep her occupied by asking her a bunch of questions about books. Her eyes lit up and she started babbling about something called tropes—apparently her favorite is something called, enemies to lovers. Sadly, it wasn't enough to keep her from being scared. Even though she was talking, she was still shaky, fidgety, and frantically looking around. We'll work on her fear and when she feels better, I'll take her back to the old office to help her work through it.

That is, if it happens within a year because after that, she'll go back home. For now, the more at ease she feels, the more she'll deliver on her work.

As I'm working, I hear a distinct knock at the door. It's not just any knock; it's a rhythmic melody of *"Shave and a Haircut"* with a deliberate pause at the end that waits for me to finish it. Ignoring the pause, I call out, "Come in, Liam."

He enters my office, with a laid back demeanor and a hint of exasperation in his voice, "You left me hanging."

Not in the mood for small talk, I ask, "What do you need, Liam?"

"*Ammo* wanted me to drop these papers off for you," he says, handing me a stack of papers concerning the office renovation.

"Great, thanks." I say dismissively, but then I remember that I need his updates. "While you're here, you can update me on the hotels. How's the one in Barcelona doing?"

He plops down in the chair in front of me. "It's going well. We had a huge bachelorette a few weeks ago while I was visiting and let me tell you, those girls were wild." A chuckle accompanies his comment, and irritation wells up within me at his foolish mindset.

"The one in Porto?"

"It's good. There was an incident but I had it under control."

I know exactly what incident he's talking about. "You mean the incident where you lost us the largest sum of revenue we could've made in years because you ruined a wedding?"

"I didn't ruin the wedding."

"You fucked the bride, Liam."

"Well, she obviously didn't want to marry the old man—I practically saved her." The nonchalance in his voice is infuriating and I try my best to not get angry.

"What a hero," I mumble before returning my focus, hoping this gets him to leave my office, but he isn't done.

"Why didn't you tell me you were getting married, or that you even met someone?" Liam asks, genuine hurt tinting his voice

"Why would I have done that?"

"Because I'm your brother."

"What a brother you've been," I mutter sarcastically, feeling a twinge of guilt for saying it out loud. Liam looks down at his hands for a moment before meeting my gaze. "Look, I know I haven't been the best brother, but that doesn't mean I don't care about you. I just wish you would've told me about this important thing happening in your life."

"I don't owe you anything," I retort, feeling defensive.

"What are you talking about?"

"Do you need anything else, Liam? I have a lot of work to do."

"I'm not leaving before you tell me why the hell you're so pissed," he almost growls.

Our eyes meet, and I can feel the fire behind mine.

I'm angry.

I'm so angry, but more than anything, I'm disappointed in him. After we lost our parents, he was—still is—my only safe place. He was only three when they died, leaving me with the responsibility of looking out for him. I've been there for every event in his life, good and bad. It's nothing to be proud of; that's what brothers are supposed to do for each other. I would never use it against him, but the time I needed him to stand by me most, he left me.

"Talk Lucas. Fucking talk. God forbid you ever did that! You haven't said a word to me for the past six months."

I stand up abruptly, my chair falling over behind me.

My voice rises with frustration, and the emotions I've been holding back finally come to the surface. "*I* haven't said a word to you?" I repeat, my finger pressing harder into my chest. "You left, Liam! As soon as we found out about Ammo's cancer, you left us. I'd hoped you would step up and share some of that responsibility with me. But instead, you chose to continue living the party life with a new woman on your arm every night." My voice cracks with hurt and a sliver of jealousy over the life he has.

Liam's expression turns defensive. "I do have responsibilities. I also have a job that I'm taking care of. Who do you think watches over all of our international hotels? It's *me*! Who sends you guys all the reports? Me!"

I take a deep breath, trying to calm down before responding. "I know you have a job, Liam. But you can't expect me to believe that you couldn't make time for your uncle, the man who raised you, when he needed you the most. You didn't even bother to call or text for months, and now you're acting like I owe you an explanation for my personal life."

Liam's expression softens slightly, but I can still see the sliver of defensiveness in his eyes.

"Lucas, I talk to him almost every day. How could you think I don't care about him?"

I didn't know that.

I didn't know that he took time out of his parties to speak with our uncle. Even so, this means Liam never went out of his way to reach out to me the way he did our uncle. He chose not to contact me, and that stings even more.

"I'm glad you do." I go to pick up my chair, but Liam is there before I can even attempt it.

"You don't get to be upset about something that doesn't

involve you." He takes a step closer to me, his hand reaching out as if to touch my arm. I move away from his touch, as if it's on fire.

"You didn't even bother to tell me that you were leaving, Liam. You left me when I needed you." My hands are shaking, and I hate that I'm getting emotional.

I hate it.

Liam takes a step back, seeming to understand my frustration.

"I wasn't supposed to leave for that long, Lucas. I needed some space and time. Everything was so overwhelming."

"Don't you think it was overwhelming for me, too?"

My shoulders slump. I'm tired. I'm tired of this constant battle—of the energy it takes to maintain it. It's as if the very essence of who I am is being molded by this unrelenting anger.

"I'm sorry I left and never reached out to you. It wasn't fair to leave you to handle everything by yourself." His eyes, filled with regret, study me like they always used to do when we were younger. Liam has always been good at reading people. He feels everything they're feeling and as good of a quality that is, I don't like it when he uses it on me.

"How long are you staying this time?"

Liam places his hand on my shoulder and smiles, "I have no return trip planned yet."

He's staying.

"What about the hotels?"

"I've got that covered. I'll get back to them eventually, don't worry."

"You're staying?"

"I'm staying."

A smile tugs at the corners of my lips, relieved that Liam is planning to stay for a while. Without thinking, I hug him, ready to let go of everything. Liam hesitates for a second before his arms wrap around me and the tension between us melt away, replaced by a sense of comfort in having him back.

He whispers the words, *"I've missed you, brother,"* I feel a lump form in my throat. The weight of his absence hits me like a ton of bricks, and I can't help but bury my face in his shoulder.

"I've missed you, too."

"Hello, husband." The sound of Leora's footsteps halts. "Oh, I'm sorry—Hi Liam."

"Hello, sister-in-law," he greets, stepping away from me and pulling Leora into a warm embrace. Leora's eyes dart toward me, a hint of surprise on her face. *"Are you okay?"* she mouths, and I nod, feeling relieved that things might finally be okay between us. When they break apart, her eyes go to his ring finger, and she shrieks, "My friend Sophie has a tattoo that looks almost identical to yours. What are the chances?" She laughs, adding, "Please don't tell me you also got it done at some dodgy back-alley parlor in Barcelona."

That's weird. If I remember correctly, he *did* in fact get his tattoo at a questionable studio in Barcelona. I remember scolding him for risking infection by not going to a professional, and he answered back with something about finding his destiny that night and nothing would get in his way of it, not even an infection. That's why he tattooed the word "Destiny" in Arabic on his finger. *Nasib.*

Liam laughs a bit nervously. "Oh, what a coincidence."

"Definitely is." Leora nods. "So, is everything good between you two?"

"Yes," both of us answer at the same time.

"Okay..." she draws out the word while casting a quick glance between Liam and me. "Great, then you'll have to join us for dinner someday soon."

"I would love to."

"Perfect, Lucas can cook."

Liam's smile spreads across his face as he looks at me. "I can't wait, but for now, I have to go. I have some work to do. See you."

With that, he walks out of my office and my focus goes back to the little firecracker standing in front of me. She's practically bouncing with excitement. I raise an eyebrow at her, silently questioning the dinner plans she's planning without my knowledge.

"So now you decide when we're having people over, Leora? I must say, you're getting comfortable with being my wife."

She laughs. "Well, I have a part to play, don't I?"

"Mhmm," I hum while I step closer to her.

She clears her throat, "I-I actually came here to talk to you about some ideas."

"Is that so?" I'm almost close enough to touch her now, but I stop myself. Instead, I sit down on my desk, facing her.

"Yes. I know we want the opening to be luxurious, but we also want it to be something the guests remember. How about live musicians? I've been looking around and I think we should consider this local jazz band. I found their Instagram and they're incredible. If you want, we can go to Promenade des Anglais and check them out."

"You want us to book musicians who play on the streets for our opening?"

Her face morphs into a look of offense. "Don't judge them before you give them a chance. They're super talented and they play different events as well."

I nod, understanding her point. "What other ideas do you have?"

"Okay, so during an event like this, we need a little bit of 'umph.'"

"Umph?" I ask, not understanding what she means.

"Yes, something extra, but let's make it something personal and beautiful. What do you think about the idea of having an exhibit with art that connects to the history of the hotels?"

She approaches me, her excitement is radiating off her like a warm glow. It's almost infectious, and if it continues, I will find myself willing to agree to anything she suggests.

"Continue," I say with an encouraging smile.

"Let's make it about Antoine, for the guests to follow his journey over the years. We can add parts of where he grew up in

Lebanon and how he became the hotel-mogul he is today. Let's honor him."

While Leora presents her idea, a surge of admiration and yearning fills me. Her creativity and enthusiasm are not only impressive but also deeply moving. The idea itself is brilliant, and I know that my uncle will appreciate it.

"I love it," I finally manage to say, my voice carrying a mix of genuine admiration and something more profound.

Her eyes beam at the approval, and I can see the spark of excitement reflected in them.

Rising from the desk, a renewed sense of purpose courses through me. The prospect of bringing Leora's vision to life resonates with me on a level that goes beyond the professional.

"How about we grab some lunch? I'd love to hear more of your ideas," I suggest, a smile playing on my lips, eager to continue this conversation.

TWENTY-FIVE

LUCAS

I take her to my favorite pizza place in Nice, *Les Amoureux*. I'm painfully aware that the restaurant name translates to *'lovers'*, but their pizza is the best Nice has to offer. In my opinion, anyway. What I had forgotten, however, is that some pizzas come in different shapes than the usual circle.

"It's a heart," Leora exclaims as she looks up at the young waiter with the biggest smile.

"A beautiful girl like you deserves all the hearts the world has to offer," he replies, with a wink that suggests there's more to the compliment than meets the eye.

As I glare at the waiter, he suddenly breaks into a mischievous smirk. "Wait a moment, you have something there," he says, reaching behind Leora's ear. With a flourish, he produces a single flower, his eyes lingering on her with a playful twinkle.

Leora gasps in delight, and the surrounding tables erupt in applause.

Is this man flirting with my wife right in front of me? I can't have other men flirting with her openly; what if someone sees or hears?

I take her hand in mine, subtly asserting my presence, "She truly deserves it all."

When the waiter leaves, Leora's eyes sparkle with amusement. "Someone's feeling a bit territorial today," she teases.

"Can you blame me? We have a facade to uphold," I reply before taking a bite of my pizza. I watch her under my lashes as she takes her first bite, waiting to see her reaction. It's anything other than disappointing. Her eyes grow as large as saucers, and she moans at the taste.

"This is the best pizza I've ever had," she hums between bites.

"It's the best pizza in Nice, but when I take you to Italy, you'll taste the finest pizza the world has to offer."

She pauses, the pizza slice dangling a few centimeters in front of her lips. "You want to take me to Italy?"

"Doesn't a married couple travel?"

"I guess." Her eyes sparkle with eagerness before she takes another bite from the pizza, a little smile hidden behind the slice.

I want to get to know her. I want to know what makes her hesitate, what makes her happy, and what her life is like. It's time for us to open up, to let each other in.

"So," Leora begins her tone more serious, "we should get to know each other better."

It's as if she's reading my mind, "I agree."

She puts down her food, and I sense a hint of vulnerability in her eyes. "Tell me about your family, Lucas."

Every time I think about my parents, about what I remember, something in me shatters over and over again. But for her, I'll try. "There's not much to say. My parents passed away when I was very young, and Antoine and his wife, Marie, became our guardians."

Leora's expression softens, and she reaches out to place her hand on mine. "I'm so sorry, Lucas. That must have been incredibly difficult."

I appreciate her empathy, but I'm more interested in her. "It was, but I had my brother with me. Now tell me about your family."

"Do you want to hear about my chosen family or biological

family?" That's not the answer I was expecting. Her expression reveals a haunted past, and for a moment, I find myself questioning why I feel this inexplicable urge to help her. I have no obligation to her. Yet, a strange desire to take away anything that has hurt her, lingers within me.

"If there's a difference," I say, my tone gentle, "I want to hear about both."

A deep breath escapes her before she speaks. "My mother died when I was born, and after that, my biological father left me to be raised by a foster family who cared more about getting their checks than taking care of us."

There's a tightening in my chest as she shares how her father left her as a child. The idea of someone abandoning Leora is incomprehensible to me.

"I'm okay, Lucas. He did me a favor," she assures me, obviously noticing the shift in me.

"As for my chosen family," she continues, a smile creeping up on her face. "Adeline and her family were our neighbors, and I spent quite a lot of time with them. They're practically my family, and later on, Sophie joined."

Her eyes meet mine, and I see a flicker of something deeper.

I don't want to push her further, but there's something in me that wants to reassure her. "If you ask me, your father made the biggest mistake a man can make by leaving you. You grew up to be a smart, resilient, and compassionate woman, and based on what I've seen between you and your friends, you're right, he did do you a favor," I tell her. "I truly believe that the people you surround yourself with say a lot about you, and your chosen family is a testament to the remarkable person you are, Leora."

"Thank you." There's a slight blush to her face as she speaks. "You're quite the remarkable person yourself, Lucas."

She takes a sip of her drink before I continue, "I don't want to pry, but why did you get fired?"

Leora coughs at the change of subject but recovers quickly, setting her glass down and taking a moment to compose herself.

"It's okay, Lucas. You're not prying," she cringes a little. "I got fired because . . . well, it's quite weird. I did something I don't remember doing."

"What do you mean?"

"According to my boss, I accidentally left out important papers during an event, and a client found them. They were not meant to read those papers, so it put the company in quite a bind. They fired me for my complacency around confidentiality."

I understand the implication. If one of my employees had lost papers, I would be very upset. What baffles me, however, is her apparent lack of recollection about it. I file it away to look into later.

"Why can't you remember it?" I ask.

Leora hesitates for a moment before replying, "I had a drink or two that night."

"A drink or two?" I repeat, questioning. Typically, a drink or two doesn't lead to a blackout.

"Yes. Only that, but I still don't remember losing those papers."

Fear rushes through my body as a thought hits me. "Did someone put something in your drink?" She immediately sees the wildness behind my eyes and shakes her head fast, "No, no. I didn't feel weird or anything like that." Leora's shoulders drop, her expression troubled. "I was tired and drained even before the event started, which must have been the reason for my forgetfulness."

I sense her frustration and confusion, and to try to offer her some comfort, I put my hand on top of hers. "Sometimes, we all have moments where our minds play tricks on us, especially when we're exhausted. It doesn't make you less capable or reliable." I reassure her, giving her hand a squeeze.

Leora's eyes briefly drop to our connecting hands, and when she looks back up, there's a subtle sheen to her eyes. "Thank you."

Then she takes a breath, and the sad, grateful look on her face morphs into a little smile. "Enough about that. Let's not dwell on my past mistakes." She leans in slightly, her voice mischievous as she continues, "Tell me about your last relationship."

I let out a laugh. "Oh, you want to talk about *my* past mistakes instead, huh?"

Leora chuckles, a melodious sound that adds warmth to the atmosphere. "We all have our share of mistakes, don't we? Besides, I'm curious."

I take a sip of my drink, considering her question. My last relationship had been with Milena. It was a whirlwind of passion and arguments, a rollercoaster ride that I'm glad to have left behind.

"My last relationship was intense to say the least. We had our moments, of course, but we also clashed a lot."

Leora raises an eyebrow, intrigued. "What caused the clashes?"

I sigh, memories of heated arguments and sleepless nights flashing through my mind. "Differences, I suppose. Different values, different priorities. We wanted different things from life, and it became clear that we couldn't give each other what we needed."

Leora nods in understanding. "Sometimes, love isn't enough to bridge those gaps."

"I wouldn't call what we had love," I reply. "I don't think I ever loved Milena. Our relationship was mostly physical, but that wasn't worth staying in the relationship."

Leora's eyes widen slightly, registering surprise at my admission. "Not love?" she echoes, shifting uncomfortably in her seat. "Have you ever been in love?"

Her question catches me off guard, and I take a moment to consider it.

"No, I haven't. Not yet," I admit, "Have you ever been in love, Leora?"

"Once, but it turned around and stabbed me in the back," she answers quickly.

There's pain in her words, and I tread carefully as I respond. "I'm sorry to hear that. Do you want to talk about it?"

She shakes her head. "Not now."

I know a little bit about her ex, the one who cheated on her. I did some research myself after our argument. The guy is a singer-songwriter according to his social media. He's got a group of adoring fans he likes to call his "angels." His songs are clichés, filled with cringe-worthy lyrics and his performances are often more about spectacle than substance.

He's a joke, a walking punchline.

As much as I dislike the guy, it seems more realistic that he lost Leora, rather than managing to make a woman like her fall in love with him. I can't wrap my head around it.

Leora deserves so much more. She deserves someone who appreciates her, someone who lives to keep the smiles on her face and someone who cherishes every aspect of who she is. Someone like . . . The thought crosses my mind, considering if I could be the one to take care of her. However, a lingering doubt persists. Deep down, I question if I would ever truly deserve her.

I glance at her, my eyes meeting hers. "I'm all ears if you ever want to talk or if you want me to send him a message."

She laughs at my comment, raising an eyebrow "As tempting as that sounds, I think I'll let the universe handle him. But thanks for offering, "

"Of course, anytime. And if you ever need a partner in crime for some good old-fashioned revenge plotting, you know where to find me."

Leora's laughter fills the room, and for a moment, the weight of her past heartbreak seems a little lighter. We may not be able to change the past, but we can certainly make the present a little brighter.

LATER, I decide to meet up with Estelle Lavigne. She took over her seat at the board after her husband passed away. But she's more than just a stakeholder; she's one of the few with a heart. Her late husband, my uncle's first investor and best friend, left a void that she's been trying to fill ever since. I grew up with both of them around, so getting her on my side in this upcoming vote, won't be hard.

"Lucas," she calls out from her office, looking up as I approach. She's in her early sixties, and her timeless elegance radiates from every carefully chosen detail of her appearance. Her silver hair, impeccably styled, frames a face that has weathered the years with grace and wisdom.

"Estelle," I greet her with a nod as I step inside, before her arms envelop me.

She gestures for me to take a seat. "It's been a while. How have you been, dear?"

"I've been managing," I reply, settling into the chair. "Especially with everything that's going on."

She nods in understanding, her eyes reflecting a genuine concern. "You know your uncle is very proud of the way you've handled things. He believes in you."

"I appreciate that, Estelle. It means a lot," I say, genuinely touched by her words. "But I need your help. Michel is stirring up trouble, and I can't afford to lose this vote."

Her expression turns serious, and she leans in slightly. "I'll do whatever I can, Lucas. I might be able to talk with Duval, to see where his mind is at. But you should reach out to Grimaldi; I think he's the one that will be manipulated by Michel the most."

She's right—Marc Duval and Louis Grimaldi are the closest to Michel, their loyalty making them potential targets for his manipulations. Which is why I have to get to them first.

She then shifts the conversation back to personal matters, "How's Leora handling everything? Being the wife of a man in such a challenging position can't be easy."

I sigh, "She's been great, always supporting me. I can't ask for a better partner."

Estelle gives me a warm smile. "Marriage is a partnership, Lucas. You need to take care of each other, especially during challenging times." She pats my hand reassuringly. "I'm sorry I missed the reception, but your uncle showed me photos. She's a beauty."

She's the most beautiful woman I've laid my eyes on. A small, unconscious smile tugs at my lips. Little do I realize, Estelle catches this moment of unguarded happiness.

"I'm happy for you," Estelle says. "Your parents would be proud."

Her words hit a chord, and I pause. Would they be proud if they knew the truth?

"Thank you, Estelle."

TWENTY-SIX

LEORA

Time moves slowly when I'm with him. I can't quite explain how or why, but I'm enjoying it. As the first month passed, I would say we've become good friends, and I truly appreciate him —in all ways. I especially appreciate his dedication to keeping his body in shape. I have to remind myself that we're just friends, however, sometimes those platonic feelings for him tip towards lust. I can't help it; he's incredibly attractive, and his body is on another level of hot.

But it seems that my body doesn't understand what the meaning of "friends" is because when I see his arms, my brain starts envisioning him holding me, and I grow flustered. When I see his back, my brain thinks about the way my nails could run down it while he's on top of me.

His hands make me think dirty thoughts, and it always ends up with me running to my bedside table to put my artillery to use. My body and brain have needs, and I'm only here to try to please them.

It's only lust, so I have moments of weakness when I entertain the idea that we should just go for it, enjoy the time we have together, and reap the benefits. I have a feeling he thinks about me in those terms as well. I've caught him looking at my legs when

I'm wearing my sleep shorts, or how his eyes will linger on my lips occasionally. I even saw him rearranging his erection one day when I was doing yoga in the living room.

Did I wear my shorts that accentuated the size of my ass on purpose?

Yes, I did.

Sue me, I'm only human.

I intentionally picked a time when I knew he would be home so that he could catch a glimpse of my ass in the air doing downward facing dog. My entire strategy revolved around making him notice me and, for once, lose his composure. I envisioned how he would grab me with those large hands before touching me in ways that would have left me screaming his name.

I think we're just two horny people that need to get it over and done with. We'll do the deed once or twice, and then we can focus on what's important, which is deceiving people until after the hotel opening we've been working on. But I don't think he will go for it. He's very stubborn, has the self-control of a monk, and often mentions how this business agreement has turned out much better than he expected because we have become such good *friends*.

Somedays I hate that word, but that's the situation I'm in, and I'm happy it's with a man like Lucas.

He's considerate. He wakes up early every morning to work out and prepares breakfast for both of us. If he has to leave for work earlier than usual, he ensures that I'm informed. Whether it's by leaving notes in the kitchen or telling me directly, he never leaves without making sure I'm aware.

He always asks me about my day, wanting to hear about it instead of only talking about himself, which is new to me. He seems genuinely interested in my life. Not to mention, he takes me out on dates. I know it's to keep up appearances and meet new people, but I like it. It feels good when he puts his arm around me or holds my hand while we're in deep conversation. It might seem crazy, but in those moments, it doesn't feel like we're faking it. It feels real.

Lucas has slowly opened up to me, and I feel privileged to be let into his world. I've learned that he's a dog person and that he grew up with a Shibu Inu named Asal, which he told me means "honey" in Arabic. He even showed me a picture of them together. It was adorable. I might have made him send it to me, to make it the wallpaper of my phone.

He also loves to spend time with his charity, to be with the kids who've lost their parents, just like him. My heart swelled when he told me about them and he even promised to take me to see them soon. I really don't know how my uterus will handle that, but we'll tackle that problem when we get there.

This morning, we slept a little longer because Lucas gave everyone the day off due to some plumbing issues in the office building. Despite that, he still wakes up earlier than me, as always, to make us breakfast. The smell of crêpes fills the air as I walk into the kitchen. Crêpes-day is my favorite; some days he makes the most delicious scrambled eggs, other days he makes me a smoothie, because, according to him, we also have to be "healthy." And apparently, to be healthy, we can't eat French toast and crêpes every day, which I disagree with, but I lost the battle the last time we discussed it, so I won't bring it up for a while.

I catch sight of him standing by the stove, his back on full display. Oh, how I love it when he cooks shirtless. I halt in my steps, gazing at him for a few moments, admiring the sculpted contours of his physique. I don't think I'll ever get tired of it; he's a masterpiece.

He turns to face me, his lips curling into a charming smile that shows off the dimples I've grown accustomed to as he greets me. "Good morning."

I settle onto a bar stool at the kitchen island and begin slicing up some fresh fruit while savoring the aroma of the steaming cappuccino in the cup he places before me.

As we sit down to enjoy our breakfast together—another

sweet moment I've come to love—his phone rings, and he excuses himself from the table after seeing the caller's ID.

"Don't wait for me, eat your breakfast." He points to the food with a nod before walking away to take the call, leaving me alone to do as I was told. I've noticed that he's quite adamant about me eating. Whenever I happen to skip a meal, or forget to drink water, he's quick to notice and immediately springs into action. He'll give me a gentle scolding and insist on buying me something to eat or drink to make up for it. It's as if he won't rest until he knows I'm taking proper care of myself.

I barely notice when he returns and says my name, startling me out of my reverie. As I turn to face him, my eyes are immediately drawn to his chiseled chest and toned biceps. His arms are crossed, making his muscles bulge even more.

My cheeks flush as I try to maintain eye contact, but it's impossible to resist the magnetism of him. He stands there, leaning against the wall, all confident and alluring, and I can't help but feel captivated by his presence as he fixes his gaze on me.

It's not fair. I've been fighting my attraction toward him for a month, and if I hadn't bought that little vibrator, I would have crumbled and embarrassed myself many days ago by either jumping him or begging him to jump me.

His gaze shifts to my lips, and a smile spreads across his face. As he takes a few steps towards me, I have to tilt my head back to maintain eye contact with him. Without a word, he raises his hand to my chin, his thumb gently brushing against the corner of my lips, his eyes locked on mine the entire time. "You had some sugar there."

His thumb brushes against my lips again, this time lingering over the fullest part before bringing his thumb to his own lips and licking off the sugar. I follow his movement, and my cheeks flush with heat as I get the overwhelming urge to lick the sugar off his thumb myself.

But just as quickly as the moment occurs, he casually sits back down on the stool next to mine and begins eating his breakfast as if nothing happened. I can't help but feel confused and flustered by the mixed signals he's sending me.

Is this what friends do in Europe? I've never experienced this level of intimacy with a friend before. Normally, people would *tell* me I had something on my face and then allow me to remove it. They don't clean it off themselves.

What is he playing at?

After breakfast, I make myself comfortable in the living room, continuing the show we started yesterday. Sitting with Lucas and watching TV shows together has become my favorite part of the day. Just having someone to share time with is comforting since I don't have my girls here anymore and I've yet to make friends in Nice. The only one I have is him, at least for a few more months.

"Are you watching without me?" Lucas makes a shocking gasp and puts his hand over his open mouth as he walks toward me. He's now dressed in a pair of jeans and a t-shirt.

Bummer.

"Oh, sorry. I just turned it on. You haven't missed much." I lie —I've watched an entire episode.

A pillow smacks me in the face as if he read my thoughts, and laughter springs out of him. "I've heard the sound of the TV for at least thirty minutes, you liar."

I pick up the same green pillow and throw it back at him, but he catches it in his hands.

"Well, why didn't you join me then?" I tease while looking at him through my lashes. He laughs as he lifts my extended legs so he can sit down and then puts them over his lap.

"Thomas called me again. I have some news."

That piques my interest. Thomas is his best friend who lives in Paris. "He's a little upset that he wasn't my best man at the wedding—not that I had one—but his wife has invited us to their home in Paris this weekend. I guess it's their way of congratulating us. Amélie is great, you'll love her. She's sweet, just like you."

"I'm sorry, what?" I don't think I heard him correctly.

"We leave this Friday."

A beat passes, then I pull my legs away from him and sit up. "Will we stay with them?"

"Yes."

This Friday, to Paris? Also known as the city of love? And then what? We'll parade around as husband and wife, trying to convince his dear friends that we're madly in love.

Oh, and let's not forget that *tomorrow* is Friday.

"We can't do that. Lucas, tomorrow is Friday! That's not a lot of time for me to prepare. You've got to stop surprising me with last minute events." I shake my head. This is the third time—first when we got married, then the brunch, and now this.

"Yes we can, and we will."

I shake my head again. "No, we can't. It's one thing to pretend in front of colleagues and stakeholders for a few hours here and there. But do you really think you could pretend to be my husband for a whole weekend?"

"Yes." His answer is short and determined.

I laugh. "You have the emotional capacity of a battery that is about to run out. There's no way you could pretend in front of them for that long. We have to look natural, and as good as I am, I don't think I could do it. They're going to find out about us, are you ready for that?"

"Like a battery that's about to run out, you say?" He smirks and turns to me.

"Yes, you can fake it for a dinner or two, maybe, but never a full-on weekend."

He looks to the side and chuckles, displaying the dimple I want to kiss. Oh, and that sound makes my whole body tingle.

"I mean we both know it. There's no Oscar on the horizon for you," I say, a giggle escaping my lips.

"What do you mean by that?"

"I just mean that we've been doing a good job so far, but we've been playing it safe. A true newlywed couple would act a little bit more obsessed with each other."

"Obsessed?"

"Yes, we're supposed to be in our honeymoon-phase. People expect us to be all over each other, I guess. But obviously, we're not going to act like that, which is why we shouldn't go to Paris. They'll see right through us."

"Oh, so you're saying I'm not affectionate enough?" At that, he moves closer to me, a lazy smile tugging at his lips as he cups my cheek. Heat rises to my face as I struggle to find the right words.

"What are you doing?" I finally get out, trying to cover up my sudden shock at his closeness. He lets out a husky chuckle and leans in closer, his breath warm against my skin, his woodsy smell makes me think all kinds of thoughts—most of them dirty.

"What do you mean?" he whispers, and it sets my nerves on edge. I try to compose myself, but his touch and proximity make it nearly impossible.

"You're getting awfully close."

"What's the matter, Leora? I just want to get a better look at you." His murmur is low and seductive. I can feel my heart hammer as I struggle to keep my composure.

"Well, you can look from over there," I say, pointing my finger behind him to the other end of the room.

"You're very funny. I never realized it before," he says, his thumb gently stroking my cheek. "I like it."

My stomach flutters at his words, his touch sending electricity through my body. I struggle to form a coherent response, my words catching in my throat. "I-I'm . . ."

"Do you want to know how funny I actually find you?" he teases, his smile morphing into a seductive smirk and his eyes taking on a darker intensity.

Yes, please tell me.

My mind races with anticipation as I nod, unable to resist the allure of his charming gaze. Before I can even process what's happening, he's leaning in so his lips are tantalizingly close to mine, paralyzing me.

"I think"—he slowly moves to my ear—"you're so funny that I want to turn that laughter of yours into screams as I bend you over my knees," he whispers, sending shivers down my spine. My mind goes blank—the intensity of his words leaving me breathless and my body aching with desire. Would he really do that? Is spanking something he's into? I've never done anything like that. My one and only partner liked it simple—at least with me. However, the mere thought of Lucas touching me, let alone spanking me, ignites a fire deep within me, and I feel the heat pooling between my legs.

"Wh-what?" I manage to stammer, feeling both aroused and intimidated by his boldness.

He grins in victory, as if he knows precisely what effect he's having on me. Before I can say anything else, he stands up and starts walking away. I catch him looking back at me with those infuriatingly charming eyes as he says, "Don't underestimate me, sweetheart. Go pack your bag."

I roll my eyes at him but as I sit here, alone and turned on, I know two things for sure: one, I'm definitely going to be in trouble in Paris, and two, I need to get back at him.

TWENTY-SEVEN

LUCAS

Thomas picked us up from the airport with a loud, *"Welcome to Paris, lovebirds."* He was all smiles as he gave us hugs.

That smile is still plastered on his face as we all sit together in their living room, with him and Amélie on one sofa, and Leora and I on the other.

"I can't believe Lucas has a wife. Never in a million years did I think he would settle down. Right, my love? Didn't I tell you that Lucas always seems too focused on work and was no fun?" Thomas turns toward Amélie and points between Leora and I.

"Oh stop it, Thomas, you've been in shock for the past month. Can't you see that he finally found the right woman?" The last part is said with a soft smile in Leora's direction.

Amélie and Thomas have been married for five years, but the three of us have been friends since university. That's where we met; we bonded over our dislike for our Strategic Management professor, whose lectures could put anyone to sleep faster than a lullaby, but we all managed to get through the class together.

"So, tell us. How did he propose?" She aims her question at Leora.

"Oh yes! It's a wonderful story." Leora looks at me with a

smirk that promises mischief. Why she does that, I don't know, because we already have a story where I proposed under the starlit sky—manly and romantic.

"He came over to my place just three months after we started talking. We were already head over heels for each other, but can you blame me?" she says, taking hold of my chin affectionately, "Just look at him. That evening, he decided to take me to a stunning rooftop terrace so we could look at the moon together."

"Oh, good job, brother," Thomas says, giving me a thumbs up.

"Yes, it was truly beautiful, but it gets better."

I glance at her, silently pleading with her to stick to the script. But she just smirks and continues, "As I get up to the terrace, I'm met by a live band that plays an acoustic version of '*Marry You*' by Bruno Mars, and Lucas, who's standing next to them, is wearing a white suit."

Thomas shifts his gaze to me, and the look on his face is making me want to scream. He's looking at me as if he doesn't recognize me. I've stated once before that I would never be caught dead in a white suit. I only wear them in black, gray, or dark blue.

Just when I think the situation can't get any worse, Leora starts talking again, and I can feel every nerve in my body telling me to make her stop.

Leora looks at me with a sly smile before turning back to Amélie, who's leaning forward in her seat with anticipation. "So, Lucas walks towards me slowly, and hands me a large box with a blue bow on top."

Amélie's eyes widen as she asks, "What was inside the box?"

Leora's grin grows wider as she continues, "Inside the box was a teddy bear, dressed in a matching white suit, holding another small box. Inside that box was a beautiful ring, and when I looked up, Lucas was down on one knee, a tear running down his cheek, holding a love letter that he read to me. It said—"

"It said, 'Will you marry me? Yes or no?'" I interject, hoping to put an end to her ridiculous story. "She said yes, and that's the end of it."

Thomas burst out laughing and I can feel my face turning bright red.

"A teddy bear in a matching suit," he echoes as he wipes the tears from his eyes. "Who are you, and what have you done with my friend?"

"I think it's sweet!" Amélie says, slapping Thomas's shoulder.

"Can I see your ring, Leora?"

"Of course." Leora stretches her hand proudly toward Amélie and I curse the day I let her keep that joke of a ring.

"It's beautiful."

I can't help but jump in. "The real one is still being resized. She chose this in the meantime."

Amélie smirks at me before taking a sip of her wine.

Leora and I exchange a glance, both of us aware of the many battles we've had about the ring, so I decide to get back at her for that horrible proposal story and the ring fiasco.

"Amélie, for dinner tonight, would it be possible to change the reservation to Restaurant Le Benkay? I would love for Leora to try it, it's one of her favorite cuisines."

Leora looks at me with a curious gaze. She's going to kill me and I can't wait.

"Of course, I'm friends with the chef's wife."

"Oh, what kind of restaurant is it?" Leora asks Amélie, sounding a bit hesitant.

"It's one of the best sushi restaurants in Paris, you'll love it. It's also very close to La tour Eiffel. Lucas told me you've never been to Paris, so of course I'm taking you to see the Eiffel Tower all lit up," Amélie replies with enthusiasm.

I can see the surprise and confusion on Leora's face. She hates sushi, and I know it.

Leora turns to me with a smile. "How lovely of you to think of me," she says, but I know what that smile conveys. She's planning my funeral as we speak.

"You have to try this one, too, Leora." This is the fourth sushi piece I've watched Leora struggle to swallow. Amélie seems insistent on making her try every single type of sushi on the menu. The look on her face is one of pure disgust, which she is trying to hide behind a smile. I'll give her credit, she's doing a decent job at it.

"Thank you," she says, attempting to eat another piece. I'm starting to feel a little bad. She really hates it, and from the look of it, she might puke soon. Her face has adopted a green sheen, but I don't want her to leave the restaurant without having a proper dinner.

Spotting a nearby waiter, I wave him over. "Bonsoir, can I order the Black Angus beef filet, please?"

Leora turns to me, a pleading look in her eyes.

"How would you like it?" the waiter asks.

My eyes go to her in question as I silently try to communicate that the meal is for her. She seems to understand because she mouths, "*Medium.*"

"Medium, please."

He walks away, and Leora lets out a sigh of relief. She leans in to me and whispers, so only I can hear, "Thank you so much. I really couldn't take another piece of sushi."

I smile at her. "No problem. I just want you to enjoy your meal."

"Well, it's your fault I'm in this situation in the first place. I haven't forgiven you yet."

I put my hand on her cheek and lean in a little closer. "Sorry about that, but it's what you get for such a ridiculous proposal story."

"Do you guys need a room?"

I straighten up and see Thomas grinning mischievously.

Amélie rolls her eyes. "Behave Thomas, let the newlyweds be."

The waiter returns with Leora's meal—cooked to perfection

—and places it in front of me, but I move it so it's in front of her. Amélie casts me a glance, because I had previously said that sushi was Leora's favorite food.

"I really want her to try this, it's my favorite," I say.

Amélie's face lights up at that. "Oh, that's so sweet."

Leora takes a bite of the meat and her face lights up with delight as she does that little happy dance of hers.

Adorable, as always. I'm never going to get tired of seeing that.

We continue our dinner, chatting and laughing together, and as we finish up, I suggest we walk to the Eiffel Tower, to help digest our dinner.

We stroll through the streets, taking in the city lights and enjoying the cool evening breeze. The Seine River flows beside us, its gentle ripples reflecting the city lights like a liquid mirror. The iconic Eiffel Tower looms ahead, its silhouette outlined against the Parisian night sky. It feels like we have the whole city to ourselves, like nothing else exists beyond the four of us.

The warmth of Leora's hand in mine, combined with the soft chatter and laughter from Thomas and Amélie next to us, creates a sense of contentment and happiness within me.

I glance over at Leora, and she catches my gaze, a small smile playing on her lips.

"What?" I ask

"I can't believe I'm on my way to see the Eiffel Tower."

I use my other hand to point up. "If you look up, you can see it." Leora tilts her head back, her eyes tracing the iconic structure as she marvels at its sheer size and beauty.

We reach the Eiffel Tower, and it's beautiful as always; its metal structure glittering in the dark night sky.

"Wow."

"It's beautiful, right?" Amélie asks and all Leora is able to do is nod.

"Come on, let's take the elevator to the top. The line is almost empty," Thomas suggests. Leora's head immediately snaps to him.

She still hasn't told me about her fear of elevators, but I'm certain of it now.

"Oh no, we don't have to go up. You guys have probably already been up there hundreds of times."

"Of course, we must. It's your first time here. Don't worry about us," Thomas insists.

I immediately notice the defeat and stiffness in her shoulders, and I try to come up with a way to get her out of this without putting her on the spot.

"Guys, let's skip the elevator ride today. I need to get back home to finish some work. I'll take her to see it another day, I promise."

They all stop, and Amélie looks at me, a bit disappointed.

"Are you sure?" she asks, giving Leora a glance.

I nod, giving Leora's hand a gentle squeeze.

"Yeah, let's save it for another time." Leora gives me a grateful smile, and I know I made the right decision.

"Okay then, but at least let me get a cute photo of you two in front of it." Amélie crouches down, lowering the phone, so she'll get as much of the tower as she can. I stand with my arm around Leora.

"Can you look any stiffer?" Thomas calls out.

Leora leans her head against me in an attempt to look more relaxed, and Amélie immediately snaps a few pictures.

"Do something else. You look awkward," Thomas chimes in again.

"Stop with your commentary, Thomas."

"He's right though," Amelié says. "Why don't you turn toward each other and kiss for the camera? That would be really cute to capture."

I clear my throat and look at Amélie. "Uh, I don't think that's necessary."

"Come on, bro, kiss your wife," Thomas says with a chuckle.

Leora and I exchange a quick glance.

"Kiss your wife! Kiss your wife! Kiss your wife!" He continues cheering.

We turn to face each other, and I swipe away some hair from her face.

My hand goes to her waist, and the other one cups her cheek before I lean down slowly, pressing my lips to hers, wanting to savor her. Leora's soft lips are inviting, and she responds to my kiss almost immediately.

With that, all thoughts of going "slow" are discarded. My other hand finds her waist, and I grip her firmly, pulling her closer. She wraps both arms around my neck to steady herself. The rapid beat of her heart against my chest becomes evident as we start to explore each other's mouths. With each movement, the intensity between us grows, sending electric currents through my body. Her fingers run through my hair, drawing me nearer as she deepens the kiss, our tongues dancing together.

I never want this moment to end, and I can't get enough of her.

Soft moans pass through her lips into mine, and I feel another surge of desire at those sounds. It's like a signal that ignites something inside of me, making me want her more.

A loud cough from Thomas breaks the spell, and we pull away, both of us blushing. I was so lost in her that I forgot they were watching us.

Amélie is giggling, and Thomas is grinning broadly. "Finally, some real action!" he says with a laugh.

"I almost thought you guys were afraid of each other."

Our breaths are heavy and labored as I stare into her eyes, searching for any sign of discomfort or hesitation, but all I see is desire and longing. Leora looks at me, her cheeks still flushed.

"That was unexpected," she says softly.

I nod, still feeling a little dazed. "Yeah, but . . . it was nice."

It was more than nice. It was electric. I can still feel the sparks between us, and I don't want them to fade away.

We stand there, caught in a moment of intimacy, before

Amélie jumps up from her crouched position. "Oh my God, you guys!" she exclaims, running toward us.

"Look at the pictures! They turned out so good. You have to get this one framed."

I look at the photo; it really is a great picture. Leora is leaning back slightly, her hair cascading down her back and I'm holding on to her waist, with our lips connected.

We look like a real couple. I think about what Amélie said and decide on printing that photo when we get home. I'll frame it and hang it in my office to make our relationship more believable, because couples take photos on vacation.

"You should post this on Instagram, Leora," Amélie says, still grinning from ear to ear. Leora nods and does just that after Amélie sends the photo over.

TWENTY-EIGHT

LEORA

"Goodnight, let me know if you guys need anything," Amélie says before leaving us in front of the guest room.

The room we will be sharing.

Lucas opens the door, and I walk in. It's a nice room that is decorated in neutral colors, and the bed is made up with crisp, white sheets and fluffy pillows. The curtains are drawn, and the soft glow of the bedside lamp creates a warm and cozy atmosphere.

Then my eyes go back to *the* bed. There's only one queen bed and no sofa for either of us to sleep on. Meaning, we will have to share the bed too.

Lucas closes the door behind us, startling me, and walks up behind me. I move to my suitcase and rummage through it until I find my pajamas.

His close presence makes me nervous. "I'll just go in there and get ready," I say, fidgeting with the hem of my shirt.

I enter the bathroom, my heart fluttering. Our lips were devouring each other not that long ago, and now I'm supposed to pretend it didn't happen and act normal?

The sexual tension between us is undeniable, and I'm not sure if I can resist the temptation, but maybe he will.

I take a deep breath and splash some water on my face, trying to calm myself down. I change into my comfortable pajamas—a soft and cozy set of shorts and a tank top—and complete my nighttime routine before stepping out of the bathroom. Lucas is standing by the bed, looking at his phone with a crease between his eyebrows.

"Is everything okay?"

He looks up at me, his eyes taking in my appearance. For a moment, I wonder if he's going to say something or do something. But then he clears his throat. "Yeah, everything's fine."

A lump forms in my throat as I nervously tuck a strand of hair behind my ear.

"I'll take the floor tonight. I don't want you to feel uncomfortable."

I raise my eyebrows, he really can't see me as anything other than a friend. He would rather sleep on the floor than next to me. However, the idea of him sleeping on the ground is almost more uncomfortable for me.

"No, no, that's not necessary," I say quickly. "We can share a bed for a weekend. I won't jump you, don't worry."

He nods slowly, ignoring my latter comment, and I can see the relief in his eyes.

"Okay then, what side do you prefer?"

"Um, I don't know," I mumble, avoiding his gaze. "I guess I'll take the left side."

"Great." He starts to unbutton his shirt.

"What are you doing?"

"Taking off my shirt?" His head tilts to the side as he looks at me with an amused expression.

I roll my eyes. "Yes, I can see that, but why?"

"We're going to bed, aren't we?"

I gesture toward his immaculate torso. "Are you planning on sleeping without a shirt?"

"Yeah, I usually sleep like this. Is that a problem? I can put on a t-shirt."

"No, no. Not a problem at all. I was just surprised, that's all," I say, feeling a little embarrassed at my reaction. "Do whatever makes you comfortable."

Lucas nods and finishes unbuttoning his shirt, revealing a toned chest with a sprinkling of hair. My eyes trail over his body, unable to resist the sight. The light reflects on his olive skin, enticing a desire to reach out and touch it. At this moment, he looks more like a piece of art than anything we'll see in the Louvre tomorrow.

"Like what you see?" There's a smirk on his face, like he knows exactly what I was thinking.

I flush and look away. "I was just . . ."

"Admiring the view?" he finishes for me, a teasing glint in his eyes.

I playfully roll my eyes. "You wish."

"You've seen me shirtless before, Leora."

"Yeah, I know."

He chuckles softly. "Then why are you blushing?"

I feel my cheeks burning even more as I try to avoid his gaze. "I mean, it's not like I was staring or anything," I mutter, mortified. "I just . . . noticed."

Lucas raises an eyebrow. "Noticed, huh? What did you notice, Leora?" he asks, his smirk growing more prominent. I must look like a ripe tomato at this point.

I clear my throat nervously. "I just noticed that you have a lot of tattoos," I reply, avoiding eye contact with him.

Lucas chuckles. "Do you like tattoos? "

I shrug, feeling flustered. "I don't know. I guess."

"Do you like *my* tattoos?" Lucas's question catches me off guard, and I find myself at a loss for words. After a moment of hesitation, I meet his gaze and reply, "I-I mean, they're nice. They look good on you." I can feel my heart pounding in my chest as I wait for his response, unsure of how he'll react.

"Just nice?" He takes a few steps toward me. "Have you seen

many tattoos like this, Leora?" His tone is low and it sounds like a challenge.

"Yes, I have," I lie, my eyes locked on his.

"Then why are you so nervous?"

He moves closer, and I can feel the heat radiating from his body. I take a step back, but he follows, crowding me against the wall. His eyes are intense as he leans in, his lips just inches from mine.

"I'm not nervous. Why would I be nervous? We're friends," I manage to whisper, my heart quickening with both fear and desire. He pauses, his gaze flickering.

"Yeah," he says, finally taking a step back and running a hand through his hair. "Of course we are . . . *Friends.*"

I let out a breath and try to steady myself, the tension between us almost unbearable.

We stare at each other for a few more heartbeats before he breaks the connection. "I'm gonna go brush my teeth."

I watch as Lucas walks away, his shirtless figure disappearing into the bathroom. My mind is a whirlwind of conflicting thoughts and emotions. We're friends, and that's for the best, but at the same time, my body aches with desire for him. I bite my lip as I sink into the bed, feeling the softness of the sheets against my skin. My body is still buzzing with the memory of his proximity, the heat of his breath against my ear. I try to push the thoughts out of my head but my whole body keeps buzzing for his touch.

No, it can't happen. I'm not putting myself in a situation where I can get rejected. I don't think I'll be able to handle that.

I grab a few of the throw pillows and set up a wall between my side and his. Nobody is touching anyone tonight.

As long as he stays on his side, I think we'll be good.

A few minutes later, Lucas emerges from the bathroom in a pair of sweatpants, looking refreshed and ready for bed. He approaches his side of the bed, and there's a subtle tug at the corner of his lips, a bemused curiosity in his eyes. "What's with the barricade?"

"Oh, uh, nothing. I just thought it would be more comfortable this way," I stammer, trying to come up with a convincing excuse that isn't *"to keep me from straddling you."* Because that is not what you say to your friends.

"I just don't want to accidentally invade your personal space while we sleep."

Lucas just shakes his head. "Sure, Leora. Whatever you say." He takes his place on his side of the bed, making no move to cross the pillow barrier.

"Goodnight, Leora."

"Goodnight, Lucas."

We settle into our respective sides, but my mind is still racing with thoughts of him. I try to push the thoughts out of my head, telling myself that it's better to just stay friends. But the more I try to ignore the feelings, the stronger they become. His scent, his warmth, his touch—everything about him is driving me insane. My body is yearning for his touch, but at the same time, I know it's not a good idea to act on it.

I try to calm my racing heart. Maybe if I just focus on getting some sleep, these feelings will fade away and I'll wake up fresh tomorrow. I close my eyes and try to drift off, but I can still feel his presence beside me, and I know that it's going to be a long night.

TWENTY-NINE

LEORA

I shift in my sleep, feeling a warm, hard body pressed against me. My eyes flutter open to see the olive skin I was fantasizing about yesterday. Lucas's arm is wrapped around me tightly, and I feel the rise and fall of his chest. My head is nestled against his shoulder, and our legs are tangled together under the sheets.

For a moment, I just lay there, taking in his warmth and the comfort of his embrace.

It feels safe. *He* makes me feel safe.

His face looks so at ease and I use my finger to trace his full lips, remembering how they felt on mine yesterday. *So soft.*

He's beautiful and looks almost boyish as he sleeps. I can't help but smile at the sight of him, peaceful and content in his slumber. Like all the stress he usually carries on his shoulders has dissipated.

As I move my hand up to brush a strand of hair from his forehead, Lucas begins to stir. His arm tightens around me, pulling me even closer as he lets out a contented sigh. I try to pull away, feeling wrong for enjoying this moment with him while he's unconscious.

His eyes open, and he looks at me with a sleepy smile. "Good morning," he murmurs huskily.

"Good morning," I reply in a low voice. I'm not sure how we ended up like this but I don't want to move. I just want to stay here with him, in his arms, for as long as I can.

Lucas stretches out his legs, making us both aware of how intertwined we are under the covers. As soon as I get a chance, I untangle from his hold and move away from him.

Lucas notices my sudden movement and his expression falls a little. "You okay?"

I nod quickly, avoiding his gaze. "Yeah, I'm fine. Sorry, I don't know how I ended up close to you during the night." I look around the room and ask, "Where are the damn pillows?"

Lucas sits up, his brow cocked up. "I threw them away during the night."

"You did what?"

"I threw them away," Lucas repeats, a small smile forming on his lips. "I couldn't sleep with all those pillows between us."

I look at him incredulously. "Why on earth would you do that?"

"I told you, I couldn't sleep." He smiles. "Are you going to make me repeat everything today?"

I can't help but roll my eyes at his teasing. "No," I say, a small smile playing at the corners of my lips.

A knock startles us. "I heard some voices. Are you decent?" Amélies voice sounds through the door.

"Yes!" Lucas calls out.

"Hey, what are you—" My attempt to protest is cut off as Lucas pulls me to him, causing me to laugh.

Amélie walks in, a grin on her face. "Well, well, well, it looks like someone had a good night," she teases, raising an eyebrow at us.

Lucas chuckles and wraps his arm around me, pulling me closer to him. "What can we do for you, Amélie?" he asks, his tone light and playful.

Amélie shakes her head, still grinning. "Just wanted to see if you guys were up for breakfast. I thought we should eat before we leave for the Louvre."

"Yes, we are," I reply, untangling myself from Lucas and sitting up in bed. "Let me just freshen up and get dressed." I jump out of bed, excitement overriding any feelings from waking up next to Lucas. "I'm so excited. I'm finally going to see the Mona Lisa and Venus de Milo with my own eyes."

Amélie beams at my excitement before exiting the room. I turn to Lucas, feeling a sudden awkwardness between us.

"Don't get too excited about the Mona Lisa. She's tiny."

"What do you mean?"

THE MONA LISA IS, in fact, tiny. I mean, come on, who made the Mona Lisa queen of the art world anyway? I've seen bigger paintings on the back of a cereal box. But hey, at least now I can cross *"See the Mona Lisa"* off my bucket list, even if she is a little underwhelming.

The look on Thomas and Lucas's faces when I finally reached her after that endless line was truly pitiful, and they reveled in my disappointment, but thankfully, Amélie had my back. She scolded them on the spot, reminding them how uncivilized it is to dampen someone's excitement, and they fell silent.

I must say, I quite like her. Whenever she walks into a room, she commands it. It's the way she carries herself, demanding respect. I could definitely learn a thing or two from her on how to wield that kind of power.

We make our way through the crowded galleries of the Louvre and I can feel my excitement building. The grandeur of the museum is awe-inspiring, and I'm grateful to be experiencing it with Lucas by my side. When we finally reach the Greek section, I can hardly contain my anticipation. The moment I see the statue of Venus in the other room, my heart swells with emotion, and a little shriek escapes my throat.

Lost in my own thoughts, I don't pay attention to where I'm walking, which is unfortunate because I don't realize there's a breeze flowing through this section of the museum floor, which, of course, lifts my dress up, exposing my underwear.

Mortified, I yank my dress down as quickly as possible.

Please say everybody missed that.

Lucas is behind me in an instant, his arm tightly circled around me as he guides me away from the air conditioning unit on the floor.

"Are you laughing?" I turn my face to him, my face burning with embarrassment.

"I'm sorry," he says, but I can tell by the teasing sparkle in his eyes that he finds the situation amusing.

"Did many people see my . . ." I trail off, unable to finish my sentence.

"No, not many people saw." He reassures me, but his tone shifts as he stops at a corner. Holding me close, he leans in until his lips hover near my ear, "But I did, and I have to say, I knew red would look good on you."

As he speaks, a warmth courses through my body, leaving me with a delightful shiver that brings a smile to my face. I turn to look at him, and our eyes lock for a moment. The intensity of his gaze makes me feel both desired and vulnerable. My heart hammers in my chest as I struggle to comprehend the meaning behind his words. Does he really mean what he's saying, or is this just his way of playing with me?

I try to compose myself, but it's difficult with him so close to me. I can smell his cologne and feel his strong body against mine. Every nerve in my body is on edge as I wait for him to speak again.

"Look, there she is, Venus de Milo." He guides me towards the sculpture, hand in hand, and my body aches for more than this innocent touch. I want him to hold me again. I steal a glance at him, taking in his beautiful features and broad shoulders. His gaze lies straight ahead but his lips are curved in a smirk, as if he knows what effect his words have on me and is reveling in it.

I really don't understand what he wants or needs from me. Is it all a joke? I try to push aside my feelings, knowing that it's not the right time or place to act on them. But as we stand there, my mind goes to every other place but the sculpture.

I want him and I think he wants me too, he might just be scared to admit it. He wouldn't say my underwear looks good if he didn't truly think that. Okay, he didn't say they looked good, he said *I* looked good in red, but my underwear is red, so it's almost the same thing.

I imagine him pressing me against the wall, his hands roaming over my body, and his lips exploring every inch of my skin. The thought makes me ache with need as a flush creeps up my neck.

I snap out of my trance when I realize Lucas is talking, describing the history of Venus. But I'm way too consumed by him to hear what he's saying.

". . . she was found on the Greek island of Milos. It's beautiful there, I think you'd love it. We'll go there someday."

Now he's planning a trip for us to Greece?

"Are you okay, Leora? You look a bit flustered."

I nod, trying to compose myself. "I'm fine," I lie, ignoring the comment about Greece. "I've always wanted to see her. She's beautiful."

"She truly is."

I turn to him, expecting to find him admiring the statue like I am, but when my gaze lands on his face, his eyes are already on me.

THIRTY

LEORA

We're both dressed to the nines, me in a sleek black dress and Amélie in a stunning red jumpsuit that enhances her beautiful blond hair and soft features. When she suggested we go out for a girls' night, I immediately agreed. It's exactly what I need right now. I need to get a break from Lucas.

As we settle into our seats at the rooftop bar, we take in the stunning city skyline. From here, I can see everything—the Eiffel Tower, the Arc de Triomphe, and the twinkling lights of the city.

It's breathtaking.

"So, tell me, how's married life?" Amélie asks, her eyes sparkling with curiosity.

I freeze, unsure of how to respond. I don't want to lie to her —she's been so kind—but I can't tell her the truth either, so I go for an in-between.

"It's been good. Lucas is incredible," I say with a strained smile on my lips.

Amélie nods, a radiant expression on her face. "I'm so happy for you, Leora. You two make such a great couple."

I feel a pang of guilt in my chest. Amélie and Thomas are two incredible human beings, and here I am, lying to their faces.

"Oh, the first year of being married is amazing." She takes a sip from her Pampelle Spritz. "I remember when Thomas and I were newlyweds, we couldn't keep our hands off each other. We fucked every chance we got. You two seem to be more civilized than us."

I cough as I attempt to clear my lungs from the drink that clearly went down the wrong pipe.

Amélie chuckles, noticing my reaction. "Oh, don't be coy. You might handle it better than us, but I saw you two this morning. And don't get me started on your kiss at the Eiffel Tower. You almost got *me* hot and bothered."

A blush rises to my cheeks, embarrassed but also amused by Amélie's teasing. "Oh my God, Amélie."

"What? We're friends, and friends talk about this stuff. Now tell me, does he relax in the bedroom? Because that man walks around with a stick up his ass." Her eyebrows raise at the word "relax."

I can't help but laugh at her blunt question. That's one of the impressions I got of Lucas when we first met. But, after getting to know him these past few weeks, my perspective has shifted. Despite his initial gruff exterior, I've discovered a layer of warmth and humor beneath. The more I learn about him, the more my laughter becomes a genuine reflection of the camaraderie we've developed.

"Some shots on the house?" A waiter comes by, saving me from answering her very private question. He sets down four shot glasses filled with an amber liquid, all topped with an orange slice and cinnamon.

I gratefully take a shot glass and raise it in a toast with Amélie. "Cheers to a great girls' night out and our new friendship," I say, clinking my shot glass against hers.

"Cheers, ma chérie." Amélie grins. "And to getting Lucas to loosen up a bit," she adds with a mischievous glint in her eye.

We both kick back our shot glasses, downing the liquid in one swallow. As soon as it hits my throat, I almost cough it up, not expecting the spirit.

Tequila.

This is going to be a wild night.

AFTER THE THIRD drink and the fourth tequila shot, Amélie relaxes even more, which I didn't think was possible.

"Okay, spill. What's the most daring thing you've ever done in bed?"

I haven't been daring at all.

"Oh, not much."

She looks at me, shocked. "No handcuffs?"

I shake my head.

"No spanking?"

I shake my head again.

"Not even a little role-playing?" Amélie raises her eyebrows expectantly.

I shake my head for the third time, feeling a little embarrassed at how vanilla my sex life seems compared to hers. Maybe it's because I've only ever been with John, but we never explored much.

"I guess I've just never been that adventurous," I admit with a shrug.

Amélie looks at me thoughtfully for a moment, then leans in and whispers, "Well, it's never too late to start trying new things. I have a feeling Lucas would want to do *everything* with a girl like you. Just tell him what you want. Communication is very important in a relationship, and in bed. Take initiative." She winks at me before downing another shot.

I'm intrigued by her words, and I wonder if maybe it's time for me to step out of my comfort zone. I don't know if it's the alcohol talking, but the way he's been acting these past few days has been very flirtatious. He touches me more when we're out, and he occasionally makes flirty comments that leave me aching.

If I'm being honest, I'm horny. Like really horny, and I need to get *him* out of my system. Us getting together once might be a good opportunity to see if there's something between us; if not, then we'll know for certain that we're not compatible, and I'll be happy using my vibrator for the rest of the year.

"Let's say I tried to initiate something, how would I do it?" I ask, and her whole face lights up.

"There's many things you could do," she says, ticking off her fingers. "You could try dressing up in lingerie or blindfolding him before taking control. Maybe you could suggest watching porn together and trying out some new positions. The possibilities are endless, really."

I listen to her suggestions with a mix of excitement and nervousness. It's one thing to talk about being daring and adventurous—actually putting it into practice is a whole different story. But Amélie's enthusiasm is contagious, and I find myself getting more and more curious. I will not, however, watch porn with him, and I will not blindfold him either. Although, the lingerie part seems to excite me a bit. I actually packed a black lace set with me and I'm wearing it now. I thought it would give me some added confidence tonight, which it did. The feeling of the suspender hugging my waist and the delicate lace against my skin actually makes me feel sexy.

"Thanks for the ideas," I say, feeling a little bolder now. "I'll have to think about which one to try first."

Amélie gives me a knowing look. "Trust me, once you start, you won't want to stop. And who knows, maybe you'll end up being the adventurous one in the bedroom after all."

WE STUMBLE through the door to the apartment, our laughter echoing through the quiet space.

"Shhh, the boys might be sleeping," I whisper, my forefinger slightly askew from the middle of my lip.

"Let's wake them. I'm hungry for some Thomas," Amélie says and another round of loud laughs escapes as we bend at the waist.

Suddenly, a voice echoes through the hallway, causing both of us to straighten up. "It's three thirty in the morning. You didn't say you'd be out this long," Thomas says, a note of sternness evident in his tone.

"Oh, don't worry Thomas, we had fun," Amélie replies with a big grin, walking towards him, her hands outstretched. He laughs, clearly not able to resist her.

He shakes his head. "You're so drunk, baby."

I might be super drunk, but not even that would make me miss the adoration in his eyes. He would do anything for Amélie, and she for him.

I want that.

"Yes, yes I am." She throws her arm around his neck. "And so is Leora."

"I can see that," Lucas drawls, his voice thick like molasses. I turn my head to the right and see him leaning against the wall. He's so damn good looking it's crazy; it's not humanly possible to look like that.

"How about we get you two some water and then go to bed?" Lucas suggests, breaking the sexual tension, flowing from only me. He leaves for the kitchen and comes back with the bottles, handing one to Thomas.

"I'll get her to bed. Good luck with yours." Thomas walks away holding on to Amélie, leaving me and Lucas alone. With his departure, my filter slowly starts to dissolve.

"You're pretty," I blurt out, looking up at him with a coy expression.

Lucas smiles at me, his eyes locking on mine. "You're pretty too, Leora."

The way he says my name is like an aphrodisiac. It could turn me on in any situation, making me wetter than the damn Mediterranean Sea.

My heart skips a beat as he moves closer to me, the scent of him making me dizzy.

"But you're very drunk. Let's get you to bed." He takes my hand and leads me toward the bedroom.

"Let's get *you* to bed," I repeat. He chuckles, shaking his head.

He sets me down on the bed and crouches in front of me, opening the water bottle. "Drink some water."

I do as he says, staring at him the whole time.

"Good girl, keep drinking." He pauses, eyeing me. "How are you feeling? Can you get dressed or do you need help?"

Amélie's words come back to me, *take control.*

"I feel great," I stand up, stumbling, and his hands go to my thighs, steadying me.

I think he wants me.

As I try to remove my dress, my drunken state gets the best of me, and I end up almost falling over. Lucas quickly stands up, catching me.

"Maybe you do need some help," he says, laughter evident in his voice.

Without another word, he moves closer to me and begins to undo the zipper on my dress.

Oh my God, it's working.

He slides the dress off my shoulders, his fingers gliding along my bare skin, igniting a tingling sensation everywhere he touches me.

"Close your eyes," I whisper as I look back, watching him as he does what I say. I step out of my dress, and I turn to face him. Wearing only my heels and lace lingerie, I command, "Open."

When he does, his eyes immediately roam my body and grow wide when they meet mine again.

The sexual tension between us is potent as he continues to stare at me, his gaze intense and unwavering.

My hands go behind my back, fumbling with my bra clasp.

"Leora," he swallows hard, making his Adam's apple bob. His voice is barely above a whisper when he asks, "What are you doing?"

My hands finally manage to unclasp my bra, and I slowly take it off. His eyes quickly move down to my exposed breasts and his eyes grow even wider before he returns his gaze to my face. He takes a step back, his eyes still locked on mine, and I can see the conflict warring within him.

Why isn't he touching me yet?

Why isn't he doing anything?

Take control, Leora, show him how much you really want him.

I take a step forward, closing the distance between us. "Lucas," I say softly, trying to read his expression. "I want you."

He doesn't move an inch as I press my body closer to him. I can sense his attraction pressed against my stomach and I finally feel his hands come up to rest on my hips, his touch sending electricity through my body.

It's working.

I try to lift up onto my toes so I can fully reach his height, but it's hard in my heels.

"Please," I whisper desperately, my breath hot against his skin. "I need you."

That seems to be all the encouragement he needs. He emits a low, hungry growl and pulls me closer, his lips crashing into mine in a fervent and hungry kiss. My arms eagerly wrap around his neck, drawing him in even closer as my tongue meets his.

His hands, strong and commanding, roam my entire body, leaving a trail of tingling sensations in their wake. I'm on fire, consumed by the passion that courses through me. I moan into his mouth, unable to control the overwhelming feeling of him. That spurs him on; he sighs into my mouth and grabs my ass, squeezing it with possessive desire.

This is it. This is what I've been waiting for.

I stumble a little as he walks me backward, and it breaks our kiss for a second. But it was a second too long, because the heat and desire in Lucas's eyes slowly morph into concern as he pulls back.

"No."

No. What does he mean by *no.*

"Yes," I despairingly answer him back, attempting to kiss him again.

"Leora, stop. I can't . . . not like this," he says, his voice strained. "You're drunk—you're not thinking clearly."

I ignore his words, reaching for him, my hands grazing his chest, desperate for his touch. "Lucas, please," I beg, my voice hoarse with desire.

He grabs my wrists, pulling them away from his body gently.

"No, Leora. I can't do this."

His words hit me like a slap in the face, momentarily sobering me up. I look at him, my heart breaking at the conflict I see in his eyes.

"I'm sorry," I whisper, tears pricking at the corners of my eyes as I raise one of my hands to cover my breasts, feeling exposed. "I didn't mean to make you uncomfortable."

He sighs, still holding on to me. "You didn't. It's not you, Leora, it's me. You're drunk and I got caught up in the moment with you, but I don't want to do anything that you'll regret in the morning. You said it yourself, we're friends, and that wouldn't be very *friendly* of me."

"Friends?" I echo back.

We're friends.

Only friends.

We stand there for a moment, the atmosphere between us thick. But he breaks it by releasing my wrist and stepping back. "I'll get you something to sleep in," he says.

The desire that coursed through my body moments ago turns into shame as I slip on the t-shirt he brings me.

I was mistaken.

I was wrong.

I've made a fool of myself.

Why did I think that I could be sexy like Amélie? Why did I think this would work? Why did I put myself in this situation? I'm not Melina, what Lucas and I have is not physical at all, we're just an arrangement to fix our own personal problems.

Of course, we're friends.

That's the only thing I am to him.

Lucas's eyes try to find mine but I can't allow myself to look at him right now. If I do, I'll cry.

His voice is soft when he speaks, as if he's afraid he'll break me into pieces.

If only he knew how fragile I'm feeling at this second.

"Let's get you to bed."

He picks up the duvet and helps me get in. I quickly turn my back to him, my tears ready to spill.

"I'm sorry, I-I shouldn't have . . ." I try to say but he presses a gentle kiss to my temple, stopping me from speaking any more.

"You have nothing to be sorry for. We can talk tomorrow. Get some sleep, *Ya Amar*."

I break.

The tears fall and there's nothing I can do to stop them.

Nothing.

It's as if the dam I built to hold them back has burst, and now I'm left exposed and defenseless. Lucas's kind and understanding words only make me feel worse. I feel like a complete fool for letting myself believe there could be something more between us.

Lucas moves away, and I think he's about to leave, but he hesitates. I need him to leave, to let me cry in peace.

"Please, leave," I plead.

With a heavy breath, he finally exits our bedroom.

I'm left alone and the weight of my own foolishness crashes down on me as I replay every interaction we've ever had, analyzing them for signs that I must have misread.

But the truth is, deep down, I knew. I knew that our arrangement was strictly for show, that we were supposed to act in public and be friends in private—that was the agreement. No touching in private was my condition, *my damned rule*. And yet, in my desperation and longing, I let myself believe that there was a chance for something between us. Something more than my lust.

I've been fooling myself this whole time, because right this second, it's not only my ego that's bruised. There's pain in parts of my heart too.

Am I starting to fall for him?

The realization makes me cry even harder. I cry and cry, my tears staining the pillow beneath me. I feel so unwanted and so naïve.

How am I going to face him tomorrow? How can I look him in the eyes without feeling the burning sting of humiliation? How can I pretend that everything is okay when I feel so broken?

I wish I could rewind time and undo this mess I've made. But I know I can't.

I'm not talking about this tomorrow. We made a deal, and I will fulfill it, but I'll keep my distance. I'm not allowing myself to fall any further.

THIRTY-ONE

LUCAS

I didn't sleep for a single second last night. After I left her alone in our room, I went to sleep in the living room. The look on her face is still etched into my mind, haunting me relentlessly. The pain and tenderness in her eyes cut through me like a knife. I never wanted to see her hurt, especially not because of me.

Last night was a rollercoaster of emotions. Her intoxication was evident, and a part of me wanted to give in to the desires that were swirling within me. I want her. Every fiber of my being is screaming for her. Since I got my first taste of her, there's been nothing else but her.

But yesterday I couldn't take action—I couldn't take advantage of her vulnerable state, no matter how much I wanted to.

I couldn't let it happen, not like that.

It took every ounce of self-control to pull away from her, to resist the temptation that was consuming me. I would never, under any circumstances, take advantage of a drunk woman. She deserves more than that—more than a hazy memory, tainted by regret. I want our first time together to be a cherished moment, one that she can fully embrace and remember with clarity. I want her to be fully aware of every touch and every word exchanged between us—if it ever happens. I want nothing less than a genuine connection; one that is built on mutual respect and, more importantly, consent.

Yesterday was not the day for us to cross that line. We both need a clear understanding of our feelings and intentions.

It was a difficult decision, but it was the right one.

The truth is, I think I might be feeling more toward her than I initially thought. In the beginning, it was only lust, a pure animalistic desire to consume her. I walked in on her doing yoga in the living room one evening and I almost lost my damn mind. Never in my life have I had to stop myself from throwing a woman over my shoulder.

Now, however, the desire is stronger, not only for her body but for everything she can give me. Anything she will allow me to have. I long for her laughter to fill the air, her touch to ignite a fire within me, and her understanding to soothe my restless soul. It's as though every cell in my body yearns for her, calling out, eagerly awaiting her response. It's as if she holds the key to unlocking a part of myself I never knew existed.

A part I never thought I'd find.

Now, I have an inkling she might want something more. Even though she was drunk yesterday, she acted on some kind of instinct. If we talk about it today, maybe we can agree to give *us* a real chance, away from all agreements and conditions.

I'M SITTING at the end of the bed, my gaze fixed on her as she sleeps. I can see the exhaustion etched on her face. After she'd told me to leave, I couldn't walk away from the door immediately. Instead, I stayed and listened to her cry herself to sleep while parts of me broke. I felt like shit, to say the least. I still do. I should have intervened before things went too far. I should have known better, or at least used better words to tell her how I feel.

Her beauty captivates me—it takes my breath away. I can't fully comprehend it; it's as though a vital piece of me is missing when she's not by my side, like the night sky without the light of the moon.

She's *my* moon. *My light.*

My body aches to be with her—to savor every second of our time together. If I'm being honest with myself, it scares me. I've never felt something so powerful toward another human being until this woman came into my grey life with her colorful sundresses and fire. She holds so much of me in her hands, and I'm afraid she'll drop me, shattering me into fragile, small pieces. That's why we need to talk about what's been simmering between us. There's something there; I know it, and she knows it too.

As if sensing my internal struggle, her eyes flutter open.

"Good morning." The sound of her vulnerable voice breaks the silence.

I take a deep breath, my gaze locked with hers. "Good morning, Leora."

There's a brief pause that's heavy with anticipation and unspoken words.

"How did you sleep?"

She shrugs, avoiding any eye contact.

"I'm sorry," I say sincerely, my voice filled with regret. "About yesterday, I shouldn't—"

Before I can finish my sentence, she cuts me off abruptly, her voice infused with self-blame.

"No, I'm sorry. I was drunk, and I shouldn't have thrown myself at you like that."

She begins to stand up, heading toward the bathroom as if trying to escape from the situation. I quickly follow her, not wanting her to run away from me. "Leora."

Her response is swift. "I'm sorry, Lucas. It won't happen again. I crossed the line yesterday. Please, let's put what I did behind us and never speak of it again."

With that, she closes the bathroom door, leaving me standing there, feeling powerless. I understand why she feels the need to distance herself from me, to protect herself from potential hurt and complications.

Our playful interactions, the way we understood each other—it all seemed so natural. And now, I fear that we may never be able to return to that ease and comfort we once had. I never wanted to hurt her, and if she kissed me sober, I would have kissed her back with everything I had. I would have savored the moment of us two connecting for the first time without an audience.

The wall she's beginning to build around herself feels impenetrable, and I can't help but feel a sense of helplessness in the face of its solidity.

THIRTY-TWO

LUCAS

The few days we've been back home have been excruciating. We barely interact like we used to—we barely interact at all.

If she doesn't have any questions regarding work, she doesn't speak to me. I've made breakfast every morning, but she's never up for it, which only confirms my suspicions that she's distancing herself from me because she adores breakfast.

Last Tuesday, I put on her favorite tv show—the one we've been watching together that always makes her run to the sofa, yelling at me to bring her a glass of wine—but nothing. Her bedroom door didn't open.

And then, yesterday, I tried to get her to go for lunch with me, but she dismissed me with the excuse that she was swamped with work.

As I sit down at my desk, trying to focus on work, my mind keeps wandering back to Leora. I can't stop thinking about her and what I can do to make things right between us. I know that I need to apologize, but I also know that it may not be enough.

To make matters worse, Louis Grimaldi has been out of the country, so I haven't been able to have a meeting with him yet. I won't get that chance either, as he returns just two days before the opening. According to Estelle, Marc Duval is leaning towards voting for me, which means I might have enough people for a majority vote in my favor. It's keeping me up at night. I can't afford to fail.

After a few hours of work, I decide to take a break and head to the cafeteria in the building to grab a sandwich, hoping to clear my mind. Just as I'm about to sit down at a table, I see Leora walking in.

Her eyes land on me, hesitating for a moment before walking over, probably to keep up the charade of our happy marriage.

"Hey," I say, probably a bit too excitedly.

"Hey." Her voice is low and guarded.

"Please, have a seat." I gesture to the chair in front of me.

"Oh, I have to get back to Camille and Simon."

Of course she does.

I try to mask my disappointment, but she must see right through me. "Maybe another time?"

She nods before looking around, catching a few of our colleagues watching us. I think that's the only reason she leans down to give me a peck on my cheek before walking away.

I watch her go, wishing I could just talk to her and clear the air between us.

"Trouble in paradise?" Liam's voice interrupts my thoughts and I jump a little in my seat. I look up to see him standing over me, a teasing smirk on his face. He's wearing his usual office-wear: jeans, a t-shirt, and a leather jacket instead of a blazer. He's never been one to follow the rules of proper office attire.

"What are you talking about?" I ask, trying to sound nonchalant.

"Don't play dumb," he says, sitting down across from me. "It's obvious that something's up between you and Leora. You two have been avoiding each other like the plague."

Is it that obvious?

"You don't know what you're talking about."

He sizes me up with a dumbfounded look, his eyes searching for the truth in my words, but I can see the doubt lingering there.

"Lucas, I'm your brother. I know when something is up."

I let out a sigh, feeling the weight of the situation. I don't want to involve him, but it might be the desperation that makes me speak up. "Things have been a bit tense since Paris," I admit.

"And what happened exactly?" Liam's eyebrow shoots up his forehead as he leans in, clearly curious.

I hesitate for a moment before speaking. "We had a little argument." Not exactly the truth, but it's as much as I'm willing to give. His eyebrows furrow as if he doesn't quite understand.

"I didn't handle it the best, and I don't know how to fix things."

Not the whole truth, but close enough.

Liam nods thoughtfully. "Well, maybe you should try talking to her about it. Tell her how you feel and try to work things out."

I nod. "I know, but every time I try, she finds ways to distance herself and avoid me—even at home."

"Why do you give her the opportunity to avoid you? Don't *try* to talk to her. If you're the reason why she's hurt, then you better be the reason why she's happy again. You have to be more assertive. *Talk* to her, Lucas."

"What if she doesn't want me to?"

He smiles at me and shakes his head. "Man, I've seen the way she looks at you. Believe me, she wants you to."

"How does she look at me?"

"As though you're the missing piece of her puzzle. It's the way her eyes light up when she catches a glimpse of you and how she tries to hide a smile every time you walk in. This girl is head over heels in love with you," Liam replies, his voice, filled with a knowing warmth that reassures me and makes my heart race all at once.

Is she in love with me?

"When did you grow up to be all wise?" I ask him, a smile tugging at the corners of my lips.

Liam pats me on the back and gives me a reassuring squeeze. "You've got this, man. Just be honest with her. Why don't you ask her to be your date to your annual charity dinner with the kids you help out? I bet she would love it. No one with a heart could say no to kids in need."

Why didn't I think of that? When I told her about my charity, her eyes lit up like a lighthouse. I had considered skipping the dinner this year, not wanting to force her to spend time with me and pretend for a whole evening when she's clearly uncomfortable and upset with me. But now, that's exactly what I want. Maybe a bit of pressure will help her see and feel the connection we truly have.

I smile gratefully at him. "That's a great idea." I stand up, squeezing Liam's shoulder. "I'll go ask her now."

With a sense of purpose, I make my way to Leora's office, my palms sweaty and a knot of nervousness tightening in my stomach. I approach her door and gently knock, waiting for her response.

"Come in." Her sweet voice welcomes me. As I step into her office, she lifts her head in greeting, her beautiful green eyes staring up at me.

"Lucas."

"Can we talk for a minute?"

"Oh, I actually have a lot to do." She averts her gaze back to her computer.

"It won't take long." I proceed to take a seat on the chair in front of her desk. My eyes go to the picture of us hanging on the wall, and her gaze follows.

It's a damn good picture.

Leora's eyes flicker with curiosity when they meet mine. There's a hint of concern behind them, but she doesn't say anything yet.

"How does your evening look?" I know exactly how her schedule looks, and she knows it. But I want her to answer me.

She reaches up, her delicate fingers brushing against the

strands of her hair, gently tucking it behind her ear. "I have no plans."

"Great, then you'll accompany me tonight for my annual charity dinner."

"I'll accompany you?" Her questioning tone, as always, adds to my already bubbling frustration. Why does she always have to fight me?

"Yes, you'll be my date."

"Is that so?"

"Yes."

My words hang in the air, and in her eyes, I see something I haven't seen in a while—something I've missed. Intrigue.

Before she can say "no," I add the most important part. "Some of the kids will be there. They would love to meet you."

As if on cue, her face morphs into that of pleasant surprise. Her eyes widen slightly, and there's a genuine smile growing on her face that brightens the room. The mention of the children seems to have touched a soft spot within her. Liam was right.

"The kids would like to meet *me*?" she asks in disbelief.

I nod, my own smile spreading across my face. "Yes, they might have heard a thing or two about you." Last time I saw them, I spoke about her a lot and they begged to meet the woman I seem to be falling for. Even after presenting her to many people, introducing her to these kids will be even more special and cherished.

Leora's expression softens even further, and a hint of blush colors her cheeks. "I would love to meet them, Lucas."

"Great, I guess we can round off the day and head home then."

A *ding* comes from her phone, quickly diverting her attention. Her brows furrow as she lets out a huff.

"Is everything okay?" I ask, my voice filled with genuine concern.

She sighs and sets her phone down on the table, the screen facing down. "Y-Yes, everything is fine. It's just some work related issues," she stammers, the pitch in her voice subtly shifting, and her eyes won't meet mine.

That's weird.

I pause for a moment, narrowing my eyes as I watch her shift under my stare.

"Really? I'll gladly help out," I offer, trying to figure out what has caused the sudden change in her.

"No, No. You have so much to do, don't worry. But I might need to stay at the office a little longer."

"I'll wait for you."

Another *ding* and her gaze goes to the phone quickly before they meet mine again. This time she doesn't pick it up.

"You don't have to do that. Go home, take a shower, and relax a bit. You deserve it. I won't stay too long. I'll just get some things in order with Camille."

Something seems odd; she's jittery and nervous. Her gaze never meet mine, and I have a sense that something is wrong. But instead of pushing her away even further, I reluctantly agree to let her stay and let her know I'll send a car.

Leora manages a faint smile, though it doesn't quite reach her eyes. It's as if she's nervous.

She's hiding something.

THIRTY-THREE

LUCAS

Leora never got into the car I sent and she still hasn't shown up at home. After I got out of the shower, I texted her and told her to be here at six thirty, which she agreed to. Now it's almost seven and I'm starting to get worried.

ME

Hey, where are you?

Is everything alright?

I pick up my phone and try to call her, but all I hear are several *beeps* and no answer.

ME

I can pick you up.

She hasn't answered any of my messages yet, and it's been almost an hour.

ME

Leora, I'm starting to get worried

Answer me!

Then I remember that she told me she would be working with Camille, so I quickly search for her contact information and press CALL.

"Hello, Monsieur Ayoub?"

I skip the pleasantries, my mind only focused on finding Leora. "Can you pass the phone to Leora, please?"

"Pardon? I'm not with Leora. I'm at home." I halt my pacing, a wave of confusion washing over me.

Okay, so she's probably on her way back home then, but that doesn't explain why she isn't answering me.

"When did you two leave the office?" My voice is harsh, but I don't care.

"About two and a half hours ago."

As the information sinks in, a knot forms in my stomach.

Leora should have been home by now.

Confusion and concern grip me, and I try to make sense of the situation. Why would she leave thirty minutes after I offered her to come with me? She told me she had a lot to do.

"Are you sure she didn't mention anything about where she was going or if something was wrong?" I ask urgently, my voice filled with worry. This is my fault. I shouldn't have pressured her to come with me tonight; she's not ready.

Camille hesitates for a moment before responding, "No, she didn't say anything specific. She seemed a bit preoccupied, but I assumed it was work-related. I'm sorry, I don't have any more information."

My mind races, considering different possibilities. If Leora left the office around the same time I did and she hasn't made it home, something must have happened during her journey back home.

"Please let me know if you hear anything."

Camille's voice trembles slightly. "Yes, of course."

With a sense of urgency, I end the call and immediately dial Leora's number again. This time, I'm sent straight to her voicemail.

"Hi, you have reached Leora. I can't come to the phone right now but please—"

I don't finish listening to her answering machine. Fire burns inside me, and I don't know if it's fear or anger that consumes me first, but in a moment of overwhelming intensity, I throw my phone against the wall. The impact shatters the screen, leaving a web of cracks in its wake.

I grab my car keys with a sense of dread and determination, and hurry out the door. What if something happened to her?

Racing to the office, panic surges through me as I frantically scale the stairs, heading straight to where I last saw her. I quickly scan the surroundings, but there's no sign of her, anxiety growing with every passing moment. I can't shake the feeling that something is seriously wrong.

Desperation sets in, and I pull out my cracked phone to call Liam, who offers to come and help me search for her. Then, I dial the police, my voice trembling as I explain the situation. They advise me to return home and wait for her, promising to inform patrolling officers to keep an eye out for her—but also informing me that until she's been missing for twenty-four hours, they can't do much. Which to me feels like bullshit and is infuriating, but the police remind me it's only been three hours, and that I should trust my wife. It's absurd; I'm calling *because* I trust my wife, and because something feels wrong.

If anything happens to her, I don't think I will ever be able to forgive myself.

THIRTY-FOUR

LEORA

I'm a liar.

I'm a disgusting liar who told my "husband" that I was going to work when, in fact, I was going to meet someone I shouldn't be meeting.

I arrived at the café we agreed on about an hour earlier than planned in order to calm myself down a little. This meeting won't take long. I'll say what I need to say and then I'll go back home to Lucas and get ready for the evening.

He surprised me by asking if I wanted to come with him. I've been hesitant around him in the past few days, especially after my awful attempt at seduction. But it feels like he's trying to make it less awkward. I'm still incredibly embarrassed, and every time I'm around him, I hear his echoing words, *"I don't want to do anything that you'll regret in the morning. You said it yourself, we're friends."*

I don't know how I misinterpreted everything to be more than it was. But he's been kind to me.

Time passes, and I find myself exchanging a cappuccino for an espresso martini—or two.

A part of me is nervous, and another part is angry, because he's late, as expected.

I reach for my phone, picking it up to double-check the

messages once more. Perhaps I misread them and I'm simply too early.

> **UNKNOWN NUMBER**
>
> Stop blocking my numbers, please.
>
> We need to talk, Leora.
>
> I made a mistake.
>
> You've been ignoring me, so I did what I had to do
>
> I'm in Nice. We need to talk
>
> Meet me at Café Paulette at 7 p.m.

I was with Lucas when I read the first message, and I tried my hardest to mask the look of shock on my face. If he knew where I was, he wouldn't be happy. Even though he doesn't seem to want me in the way that I want him, there's a possessiveness in him that leaves me to believe he wouldn't take lightly to me going for a coffee with another man, in public. As long as I wear his ring, there's an unspoken understanding between us that we're bound by vows and promises.

After Lucas left, I glanced at my phone to read the messages and I almost had a heart attack on the spot.

John's here—in Nice.

This is the fourth number he's texted me from, and I've blocked every single one thus far, but I've had enough. I need to hear what pathetic speech he has practiced. My cheating ex-boyfriend is here to beg and I'm all for it.

Another half hour passes before I get a message from Lucas this time, asking where I am. I don't answer. Then another message arrives, followed by a call.

Fuck. Should I answer? He might be worried. I think about it for a second and decide not to. I let it ring because I can't bear to lie to him this second.

"Leora?" A voice I know all too well snaps me out of my thoughts and I turn around to face *him*.

His hair is longer and he has a beard now. The blue t-shirt he's wearing is a size too big for him, making him appear slightly disheveled. The sight of him brings back memories of how he used to present himself. He used to care so much about his appearance, but now he certainly doesn't look like the John I left behind.

"Can I sit down?"

Say no.

"Sure."

You fool.

"I've tried to reach you so many times."

He takes a seat, keeping his pleading blue gaze on mine.

"John," I say, my voice slightly strained. "Why are you here?"

His presence is stirring up a mix of emotions I thought I'd buried. I try to maintain a composed demeanor, but inwardly, I'm bleeding. All the wounds I thought were starting to heal are now ripped open once again. The memories of our past relationship resurface, reminding me of the mistakes and heartbreak I endured.

"After I saw that photo you posted, I knew I needed to see you, Leora," he says, his voice trembling with sincerity. "You haven't returned my calls, messages, or emails. This was the only thing I could do to reach you. I miss you."

He fucking misses me.

"You miss me?" My voice is sharp, almost sounding sardonic.

"Yes, more than you know."

"You didn't seem to miss me when you were shoving your tongue inside that redhead." The words slip out of my mouth before I even know what I'm saying. The bitterness and anger that has been simmering within me finally find their release as I stare at John, his mouth dropping slightly at my crude words.

The image of him with someone else still haunts me, a constant reminder of our broken trust.

I'm not sad anymore. I'm just angry.

He opens his mouth, but no words come out. Guilt and regret flash across his face, and I can see the weight of his actions finally sinking in. The truth of my words hangs heavy in the air between us.

"I'm sorry, Leora," he finally manages to say, his voice heavy with remorse. "I messed up. I made a terrible mistake, and I regret it every day."

I shake my head, a mix of frustration and disbelief coursing through me. "Regret doesn't undo the pain, John. It doesn't erase the fact that you betrayed my trust—that you shattered our relationship."

He reaches out a hand, as if to offer some form of comfort, but I quickly pull it back, creating some space between us instead. I can't allow myself to be pulled back into his web of manipulation and broken promises.

My phone dings again with two new messages from Lucas. He's worried and I feel like shit, but before I can respond, my phone dies. *Just my damn luck. Why is this happening?*

"I'm sorry for what I did to you," John says, his voice tinged with desperation. "But I still love you, Leora. I never stopped loving you."

At those words, my eyes snap back to his. The sincerity in his voice momentarily catches me off guard, but I quickly remind myself of the countless nights I spent crying and the sleepless nights I spent wondering why I wasn't enough for him. Love shouldn't come at the cost of my own happiness and well-being. It shouldn't break me down to a minuscule version that does everything to fit his mold.

"I've changed, I promise. I know how much I hurt you, and I was wrong. I don't know why I even did it," John pleads, his voice filled with remorse.

I pause for a moment, contemplating his words. Part of me wants to believe that people can change, that he could be sincere in his remorse, and that there's a future for him. But deep down, I know that the issues in our relationship run deeper than just the act of cheating.

"Do you think your only mistake was cheating?" I ask.

His brows are furrowed as he nods. "I was lost. We weren't in the best place and I was looking for something I thought I couldn't find with you. But I was a coward. I didn't look hard enough."

I let out a bitter chuckle, shaking my head in disbelief. "John, blaming our relationship problems solely on me is a cop-out. Yes, we were going through a rough patch, but instead of communicating and working through it together, you chose to seek fulfillment elsewhere. That was your decision, not mine."

I take a deep breath, my voice steady but filled with determination. "I refuse to be held responsible for your choices and actions. I refuse to accept the blame for your lack of commitment and loyalty. It wasn't just about the cheating, it was about how you made me feel, as well as the lack of respect and attention in our relationship. It was about the emotional neglect and the constant feeling of being second best." I meet his gaze squarely, my eyes reflecting a mix of disappointment and what I hope is strength. "Relationships require effort, honesty, and trust from both sides, and you failed to uphold your end of the bargain."

"I never disrespected or neglected you." He's defensive, but I can see a tiny hint of realization in his eyes.

And desperation.

I maintain my composure, determined to express my truth. "John, maybe you didn't realize it at the time, but the way you prioritized other aspects of your life over our relationship made me feel neglected. The constant feeling of being an afterthought took a toll on me emotionally."

He leans back in his chair, his expression a mix of contemplation and denial. "I'm sorry you felt that way, Leora. I had my own struggles and my own ambitions, and I thought I could balance it all."

"Being sorry *I* felt a certain way is not an apology, John. Take responsibility." I pause, allowing my words to sink in and hoping he truly comprehends the gravity of my statement. For a moment, I sense a glimmer of understanding. But as quickly as it appears, it fades into defensiveness.

"I did the best I could, Leora. I never meant to hurt you."

I shake my head, unable to accept his excuses any longer. "Your best wasn't enough, John. It's time for you to acknowledge that and move on."

His shoulders slump with resignation. "I guess I can't change the past."

"No, you can't," I respond, firmly. "I deserve someone who values me enough to be faithful and who is willing to put in the effort to make our relationship work. I deserve more than just empty apologies and promises. And I'm not willing to settle for anything less."

"You mean with your new *'husband.'*" He uses his fingers to emphasize *husband*.

I stiffen a little at his words, my mind going to Lucas. "Yes, with my husband. I've moved on."

"I don't believe you."

I meet his skeptical gaze with unwavering determination. "Believe what you want, John. But the truth remains that I've found happiness with Lucas."

A flicker of doubt crosses his face, as if he's grappling with the idea that I've truly moved on.

"We're not going to get anywhere with this John, and I have a dinner to get to." I try to rise up but before I'm able to stand, his hand flies out, grabbing my wrist, *hard*.

I try to pull my hand away from his grasp, but he's holding on to me too tightly and the way our skin is rubbing together is starting to hurt.

"John, let go of me." I hiss through gritted teeth. Feeling his grip tighten on my wrist, a mix of fear and frustration washes over me. I struggle to free myself from his hold, the pain becoming more pronounced with each passing moment.

"I apologized, Leora. I made a mistake. What more do you want from me?"

"Let me *go*, John," I grit out.

But he doesn't release his grip on me. His face contorts with desperation as he speaks. "We're not done talking, Leora. You can't just walk away from me like this."

I attempt to break away from him again, but it only makes things worse. A sensation, close to a thousand needles, spreads across my wrist, and I'm fervently hoping it doesn't leave a mark.

"John, let go of me, now. You're hurting me."

For a brief moment of shock, his grip loosens, and I seize the opportunity to pull my hand away. I step away, my heart pounding in my chest. The café patrons glance at us curiously, sensing the tension in the air.

"What is wrong with you?" My voice grows louder.

"I'm s-sorry, I didn't mean to."

No, I'm not allowing him to feel sorry about himself or his actions.

I take a step toward him, pointing at him. "Don't you ever touch me again."

"Leora."

"Fuck you, John. For everything," I declare firmly, my voice unwavering. "This conversation is over. Seek help, work on yourself, and find a healthier way to address your emotions."

He looks away, his expression a mix of resignation and bitterness. "I guess I really lost you then, huh?"

I nod, my voice filled with finality. "Yes, you did—a long time ago."

Without waiting for his response, I turn and walk away, leaving behind a chapter of my life that was now tainted by pain and disappointment.

I don't remember the way home. Lucas usually drives us and my phone is dead which means calling an Uber isn't an option. I scan my surroundings, searching for any sign of transportation and unfortunately, there doesn't seem to be a single, available taxi in sight. Frustration wells up within me, but I push it aside, focusing on the one thing that matters—getting back to Lucas as fast as possible. I'll just put on a dress and we'll be on our way to the charity dinner.

I continue walking, relying on my memory to guide me. I occasionally stop to ask for directions from passersby.

Finally, after what feels like an eternity, I recognize a familiar landmark. I'm exhausted, my body is screaming for rest, however, that doesn't matter. Relief washes over me, pushing away the fatigue when I spot the building.

Home. I quicken my pace, and I even choose to take the elevator. It's faster than the stairs.

Lucas has been quietly supportive of my fear of elevators, even though he hasn't openly acknowledged it. Whenever we find ourselves in an elevator, he distracts me by engaging in light conversation, shifting my focus away from my fear.

It's one of his many sweet sides.

I keep my mind on him as the elevator ascends. I'm not completely fearless; my heartbeat still quickens and nausea hits me, but I'm still doing it. If this were a month ago, I would have never stepped in all by myself.

The elevator dings, signaling my arrival at the desired penthouse. Taking a deep breath, I step out and walk toward our apartment, eager to see Lucas.

The sound of his voice fills the hallway as I approach. I can sense the urgency in his tone as he speaks to someone, but as soon as he catches sight of me, his expression transforms from worry to relief. The conversation is seemingly forgotten as he rushes towards me and envelops me in a tight embrace.

"You're back," he says, his voice carrying both concern and

relief. His hold on me is strong, as if he's afraid I might disappear. "Are you okay?"

I'm taken aback by his reaction, unsure of what has transpired in my absence. I take a moment to gather my thoughts before responding. "I'm here, Lucas. I'm okay," I assure him, feeling a sense of comfort in his arms.

He releases his embrace slightly, his hands finding their way to my shoulders as he scans my face and body, searching for any signs of harm or distress. His concern is palpable, and I'm grateful for his care.

"Are you sure? Why didn't you take the car I sent? Where have you been? What happened?"

He looks at me with so much care and worry etched on his face, his eyes searching mine for answers. He shoots his questions at me with urgency. I take a moment to gather my thoughts, torn between telling him the truth and not wanting to upset him at seeing John.

I hesitate, my mind racing with conflicting emotions. I fear my recent encounter with John will push him further away from me, and I don't think I can handle losing him as a friend. I decide to shield him from the truth, at least for now.

"I'm sorry, Lucas," I say, my voice tinged with remorse. "My phone died, and I was working with Camille. It took longer than expected, and I couldn't reach you. I didn't mean to worry you."

Lucas's expression changes from concern to confusion. Skepticism lines his furrowed brow as he tries to make sense of my explanation. He takes a step closer, his voice laced with skepticism.

"With Camille? Until this late in the evening?" he questions.

I can feel the weight of his doubts pressing upon me, and my mind races to come up with a convincing response. Panic starts to well up within me, but I push it down, determined to maintain the charade.

"Yes, with Camille," I reply, my voice steady but my words

betraying a hint of defensiveness. "We had a last-minute project that required us to work late."

Lucas's gaze intensifies, and I can see the flicker of suspicion in his eyes. He crosses his arms. "It's nine thirty in the evening, Leora."

When did it get so late, and how long was I walking?

"You're telling me you worked so hard you missed the dinner you were so excited to go to?"

I take a deep breath, realizing that my lies are crumbling under Lucas's questioning. I can sense the disappointment in his voice as his words pierce through my defenses.

"No, it's not like that," I stammer, my voice filled with frustration. "The project . . . it just got really intense, and I lost track of time. I didn't mean to miss the dinner, I promise."

Lucas's expression doesn't soften in the slightest, and his skepticism remains. He uncrosses his arms and steps closer, concern evident in his eyes.

"Why didn't you call me? We could have figured something out. I could have helped you."

"I told you my phone died."

"Did Camille's phone die too? Or was she busy charging it at home?"

He knows I wasn't with her. My mind races, palms growing sweaty. I've already dug myself a hole deep enough for the both of us, and I have to stick to my lie. At least until he's calmed down. Then I can tell him why I had to meet John alone and why I didn't tell him. Until then, I'm entangled in the web of my own making.

"I should head back home. You guys talk this out," another voice says, and both Lucas and I turn toward it—toward Liam.

"No, stay," I almost beg.

"Thank you, brother," Lucas says.

"Glad you're safe, Leora," Liam says before he's gone, ignoring my plea for him to stay.

"Now, Leora, tell me where you were," Lucas demands, his

eyes searching mine for the truth. A truth I'm not ready to share while he's upset.

"I already told you. I was working with Camille, and my phone died. That's all there is to it. Can we please drop it?"

"Leora, I know you're lying to me, but I don't understand why."

"I'm not lying!" I raise my voice, my frustration boiling over. I hate the way the lie tastes on my tongue.

"I *know* you, Leora," he says firmly. "I know when something is bothering you, and right now it's written all over your face. Besides, I called Camille earlier, and when she answered, she was at home. So, let's try this again. Where were you?" Lucas's expression hardens and his eyes narrow. The look on his face is like a stab to the heart. Making more guilt settle in the pit of my stomach.

"I was working with Camille then she left and I stayed behind."

His eyes harden even further as he takes another step toward me, his proximity heightening the tension in the air. I can sense that he's reaching his breaking point, his patience wearing thin.

"Leora," he says, his jaw clenched so hard it's almost breaking. "You're telling me that you chose to stay at the office until now, an office with multiple clocks and ways of reading time? Meaning you missed the dinner on purpose—the dinner you knew was important."

"I didn't know—"

He moves his hand up in a stop gesture. "I'm not finished! You didn't send me a message or call me to tell me you couldn't come. You left me worrying at home, going mad, thinking something had happened to you. You could have told me that you didn't want to spend the evening with me. I could have been at the charity dinner without you." Lucas's words sting, and I feel deep regret for the choices I've made.

"I've been worried sick waiting for you, do you understand that? I called the damn police, Leora. That's how worried I've been. I thought you were hurt." Lucas's voice quivers as he pours out his frustrations. His brows are furrowed, and his lips press into a thin line, betraying the emotional toll the situation has taken on him. His hair is all tousled, he's probably run his hands through it a hundred times this evening, because of me.

The tension radiates through his body, his muscles visibly taut as he takes a step closer, closing the gap between us. The intensity of his presence sends a jolt through me.

Each one of his words is a painful reminder of the impact my actions have had on him. The weight of my choices crashes down on me with full force. I search for words, desperate to say something.

"I . . . I'm sorry," I manage to say, my voice barely above a whisper.

Tears well up in my eyes as a result of my own hurtful choices. I turn away from him, not wanting him to see me cry as I run a hand through my hair.

His hand grabs my arm. "Leora, is that a bruise?" I frown at him, but Lucas's gaze is fixated on my wrist, where a faint mark from John's grip lingers.

Caught off guard, I quickly try to pull my hand away but Lucas's grip tightens on my arm. His touch is unyielding as he forcefully pulls down my blazer to reveal the full bruise on my wrist. His eyes widen in shock, transforming into a storm of fury and his brows furrow with an intensity that seems to radiate palpable anger, a storm brewing beneath the surface.

His voice carries a note of urgency as he lets go of my arm. "Leora, who did this to you?" There's a fire in his eyes—a fierceness that I've never witnessed before. It's evident that he won't let this slide, that he's prepared to fight for me and confront the source of my pain.

"It's nothing," I mumble, but he doesn't back down.

"Who did this?"

"No one did. Please just let it go." I hadn't expected him to see the bruise, and now there's no way I can tell him the truth. From the look of it, he'll ruin John if he ever finds out.

His voice, though strained, remains firm as he replies, "Leora, I can't just let it go. Tell me!"

"Stop pretending like you care."

"Are you serious? Of course I care! I can't stand the idea of anyone hurting you. I care about you." His voice is raspy with a hint of desperation behind it, as if he's pleading for me to understand his perspective.

I'm experiencing a mix of conflicting emotions—fear, shame, and confusion. Why is he pushing me, why does he care this much?

Because we're friends.

Yeah, friends. *Only* friends, and we will stay that way until we divorce and I go back home.

Alone.

"I hit my hand, okay. I was clumsy."

"No, you didn't."

"Yes, I did."

"Leora, I know you're lying. I can see the finger marks clearly, so quit lying and tell me the truth, so I can find the person who did this to you." Lucas's voice rises, matching the power of our argument.

I keep quiet, not giving him an answer.

His jaw tightens, his voice edged with anger. "You think shutting me out and pushing me away will make it better? Like you've done for the past few days."

"I'm not pushing you away."

"Yes, you are. You've been doing it since that stunt you pulled in Paris." He almost spits out the words.

That stunt you pulled in Paris.

Is that what he thinks of it as? Is that what he thinks of me being vulnerable and putting myself out there? Of me wanting him? That it was all a stunt?

I was already humiliated, and now he's throwing it back at me. The hurt and frustration fuels me, pushing me to retaliate.

"Fuck you, Lucas."

"Last time I checked, that's exactly what you were begging me for," he says through gritted teeth, his words like a slap to the face.

The heated exchange hangs in the air, filling it with tension and raw emotions. A flicker of regret dances on his face, like a passing storm cloud momentarily casting a shadow on his features. His brows are slightly furrowed and there's a glimmer of sadness in his eyes, as if he's just realized the depth of his hurtful words. It's a fleeting moment, one that doesn't seal the open wound he left behind.

His lips part as if he wants to speak, to take back the hurt he inflicted. But he hesitates, I watch as his jaw tenses and then relaxes, a visible struggle playing out on his face. His shoulders slump slightly, as if the weight of his regret is physically beating down on him.

Say something.
Take it back.
Say that you didn't mean it.
Please.

As quickly as the regret appears, he masks it behind a stoic facade. His features harden, and the regret retreats, leaving only a trace of longing in his eyes. I wonder if it's too late to mend the damage this fight caused, but not a single word leaves his lips. Tears threaten to spill from my eyes, but I hold them back, refusing to let him see how deeply he has wounded me.

I push myself past him and walk to my room. This time, he doesn't stop me.

THIRTY-FIVE

LEORA

I wake up feeling exhausted. Lucas's words and my lies were haunting me in my sleep. I have to tell him the truth, but his words still hurt. So, instead of starting the conversation we need to have, I decide to go down to the café next to our apartment for a coffee and something sweet to calm my nerves before opening the discussion again.

When I leave my room, I'm met by Lucas sitting at the kitchen island, his head tilted toward the ceiling. He turns his face towards me and it doesn't look like he slept much either. His face is etched with exhaustion and the hint of remorse is back. Our eyes meet, and a heavy silence hangs in the air. His lips are slightly parted, hinting at the words he wants to say, but the tension between us keeps him quiet. He knows that I lied; he told me he called Camille, and she told him I wasn't with her. I'm in the wrong for lying but his words cut deep and I need some space before opening up the discussion. But even so, seeing him like this —almost broken—hurts. It's my fault he didn't get any sleep. It's my fault he's upset, and the feeling of guilt gnaws at me.

"I'm going to Jean Paul's. Do you want anything?" I ask, reaching my hand out. He adores their pain au chocolat and I can't for the life of me go there without getting him one.

He stills, his back going rigid, and the broken look in his eyes is completely gone. "Who the fuck is Jean Paul?" Rage and a hint of something else—possessiveness, maybe—simmer behind his black eyes.

"I'm sorry?" I ask, trying to keep my voice calm.

It only takes him two seconds to get out of his chair and to eat up the distance between us. "Who. The. Fuck. Is. Jean. Paul?"

I let out a little laugh, unable to control myself. Lucas's eyes widen even further, his confusion evident on his face.

"Jean Paul's"—I emphasise the "s"—"is the name of the cafeteria down the street."

He doesn't calm down in the slightest. I turn to walk away, but he catches up with me and twists me around, his hand gently gripping my bicep. His eyes are still burning with anger and his chest is heaving with each breath he takes.

"I don't believe you, Leora," he growls, his voice dark. I didn't think it was possible but he's even more furious today.

"Where were you yesterday?" His subject change catches me off guard.

"I told you, I was working and lost track of time."

"Let's try that again." He challenges. "Where were you yesterday, Leora?" My name on his tongue feels like a threat, a promise of something deliciously dangerous to come.

"The *truth* this time," he persists, voice low and menacing as he takes a few steps toward me, making me walk back until my back collides with something solid. His arms cage me against the wall.

His body presses closer, flush up against mine, making it difficult to concentrate on anything other than him. Or his smell. Why does he smell so damn good? I can't think clearly with him this close, his scent all around me—consuming me. He smells like a man who's embraced his masculinity, a tantalizing blend of earth and untamed nature.

"Who gave you that bruise?" His gaze flickers down to my

wrist, his finger following his perusal. He caresses the marks gently, leaving goosebumps in its wake.

"I, um, I bumped into a table. It's nothing," I say, feeling my cheeks heat up.

I can see the look of disappointment in his eyes, and it makes me feel incredibly guilty.

"A table, hmm? I don't know who you think I am Leora, but if I want to find something out, I will."

The blood drains from my face as I struggle to find the right words to say. But before I can attempt to explain myself, he continues speaking. "I know where you were yesterday. You went to see that ex of yours."

My eyes widen as I hear the accusation in his voice. How could he have known? I had been careful, but it seemed that Lucas was one step ahead of me. I open my mouth to speak, but no words come out. Caught in the silence, I struggle to find an explanation that could undo the damage already done

"Don't try to lie to me, Leora," he snarls, pinning me with a hard glare. "I have eyes and ears everywhere."

My mind races, trying to come up with an explanation, but I know it's no use. I can see the anger and hurt hidden behind his words, and I break. I do what I should have done yesterday—I confess.

"I-I only met him because he showed up here, out of the blue. I had to tell him to leave me alone and to move on."

"You lied to me." Lucas's body is still pressed up against mine, and I can feel every hard ridge of his torso against mine.

"I'm sorry," I murmur.

His eyes go back to the bruise on my arm.

"I'm okay, Lucas. It's just a bruise."

"No, he hurt you, and if that coward hadn't left the country yesterday, I would have hurt him too." His hands clench into fists on the wall, and the anger in his eyes is palpable.

I can't believe my ears, why would he do that. Why would he go after John?

To be honest, I'm happy John left France. Even though he's hurt me in several ways, I don't think my conscience could handle Lucas hurting him.

I swallow hard, the air between us heavy with tension. "You went to see John?" I cautiously inquire, my voice barely above a whisper.

"I had to make sure he understood the consequences. No one hurts you and gets away with it. But I was too late."

"I appreciate that you want to protect me, Lucas," I say, meeting his eyes, "but I didn't ask you to go after John. I can handle him."

His brows furrow, frustration in his expression. "I don't want you seeing him again, Leora."

I understand where he's coming from, but it's not his decision who I have coffee with. It's not like I'm planning on meeting John in the future; I never want to see him again. But Lucas's possessive ego is starting to annoy me and as much as I want to belong to him, I don't. He's made sure of that.

"You don't get to decide that," I retort, lifting my chin in defiance.

He lets out a deep laugh. "Yes, I do." He pulls my hand up and we both glance at the ring on my finger. "As long as this pathetic excuse for a ring is on your finger, I decide," he asserts, his tone filled with possessiveness. The audacity of his claim fuels the fire burning inside me.

Who does he think he is? What the fuck is wrong with him?

We're only friends, Leora.

You look good in red, Leora.

You're funny, Leora.

You can't meet him, Leora.

What does he want from me?

"No, Lucas," I retort, my voice filled with defiance. "A ring doesn't give you ownership over me and who I can see. We're just friends, remember?"

His face contorts in frustration, lines etching deep furrows across his forehead. "Friends?" he scoffs, his voice laced with disbelief.

"Yes, Lucas," I respond, my voice steady despite the surge of emotions coursing through me. "That's what you said, remember? During my *stunt* in Paris."

His eyes search mine, the turmoil within him mirroring my own, and the pull between us grows stronger.

He completely ignores my words. "I won't tolerate you meeting up with anyone behind my back, and I sure as hell won't tolerate anyone touching you—leaving a *mark* on you."

"Oh, really? And what are you going to do about it, hmm?" I challenge.

A wicked smile curls his lips, his eyes gleaming with a hint of danger. His hand finds its way to the small of my back, pulling me flush against his chest.

"You have no idea what I'm capable of, darling. But I promise you, if you continue testing my patience, I will take you up on my promise to take you over my knees." His voice drops to a low, husky whisper, filled with an intoxicating blend of authority and desire.

The magnetism between us is almost unbearable. But I refuse to back down. "I belong to myself, Lucas. No one owns me. Not you or anyone else."

The air crackles with tension as our bodies remain locked in proximity, the invisible boundary between us blurring with each passing moment.

Scratch that. There are no boundaries.

He presses his hips to me and I feel—

Oh, shit.

This is turning him on.

My hips push forward of their own accord, and I curse myself as Lucas returns my movement with a smile because now he knows I'm turned on, too.

His hand moves up to grasp the back of my neck, his fingers digging into my skin.

"Is that so?" I can feel his lips brushing against my ear, and I know I should push him away, but I can't. My body is responding to him, and no matter how hard I try, I can't resist it.

"Yes," I whisper as an answer.

Just friends.

Just friends.

Just. Friends.

His hand continues its movement from my neck to my hair, tangling his fingers in the strands and pulling my head back, forcing me to look up at him.

"You belong to me, Leora. It's in our agreement," he declares with raw desire. His eyes darken, revealing a side of him I've never fully seen before—*but oh, how I've dreamed of it.*

My breath catches in my throat, anticipation and apprehension filling the air. The intensity of his touch and the commanding authority in his voice sends a rush of heat through my veins. I'm on fire. As much as I want to deny it, there's a part of me that craves his dominance, and longs to surrender to his power. I've known this for a while—I knew it in Paris, and I threw myself at him, wishing for this response, but he didn't want me.

"*You* told me we were only friends. *You* denied me. You don't get to claim me or control me," I assert.

"I didn't mean it."

An amused laugh escapes from my throat. "Well, Lucas, it seems you have a lot of catching up to do if you think you can just flip the switch like that," I respond, raising an eyebrow.

His eyes flicker between mine, and he takes a deep breath before he speaks again. "I never flipped the switch, it was always on for you."

"You're not making any sense."

He presses himself into me even harder, making a point. "I mean, I. Want. You."

I feel his *want* for me, and I want to believe him, I really do, but what if this is a test?

"And *you* want me, too," he continues, his voice husky and filled with raw honesty.

Is it that obvious? I can feel the heat rising through my body, most prominently between my legs, and I'm probably dripping at each and every word that leaves his tongue.

He leans down again, leveling his gaze to mine, so close that our lips almost touch.

I shake my head and say, "I was drunk."

He tsks. "No more lying." His grip on my hair tightens, a spark of both challenge and longing flickering in his eyes. The charged energy between us becomes almost tangible.

His eyes roam my entire face and they land on my lips. His chest is heaving and the look in his gaze could make any woman fall to her knees. But before I get the chance to say anything, he lets out a breath muttering, "Fuck it," and then his lips crash down on mine.

His kiss is rough and demanding—almost punishing. I'm caught off guard for a moment, but then I give in. I wrap my arms around his neck, pulling him closer as our kiss deepens.

He slows the kiss, teasing my lips, and sweeps his tongue into my mouth in a dance, and I follow his every leading step. My hips are rocking against his—I can't help it, and I earn myself a groan that sends a surge of pleasure through me.

"You are *my* wife." His lips move to my neck and he finds the sweet spot that makes me moan out loud. "No one touches *my wife.*"

I don't know if I'm once again dreaming, but this, between us feels right. It feels perfect.

"You're mine," he growls against my neck and his hand in my hair tightens. "Say it." And I give in almost immediately.

"I'm yours." There's no denying it—I'm his, and he's mine.

"That's right," he murmurs while his hands slide down under my ass and he lifts me up, pushing me flat against the wall.

His lips find mine once again in a toe-curling kiss, and I wrap my legs around his waist, pressing my hips deeper into him.

Another throaty groan escapes his lips as I grind against him, feeling how hard I'm making him. It makes me smile against his lips. It feels like an award—it's *me* making *him* feel this way.

We keep kissing and I don't realize we're moving until my back bounces on something soft—a bed.

He breaks the kiss, his lips trailing a path of fiery kisses along my jawline. His voice is a seductive whisper against my skin, filled with a hunger that matches my own. "You have no idea how long I've wanted this."

His hands roam slowly, teasingly, over my body, igniting a trail of electrifying sensations wherever they touch. His fingertips glide over my dress, and the warmth of his touch against the exposed skin of my neck feels incredible. I arch my back, seeking more of his touch, my fingers grazing the fabric of his well-fitted shirt. As our bodies intertwine, I'm acutely aware of the subtle details—the play of fabric, the contour of muscles, and the irresistible force drawing us closer.

My hands reach for him and I slam my lips back on his. This time, I'm in charge, and I want more. My tongue finds its way into his mouth and he welcomes me with his. I wrap my arms around him, pulling him closer, wanting to feel every inch of him against me. Our bodies move together in a rhythm that is both familiar and intoxicating, as if we were always meant to find each other, in this moment. But that feeling is quickly lost as he pulls away, breaking our connection.

"No!" I breathe at the loss of his lips.

"I need you to tell me I can touch you in private."

A small giggle escapes my lips. "Haven't you been touching me?" I rise up, leaning back on my arms. My giggle fades when I find his face all serious.

"No, I want to *really* touch you. I want you to feel me every-where for days to come."

"Yes, please. *Please* touch me."

That seems to satisfy him because he nods and takes off his shirt, and I'm stunned again. Even though I've seen him shirtless several times, this time is different. His tattoos feel like a newly discovered secret, even though I've seen them many times. It's the way they seamlessly transition from his full sleeve onto his chest creating an intricate tapestry of Arabic scribbles and symbols. Each mark appears to hold a unique story, and I'm filled with an irresistible curiosity to decipher every single word.

As I trace the lines with my eyes, I can't resist the urge to reach out with my hand. At my touch, his whole body shivers, and I look up to find him focusing intently on my finger, his eyes igniting with desire. My finger continues down his stomach, following the faint line of hair that trails down his incredibly muscular abdomen and disappears past his waistband. A waistband I want to pull down right this second.

He's so damn perfect.

"Thank you." He laughs as he leans down, hovering over my lips. "You're quite perfect yourself."

Did I say that out loud? I don't even know how to exist normally, he's making me malfunction.

His hands find the hem of my dress and he sucks in a breath when he slowly slides the material up my thighs and over my stomach until my breasts are completely on display for him.

His lips immediately lower to them and he sucks on one of my nipples while massaging the other—switching back and forth between them. It feels so good, but I need more. Much more. Several whimpers leave my lips and before I know it his hand trails down my stomach, leaving goosebumps in its wake. The anticipation builds with each caress, as his hand ventures lower, inching closer to the place that aches for his touch the most. My breath hitches in my throat, eagerness coursing through my veins.

"Are you already wet for me, Leora?" He's smirking because he knows the answer. He knows he'll find me completely and utterly soaked for him.

"You'll have to find out for yourself," the words come out as a whisper—a whisper filled with the exact need he's asking about.

He's so close and all I want to do is scream at him to touch me.

I'm on edge, and if he doesn't quench my thirst for his touch soon, I might have to put his hands on me myself, guiding him.

But there's no need for that.

His fingers slide over my red underwear and when he finally feels the wetness that has been pooling there, he swears under his breath.

"Fuck, is this all for me?" His fingers caress me through my drenched underwear, making my head fall back. These past weeks have been foreplay—the arguing, the pushing each other's buttons, the flirting, *everything*. There's been something in the air since the first day I laid my eyes on him in the lobby, and even though I didn't like it, I've wanted him since.

His caressing stops and my eyes meet his in a plea to continue.

What is he doing?

"Answer me. Is this all for me, Leora?"

This man is going to be the death of me. The smirk on his face is both enticing and infuriating, a dangerous combination that leaves me almost breathless.

"Yes, who else?" I snap, and the only response he gives me is a devilish smile right before his caressing fingers return. This time, to slide my underwear to the side and finally, finally touch me.

Skin to skin.

He uses his finger to gather my wetness and spread it around, teasing me and driving me crazy.

"Lucas, please," I plead

He studies my face, a playful glint in his eyes. "Patience, *Ya Amar.*"

His finger moves to my entrance and he slowly slides it in, a deep groan leaving his lips. My back arches even more, and his eyes dart to mine, studying me. He stops his movement looking completely in awe.

"More," I breathe and he rewards me, sliding a second finger inside, slowly pumping them in and out.

His lips find their way back to mine, where they belong. It feels as though my whole body is on fire, engulfed in a blazing inferno that consumes every inch of my being and he's the only one who can quench the flames.

His touch quickens, and I'm so close. *So close.*

Another moan leaves my lips as his thumb draws circles on my clit.

"I need you to come all over me—my hand, my tongue, and my cock."

I'm momentarily shocked over his words, but they fuel me even further. He curls his fingers hitting the right spot as he applies more pressure on my clit. Every touch, every kiss, sends waves of desire coursing through me, igniting a hunger that can only be satisfied by him. The intensity of our connection is pushing me to the edge of an abyss I'm desperate to plunge into.

I come with a deep moan as I feel myself pulsing on his fingers as he continues pumping into me while his lips suck on my neck. My whole body is shaking and when I come down from my high, and I open my eyes to see he's sitting back on his knees, his abs flexing as he watches me in awe.

"Good girl." He slowly licks his lips. "That's one."

Good girl.

I don't understand how he just fucked me with his fingers, but him using the words *"good girl"* is what causes me to blush.

Instead of waiting for him to come to me, I push myself up and try to grab at him, needing his weight on me, but he doesn't allow me to.

Another *tsk* leaves his lips. "Now, now wife . . . patience. I have other plans first." He rises from the bed and stands at the edge of the bed frame. I frown at his words. What is it that he doesn't understand? I want him *now,* but of course, he has some "other plans" because he likes to annoy me.

"What kind of pla—"

His hand clutches my ankles and he drags me down the bed making my legs dangle at the end.

"What are you doing?" I say with a laugh

"I told you, you're coming on every part of me today," he says with such authority as he lowers himself down on the floor, kneeling between my legs. "I want to taste you." His lips hover close to my core and his breath reaches the right places, but he's not touching me just yet.

"I don't kneel for anyone, Leora." He turns his head left and right, kissing my inner thighs. "But for you." *Kiss.* "I'd kneel every second of the day. If it meant having you spread out like this." *Kiss.*

I feel his teeth biting down on my inner thigh—leaving a mark—so close to my core and I moan at the hint of pain.

"That's the power you hold over me."

Oh my god.

The sight of him between my legs is surreal, and when he leans in to take his first real taste, we both moan at the same time. Then my world spins off its axis as he begins to devour me.

THIRTY-SIX

LUCAS

The first taste of her feels celestial.

Leora is better than any dessert I've ever had, and I don't think I'll ever forget the taste of her. And every time she moans, my cock grows harder. It should be impossible to be this turned on, but with her, I'm learning that nothing is impossible. As soon as my tongue touched her pussy, I was welcomed by a flood of desire. I wish I could bottle her up.

I want to take my time. I need her to crave me again and again after this, because I know I will remain starved for her.

"Lucas," she breathes out my name in a way that makes me want to record it and play it on repeat forever.

I slow my pace and pull away for a second. "Tell me what you want and I'll give it to you." The heat in her gaze is mesmerizing. "I'll give you the world if you ask for it."

She smiles at my words. "You. I want *you*."

I dive back down, this time to wrap my lips around her clit and suck. I want her squirming under my touch.

"Lucas," she says, this time with much more need. "I'm close."

I pull away.

"No. What are you doing?" I'm met by furrowed brows and a parted mouth, and I smile. As much as I want her to come on my tongue right this second, she also needs a little punishment after yesterday.

"You didn't think I would make it that easy for you."

Her brows furrow and eyes narrow as she speaks, "Lucas!" She's becoming increasingly annoyed, and that's exactly what I want. I want her frustrated, and I want her angry. I want her filled with so much need she'll almost burst. Exactly like I've been feeling.

"You didn't think you could shut me out and then meet another man without being punished, did you?"

"Punished? I already said I was sorry."

I grab her and pull her along with me. I make her stand up in front of me as I sit down at the edge of the bed, her confused green eyes scrutinizing me. She's gloriously naked and before I tell her what I want to do to her, I take in every curve.

"Not enough. I need you to lay down over my knees."

Her eyes grow wide when she catches on to what I have planned for her.

"I'm sorry?"

"Do I need to repeat myself? Over my knees, *wife*."

"You want to *spank* me?"

"Didn't I promise you that I would turn your laughs into screams? I keep my word, Leora. Now, lay down if you want me to consider fucking you."

She hesitates, but before she gets a chance, I pull her down on me so that her stomach is lying flat on my knees, her ass gloriously presented to me.

It's begging me to take a bite—so I do.

"Did you just *bite me*?" She turns her face to me, frowning, but she can't hide the little curious smile that curls the corner of her lip. She wiggles her body on my knee and I put an arm over her back to keep her still.

"I couldn't help myself." I shrug.

I use my other hand to caress her full ass, massaging and squeezing it.

"Do you remember your safeword, Leora?"

"W-what?"

"Your safeword, say it to me," I say, needing her to understand the rules before I continue.

"Amaretto."

"Use it if you need me to stop, okay?" I reassure her.

"Okay."

My hand continues massaging her, trying to relax her. Just as she does, I raise my hand and land a slap on her left cheek, the *crack* echoing in the room together with Leora's gasps. She doesn't use the safeword, but I need to check in to see if she's still alright with it. "Do you want to use your safeword?"

She takes a few seconds, her eyes on me before she shakes her head. "No."

"Are you sure?"

She nods.

My hand lands two more slaps, moving between her left and right cheek, before my fingers find her even wetter than she was before. She's dripping wet, her need soaking my leg.

"You're liking your punishment, aren't you?" Her body tries to move against my fingers, but I hold her in place. She's not in control here—I am, and I decide how much pressure she can have.

I remove my fingers, and she blows out air. "Lucas, please."

"Please what, Leora?"

"Just stop teasing me."

"Do you want to use your safeword?"

"No." She huffs in frustration and I land three more slaps on her ass, leaving it red with my handprint. She hisses, but when my palm sooths her ass, she melts into me before I grab her waist and throw her back down on the bed.

I climb over her, hovering as her eyes meet mine. Her brown hair lays like a halo against the white sheets. Beautiful.

I bend down, dragging my teeth over her earlobe. "Tell me what you want, Leora."

"You know what I want," she says, breathlessly.

"Tell me," I insist, my gaze locked on her.

A nervous smile spreads across her lips before she hides her face under her hands.

"No. No hiding from me," I whisper, gently pulling her hands away, my need for her clear in my eyes.

"I—" she starts, but she stops herself, taking her lips between her teeth.

"Say it," I command.

"I want you," she finally confesses, her voice trembling with desire, "inside me."

Fuck.

Hearing her say those words stirs something deep within me, and I want that, too. I want it so bad. But not yet. I told her what I was going to do, and by the looks of her, she's ready to come again.

"If you want me inside you so badly, then I need you to come for me." My mouth finds her pussy again, and this time, I'm not gentle or slow. I devour her as if she's my last meal, needing her to come on my tongue right this second.

She grabs a handful of my hair as she presses herself tighter against my mouth, her whimpers coming faster.

"Now, Leora," I order as I wrap my arm around her thighs to keep her in place. I suck her into my mouth while pushing two fingers inside her, curling them to hit the right spot.

She comes with a scream, my name on her tongue and her arousal on mine.

I want more.

I *need* more.

She's the drug I never knew I craved, and now I'm addicted.

"That was . . . amazing." Her lips twitch and there's a slight blush on her face, as if she's embarrassed.

"That's two," I say as I climb back up to kiss her. When we pull apart, she licks her lips. The sight of her tasting herself lights an even bigger fire within me.

I look down on her, mesmerized by what I see. The light from the windows shines on her naked body. "You are the most beautiful being I've ever laid my eyes on."

"Condom. Get a condom, now." Her demanding tone spurs me on.

"So needy," I laugh at her impatience as I grab one from my nightstand and step out of my clothes before I roll the condom on. When I look back up, I find her staring. Not at me directly, but at my cock.

"Is something wrong?"

I can't help but smile at the look on her face. Her eyes are large and her mouth is slightly open. "You're huge."

I slowly climb back onto the bed, my gaze fixed on her. As I reach her side, my lips find her nose. "You can handle it."

Her eyes shimmer as she looks at me, and all I can think about is having them on mine when I fuck her.

I slowly spread her legs, rubbing my cock against her, coating it in her arousal.

Leora sighs deeply. "Lucas, stop playing with me."

She's so frustrated, and I love it. I answer with a laugh as I line myself up. "You want me that bad?"

Her hand strokes my cheek. "Yes."

"Yes, *what*?" I press.

Her hand leaves my cheek. Instead, she grabs my chin between her thumb and forefinger, her grip firm.

"Yes, please. Can you fuck me now?"

I grab a hold of her hips with both my hands as I press forward, slowly sinking into her. Her eyes close as we both groan together in harmony.

"Just like that, baby. Take it all." I bury myself fully inside. Her nails dig into my back, drawing a raw, animalistic growl from my throat.

She feels incredible—better than anything I've ever felt before. I try to be still, letting her get accustomed to me before I start moving, but *fuck*, it's like she was made for me—like we're perfectly molded for each other.

I should tell her that she's the best person I've ever been with. But at this moment, words defy me.

I wait for her to open her eyes, giving me an indication that she's ready. When those big green eyes meet mine, she smiles. It's then that I begin to move, fucking her into the bed as my eyes go to where we're joined. It's so hot, and the sounds of our bodies slamming together, mixed with her moans, will be tattooed in my brain forever. This girl's not getting away, not after this agreement is over, not ever.

"Fuck." I breathe, and she groans in response.

Her breasts bounce with each thrust and I take pleasure in every single second of it.

"I can feel you everywhere," Leora moans, her head tossed back as I start fucking her harder.

"And you'll feel me for days to come." My thrusts grow more intense and her breaths quicken. She lets out sweet whimpers, making my whole body shiver.

"That sound," I whisper against her neck. "I'd do anything to hear that sound every single day."

Leora throws her head back, showcasing the length of her neck and I take advantage of it, kissing and licking every part I can reach. When my teeth graze the sensitive part where the neck meets the shoulder, she shivers.

"If it's always like this, then please do," she utters in a breathy voice.

I grab a pillow and slide it under her hips. When I thrust into her again, I hit a different angle that she clearly enjoys, because she pulls me closer and drags her nails down my back.

"You're taking me so well. I'm so proud of you." Her walls squeeze at the praise. "Such a good girl, loving how I fuck you."

"Oh my god." She sighs.

"Not God, *Ya Amar*, only me."

I clamp down on her hips and continue at the same pace.

"Please, Lucas."

I find her eyes, and the look in them is feral. I reach down to circle her clit. "Again. Say my name again."

"Oh fuck, Lucas. I'm close."

I'm close too. I'm doing everything in my power not to come before her. The look on her face is filled with the same burning desire within me. I keep rubbing her clit as I thurst her into the matress. Her inner walls tighten, clutching on to my cock and I know she's right there.

"Come for me."

My mouth finds hers again, and we both inhale deeply, savoring the moment. Each breath she exhales becomes my own.

"Now, Leora," I demand.

Her whole body tenses as her eyes roll back. I've never seen anything so beautiful in my whole life. She comes with the most erotic scream I've ever heard, and her walls squeeze me so hard. Before I know it, I'm following her into oblivion, roaring her name. My whole body is on fire with my head tossed back, as I come harder than I've ever had before.

I sink down on her, breathing hard against her throat before I lay down next to her collecting her in my arms as we both calm our panting breaths.

Leora's eyes meet mine, her bottom lip caught between her teeth—a telltale sign of her nervousness that I've come to recognize.

There's a slight sheen to her forehead as she scrunches it. "Did you enjoy that?" Her question lingers in the air. Was she not in the same room with me? Did she not hear me roar her name like an animal when I came?

"Was I . . . was I good?" Her words trail off.

I hold her chin between my fingers, making her look at me again. "That was the best sex I've ever had. I don't think I'll ever get my fill of you."

"This is not how I expected the morning to go," she says with a chuckle against my lips, her finger going to my tattoos again.

"Me neither, but it's what I hoped would happen. I've been wanting this for so long."

Her finger circles the tattoo on my chest. "What does nineteen ninety five represent?" My heart drops for a second as I remember why I got the tattoo in the first place.

"It's the year my parents passed away."

She doesn't say anything for a moment, her touch lingering on the inked tribute to a painful chapter of my life. I can feel the weight of unspoken sympathy in her gaze.

"I'm sorry," she finally whispers, her eyes reflecting a mixture of understanding and compassion.

I nod, appreciating her silent support. "It was a long time ago. They would have loved you though."

"You think so?"

"I know so." She cuddles closer to me, and I press her tighter to my chest.

Her voice changes, and she brings up another topic. "Why didn't you take the chance in Paris? I practically threw myself at you." Her voice carries a tinge of embarrassment, and it makes me feel like the smallest person on earth. I handled that whole situation so poorly; I should have let her know how much I wanted her, instead of calling her my friend.

"Believe me, I wanted to, but I would never take advantage of you while you're drunk, Leora."

"You wouldn't have taken advantage of me. I wanted you," she says matter-of-factly

"I wanted you, too—sober."

She doesn't answer.

"I'm sorry, I should have handled it better," I say, and her fingers graze lightly over my skin in a reassuring gesture.

"And I'm sorry I lied to you."

Her apology hits home this time, even though there's still a kernel of disappointment somewhere deep inside the pit of my stomach. "All I want is to move forward. Are we okay?"

"We're more than good." She shifts her position, moving

around until she's on top of me. Her breasts are now on full display, and I sit up to kiss them.

"I have a question."

"Shoot," I say, curious about what's on her mind.

"What does '*Ya Amar*' mean?"

"It means that you're my moon." Because, at this moment, she is the light that guides me in the dark. My one true moon.

She smiles, seemingly happy with the answer as she bends down, her lips finding my neck. The warmth of her touch sends shivers down my spine as she leaves a trail of gentle kisses along my neck.

Her tongue finds my earlobe and I shudder. "Can I ask you something else?" she asks .

"Absolutely."

"Do you have any fantasies?"

"All my fantasies include you." My answer seems to have been the right one because she captures my lips in hers, kissing me infuriatingly slowly.

"You on top of me is the first one," I breathe against her lip, slapping her ass, holding her, while she grinds against my, now fully-awake, cock.

"You want more?" I ask her.

"I need more. I need *you.*"

LUCAS

After fucking her again in my bed, and then in the shower— my new favorite activity, I must add—we both got dressed and made our way to the office. This time we walked hand in hand, and it felt real. Like we're not putting up a front anymore. Her hand fits in mine perfectly, and that's where I want it to stay.

"Bonjour," Camille greets us with a smirk on her face.

"Bonjour," both Leora and I answer at the same time.

"Your uncle is waiting for you in your office."

I frown, what is he doing here? He's supposed to be resting. Liam called me two days ago and told me that he'd been very tired. Fluid has started to accumulate around his lungs and in his chest, which the doctors drained, but they told him to rest. Being in my office is not resting.

We walk into my office and I spot him rising on unsteady legs. His arms open, welcoming us, and we take turns greeting him.

"Hey, *Ammo, kifak lyom?*" I ask him, curious to know how he's feeling today.

"*Ahsan, ebni,*" he responds.

Leora's attention moves to me in question, and I translate. "He's feeling better."

Her hand gently envelops mine once more as we take a seat. I can sense uncle's watchful gaze, observing our every move. The corners of his mouth turn up, forming a gentle curious smile. "You two seem to be getting along."

I exchange a glance with Leora and she tries to hide her smile behind her hand. We finally are.

"As much as I love seeing you, is there a reason you took time to come down here when you should be resting?"

"Oh, I'll rest when I'm dead," he says like it's a joke, but it's not funny because according to the doctors, he will be soon.

"Don't look at me like that, I'm joking. I'm here because I wanted a change of environment, and seeing you always makes me happy."

A knock on the door, followed by Liam's voice, interrupts us.

"Look at that, the whole family is here," he says with a huge smile on his face. As tired as my uncle looks, seeing Liam brings a certain glow to him. He looks between us, his eyes starting to well up, and Leora catches on.

"How about I go and get us some coffee?" she suggests, leaning over and placing a gentle kiss on my cheek before turning to head out of the office.

"I guess the fake marriage has turned into a real one," Liam states, his comment taking me by surprise.

"Wait, how did you . . ." I begin, but Liam chuckles, cutting me off.

"Relax, Lucas. I may have been gone for a while, but I'm not oblivious. I know you, brother, and I've been observing the two of you," Liam says with a mischievous glint in his eye. "I also may have found a copy of your contract while I was helping Ammo with some paperwork after your so-called wedding."

I'm taken aback. "You've known for that long?"

He nods. "Yes."

"But you never said anything," I murmur quietly.

"Why would I?" Liam responds with a knowing smile. "I saw the way both of you looked at each other. It was real from the start. You two just didn't realize it."

His words wash over me, filling me with a warmth that I hadn't realized I'd been missing. The tension that's been gnawing at me for months seems to release, and a genuine laugh escapes my lips. It's been too long since I've shared a laugh like this with Liam.

"So the whole thing about me asking her to the charity dinner was just you trying to do what?" I ask him.

"It was me trying to urge you to do the right thing, which is to not let your pride get in the way of something I know is meant for you."

"You never cease to amaze me, brother," I tell him, getting up from my chair and walking over to him. I pull him into a tight hug, grateful for his understanding and support. I've missed this.

When we finally release each other, we both turn to look at our uncle, who's still seated in his chair.

His eyes glisten with unshed tears. We exchange a meaningful glance, realizing that this moment has touched not only us but also our Ammo, who's been on both ends of mine and Liam's rocky relationship.

"This is what I've been praying for," he says, his voice trembling with emotion, "that you two find your way back to each other's lives before I leave mine." His words resonate deeply within me. Detecting a hint of fear in his voice, a pang of regret washes over me for the months of estrangement between Liam and me. As the older brother, I should have been the one to bridge the gap, to set aside my ego and pride in favor of family. Instead, I allowed misunderstandings and hurt feelings to fester, driving a wedge between us. The realization that he had been silently praying for our reconciliation strikes me deep in the core.

Liam and I turn in unison and reach out to grab our uncle's hands.

His eyes, once filled with worry, now reflect relief and gratitude.

"And Lucas, when it comes to Leora, I always knew you two would find your way to each other. There's an Arabic proverb that fits you both perfectly: *In love, the heart always knows the way.*" The wrinkles around his eyes deepen, a knowing smile tugging at the corners of his mouth.

"Well, look at that. Am I barging in on family time?" The atmosphere in the room takes an abrupt shift as Michel Beaumont makes an unexpected entrance with Camille in tow. I exchange a quick, puzzled glance with Liam.

"Monsieur, I told you they were in a meeting," Camille huffs between breaths, clearly flustered by Michel's intrusion.

"Really? I thought you meant they're waiting for *my* meeting," Michel mocks.

"We don't have a meeting today," I state firmly, my distaste for Michel becoming more evident by the second.

"We don't? Well, since I made the effort to come down here, why don't we?" Michel's suggestion holds an air of arrogance.

"Of course, please come in and sit down," my uncle intervenes, attempting to diffuse the mounting tension.

I watch as he takes a seat. There's a subtle shift in his posture and a guarded look in his eyes. He's hiding something.

He directs his attention at me. "Let's cut to the chase. I don't think you're cut out to take over the hotels."

"I'm already aware of your opinion, Michel. But you're wrong, I'm more than capable of running this company."

"Michel, this is neither the time nor the place for such discussions," my uncle replies, his voice measured and firm.

But Michel doesn't seem inclined to back down. He leans forward, his eyes locking onto mine for a moment, and then he addresses my uncle directly. "I, on the other hand, have a good head for business. Just step down, appoint me as the new CEO, and we won't have to vote. I promise I'll keep Lucas and Liam in their current positions."

My uncle exchanges a glance with me, and we both know that Michel's proposition is far from genuine. Trusting him with the position would be a grave mistake, one that could jeopardize everything we've worked for.

"I appreciate your confidence in your abilities, Michel," my uncle says, maintaining his composed demeanor. "But the decision has already been made on my end, and I stick by it."

Michel's smirk turns into a snarl, his voice dripping with menace. "You have no idea what's at stake here. You will see this empire you're so proud of slip through your fingers. The vote will be just the beginning, and you'll be left with nothing."

I clench my fists, struggling to contain my anger. My uncle, however, remains remarkably composed.

"Michel, threats won't get you what you want. We'll face the vote, and the stakeholders will decide. But mark my words, as long as I'm alive, I'll never hand this company over to you."

Michel's tone takes on a more threatening and aggressive edge, his desperation to seize control of the company palpable. "Be careful, Antoine. We all know your time is ticking," he hisses, leaning even closer, his voice a venomous whisper. "I also know things that you and your dear nephew might not want people to know about."

Anger bubbles up inside me as Michel's threats become more intense. My patience wears thin, and I'm ready to take action.

"That's enough," I declare firmly, my voice trembling with restrained anger. "Leave my office, now."

My uncle doesn't say a word, but his stern expression mirrors my sentiments. Does Michel know about Leora and my agreement?

A cold shiver runs down my spine as his words hang in the air. Michel has always been willing to go to great lengths to achieve his goals, but it's taken a sinister turn.

Michel stands up, a small, taunting smirk on his face. "I think I'll repaint this office and make it more to my taste."

Liam steps forward. He's taller and broader than Michel, and his imposing presence makes Michel take a step back, a flicker of fear crossing his face. Liam's message is clear—Michel should think twice before taking any drastic actions.

Once Michel is out of the office, my uncle slumps into his

chair, an air of weariness about him. Concern laces my voice as I ask, "Are you okay?"

My uncle attempts to reassure me, but his words are cut short by a sudden fit of coughing. When he removes his hand from his mouth, it's stained with blood.

"I'm fine," he insists, trying to downplay the severity of the situation.

Liam, however, is less composed. Panic flashes across his face, and he interjects urgently, "We need to get you to the hospital. This isn't something to take lightly."

Despite his concern, my uncle rises from his chair. "I told you, I'm fine. Now let me be," he repeats firmly, his voice carrying a sense of stubborn determination. He begins to walk toward the exit, where he almost bumps into Leora, who has returned with coffee and desserts, a look of confusion on her face.

As my uncle walks past her, Liam calls after him, his voice tinged with concern and urgency, "*Ammo*, please, let us get you checked out. This is serious."

Leora's eyes widen in alarm as she listens to our exchange, and she sets down the tray.

My uncle raises his hand, signaling that he's not willing to entertain the idea of seeking medical attention. Liam and I exchange worried glances, but there's little we can do when our uncle is so insistent. We watch as he continues toward the exit, his steps steady but his face slightly pale.

Leora approaches us cautiously, her gaze fixed on my uncle's departing figure. "What happened?" she asks, her voice filled with genuine concern. We tell her everything, including my suspicions that Michel knows . . . everything.

As soon as we step foot in the elevator, Leora's anxiety skyrockets, as it always does. For someone so afraid, she has to be one of the most courageous people I know. To fight fear the way she does is remarkable. No matter what the fear is, conquering it takes strength and determination—two qualities Leora possesses.

However, sometimes a person needs a little push, and that's what I'm here for.

I don't try to start a conversation to take her mind off the moving elevator, like I usually do. I've attempted that a few times, and I think it's been working. But right now, I have another idea that I hope will help her associate better memories with elevator rides. It will also help me relax after the shit day we've had.

Her back is pressed up against the wall and I move closer to her—close enough that she has to tilt her head back. She watches my every move, unsure of what I'm doing, but as I raise my hand to press the red button on the control pad, her whole face changes.

"What are you doing?" But it's too late. The elevator stops with a sudden jolt, and I can see the panic in her expression but I quickly reassure her.

"Just trust me," I say, my voice calm and steady, even though I'm nervous. If this doesn't make her relax, I'll probably have caused more damage than good.

Her eyes are squeezed shut, and her chest is heaving with every breath she tries to take. "Lucas. Please, make it move again," she says in a low voice. "P-please."

I reach out and gently cup her face, making her focus on me. "I would never do anything to hurt you. We're going to create a new memory here," I explain. Her eyes snap open and lock on mine. "Something to replace the fear with something better. Call it cognitive behavioral therapy. Something you'll enjoy, okay?"

She swallows hard but nods, her trust in me evident, causing my own heart to beat faster. With the elevator at a standstill, I lean in and capture her lips in a soft kiss. At first, she's tense, but as the seconds tick by, she eases into the kiss, her body melting against mine.

Her arms find their way around my neck, pulling me closer—a silent plea for more. I respond by pressing her into the wall with a bit more urgency, allowing our bodies to meld together. A soft, melodious moan escapes from her lips, and I seize the opportunity to deepen our kiss. She allows my tongue to explore every part of her mouth, tasting her sweetness and hunger.

I move from her lips to her neck, savoring the taste of her skin. My lips find the sensitive spot, and I press gentle kisses there, eliciting a low moan from her.

Her fingers tangle in my hair, urging me up to find her mouth again in a fervent, hungry kiss. Her taste is addictive—I can't get enough of it, and I curse myself for not allowing this to happen sooner. I want to worship her every chance I get, to make her feel cherished and adored. Every sigh and moan that escapes her lips fuels my own need, driving me to seek more of her and to give her everything I have.

I break the kiss once more, my gaze locked on hers. The fear that flickered in her eyes a few minutes ago has vanished, replaced by a fiery desire. Her ragged breaths now rise and fall in rhythm with mine, the earlier elevator-induced anxiety completely forgotten. It seems my idea has been working, but I'm not done just yet. I'm still hungry.

"So, this is the medicine I've been needing?" she asks with a giggle, a rosy blush adorning her cheeks.

"You're so beautiful when you're flustered," I murmur, my lips hovering near her ear. "But we're far from finished."

A curious yet assertive smile dances across her lips as my hand trails down her hip to find the hem of her sweet dress. It has been driving me insane since we left the apartment.

"We can't," she whispers, her voice trembles even as her body leans into mine, telling a different story. Her hands grip my shirt, fingers clutching the fabric tightly. "Not here." Her breath is unsteady, even as her body betrays her.

I chuckle softly, my breath hot against her skin. "We absolutely can. Who's going to stop us?" I murmur, my fingers slipping under the fabric of her dress. Slowly, I trace her delicate, soft inner thigh and stop when my fingers brush against her underwear.

When I feel how wet she already is, I groan loudly and lean my forehead against hers. "You're killing me, Leora." She bites down on her lip, trying to stifle the moan that threatens to escape.

My good girl.

"I think it's you who's actually trying to kill me," she says into my lips as I lean down to capture them again.

I'm too hungry to be gentle right now. She gasps when I grab her underwear and rip them off, placing the ruined piece in my breast pocket. Then I kneel, my tone commanding, "This is what I want you to remember every time you step into an elevator." I don't wait for her to answer. Instead, I shove my face forward, devouring her as her moans sing symphonies that echo in the small space.

THIRTY-EIGHT

LEORA

I've made him watch both *Mamma Mia* movies today, one after the other, and now we're watching a third movie, which, to my surprise, he's never seen. It's a disgrace, but I'm doing my best to fix him.

"So you're telling me he dies because she's too lazy to move?" he asks, completely enthralled with the movie, his eyes fixed on the screen. I nod, not able to speak as tears run down my cheeks. The movie *Titanic* always makes me emotional and the end makes me cry every single time.

"That's complete bullshit. They both could fit on that door. She can't leave him freezing to death!" he exclaims, shaking his head in disbelief. I mean, he's right, if Rose had just scooted over a bit, Jack could have climbed up, and he'd never have died—and yes, that's the hill I'll die on.

I wipe away my tears and look at him with a mix of amusement and agreement. His brows are furrowed, his hand pointing toward the TV as if he's trying to tell Rose to scooch to the side.

I laugh a little bit at him. "You're so right, they would have fit. I wish they did, those two were soulmates. But hey, it's the age-old question that keeps everyone coming back to the movie."

Lucas chuckles, shaking his head. The dimple I love more

than anything on full display again. "Soulmates wouldn't let each other die without *trying* to save each other." His hand goes to my back and moves in a soothing motion before he murmurs, almost as if to himself, "I would have made room for you."

He must feel the way my heart starts to pound. It's almost as if it's trying to break out of my chest in an attempt to reach his.

I would have made room for him, too.

When the credits roll, exhaustion washes over me, and I let out a big yawn. Lucas looks at me, amusement twinkling in his eyes.

"Right, it's time for bed," he declares.

I nod in agreement. "It really is. It's been a long day, especially after Michel's visit." But I don't move; I snuggle against him even further and Lucas's arms wrap around me, my head resting against his chest. His heartbeat is a soothing rhythm against my ear.

Leaning in, our lips meet in a sweet kiss. The taste of something like home lingers as we pull away. I yawn again and he whispers, "Okay, Sleeping Beauty, let's go."

Lucas unwraps his arms from around me as we both get up, me walking towards my room and him behind me.

"Where do you think you're going?" he asks curiously.

"To sleep," I reply, confusion etching my face.

"Yeah? Well, you're not sleeping in there."

Confusion turns into surprise as I try to comprehend his words. "What do you mean?"

Determination surges within him, and he quickly closes the distance between us, wrapping his arms under my knees and effortlessly lifting me up. "From now on, you're sleeping in *our* room. There's no chance in hell I'm letting you sleep far away from me again."

A smile slowly spreads across my face as I wrap my arms around his neck, my excitement mirroring his. "I'd love that," I say, my voice filled with joy.

I WAKE up with his arms tightly wrapped around me; as if he's scared I'll run away. Which is something I would never do because being here, enraptured by the essence of him, feels like home.

It feels *right,* and it scares me.

Because the last time I felt happy, everything changed and I got stabbed in the back. However, it's different this time; it's as though my whole body knows it. It feels different with Lucas.

Yet, I can't help but worry about the reality that we've signed papers stating that this will end. These feelings have a deadline—a deadline I'm hoping we will extend.

"I can hear your thoughts brewing in there."

If I found his dark voice sexy before, it's nothing compared to the allure of his raspy morning voice whispering in my ear.

He releases his tight hold on me, and for a second I miss the heat, but it quickly comes back as he turns me to face him.

"Good morning, beautiful." Lucas presses me closer to his chest, sealing the moment with a sweet kiss on top of my head, eliciting a contented sigh from deep within me

"Morning." My answer is enough for him to lean back and grab my chin, forcing me to look him in the eyes.

"What's wrong?" Lucas asks with worry in his voice

"Nothing is wrong,"

"Leora?" Just him saying my name in that caring voice of his makes tears spring to my eyes. *What is wrong with me?*

His eyes search mine and for a second he looks confused. But then it morphs into some kind of fear before both of his hands go to my cheeks and one of his thumbs wipes away a single tear that escaped.

"Tell me so I can make it right." His words are low. There's so much emotion behind them and it makes more tears fall.

"I'm sorry," I whisper back, but he takes the apology the wrong way.

His eyes move frantically over my face while he slightly moves away to look at me. "Did I do something?" he asks, his voice a bit shaky.

"No, it's not you—"

In his stressed state, he interrupts me, "What did I do, Leora? I don't want to hurt you so please tell me what I did, because I'm the one who should be sorry for your tears."

This time, it's me who grabs his face, grounding him.

"You haven't done anything wrong. It's the opposite. You've done everything right and it scares me."

"What do you mean?"

"I'm happy. Everything with you feels right and it scares me so much because the last time I was happy, everything changed and it broke me into pieces. Pieces I've been slowly putting together again while being around you."

"What are you afraid will happen?"

"I'm afraid I'll break again, and this time, I won't have enough energy to put myself back together." I look him straight in the eyes, and his frantic gaze softens. He turns his head and kisses both of my palms.

"I won't break you, Leora. If I ever hurt you, I hope the ground opens up and swallows me whole." Lucas uses his hand to push away the hair that has fallen in front of my face. "I'm happy, too." His confession hits home. It's the words I've been wanting to hear for a while.

"You are?"

He leans down and kisses my nose. "Yes, you make me very happy, Leora Ayoub."

Not Leora Davis. Leora Ayoub.

It's the first time he's called me that.

He gave me his name.

THIRTY-NINE

LEORA

As the following days pass, we slip into a routine. The rhythm brings a comforting stability as each day is painted with shared laughs and intimate moments. There's a sense of security and belonging, like I've passed the point of no return with him.

He doesn't know it yet, but in a way, Lucas is healing everything broken inside of me, and I'm finally starting to feel like a whole person again.

Never had I thought that I would feel this way about him, or that he would feel anything other than annoyance against me. Ever since our argument, that led to us finally expressing what we felt, everything has been like a dream. It's like a switch has been turned on. With every tender gesture and every stolen glance, he shows me something I never thought possible. It's as though our connection runs deeper than words can express, like he's mending the pieces of my soul that were fractured long before he came into my life.

He has a way of making me feel cherished, seen, and valued. Not just for who I am in his eyes, but for who I am becoming with him by my side.

But will this last? Should I be happy in the moment and not think about the agreement and the ticking deadline?

I have so many questions. I wish I had my girls here; I need them to push me, to help me, and to tell me what to do. So I pick up my phone and text them.

ME

I miss you.

ADELINE

I miss you more, babe.

SOPHIE

I miss you too, hun.

How are you?

ADELINE

Yeah, how's it going with the husband?

Still annoying?

ME

Well, actually...

ADELINE

DID YOU SLEEP WITH HIM?

My phone immediately starts ringing and I laugh when I see Adeline and Sophies name pop up in a group call.

"Hello!" I answer with a smile.

"Spill it," Adeline quickly says, and I do. I tell them everything that's happened, starting with the events in Paris and how John showed up and Lucas found out. Then I tell them about our argument and how it finally pushed us to be together. I finish with my name on his lips: *Leora Ayoub.*

Nobody speaks for about ten seconds.

"I knew it. I knew this would turn into something more after I saw how he looked at you during the reception. I knew it was only a matter of time," Sophie says, and I can hear the smile in her voice.

"How did he look at me?"

This time Adeline speaks. "As if you were something conjured up by his dreams."

That's impossible. During the wedding, it seemed as though I was a burden he couldn't wait to get rid off.

"Have you fallen for him?" Sophie asks. I don't answer for a few heartbeats, and I think that is what gives the truth away. I know I have, but can't bear to say it out loud.

"Oh, *Habibti*," Adeline starts, her voice so soft it makes me shaky. "Have you told him?"

"No, not yet," I finally whisper. "I don't know how to. We still have the agreement. What if this is only until the one-year deadline hits us? Also, there's so much to do before the opening and his uncle is really sick. I don't want to add to his stress."

Both of them sigh, but seem to understand. "I understand, and you do it at your own pace, but from what I've heard, this man is completely in love with you. How can he not be? You are incredible Leora. When a person truly gets to know your heart, there's nothing not to love."

Adeline's words make my whole body warm. I'm so lucky to have the privilege to call them my best friends—I don't know what I would do without them.

"I love you," I tell them, because I really do.

"We love you too," Sophie replies before changing the subject. "Now, tell us the details. How big is he?"

I'm too shocked to answer immediately. I never thought Sophie would be the one to ask this question; I had expected it to come from Adeline.

Before I can answer, Adeline chimes in, urging me to answer the question which I do.

"Huge."

THE HOTEL OPENING is in three days and I have nothing to wear.

I've moved into his room, but I've kept some of my clothes in my old room, this way I have two wardrobes. I rummage through my wardrobe, filled with incredible items, yet nothing seems good enough for this event.

Lucas leans against the doorframe, his signature smirk playing on his lips. After I moved into his room, he helped me move my everyday clothes. I guess I should say, *our* room—he gets upset every time I use the word *"your."* We relocated his fancier suits to hang next to my dresses in the guest room, leaving us with two walk-in closets."

"I don't know what to wear," I grumble, my voice tinged with a mix of frustration and anxiety.

He chuckles softly, clearly amused by my panic. "Leora, you have more clothes than most people. I made sure of that myself. I'm sure you'll find something."

I huff, throwing a rejected dress onto the bed. "That's easy for you to say, Mr. I-Have-Everything-Under-Control."

"I don't have everything under control, didn't I tell you? Apparently, Michel convinced the whole board that the perfect time for the vote would be during the long awaited opening." I've never hated a man as much as I hate Michel.

Lucas has been telling me he's alright, and not stressed at all. But every time I catch a glimpse of him working, his knee is bouncing up and down and he's always fidgeting with something.

"How are you feeling about it?" I ask as Lucas pushes himself off the doorframe and strolls toward me.

"There's nothing I can do at this point. Whatever they decide, that is how it will be. I've done my best," Lucas says, but his words don't match the tension etched across his face.

I reach out and take Lucas's hand, pulling him closer. "Lucas, you've worked tirelessly for this. Your best is more than enough, and everyone knows it," I reassure him, trying to convey the strength and confidence I have in him through my touch.

His eyes meet mine, and I can see the doubt that still lingers. His shoulders, burdened with the weight of responsibility, slump slightly. "I just don't want to disappoint you."

I gently lift his chin with my finger, forcing him to look directly into my eyes. "You will never disappoint us. I'm more than proud of you, Lucas. We all are."

A warm, grateful smile spreads across his face, and he pulls me close. "While I can't do anything about their opinions of me," Lucas continues, his voice lighter now, " I can at least help you. I have something for you. In fact, I've had it for about a week now." His eyes sparkle with mischief.

My curiosity piqued, I stop my frantic search and turn to face him. "What are you talking about?"

He grins. "You'll see. Just wait here." He leaves the room, and I'm left to wonder what on earth he's up to.

A minute later, Lucas returns, holding three boxes. One is larger than the others. He sets them down on the bed and starts handing them to me, one at a time.

"Open," he urges.

I tear into the first small box and find a beautiful diamond necklace. This must have cost a fortune. My heart flutters, and I look up at him in surprise. Lucas nods. "That's for you to wear at the opening." He hands me the second of the smaller boxes and I open it, revealing a pair of elegant silver earrings that match the necklace perfectly.

"Lucas, these are stunning," I whisper, touched by his thoughtfulness. "But it's too much, I can't—"

"You can," he says matter-of-factly, and I must have a funny expression on my face because he chuckles again.

"Do you like them?"

"I love them."

"I'm glad, but we're not done yet." He gestures to the large box, and I eagerly lift the lid.

Inside, I find the most beautiful evening gown I've ever seen. It's a deep, blood red, with intricate lace detailing around the chest and a flowing, ethereal skirt that shimmers in the light. I'm rendered speechless by its beauty.

Lucas grins proudly. "You'll wear this," his voice soft and filled with affection. "You know what I think about you in red," he says, and I feel my face flush. I'm so overwhelmed with gratitude and love that I can't hold back my tears.

"Lucas, you didn't have to do all this."

He takes my hands in his and looks into my eyes. "I wanted to. I wanted to make sure you felt like the most beautiful woman in the world—exactly the way I see you."

I wrap my arms around him in a tight embrace, my heart bursting with what I can only describe as love. "You're amazing, Lucas."

He kisses the top of my head. "I try."

I sigh and press myself against him further, and he turns rigid for a second before he leans down and whispers in my ear, "After the opening, I'm going to take you back home and I'm going to rip that dress off of your body."

My breath hitches when he kisses my neck. "Then, I'll remove the lingerie you'll be wearing—using only my teeth—until the only thing you'll be wearing is the jewelry and your heels." He licks the shell of my ear and my breathing ceases.

"And then?" I ask with a shaky breath.

"Then, I'll—" His phone interrupts the moment, and when he looks at it, he swears under his breath. He angles the phone so I can see the name on the display, *Ammo Antoine*.

"I have to take this," he says as he leaves me standing in my room, all hot and bothered. But not before I got a good look at him; he was also all hot, bothered, and hard.

FORTY

LEORA

We did good—no, we did *great*.

As soon as I step out onto the rooftop terrace, my mind is blown. It's exactly how we planned it to be. String lights hang gracefully above, casting a soft, warm glow that dances in the evening breeze. Tables are adorned with fresh flowers and flickering candles, offering intimate nooks for conversation. Plush, cushioned seating arrangements invite guests to linger and savor the moment. The open sky above and the cityscape below make for a breathtaking view as the starlit sky enchants us.

But what makes me the most excited is the big wall that welcomes the guests as they step in. It's filled with a collage of framed photos of Antoine's life—a rich tapestry of memories starting from where he grew up in Lebanon, to him standing outside the entrance of his first hotel in France. The photos have already welcomed an audience and they all share smiles as they take it all in. I can't wait for him to see it.

All the stakeholders seem to be here as well, but I haven't spotted Antoine yet. I caught a glimpse of Milena and Michel a few minutes ago and, telling by the look they threw my way, both seem to still despise me. It doesn't matter though; the only thing I'm praying for right now is that all the stakeholders see how beautiful this new hotel is and know how much work Lucas has put into it. Everything he does, he does with passion. He loves these hotels, and he has so many amazing plans. I just hope I haven't ruined it for him. They have to let him and his uncle stay.

Lucas had to leave before me, and I haven't spotted him yet. I'm wearing the dress he got me, and it fits like a glove. It's the most beautiful dress I've ever worn and when I put on the necklace all I could visualize was Lucas's whispered promises and the curiosity of what he would do to me. My hand instinctively goes to the necklace and I smile to myself.

"There you are," a soft voice whispers in my ear, sending shivers down my whole body. I quickly turn around to find the most gorgeous man in front of me. "You look beautiful, Leora." It's hard to describe the way he looks at me, as though he wants to cherish me while still ripping my dress off and devouring me whole.

And I want both—more than anything.

He's wearing a black tuxedo with a bow tie that matches the color of my dress, and when he smiles at me, the confidence in his gaze and the subtle curve of his lips exude a captivating blend of power and masculine charm. My mouth almost falls open and I think I might be drooling. "You don't look so bad yourself. If there weren't so many people around, I think I would go for one of those fantasies of yours," I murmur as I throw my arms around his neck.

"Don't make promises you can't keep, *Ya Amar*." He kisses me softly. "Because I will be taking you up on that offer." Then he kisses me again, this time not as soft and when we break away he looks back towards the bar, and there's a hint of a smile on his lips. "Come, there's someone I would like you to meet." His hand grabs mine and he walks me toward a woman dressed in a black dress that reaches her knees. *Who is that?*

I wish I never found out, because when she turns around, my stomach drops.

"Agnes, what are you doing here?"

Her eyes widen in surprise. "Did you forget the invitation you sent me? You told me this was your way of apologizing for how you acted when you worked for Momentum Marketing. I couldn't say no to that or an all-expenses paid trip to France," Agnes says with a leering smile on her lips. I turn to find Lucas looking at me with a smile of his own. There's a knot forming in my stomach at the sight of her. I don't understand; why is she here? Why is she saying that I sent her an invitation asking to apologize? Because I didn't, and I wouldn't. I still can't wrap my head around the whole situation. I don't remember.

"Leora didn't invite you. *I* did. Not for Leora to apologize, but rather for you to apologize to her."

I turn to Lucas and his face is stone cold, anger brewing behind his eyes.

"Why would I do such a thing?" Agnes replies.

"I'm happy you asked." He takes his phone from his pocket and shoves it in her face. "If you take a look at this video, you'll see the papers that Leora misplaced are in the hands of *your* client."

Why is he showing her this? I experienced this embarrassment once, I don't need to do it again.

"But do you know what I found odd? If we rewind this video a little bit, we'll both see that it wasn't Leora who misplaced the papers." He pauses. "It was you."

Ice washes over my whole body.

It was *her*?

I watch, captivated, as Agnes stumbles to a table, holding on to a folder. In the background, people are cheering, and for a brief second, I see Mike and I walk by. We wave to her but she dismisses us.

A few heartbeats pass, and then she walks away, leaving the folder on the table.

The folder I supposedly left behind.

I don't know what to say or think. All this time, I've thought I made that mistake. All this time, I thought I was fired for a reason caused by me, even though I could have sworn it wasn't me. Now it all makes sense, why I didn't remember it. How would I, if it never happened? My mind continues to drift, if it was Agnes's fault, why would she fire me and make me believe I was in the wrong?

"I-I don't know," she stutters.

"You didn't think you'd get caught, did you? Now, listen carefully. Unless you want your entire world to unravel, you will personally reach out to every individual you've ever uttered a word about Leora to. Tell them it was all a colossal misunderstanding and that you mistakenly terminated the employment of the best damn worker you ever had." His eyes narrow, and a menacing smile plays on his lips as he leans toward Agnes. "Understand this: I won't allow anyone to tarnish my wife's name. Do you understand? Because if you don't, this video will find its way to every corner of my network, and you'll find yourself blacklisted from the marketing industry, and any other industry that doesn't involve flipping burgers."

Her face, once smug and alive, is now white as a ghost as she nods hysterically. She starts to turn to get away from us, but Lucas stops her and tsks. "Agnes, you forgot the most important part"—he nods his head toward me—"beg Leora for forgiveness."

She turns to me and speaks so low, I almost can't hear her. "I'm sorry, Leora."

"No, Agnes, I said *beg*. On your knees," Lucas commands.

On shaky legs, she bends down, her knees hitting the marble floor.

"Lucas, this isn't neces—"

"Now beg for forgiveness, Agnes," Lucas demands.

I look at him and what I see in front of me is shocking. His eyes are furious and hard; they would make even the strongest bend to his will. His back is completely straight, demanding respect, and that's what he'll receive. This is the powerful man I've seen glimpses of—the man who is destined to run an empire.

"I'm so sorry, Leora. What I did was wrong."

"Why did you do it?" I whisper in response to the humiliating scene.

"I panicked when I found out I misplaced the papers and when it came out to the board that a customer had found the papers, I knew they would fire me on the spot if they ever found out, so I chose someone else."

"Why me?" I whisper.

"I worked twice as hard as you, yet no one ever praised me as they praised you. No one ever liked me the way they liked you. I never thought the board would actually fire you. I thought they would discipline you a bit and maybe give me some of your accounts, but they wanted you gone. But at least it wasn't me, because I knew you'd find another job. I mean, look at you now."

That fuels a fire within in.

"But you continued speaking ill of me to anyone who would listen and—" I cut myself off, my voice rising with anger. "You sabotaged my career. You let me believe I made a terrible mistake, and then you proceeded to destroy my reputation. And all because you were jealous? Because you thought I got praise that you deserved? You chose to ruin my life!"

I take a deep breath, struggling to contain the fury building within me. "And you think it's okay? That I should thank you? No, Agnes. I don't owe you any gratitude. I've worked hard for everything I have, and you tried to take it away from me."

"I know what I did was wrong, Leora. I messed up, and I regret it. But you have to understand the pressure I was under."

"It doesn't matter, it doesn't justify your actions. But for what it's worth, I know what I deserve now." I grab Lucas's arm and he puts his hand over mine.

"That's all, Agnes. You're dismissed," he says before seizing my waist, effortlessly spinning me around and locking his intense gaze with mine. He leans in and kisses me right there, in front of Agnes, who remains on her knees, and our assembled guests. He kisses me with such passion and pride, that I almost lose my footing, but I won't because the hold he has on me is as strong as the tide, pulling me into his embrace with an irresistible force.

When we break away, his eyes look at me with animalistic need and I'm sure mine mirror his.

"Do you still want to recreate one of my fantasies, Leora?" he whispers and I nod, because I do. I want to recreate every single one of them.

"Then let's go." Without another word, he entwines his fingers with mine, and suddenly, we're in motion, leaving Agnes and the past behind. He strides purposefully, and I can barely keep up, my laughter bubbling out like the giddiness of a schoolgirl. We descend two flights of stairs in a hurried descent, and as we reach the bottom, he swiftly enters a code to unlock a door. It swings open to reveal what appears to be a small office space. He leads the way into a room, gently pushing me inside before closing the door behind us. My eyes take in the space before me. There's an imposing desk with an elegant chair positioned in front of it. Behind the desk, a floor-to-ceiling glass wall offers a captivating view.

"You're breathtaking," he murmurs, his eyes tracing every curve as he circles me like a wolf stalking its prey. He takes a seat on the desk, his eyes locked onto mine, his gaze filled with a hunger that matches my own.

"I love that dress on you."

"Thank you," I respond, feeling a rush of warmth flooding my cheeks.

"Take it off." His voice drops to a husky whisper, and a thrill of anticipation immediately rushes through my body.

I can see the desire in his eyes, feel it in the way he watches me. I want him, too, but I can't resist the urge to be a little bold—to try something new.

I take a step closer, the heat between us almost unbearable. My fingers move to the zipper of my dress, slowly dragging it down as I maintain eye contact with him. The anticipation grows with each inch of exposed skin, and I can see his restraint slipping away.

But I pause, the dress hanging off my shoulders, revealing more of my body yet still leaving much to the imagination. His jaw clenches, and I can tell he's struggling to contain himself.

"What's the matter, Lucas?" I tease, my voice dripping with what I hope is seduction. "Didn't you say you'd want to rip this dress off my body?"

His eyes burn as he watches me, his breath coming faster. I revel in the control I have over him in this moment, a heady sensation that sends shivers down my spine.

I let the dress slide down my body, letting it pool at my feet, and I stand before him in a set of delicate lingerie that matches the fiery passion in his gaze. The room seems to crackle with electricity as I take slow, deliberate steps toward him.

His hands reach out to touch me, but I dance just out of his reach, enjoying the game we're playing. I want to savor this moment, to make him ache for me even more.

"Come here," he growls, his restraint finally giving way to raw desire. He grabs my waist and pulls me to him, crashing his lips against mine in a searing kiss. The hunger and urgency between us ignite into a blazing fire. Our hands and lips are everywhere, exploring, igniting, and stoking the flames of our desire. The taste of his lips, the feel of his hands on my skin, it's all I've ever yearned for.

He turns us around and sits me down on the desk, a piece of furniture meant for work now transformed into an altar of passion. I arch my back, inviting him closer, and he follows. My fingers reach for his belt and I swiftly undo it, the anticipation building with each passing second. As I slowly unzip his pants, his breath hitches, and he watches me with dark, hungry eyes. With deliberate slowness, I slide his pants down, revealing his desire straining against the fabric of his boxers. I take my time, savoring the moment, and when I finally free him, he lets out a low groan of pleasure, as if he were in pain before. I grab him, and slowly move my hand up and down, my thumb brushing gently over the sensitive tip, eliciting another deep moan from him.

He's completely at my mercy, and it's driving him wild. I continue my exploration, my touch becoming bolder and more demanding. Every stroke and caress is a symphony of pleasure that we create together.

He arches his back, his hands gripping the edge of the desk as he leans against me, his knuckles turning white. I want him to know just how much I crave him. "I want to taste you," I whisper. His eyes widen in surprise.

His breath hitches at my words, lust burning even hotter in his eyes, but he doesn't move away so I can climb down. "Please," I respond, my voice filled with need. He moves, turning so he's leaning against the desk and I smile, a wicked gleam in my eye, my lips trailing a path of fire along his abdomen as I make my way down to the floor. His eagerness is tangible as he watches my every move.

With tantalizing slowness, I reach his throbbing cock, and I give him what he craves. My lips, soft and warm, meet his heated skin, and I take him into my mouth, indulging in his taste and the way he trembles beneath my touch. I moan as I suck and lick the drop of precum that's leaking from him.

His fingers thread through my hair, a silent encouragement as I continue to pleasure him. The room is filled with the intoxicating sounds of his moans, urging me on.

The sound of a man being comfortable enough to moan and actually make sounds might be the hottest thing ever, and I can feel how it's making me even wetter, ruining the expensive under-wear I'm wearing.

"If you don't stop, I'm going to come."

Those words compel me to intensify my action even further, but his hand in my hair pulls me away from him. I almost protest when he drags me up so I'm standing leaning against him. "The only place I'm coming is inside of you."

Suddenly, I'm bent over the desk and he's positioned behind

me, my hair wrapped around his fist. With skillful fingers, he teases me, making my breath hitch and my heart race.

Every touch, every caress, sends electric currents of pleasure through my body, and I can't help but press against him in a silent plea. I want him, need him, in ways words can't express.

He kisses his way to my ear, "I want to be inside you, but–"

"But nothing. I need you now."

"I don't have a condom."

Fuck, we haven't had this conversation, but I don't care if we use a condom or not.

"I'm clean and I'm on the pill," I answer, my voice needy.

"I'm clean, too."

I push my ass a little higher. "Then we don't need a condom."

His grip on my hair tightens, and I can feel his breath on my skin, sending shivers down my spine. His fingers, still slick with my desire, find their way to his mouth as he licks them clean, and I gasp at the vulgar scene.

"You're perfect," he murmurs, his voice husky with need. "Always so ready for me, and so damn sweet." His words wash over me like a caress before his fingers move my underwear to the side, and I sense him against my core. A low, guttural moan escapes my lips as his cock enters me inch by glorious inch. The sensation is electrifying, like a thousand stars igniting in the night sky at the same time.

He moves with primal intensity, each thrust taking us higher and higher, pushing me into the desk. I can feel the tension coiling within me, ready to explode. I lose myself in the sensation of him, in the way he moves, in the delicious friction of our bodies meeting again and again. The room is filled with the sound of our ragged breaths and the slapping of skin against skin. His hands move to my hips as his thrusts grow more ferocious.

"You're mine," he says as if he's staking a claim, his voice low and possessive. As if he didn't already know he'd ruined me for all other men. I turn my head to watch him and I'm met with his dark eyes boring into mine. It's a declaration of ownership, but not in a way that diminishes me. Instead, it's a promise, a reassurance that, in his arms, I'll always be cherished and protected.

"And you're mine," I reply, my voice filled with the same conviction.

He pulls out of me growling, before he turns me around to lift me up, as he enters me again. Lucas leans in, capturing my lips as he keeps pounding into me.

He sits me down on the desk, so one of his hands can leave my ass before he reaches down between us. His two fingers find my clit, and I don't need much; I'm so close to coming.

"Leora," he breathes against my lips, and I know he's close too

In a moment of pure ecstasy, we shatter together, our bodies convulsing in pleasure.

As we come down from the heights of passion, he holds me close, his strong arms wrapped around me, creating a cocoon of warmth and home. My head rests against his chest, and I can hear the steady rhythm of his heart.

And then he breaks the silence with words that send a jolt of shock through me, making me panic. "I want us to end the agreement."

I try to pull away to create distance, but Lucas doesn't let me go. His grip tightens, and he holds me firmly against him, as if afraid that I might slip away. Then he speaks, his voice gentle yet resolute, "I don't want to have an end date with you."

I freeze, my heart pounding in my chest. I turn to look at him, my eyes searching for any sign that he might be joking or playing with my emotions. But all I find in his gaze is sincerity and vulnerability.

"Why?" I manage to whisper, my voice trembling.

He smiles a soft, tender smile that makes my heart ache with longing. "Because you make me feel alive, Leora," he says, his voice filled with emotion. "You make me happier than I've ever been. It's as though you brought color into my gray life."

His words wash over me like a warm embrace, and I feel tears welling up in my eyes. In that moment, I truly believe that what we have is real. He's not just a passing chapter in my life; he's become a part of my story.

"I think I'm falling in love with you," I blurt out the words that have been haunting me for a long time, not expecting a response.

"I'm falling in love with you, too."

FORTY-ONE

LUCAS

"Where the hell have you been?" Liam spots us as soon as we sneak back to the party—apparently, we're not discreet at all. "And why does your hair look like that?" he continues, and then he peeks at Leora. "You too? Why is it all tousled? It almost looks like you've just—" He laughs but when he notices the red hue creeping up Leora's neck, understanding settles in and he looks back at me.

"Really? You just had to sneak away like two horny teenagers this evening?"

Leora is biting her lip, holding back laughter while her face is red as a tomato and I just shrug. "Stop acting jealous. When and what we do is none of your business, brother. Now, where's *Ammo*?"

"He came a few minutes ago. He's by the pictures. But please fix your hair before you go up to him. He's already stressed enough, he doesn't have to look at your sex-hair."

I rake a hand through my hair, trying to smooth back the locks and Leora does the same, combing her fingers through her beautiful waves that were wrapped around my fist a few minutes ago.

The way she took control just now might have been the sexiest thing I've ever seen. Little did I know that beneath her poised exterior, a fiery vixen resided. Seeing her confident and bold like that would have brought me to my knees if she hadn't asked to taste me first, and what a taste it was.

I look at her, and when our eyes meet, there's a particular gleam in them that makes me sure she's thinking the same thing as me.

"Do you want me to hold your hand and take you to him?" Liam says with a mocking tone and I just shake my head at the smugness on his face.

"Let's go." My hand reaches for Leora and we walk to meet my uncle standing in front of Leora's picture wall. I haven't seen it yet. She showed me some of the photos she found when she was planning this whole thing but seeing this live is something completely different. Seeing my uncle's eyes light up with gratefulness and nostalgia as he gazes at the pictures—it's as if a bridge between the past and present has been built right here in this room.

He feels our presence and turns around, moving slower than he usually does. He greets us both and then he turns to Leora, a tear glistening in his eye. "You have given me a gift beyond measure, my dear. To see these memories come to life again, to feel their warmth once more. I cannot thank you enough."

Leora's smile mirrors the mistiness in her eyes. "It was an honor, Antoine. These memories deserve to be cherished."

We all continue to gaze at the photos as he points to them, sharing stories of his old friends and the little village where he grew up. When he reaches a particular photo, he pauses, his voice quivering with emotion. It's a picture that I've come to know well, but today, it takes on a new significance as I see it through his eyes.

"That's me and . . ." Antoine pauses, his voice nearly breaking.

His eyes linger on the image, and I gently complete his sentence, "You and Mum."

A wistful sigh escapes his lips, and he nods, the tears welling up but not spilling over.

"I miss her."

"I miss her, too," I reply softly, my own emotions bubbling to the surface.

Leora leans into me, squeezing my hand. "She's beautiful."

My uncle smiles. "She was, indeed."

He clears his throat, "Lucas, I want to talk to you before the—"

"Antoine," Michel greets, his tone lacking genuine warmth. My uncle is interrupted and the tranquility is shattered by Michel, accompanied by Melina. She walks up to us with an air of entitlement, and her disruptive entrance draws our attention.

He responds politely, although his face remains devoid of emotion, "Michel."

"You look tired. Are you sure you're up for this tonight?" I can feel a nerve starting to twitch in my jaw, almost making me lash out at Michel. I'm still not over how he treated Leora during the brunch, and one misstep from him might just earn him a bruise or two. Which will not bode well for the meeting we'll be having tonight.

Tonight is the night when the crucial vote takes place, determining whether I'll take over after my uncle or if they'll elect someone else to fill the seat. My palms are clammy as I glance around the terrace at the faces of the stakeholders—they hold our future in their hands. The anticipation hangs heavily in the air, and I can't help but feel a nervous knot tightening in my stomach. From my end, I truly believe they've been happy with how I've taken care of the company by my uncle's side. I've encouraged many changes and I was the reason for us starting to branch out, well, outside of Europe. It should be enough for them to see the potential in me. If they don't, I'm not sure I'll know what to do.

Leora has been a sweetheart this past week, she seems even more nervous than I am. She's been acting in the most endearing ways, trying to alleviate my own anxiety, though her own nerves were palpable beneath her composed exterior. She'd surprise me with my breakfast in bed and by leaving small notes all over the apartment. With her I can be honest, and I can tell her about the fear I have of losing, but here, in front of my uncle and Michel, I can't afford to show weakness. Not when the future of the company, my uncle's legacy, and my own destiny hang in the air. I know Michel has never liked us but I'm afraid he's used his poisonous tongue to get the other stakeholders on his side.

"Don't you worry about me. I'm feeling great," he answers.

"Dad, can we go now?" Milena complains, impatient as always. "This place is so boring."

"I'll see you soon gentlemen," Michel says before they both walk away.

I SIT in a stately conference room, the floor-to-ceiling windows offering a view of the city's skyline. The room exudes formality, with dark mahogany furniture and plush leather chairs surrounding a long, polished wooden table. Crystal chandeliers hang from above, casting a warm, golden glow.

At the head of the table, Antoine sits, looking composed but bearing the marks of his declining health. To his left, my brother Liam, and to his right, myself.

Liam can't help but fidget subtly in his seat, his nerves betraying him. I glance around, my eyes meeting Michel's. He sits among the other six stakeholders, a sly smile playing on his lips. His gaze locks onto mine, and he raises a taunting eyebrow at me. The other stakeholders maintain a stoic demeanor, fully aware of the gravity of this meeting.

Antoine calls the meeting to order, his voice firm but carrying a hint of strain. As the discussions commence, I can't shake the feeling that Michel is plotting something, and it keeps me on edge throughout the proceedings.

When it's Michel's turn to speak, he stands up. "We all know this meeting was called upon by me. As we're all aware, our long-time friend Antoine is sick, and his health has been deteriorating." There's a hidden agenda lurking behind his carefully chosen words and I grip the edge of my chair, my knuckles turning white.

"As we face this challenging situation," Michel continues, "we must consider the future of this business. It's clear that decisions need to be made, and I believe it's time for us to plan for a smooth transition. Perhaps it's time for new leadership." My heart races as I watch him manipulate the situation.

Liam leans over and whispers to me, "Stay calm, Lucas. We expected this."

Antoine addresses the room, his voice carrying the weight of years of experience and dedication. "I appreciate Michel's concern for the well-being of the company, but rest assured, I have a succession plan in place. Lucas will take over and the business will continue to thrive under his leadership."

Michel's smile widens, and it's clear he's ready to challenge whatever plan Antoine has set in motion.

"You mean the man who pretended to marry a girl to fool us all?" Michel's voice drips with mockery. I try to maintain composure because Michel can't know about me and Leora. He can't have any proof, no one will believe him.

"Enough," Gérard Moreau speaks up this time, his tone firm and commanding. "This is neither the time nor the place for personal vendettas."

"What do you mean by pretend?" Louis Grimaldi asks. He's the oldest and probably the most old-fashioned of all people involved today so I'm not surprised he took Michel's bait.

"I happened to have the incrementing agreement, signed by both Mr. Ayoub and Miss Davis. Filled with different kinds of conditions and a sum she would be paid at the end. If that doesn't speak of both their character, I don't know what would. Is that the man you want to handle the hotels and your investments?" He holds up our agreement in his hands, with a smirk on his lips.

The room spins as Michel's words cut through the air, and a

chilling panic takes hold of me. *How the hell did he get a hold of those papers?*

I glance around the room, meeting the eyes of the people who have the choice to change my life today. They now wear expressions ranging from shock to skepticism. Their trust in me hangs by a thread, and I can feel it slipping away with every passing second.

My mind races, contemplating the repercussions. This revelation not only jeopardizes my chances of taking over, but it also has the potential to cast a dark shadow over my family, over Liam. We all knew there was a risk of them not choosing me, but never about them finding out about the agreement with Leora.

Leora. The woman I've come to love, whose name is now associated with a scandal that threatens to tarnish her reputation. There would be no fixing it; these people would speak to everyone they know, and word would travel. That can't happen. She's my wife. No matter how the marriage started, she's my wife now, and it will remain that way.

"It's Mrs. Ayoub," I interject, unable to remain silent any longer.

"Excuse me?" Michel responds, feigning ignorance.

"I said it's *Mrs. Ayoub*. Not Miss Davis," I assert firmly. "I've told you this before, and this will be the last time, but you don't speak about my wife, Michel. Not now, not ever. Do you understand me?"

"Is she truly your wife if you had to find her on the streets just to fulfill your desperate, selfish needs to uphold a clause?"

I stand up quickly and move toward him and Liam follows me. "Did you not hear what I just said?"

"Your wife is—"

"I would be very careful how you finish that sentence, Michel," Liam says in a low, threatening tone.

"Is it true, Lucas?" Estelle Lavigne's question pierces through the room, her eyes searching mine for an honest answer. I meet her gaze, recognizing the genuine concern etched on her face. In this sea of scrutiny, she stands out as one of the few stakeholders who genuinely cares.

She was always there, a constant presence as I grew up, a witness to my journey. Now, her inquiry demands a truth that could shape, not only the company's future, but also the perception of my character.

"Yes, it's true. Both him and that wife of his are liars." Michel speaks up again and I have to stop myself from grabbing on to his collar.

"Leora *is* my wife," I declare firmly. "It doesn't matter how she became my wife, just that she is and will stay so." I run my hand through my hair, frustration filling me. "You all forced me into this."

Louis' stern voice echoes through the room, "Your actions are set on your shoulders, son. There's no room for blaming others."

I meet his gaze, acknowledging the weight of his words. The responsibility for my choices rests squarely on me, and no amount of justification can change that.

"That clause shouldn't even be there. Haven't I proven to you what I'm capable of?" I retort, frustration seeping into my voice. The achievements and dedication I've demonstrated seem to fade in the face of this traditional constraint.

"It's tradition," Michel interjects.

"But traditions can evolve, can't they?" I challenge, attempting to plant a seed of doubt in their adherence to the old ways. Michel's smirk persists, but there's a flicker of doubt in his eyes.

"It's true that circumstances led to a unique marriage arrangement," I begin, addressing the elephant in the room head-on. "But let me be clear, Leora is not just a means to an end. She's my wife, and I care deeply for her. The agreement is a part of a complex situation that doesn't define the entirety of our relationship. But that shouldn't matter to you. My uncle has taught me everything he knows and I'm certain I can continue on in his footsteps."

Liam stands by my side, a silent pillar of support, and I sense his unspoken determination. The stakeholders remain divided, some still skeptical, while others seem swayed by my sincerity.

Estelle, with a thoughtful expression, speaks up again, "In matters of the heart, perhaps we should focus on the commitment. After all, it's not unheard of for marriages to begin under unconventional circumstances."

Michel attempts to interject again, but Gérard, with a raised hand, silences him. "We're all aware of the clause, and from where I'm standing, Lucas has followed it. Now, let us proceed with the vote. This meeting is not the forum to pass judgment on personal matters. We are here to decide the future of the company." He takes a break and looks Michel in the eyes. "Lucas has consistently demonstrated his capabilities in his role, the hotel we're sitting in today is open because of him. He's the reason we're planning to venture into the United States, with not one, but three, hotels. One set to open its doors in New York in three years. Antoine has chosen him as his successor and it's our job to accept it or not. So let me start . . . I accept."

Gérard's words offer some relief. His support reminds me that there are people in the room who recognize the depth of my commitment to the company and my integrity. While it's true that Leora and I didn't start off on the most honest footing, we couldn't have predicted how our relationship would evolve, and ultimately strengthen our resolve. I'd make the same choices again if it meant keeping Michel away from our company and Leora in my life. I don't regret it and never will.

Michel leans back in his chair, his sneer fading into a scowl. "I do not accept."

My eyes travel to Estelle, and the look on her face is warm when she speaks, "I accept."

Then it's Louis's turn, "I do not accept."

Two, on our side

Two against us.

Three votes left.

FORTY-TWO

LUCAS

My search for Leora begins almost instinctively. I need her by my side, now more than ever. As I exit the room, she suddenly appears, rushing towards me with open arms. Leora wraps herself around me, her arms secure around my waist. It's a welcome embrace, and I hold her just as fiercely, feeling the warmth of her presence wash over me. When she lets go, I glance around. Gérard and Estelle walk by with warm smiles, acknowledging us. Their support is comforting. Michel, however, pushes his way through the crowd, his face contorted in a scowl. Without a word, he grabs Milena and forcefully leads her away. Milena's bewildered expression adds to Leora's confusion.

Her worried voice breaks through the chaos. "What happened in there, Lucas?" Her eyes are filled with concern, and there's unease in her tone.

I let out a sigh, my fingers running through my hair. "Will you stay even if the news is bad?" I ask, my voice heavy with insecurities. I can't help it, Leora is everything. She's everything I've been missing and everything I need. How I've lived thirty-four years without her, I don't know. But now that I have her, I'm never letting her go. She's the only woman who's made me think about having my own family—the only woman I would want as the mother of my children.

She hugs me again while she leans her head against my chest. "Of course I'll stay with you. I just want you."

I kiss the top of her head. "Good, because we won."

"What?" She looks up at me, tears forming in her eyes. "They voted for you?"

I smile at her, cupping her face gently with my hands. "Yes, they did. Gérard Moreau and some others spoke up for me, and Michel's attempts to tarnish us backfired. We're in the clear, Leora. Antoine's plan worked."

In the end, five out of the seven stakeholders accepted me as the successor, and after Michel's actions, I doubt he'll stay with us for long. This might have been the last straw. Many have been displeased with him for the past years, and now there might be enough people to collectively vote him out. Louis, on the other hand, will soon forget about this, as he enjoys making money, and with my future plans, he will.

Leora wraps her arms around me once more, tears of joy replacing the worry in her eyes.

"This is all I wanted," Antoine says, and we both shift to look at the smile on his face. His eyes glisten with unshed tears and I go to hug him tightly before I move to hug Liam.

But when I look back at my uncle, his expression has transformed. It's no longer the prideful smile I just witnessed; instead, it's a serene and content one that radiates profound fulfillment. His eyes convey a depth of gratitude and love that strikes a chord deep within me. Before I can fully comprehend the moment, time seems to accelerate, and with a sudden thud, he collapses to the ground.

"*Ammo*," Liam and I scream as we rush to his side, panic plastered on all of our faces.

"Call 112!" I urgently shout, and Leora springs into action, swiftly dialing the emergency number before following us to the ground with remarkable speed.

"He's going to be okay," she whispers, her voice a soothing melody in the midst of the frantic symphony surrounding us. Yet, her eyes betray a shared fear, a reflection of the uncertainty that hangs in the air.

"It's okay. I'm ready." My uncle's voice is low and we bend down to hear him better, but he doesn't speak again. His eyes flutter shut, and his breathing worsens, getting more labored. Every second feels like an eternity as we await assistance.

"Where's the damn ambulance?" The pain in Liam's voice reverberates in my own chest. As if on cue, the paramedics rush towards us, pushing us all to the side so they can get to work. Leora takes my hand in hers, tears streaming down her face. I can't seem to understand the severity of the situation; I'm numb. I'm scared, and the stabbing panic in my chest is increasing, but I can't allow it. Because he's going to get better. He must get better. He can't leave us.

He can't leave me.

"His lungs have accumulated a lot of fluid, a condition known as pleural effusion," Dr. Rousseau explains, her tone measured. "The cancer has invaded the pleura, causing inflammation and disrupting the normal fluid balance. This led to the excessive buildup of fluid in the pleural space surrounding the lungs. As a result, his respiratory function was compromised, and he collapsed."

Leora's soft voice wavers as she asks, "Will he get better?"

The doctor takes a deep breath before continuing, her eyes conveying a mixture of empathy and sorrow. "I'm sorry," she says gently, "but his cancer has spread extensively. At this stage, the prognosis is not favorable, and we won't be able to cure it. Our focus now is on providing the best possible care to manage his symptoms and make him as comfortable as we can during this time."

My mind races with "what-ifs" and "if-onlys," tormenting me with the possibility that I might have altered the course of events. Why didn't he tell us? Why didn't we push for more answers? The waves of guilt crash over me, each one carrying the weight of missed opportunities.

Leora's hand on mine provides a small comfort, but the guilt gnaws at the edges of my consciousness. The doctor's words echo in my mind, and I can't escape the haunting thought that I might have let him down.

"Can we see him?" Liam asks.

"He's sleeping at the moment, but you can go in," the doctor replies, her voice gentle.

The door creaks softly as Liam pushes it open, revealing the dimly lit room where our uncle lies motionless. The rhythmic beeping of machines is the only sound that breaks the heavy silence. I follow Liam, my steps cautious, as we enter the room. Liam approaches the bed, looking down at our uncle, who appears more fragile than ever beneath the pale hospital lights.

A soft sigh leaves Liam's lips as he whispers, "Hi *Ammo*," his voice barely audible. He turns to me, unshed tears glimmering in his eyes.

"What if he never wakes up, Lucas? What if—" He breaks. Tears stream down his eyes and I immediately wrap him in my arms, cradling his head to my shoulder. The same questions are on repeat in my head, but for Liam, I have to be strong. I can't break too.

"Lucas, Liam," Uncle's weak but genuine smile reaches us, as he speaks. "You boys, you've been a gift to me."

Tears brim in my own eyes, but I blink them away, "You'll be alright," I soothe, my voice cracking with emotion as I sit beside him. Liam joins me, and together, we encircle him with our presence.

I watch, a knot forming in my stomach, as our uncle gathers his strength to speak. His eyes, though tired, convey so much love. "Promise me that you'll take care of each other."

Liam and I exchange a glance. "We promise, *Ammo*," Liam chokes out. I nod in agreement, my own voice catching in my throat. He tries to smile in response, but a cough interrupts, leaving some blood stains on his lips. Liam's expression shifts from tentative hope to concern as he glances at me.

"Easy, *Ammo*," Liam says softly, his voice a comforting murmur. "Don't strain yourself."

His gaze locks onto mine, and he musters a frail but affectionate smile.

Suddenly, the machines start beeping, interrupting the delicate exchange. I squeeze Uncle's hand, desperately hoping for a sign that he's still with us.

Liam's eyes widen, panic flashing across his face as he looks at me, searching for reassurance. The room seems to close in on us, and the air grows thicker with the weight of uncertainty.

Liam releases his hand and rushes toward the door, yelling for assistance from the medical staff waiting outside.

I stand unwavering by Uncle's side, my heart thundering in my chest. "Not yet. *Ma tetrekna, Ammo, bisharafak, ma tetrekna.*" I beg him not to leave us, to stay with us a little longer. I feel like the little boy who was pleading for his parents to stay, to not leave him alone. There's desperation in my voice, a fear of losing the man who has been a pillar of strength and love in our lives.

The room falls into an unsettling hush as the medical team swarms around my uncle, desperately urging Liam and me to clear out. But their words are lost in the chaos. I can't hear them; there's a humming in my ears that seems to intensify for every second that passes. My eyes are only glued on my uncle, watching as he struggles to stay awake.

Resisting the push to leave, a hand clamps onto my arm, yanking me away from the room.

The corridor offers no refuge. It's sterile, cold, and the antiseptic smell now cuts through me. Leora runs up to me immediately, her eyes scanning my face, concern etched on her features. Yet, her words dissolve into the turbulence in my mind.

FORTY-THREE

LUCAS

"You haven't said a word since we left the funeral. Please say something, anything. What can I do?" Leora's voice pierces through the heavy silence that's settled between us.

The funeral was a testament to the impact my uncle had on people's lives. Friends from all corners of the world had come to pay their respect. The church echoed with stories of his adventure, the laughter he'd brought to people and their shared memories.

Not an eye was dry. It was a beautiful goodbye, a celebration of a life well-lived, and a reminder that he'll always be with us. As empty as I feel right now, at least I know I've been loved by him my whole life, and it will continue with Leora.

The dim, cold lighting of the parking garage casts eerie shadows on our faces. I turn my gaze to her, and her red, puffy eyes mirror the grief that weighs down on my chest like a leaden anchor. All I want to do is console her, hug her, and tell her that everything will be alright but there's no energy in me to do anything.

"Having you by my side is enough," I manage to choke out, my voice trembling with the weight of sorrow.

It's true.

She's everything. Having her by my side is the greatest comfort I can find in this overwhelming darkness. She's the most precious gift my uncle could have ever left me, a gift I didn't appreciate when he first introduced us.

I reach into my suit pocket and take out the letter that was handed to me by our lawyer after the funeral. Both Liam and I got one. He read his on the spot and broke down. I wasn't ready then —I didn't want to break down in front of him. But now, for some reason, sitting in the car with Leora, I am ready to face whatever is inside this letter.

Leora reaches out and places her hand over mine. "You can do it. I'm with you, all the way."

With trembling fingers, I carefully open the envelope. My heart races as I begin to read, every word a poignant reminder of the man who's no longer with us.

My Dearest Lucas,

My pride and joy, as I sit down to write these words, my heart is heavy with the knowledge that this might be the last time I get to express my feelings to you in this way. Life is a fragile and beautiful thing, my son, and it's in moments like these that we truly appreciate its fleeting nature.

I want you to know, Lucas, how much you mean to me and how immensely proud I am of the man you've become. You've grown into an amazing individual, a person of remarkable character and unwavering strength. I've always known the potential you held within you, even if I didn't always express it in the gentlest of ways. I pushed you because I believed in you, and I knew that you had the capacity to achieve greatness. You've exceeded even my highest expectations.

Your parents, may their souls rest in peace, would be bursting with pride if they could see you and your brother now. You have your mother's eyes, Lucas, and every time I look into them, I see a reflection of her warmth and kindness. I see her spirit living on in you. When I look at Liam's determination, I see your father. You two are the living legacy of the love your parents had for each other.

Before I met Leora, I must confess, I was worried about you. I was afraid that you would continue to bear the weight of the world on your shoulders and that you wouldn't allow anyone to share your burdens or your joys. But then, when Leora came into your life, I witnessed a transformation. She fit with you in a way that was truly remarkable. I saw how she helped you carry the world, how she eased the burdens that you've carried for so long. Most importantly, she showed you how to accept love. You, my dear son, have always been a giver. Your heart is boundless, and your capacity for love knows no bounds. However, I understand that receiving love has often been a challenge for you. It takes a special kind of *person to break down those barriers, and Leora is that person. She has shown you that it's not just about giving love, it's about allowing yourself to be loved in return.*

As I write these final words, please understand that my love for you is eternal. I've loved you all your life. Don't think that just because I'm gone, I'll stop loving you. I'll be watching over you, my dear Lucas, guiding you from above.

With all my love,
Ammo Antoine

P.S: Lucas, ya ebni, don't delay in giving Leora the gift you've been wanting to give her. Life is too short to wait, and she deserves all the love and happiness in the world. Make every moment count, and let your love for each other shine brightly.

"Lucas . . ." Leora's voice falters, and when I look into her eyes, I can't see her clearly. Everything blurs into a haze of grief and loss. Something warm runs down my cheek, then another and another. Before I know it, Leora grabs me. Her hand envelops my head as she hugs me to her chest, and I feel a strange mix of vulnerability and strength. Vulnerability because I'm allowing myself to break down, to admit that I need comfort, and strength because her love is the buoy that keeps me from completely drowning.

I allow myself to truly mourn. I sob for the man who has been not only my guardian, but also my guiding light. His unconditional love has shaped me into the person I've become, and his absence leaves an irreplaceable void.

Leora holds me through it all, her arms a sanctuary of solace and understanding. She whispers soothing words, the gentle cadence of her voice a balm to my broken soul. Her fingers stroke my hair with tenderness, and in her embrace, amidst the torrents of my grief, I realize something. It's a truth I've known for a while, deep in my heart, but now, in this moment I find the courage to voice it.

"I love you. I'm *in* love with you," I whisper, the words escaping my lips like a secret finally revealed. "I've loved you for a long time. I should have told you sooner."

Leora's grip on me tightens, and I feel her heart beating in sync with mine. She doesn't say anything for a moment. Then, she lifts my head gently with her hands while her fingers wipe away the tears that fall. Her eyes are filled with tenderness, and she says those three words that bring warmth to my heart.

"I love you, too," she says softly, her voice carrying the weight of her own emotions. I lean in and capture Leora's lips with mine. Our kiss is a gentle dance of emotions, a silent confession of the love that has silently blossomed between us. We went from being two selfish people bound by an agreement to becoming something much more. Something I never in a million years thought I would find. We've become what I always saw between my parents. I finally found it.

As our kiss deepens, the world around us fades into the background, its significance diminishing. The weight of grief is momentarily lifted, replaced by the sweet, comforting embrace of her.

In this kiss, we find strength, and the promise of a brighter tomorrow.

In this kiss, I know that whatever mountain life wants to throw at me, I can climb it together with Leora.

EPILOGUE

LEORA

2 YEARS LATER

Two years have passed since Lucas and I renewed our vows—getting married for real this time. Lucas's proposal had been nothing short of magical, a moment that belonged in the pages of a romance novel. He did it during our first vacation together, or what he fondly called our "Delayed Fake Honeymoon," by whisking me away to Lebanon.

The beauty of the country, the richness of its history, and the warmth of its people left an indelible mark on my heart.

Lucas took me to his favorite spots, guiding me through the entire country. Yet, it was our visit to Harissa, his absolute favorite place, that held a moment I'll cherish forever. On the bumpy cable car ride to the top of the mountain, with my heart pounding in both excitement and fear, Lucas went down on one knee and proposed to me again—this time he gifted me his mother's ring. It's a gold band adorned with a captivating blue sapphire in the middle with two diamonds hugging it.

I thought I was going to die, not only from the height but from the overwhelming rush of love and joy. In that thrilling, terrifying moment, I knew I'd gladly face anything as long as we were together.

Now, as I prepare for my thirtieth birthday party, I can't help but reflect on the incredible journey that brought me here.

"Happy birthday, *Ya Amar*," Lucas whispers as he bends down to kiss my lips and I relish in the feel of him.

"Thank you," I whisper against his lips before I bend down so I'm at eye level with our little Antoine, who's currently the center of our world. "Are you finally going to say your first words? Say, 'Happy Birthday, Mama.' Please, just say 'Mama,' 'Mama.'" I playfully urge our one-year-old. He came as a complete surprise, one I cherish more than life itself. We found out I was pregnant during our first Christmas together. Apparently, Lucas knew before I did. I've never had a regular period cycle, so I didn't think about it being late. He mentioned that he noticed my mood changing significantly and that I seemed constantly tired. I remember the moment he gently brought it up, his eyes filled with excitement and a warmth that made my heart swell. He's an incredible father.

Lucas chuckles at my feeble attempt. "He's already said his first word. You're just upset that the word was 'baba.'"

"I don't recall," I tease, and right on cue, Antoine decides to chime in.

"Baba, baba, baba," he repeats, the little traitor.

When I look back up, I find Lucas with his amused look and a mischievous grin plastered on his face. "You don't recall what, darling?" he asks innocently.

"Okay, you won this one, but just wait, he'll be a momma's boy soon enough." This is a long-term game and I'm ready to play it.

As I put the finishing touches on the decorations for the party, I can't help but smile at the anticipation. Sophie, Adeline, and Liam are all flying in. I've missed them so much. Liam is back home about every three months, but I haven't seen Sophie and Addie in a year—not since I gave birth to my little boy, who's brought an even deeper sense of joy and love into our lives.

They're already spoiling him with gifts, making me nervous for what's to come.

The elevator doors open, and I turn to find Adeline rushing toward me—no scratch that—she rushes by me to greet her favorite nephew.

"Hi, my sweet baby," she coos at him as she takes him from Lucas, showering him with kisses and affection.

Meanwhile, Sophie and Liam walk toward me, but there's something awkward about them as usual—something in the way they exchange glances that makes me curious.

"Happy birthday, beautiful. I've missed you," Sophie says as she hugs me tightly, her voice filled with genuine warmth.

Liam chimes in, "Happy birthday, sister-in-law."

When all of them shift their attention to Antoine, I turn to Lucas and whisper, "Stop hovering. You're making it obvious."

"I'm not hovering," he whispers back, a proud glint in his eyes.

"Yes, you are. Now stop it."

"We're telling them today, right?"

His hand moves toward me but I push it away as I walk away, muttering, "So discreet." Lucas follows and when we reach Sophie I look at him and give him the nod, urging him to ask her what we discussed.

"Why are you acting weird?" she asks us.

"We're not acting weird. Lucas just has a question he would like to ask you. Right, Lucas?"

"Right." Lucas clears his throat before continuing. "I've heard you're a great interior designer, Sophie, and as you might be aware, we're opening up a new hotel in New York." He clears his throat again, and my eagerness takes over. "What he's trying to ask you is if you would feel comfortable working on the interior project?"

Sophie blinks, still processing the unexpected offer. Her eyes dart between Lucas and me, as if trying to gauge whether this is some kind of joke. Finally, an infectious smile spreads across her face, transforming it into one of genuine delight.

"Lucas! Leora!" she begins, her voice filled with gratitude, "I can't believe you'd trust me with something this monumental. Of course, I'd be honored to take on this project. You won't regret it."

Lucas and I share a triumphant look. This was a surprise we had been planning for months, and we couldn't have asked for a better reaction. She walks toward Adeline, happy with the news and I lean into Lucas, whispering, "Should we have told her that Liam will be overseeing the new hotel?"

"Why would we do that?"

"Because they're always so weird around each other," I say, a bit worried about how they'll *actually* work together. I don't know exactly why they're awkward, but they just haven't clicked. Which is weird because Sophie is amazing, and so is Liam. He and Adeline already act like siblings toward each other, so I truly don't understand why they seem to have issues, but I'm doing my best to fix things.

"Let's keep it a surprise. That way she can't run away, and they'll all be friends soon enough," Lucas says, happy with his plan.

Let's just hope it works, because I don't have much patience for any more awkward parties.

As I blow out the candles on my birthday cake, surrounded by the people I love most in this world, I make a silent wish. It's a wish for more years filled with love, laughter, and adventures with Lucas and my people by my side. Our journey together has only just begun, and I can't wait to see where it takes us next.

"What did you wish for?" Adeline asks.

"Another nephew or niece," Liam suggests, his finger stuck in little Antoine's grip. This time, when Lucas reaches out for me, I don't push him away. Instead, I lean into him when his hand cradles my little bump.

"No need to waste a wish on that," he says with so much pride that it lights up the entire room and makes my heart burst. "We're actually expecting another baby."

Gasps and cheers erupt from our friends and family, and I

can't help but laugh at their reactions. The joy in the room is palpable, and I feel like the luckiest person in the world.

In the midst of the celebration, Lucas leans over and whispers in my ear, "I love you, Leora."

I turn to him, my heart swelling with affection. "I love you too, Lucas."

And in that perfect moment, I know that I'm exactly where I'm meant to be.

THE END

COMING SOON BY M. PAMELA

Unexpected Love

Book 2

ACKNOWLEDGMENTS

I find it surreal to grasp that I've written a book. It has always been a dream of mine, and achieving this goal feels incredibly rewarding. English is not my first language, but it's the only language I read and write in. I was born and raised in Sweden to two incredible Lebanese parents, who taught me to reach for my goals. So to mum and dad, despite keeping this book and its content a secret, you've consistently encouraged me to pursue my dreams, and I'm utterly grateful for that.

My dad used to tell me, "It doesn't matter if you're a Renault Kangoo or a Ferrari; you'll reach the goal eventually. The important part is the drive, not the speed." That stayed with me and I truly believe it. So for everyone who ever compares themselves with others, *don't*. You'll reach your goal eventually. Everything happens for a reason. Also, thank you mom and dad for sharing your beautiful love story, from your meet cute to Dad's proposal in the cable car on your way to Harissa (Our Lady Of Lebanon). Your love for each other is what drives me to find my future soulmate.

Ever since I learned that my grandfather was a writer in Lebanon, specifically a poet, I've dreamt of this moment. So, thank you, Jeddo, may you rest in peace. This may not be the story you expected me to write, but hey, I wrote a book.

To my amazing best friends, Merna and Rebecca, thank you for your unwavering support and for cheering me on when I doubted myself. Thank you for listening when this book was just a concept.

A heartfelt thanks to my cousins, my *soulies*; you might not know that I've written this book yet - or if you do, surprise I love you. Your constant support in everything I do made me believe in myself enough to embark on this little project. Also, thank you for patiently enduring my rants about books.

Norhan, Karla, and Ronnie, I don't know where to begin. You three have been my cheerleaders from the start. Thank you not only for being alpha/beta readers but for being great friends who took the time to listen to my voice notes about ideas and all my insecurities. What would I have done without you? And to the rest of my betas, Emma, Sydney, and Grayson, thank you for your honesty and the time you spent on my draft. You are all warriors, and each one of you brought something unique to this process.

To my amazing editor, Cait, you are magic and one of the sweetest souls I've ever encountered. Thank you for pushing me, being honest, and helping me mold this draft into the book I have today.

To Grace, thank you for saving me. I was on the verge of burnout, and the idea of formatting this book terrified me. Then you swooped in and helped me out, and I'm so thankful.

To the incredible team at Books and Moods, especially Julie, thank you for bringing my cover to life exactly as I envisioned it.

Rosana Rainhart, I'm so thankful to call you an author friend in this community/industry. You've helped me through it all with motivating, supportive and real words. Thank you!

Thank you to the sweet Taylor, who made my gorgeous divider.

Thank you to Bookstagram and all of you for joining me on this journey and allowing me to tell this story. Lucas and Leora will have a special place in my heart forever.

PS. Do you remember the scene in the Louvre when Leora's dress blew up? Well, that actually happened to me when I visited in 2022. Unfortunately, I had no Lucas to whisper in my ear.

ABOUT THE AUTHOR

Meet M. Pamela, a romance enthusiast who has been writing since the days when high school was more than just a distant memory (but let's not get into the specifics).

She loves to write all kinds of romance and loves to read them as well. - she likes to ramble about here favorites...a lot.

When she's not writing, reading or daydreaming, she's either traveling around the world in search for new inspiration or enjoying time with her family and cousins.

Socials
Instagram: @Authormpamela
Tiktok: @Authormpamela
Goodreads: M.Pamela